Praise for DANIEL

D1009562

"Without any doubt, I can alrea
will end up on my and many other lists of best novels for
young adults published in 2014. What did I like? The list is
a mile long."
   YA Books Central

"*Stolen Songbird* is an enticing beginning to a magical new
trilogy. The passion between Cécile and Tristan simmers
tantalizingly beneath the surface, anticipating the slightest of
sparks that will fully ignite it. Jensen has created a vivid and
complex world that readers will be eager to explore further
in the next two installments."
   Teen Reads

"*Stolen Songbird* is a fantastic debut. The book had an
amazing cast of developed characters, an intriguing plot,
an swoon- worthy romance and an ending that'll have you
itching for the next book. I'd definitely recommend it."
   YA Midnight Reads

"*Stolen Songbird* is an absolutely wonderful addition to the
fantasy genre. The book is full of magic, adventure, outlandish
creatures, and at its heart is one of the most touching love
stories I have ever read."
   Avid Reviews

"The writing style was superb. I was transported to the world
of Trollus and I walked side-by-side with Cécile. The setting
was magical and I was sucked into the story, which has a very
interesting and complex plot without being overwhelming."
   The Daily Prophecy

DANIELLE L JENSEN

Stolen Songbird

The Malediction Trilogy I

ANGRY
ROBOT

ANGRY ROBOT
An imprint of Watkins Media Ltd

Lace Market House,
54-56 High Pavement,
Nottingham,
NG1 1HW
UK

www.angryrobotbooks.com
twitter.com/angryrobotbooks.com
Feed the trolls

Originally published by our Strange Chemistry imprint 2014
This Angry Robot-badged reprint published 2015

Cover by Steve Stone at Artist Partners
Set in Sabon and Princess & the Frog by Argh! Oxford

Distributed in the United States by Random House, Inc., New York.

ISBN 978 1 908844 96 5
Ebook ISBN 978 1 908844 97 2

Printed in the United States of America

9 8 7 6 5 4

For MB, *who started me down this path.*

CHAPTER 1
Cécile

My voice rose an octave, resonating through the Goshawk's Hollow marketplace, drowning out the bleating sheep and the hammer of the blacksmith down the way. Dozens of familiar faces abandoned their business, expressions uniform in their nervousness as they anticipated the note I had dreaded daily for the past month. *She* liked an audience for my failures.

A tremor raced through my body, my palms slicking with sweat. Madame Delacourte's gaze burned between my shoulder blades, her low expectations only fueling my resolve. I would not break.

Resisting the urge to ball my hands into fists, I pushed my last breath into the crescendo of the piece. Almost there. Several people stepped forward, the words of encouragement on their lips drowned by the enormity of my song. This was when my voice broke. Always, always.

But not today.

The market erupted with cheers as I finished. "Well done, Cécile!" someone shouted, and I bobbed a little curtsey, my cheeks flushed with a sweet combination of embarrassment and delight. The echo of my song drifted off through fields and valleys tinted green with spring, and everyone went back to their business.

"Don't go getting all puffed up in the head," Madame Delacourte sniffed from behind me. "Impressing that lot of backwards country folk is no great feat."

My back stiffened, and I turned to meet her wrinkled glare.

"You're good," she said, lips drawn tight to the point of invisibility. "But not as good as her."

Her. My mother.

For most of my childhood, I knew almost nothing of her – the woman my father spoke of with such reverence that one would have thought her a queen. Knew only that my father had run off to Trianon in his youth, fallen in love, and married a young stage soprano named Genevieve. But when my grandfather died and my father inherited the farm, she'd refused to return with him.

"City girl who couldn't stomach the thought of country living," Gran always grumbled when asked about my mother. "Though what kind of woman abandons her husband and three children is beyond my reckoning."

Abandoned was a strong word. She did visit. Occasionally. I thought for a long time she'd neglected us because she didn't love us enough, but now I understood the decision my mother had made. A farmer's wife had no respite from work – up at dawn and last to bed. Tending animals, making meals, churning butter, doing laundry, cleaning house, raising children... the list was endless. The wives in

Goshawk's Hollow all looked old before their time, with chapped hands, weathered faces, and permanent frowns, whereas my mother remained beautiful: a star of the stage. She looked more like my older sister than my mother.

"Are we finished for today, or would you like for me to sing it again, Madame?" My voice was saccharine and contrasted mightily, I knew, with my flinty expression. She'd been a thorn in my backside for nigh on four years now, doing her best to turn what I loved most into a dreaded chore. She'd failed.

"By this time next week, you'll be begging to come home." Turning on her heel, she strode off the porch and back into the inn, black skirts swishing. With any luck, this time, this week, would be the last time I laid eyes on my vocal teacher. In a week's time, I would be learning from the best opera singer living on the Isle of Light.

Unbidden, my mother's image rose to the forefront of my mind, and along with it the memory, four years ago to the day, when she'd sealed my fate. "Sing," she had demanded, and I'd chosen a tune popular at barn dances, the only song I knew. When she scowled, I thought my heart would break from disappointment.

"Any talentless wretch could manage that," she said, blue irises identical to mine except that hers were cold as the winter sky. "Repeat after me." She sang a few lines from an opera, her voice so lovely that it brought tears to my eyes. "Now you."

I imitated her, hesitantly at first, but then with more confidence. She'd sung and I'd repeated, trilling like a songbird mimicking a flute.

She'd smiled. "Well done, Cécile. Well done." Turning to my father who'd watched from the corner, she'd said, "I'll take her when she's seventeen." When he'd started to argue, she raised a hand, silencing him. "She's strong, clever, and, once she's grown out of this awkward stage, she'll be fair enough. And her voice is divine." Her eyes had gleamed. "She's wasted out here in the country where no one would know talent if it kicked them in the face. I'll arrange for tutors to come out to Goshawk's Hollow to teach her – I'll not have her arriving with the manners of a milk cow."

Turning to me, she'd unclasped a golden pendant from her neck and fastened it around mine. "Beauty can be created, knowledge learned, but talent can neither be purchased nor taught. And you've talent, my dearest girl. When you stand on stage and sing, the whole world will love you."

I clutched that pendant in my fist, now, staring at the door Madame had closed behind her. The whole world would love me.

The sound of my name caught my attention. Scampering down the wooden steps, I dodged puddles as I made my way over to where my best friend, Sabine, was leaning against a fencepost, playing with a coiled lock of hair. She grinned and handed me a basket of eggs. "You finished it."

"Hundredth time's the charm." Taking hold of her arm, I tugged her in the direction of the stables. "I need to hurry back to the farm. Gran needs these eggs for the cake she's baking for my going away party tonight."

Sabine's face fell.

"I did invite you," I reminded her. "You can come back with me, if you like. Spend the night. The coach will have to pass through town on the way to Trianon, so it would be easy enough to drop you back in the morning," I said casually, as though I traveled by hired coach every day of my life.

"I know…" She looked down. "But my ma took the gig to the Renard farm. She said not to expect her till the morning."

I made a face, not bothering to suggest she saddle her pony and ride with me. Sabine was terrified of horses. Bloody stones and sky, why hadn't I thought ahead this morning and hitched Fleur to the buggy instead of riding to town? And where on God's green earth was my brother? Frédéric was supposed to have arrived from Trianon hours ago. Sabine might have conceded to ride behind *him*, if only because she'd fancied him since time eternal.

"I can't help but think this is the last time we'll see each other," Sabine said softly, interrupting my thoughts. "That once you're in Trianon with your mother, performing and going to all those parties, you'll forget about the Hollow. And me."

"That's utter foolishness," I declared. "I'll be back so often to visit, you'll be right sick of me. You know Frédéric comes back whenever he has leave."

"He hasn't been back since the new year."

It was true that since Fred's most recent promotion to second-lieutenant, he'd found less opportunity to visit. "Then I'll ride by myself."

"Oh, Cécile." Sabine shook her head. "You can't be doing that anymore – it's unladylike. People will talk."

"But it's in your best interest," I reminded her. The stable boy was leading Fleur towards us, but I found myself not wanting to leave. Sabine and I had been best friends our whole lives, and the thought of not seeing her every day formed a cold pit in my stomach.

"I'll ride home, give Gran the eggs, and then hitch up the buggy and come back for you," I decided. "Go put on your blue dress. I'll be back in no time at all."

She bit the ends of her hair. "I don't know…"

I caught her gaze for a long moment. "You're going to come back with me in the buggy and attend my party," I said firmly.

Sabine's eyes went blank, and for a heartbeat, everything came into sharp focus for me. The sounds of the market. The solid earth beneath my feet. A breeze rushed past us, ruffling Sabine's hair. She smiled. "Of course. I wouldn't miss it for anything."

Nothing a bit of willpower couldn't accomplish.

Swinging into the saddle, I twitched the reins to calm my frisking horse. "I won't be more than an hour. Watch for me!" One hand clutching the basket of eggs, and the other the reins, I dug in my heels and galloped out of town.

Our farm was close enough to the Hollow that we were almost considered town folk, but far enough that the smell of pigs didn't offend the noses of those less used to country life. I could have galloped the entire way there, but I let Fleur stop and catch her breath about halfway. Her hooves thudded softly against the damp earth as we walked down the road. The smell of pine was thick in the air and a cool breeze rushed down from the mountains, blowing my long red hair out behind me.

A flash of movement caught my eye, and I stopped, scanning the forest to either side of the road. Bears and mountain cats were common enough around here, but if the horse had scented a predator, she'd have been uncontrollable. The wind gusted through the trees and I thought I heard the crackle of breaking underbrush, though I couldn't be sure. My pulse quickened, a prickle of anxiety running down my spine. Highwayman? Robbery wasn't common this far north of the Ocean Road, but it was possible.

"Hello?" I called out, gathering up the reins. "Is someone there?"

No answer, but anyone intending to rob me was unlikely to reply. My trepidation grew. I'd ridden this road rain, snow, and shine, and never felt a moment's fear before. Fleur pranced beneath me, sensing my anxiety.

The wind rose again, no longer gentle, but like angry fingers tugging at my hair. The sun ducked behind a cloud, turning the air chill. My eyes unconsciously turned to Forsaken Mountain, looming in the distance. I was halfway between home and town, but Jérôme Girard's farm was nearby. I could ride there and ask his son Christophe to accompany me the rest of the way.

But what if he laughed at me for being such a ninny, scared of noises in the underbrush that were probably from a squirrel or a snake? Despite a lifetime proving to the contrary, everyone acted like I was already a city girl, and this would only prove their point. I circled and stared back the way I came. I could ride back and wait for my brother, but what if something had kept him in Trianon and he wasn't even coming?

I'll gallop home, I decided. Let whoever's lurking in the woods try and catch me. Turning Fleur around, I abruptly hauled on the reins. The basket slipped from my hand and smashed against the ground, yellow yolks mixing with the mud.

A cloaked rider blocked the road.

My heart leapt. Fleur wheeled around, and I laid the ends of my reins to her haunches. "Hah!" I shouted as she surged forward.

"Cécile! Cécile, wait! It's me!"

A familiar voice. Gentler this time, I reined in and looked over my shoulder. "Luc?"

"Yes, it's me, Cécile." He trotted over to me, pulling back his hood to reveal his face.

"What are you doing sneaking about like that?" I said. "You scared the wits out of me."

He shrugged. "I wasn't certain it was you at first. Sorry about the eggs."

An apology that didn't explain at all why he'd been lurking in the bushes in the first place.

"I haven't seen you in quite some time. Where have you been?" I asked the question even though I knew the answer. His father was gamekeeper on an estate not far from our farm, but several months ago, Luc had taken off for Trianon. My brother and other townsfolk had caught wind that Luc had had a bit of luck betting on the horses and playing at cards, and was now living the high life spending his winnings.

"Here and there," he said, riding around me in a circle. "The gossips say you're moving to Trianon to live with your mother."

"Her carriage is coming for me tomorrow."

"You'll be singing then. On stage?"

"Yes."

He smiled. "You always did have the voice of an angel."

"I need to get home," I said. "My gran's expecting me – my father too." I hesitated and looked down the road. "You may ride with me, if you like." I rather hoped he wouldn't accept, but riding was better than standing here alone with him.

"Today is your birthday, isn't it?" His horse sidled tight against mine.

I frowned. "Yes."

"Seventeen. You're a woman now." He looked me up and down as though inspecting something that could be bought and sold. A horse at market. Or something worse. He chuckled softly to himself and I cringed.

"What's so funny?" My heart raced, my instincts telling me that something was terribly wrong. Please, someone come down the road.

"I was just thinking about how sometimes fortune finds us when we least expect," he said. Before I could react, he reached down and seized Fleur's reins. "I need you to come with me. There are some individuals who would very much like to make your acquaintance."

"I'm not going anywhere with you, Luc," I said, trying to keep my voice steady – I did not want him to know I was afraid. "My brother won't take kindly to hearing that you caused me trouble."

Luc glanced around. "Funny, but I don't see Frédéric about. Seems it's just you and me."

He was right about that, but wrong if he thought I'd go without a fight.

I jammed my spurs into Fleur's sides and she reared, hooves striking out and knocking away Luc's hand. "Hah!" I screamed and plunged down the road at a gallop. Sensing my terror, the horse ran faster than ever before, ears pinned back. But Luc's stallion was bigger – if I kept to the road, he'd catch us easily. A game trail appeared ahead, and I swung down the path.

Branches tore at my hair and skirts as we leapt over fallen trees and crashed through the underbrush. I let the mare have her head, concentrating on staying low and keeping my seat. Behind us, I heard the big horse's hooves thundering against the ground along with Luc's curses and vile threats. We were nearing the Girard farm. Ahead, the break in the forest was visible, and beyond lay their fields. "Chris!" I screamed, knowing I was still too far for them to hear me. "Jérôme!"

A glance behind showed Luc in fast pursuit. He was near enough for me to see the fury written on his face. I could not let him catch me. I would not. Then a branch smashed across my chest, launching me backwards. Fleur disappeared from under me and I was falling, my eyes fixed on the sun filtering through the green leaves of the trees.

Then, nothing.

CHAPTER 2
Cécile

A grey-furred foreleg was all I could see when I opened my eyes, my body bouncing up and down with the trotting motion of a horse. The pommel of a saddle dug painfully into my stomach and my head felt like a hundred angry giants were trying to hammer their way out. Where was I?

I squirmed, but I couldn't move far. My hands and feet were bound to the horse, my mouth gagged.

Luc.

Terror surged through me like water through a broken dam, and I thrashed and jerked about, trying my hardest to get free. The stallion shied sideways and I caught sight of thick forest.

"I wouldn't do that if I were you." Luc's voice was companionable, as though we were out for a ride in the park. "He has the unfortunate habit of going over backwards when he spooks, and that wouldn't go well for you."

I froze.

"You're probably wondering where I'm taking you. I'd love to say, but unfortunately my associates have placed a number of restrictions on me."

Tears of frustration ran down my forehead as I painfully craned my neck to look up at him. He smirked and patted me on the bottom. "You didn't really want to go to Trianon anyway, did you? The stage girls are all just highly priced harlots, and you never struck me as that sort of girl. Better suited to the Hollow than the big city."

My head dropped, and I rested my cheek against the horse's shoulder. Bile rose in my throat and I struggled to keep my stomach contents down. If I threw up while gagged, I'd choke on my own vomit. *Think, Cécile! Think!*

"Here we are."

He dismounted, and I stared at his hands as he untied the knot binding me to the horse. When the tension on my legs gave, I kicked out hard, catching him in the face.

"Damn you!" he howled.

I slid to the ground, landing with a thud. Seconds later, a boot caught me in the ribs, flipping me over. I yelped against the gag, my gaze fixed on Luc's bloody face. My wrists and ankles were still bound – the best I could do was roll into a seated position.

"You can make this easy, or you can make it hard," he hissed, wiping his nose with a filthy handkerchief. "Either way, you're coming with me."

"Where?" I managed to make the word audible around my gag.

He jerked a blood-smeared chin forwards and I looked over my shoulder. Forsaken Mountain loomed menacingly above us. Its glittering southern slope was sheer as a knife slice through butter, the broken half a crumbled slide of rock stretching down to the ocean. I felt my eyes widen. Old men always talked about treasure troves of gold lying beneath the fallen rock, but they also said the mountain was cursed. Treasure hunters had a way of disappearing when they went poking in amongst the rocks and, for every story concerning a man gone missing, ten more speculated on those who'd taken him.

Luc left me gaping at the mountain while he led the horse over to a rough wooden paddock. I clawed at the knots binding my ankles, but they were tight and my fingers were numb. Luc was unsaddling the animal now, distracted. I tried to crawl on knees and elbows, but quickly realized it was a waste of time – I couldn't move fast enough and my legs left obvious marks in the dirt. Crouched on my knees, I reached up and pulled off my gag. Taking a deep breath, I screamed, my voice thundering down the mountainside. The horse squealed and leapt away from Luc, galloping to the far side of the enclosure. I screamed again, praying there would be someone near enough to hear.

Luc sprinted in my direction, but I managed to howl for help one last time before his fist caught me in the cheek. I toppled backwards and he grabbed my dress, hauling me upright and hitting me again. My face throbbed, my vision hazy.

"Quite a set of lungs on you!"

I tried to crawl away, but he snatched up the rope binding my legs and dragged me down a slope, my skirts riding up around my waist. Sitting on my bare legs, he unbound my ankles and retied the rope to one of them. Then he flipped me over and untied my wrists, leaving them free.

"You need to be able to swim. It's the only way under the mountain." One hand grasping the bodice of my dress, he tore it down the front, brushing aside my arms as I attempted to fight him off. "Don't worry, Cécile. They were specific that your virtue remain uncompromised."

"Who?" I demanded. "Who are you talking about? Where are you taking me? Why are you doing this?"

He shook his head. "You'll learn soon enough." Taking hold of the rope attached to my ankle, he hauled me into the icy pool of water lying at the base of the rocks. I had to start swimming or risk drowning. My breath came in great heaving sobs, my terror building to the point I thought I might drown myself and save Luc the trouble. He must have noticed as much, because he swam back and snatched hold of my arm.

"Pull yourself together, Cécile! I didn't drag you all the way up here so you could cry yourself to death. Now on the other side of this rock is a cave. To get inside, you must swim down about four paces and slip under the edge of the rock. Do you think you can manage?"

"This is madness," I croaked.

Luc dove beneath the surface. I barely had the opportunity to take a deep breath before the rope binding my ankle jerked me under. The rock was slimy under my hand, and seemingly endless. I swam hard, the rope slack enough now that I could kick. Where Luc was, I couldn't say. What I did know was that his grip would keep me down here until I found the opening or until I ran out of air.

Bubbles trailed from my lips, floating freely to the surface. My lungs burned, desperate for breath. My heart hammered faster and faster. The pressure of the water overhead built until my ears popped. Then the rock disappeared, leaving me disoriented and grasping about in the darkness.

I found the edge of the rock. But as I slipped underneath, the water thickened like glue for a moment, holding me in place for precious seconds. My skin tingled as though I stood on the top of a mountain in the middle of a thunderstorm, lightning crackling down all around. Shuddering, I struggled through and pressed upwards.

The rope pulled hard on my ankle, flipping me upside down. Hands grabbed hold of my wrists and my head broke the surface. I sucked in sweet life-giving air. The darkness was absolute. Grasping about, I found a rock protruding from the water and I clung to its slick edges, afraid to let go.

I felt the icy cold of the water on my body and the rough stone beneath my fingers, smelled the stagnant damp air, and heard the faint splashing of Luc as he paddled towards me. All my other senses combined seemed insignificant compared to the loss of sight. I shivered, waiting.

"Are you all right?" Luc's voice broke the silence.

"No."

Tension radiated between us and I cursed every decision I'd made that had led to this point. If only I'd galloped straight home, or fought harder, or had bloody well watched where I was riding, then maybe I wouldn't be here.

But I was here. And a morbidly curious little part of me wanted to know why. "You owe me an explanation," I said.

"Aye, I reckon I do," he said. "But first let's have some light."

I listened as he scrambled out of the water, fumbling around in the darkness. Then the sound of a flint being struck and the faint glow of flame, as welcome to me in that moment as a hand plucking a drowning sailor from stormy waters. Carefully, I climbed out of the pond and made my way towards it. Luc held a burning splinter to a storm lantern. When the wick caught, he turned it up high, illuminating the cavern with its blessed glow.

We were in a small cave of sorts, rock encasing us on all sides. Apart from the watery entrance we had come through, the only exit was a dark tunnel leading away from the water. There were no signs of treasure, gold, or of anything other than a pile of supplies and the lantern, which Luc had obviously brought on a prior occasion.

"Well," I said, wrapping my arms around my icy body. All I had on was a shift and boots, and the damp fabric concealed uncomfortably little. I hadn't truly expected him to answer, but Luc had always been excessively proud of himself, so I shouldn't have been surprised when he did.

"Of course, of course." He leaned closer to me, the lamp casting shadows on his face. "It is the most incredible of things. I'd scarce believe if I hadn't seen it myself."

"Get to the point, Luc!"

He laughed as though something I'd said was beyond amusing. "You never did appreciate a good tale. So, fine, I'll get straight to the point. I've found the lost city of Trollus."

Silence hung between us for a long moment. I certainly hadn't expected his motivations to have anything to do with a mythological city. "Do you think this is some sort of jest or have you lost your mind?" My voice echoed through the cavern. *Mind... mind... mind... mind...* We both flinched and looked about uneasily.

"The city wasn't lost, Luc. Trollus was buried by half a mountain worth of rock."

"Aye," he said, his eyes narrowing. "Buried, but not destroyed. At least not completely."

"Impossible. Nothing in this world is strong enough to withstand the weight."

"That is the best part." He leaned closer to me. "Just like in the stories: they've been living here under the mountain this entire time!"

"Who?" I asked, afraid but desperately wanting to know.

Luc's eyes reflected the orange glow of the flame, and he licked his lips, relishing the moment. "The trolls, Cécile. They're here!"

"Fairy tales," I whispered. "Stories told to scare naughty children."

Luc laughed. "Oh, they're plenty real and plenty monstrous. And happy enough for us humans to think they're shadows in the night. Keeps people from troubling them and trying to steal their treasure."

"Treasure."

"Aye. Chambers heaped with gold and jewels."

"If they dislike humans, why would they let you anywhere near their wealth?" I asked, discreetly taking stock of my surroundings. The pool lay directly behind me. If I caught Luc off guard and managed to get into the water, I might have a chance. I could hide in the trees until nightfall and then make my way to the farm, if my father didn't find me first.

"His Majesty showed me during our... negotiations."

"His Majesty?" With a maniacal laugh, I leaned back on the palms of my hands. The stone floor was sloped. If I threw my weight backwards, I'd roll into the water. "I didn't realize trolls had royalty!"

"Oh, yes," he said. "They are the ones who purchased you." I gasped. "For what?"

"With gold," he said, mistaking my question.

"What do they want with me?" I whispered.

Luc shrugged. "With what they agreed to pay, they can throw you in a cooking pot for all I care."

Because according to the fairy tales, that was what trolls did. Put you alive into a pot of boiling water and then gnawed your flesh until all that was left were bleached white bones.

I clawed my way back towards the pool, my fingernails tearing on the rocks. All I could think about was that I was being marched towards the most horrific of deaths. Nothing Luc could do to me could possibly be worse than being eaten. I struggled with single-minded purpose towards the pool, but Luc had a tight grip on my leash and I was no match for his strength. "Help!" My voice echoed off the water and the rock until it seemed I had a dozen doppelgangers, all of them taunting me with the futility of my screams.

Luc slapped me hard. "Shut your mouth, or I'll gag you again." One finger pointing towards the glowing lantern, he said, "Pick that up, and start walking."

Hands numb with a cold that was far more than skin deep, I followed Luc's order.

What I had thought would be a straight walk into the deep was anything but. Instead, a labyrinth of tunnels, crevices, and dead-ends lay beneath the mountain of stone. The floor was an uneven carpet of boulders and rocks, riddled with cracks that could break your ankle or swallow you whole. I took each step with caution, a kidnapper at my back, and the risk of a broken neck at every turn. My shift clung to my body, refusing to dry in the damp darkness and providing nothing in the way of warmth. The light from the storm lantern shivered along with me, casting strange shadows on the rock and setting my heart racing until I was convinced it would beat itself out of my chest.

At each intersection countless rough markings were carved or chalked on the stone. Some were clearly directions or warnings, but others were meaningless symbols. Logic crept past my fear, and I knew that if I had any chance of escaping, I'd need to know how to find my way.

"Who made these?" I asked, my voice seeming loud after the long silence. I kept my tone quiet and non-confrontational. Luc got his back up easily at the best of times and I needed to keep him talking.

"Treasure hunters." Luc tapped his knife against one of the strange symbols. "Each of the pathfinders has his own mark leading the way he deems fastest. Or safest, most like," he amended.

An arrow next to a symbol carved into the stone pointed to the right, where a narrow, slot-like tunnel promised a tight squeeze, even for me. Half a dozen symbols had arrows pointing to the passage on the left, which seemed wide open and inviting by comparison. "Why not the other way?"

Luc shook his head and tapped two wavy lines scratched below the markings. "Means sluag been sighted down that path. Or their leavings, at least."

"What's a sluag?"

The uneasy expression on Luc's face did not ease my fear. "Something big and something best to be avoided," he said. "I asked the trolls about them. They said that if I ever got close enough to spot one, t'would be unlikely I'd live to tell the tale. Even they are afraid of sluag." He pointed towards the right. "The tight spaces are safer."

I shone the light down the left passageway, but the scant few feet of visibility gave me no comfort that there weren't sluag or worse lurking beyond. My back against the wall, I reluctantly squeezed into the crack.

The crevice remained tight for a long time and progress was both slow and exhausting. When the passage finally opened up into a bigger space, I sank down on the damp rock with relief. Luc emerged soon after, his face as filthy and exhausted as I assumed mine to be.

"We need to keep moving," he said, after taking a long swallow from his water skin then passing it to me. "The trolls are expecting us by nightfall."

Needless to say, I didn't find the reminder particularly motivating. "Who told you about these tunnels, anyway? Or would you have me believe you decided to crawl to the center of the earth one day to discover if you might pop out the other side?"

Luc sneered at me. "No one can tell anyone about this place – the trolls ensure that. If you make it all the way to Trollus, and if they decide you're useful enough not to kill on the spot, they make you swear magic oaths binding you to secrecy. S'why I couldn't tell you anything until we got under the rocks. The trolls, they're big on oaths. Don't take too kindly to those who break their word, so we best be moving right along."

I sat rooted, refusing to move.

Luc tossed up his hands in exasperation. "Fine. I took to noticing that old Henri seemed to have unlimited coin to do his drinking in town, though he ain't never worked an honest day in his life. So I followed him, thinking he had a stash buried in the forest somewhere. Turns out he's been trading with the trolls all these years and no one the wiser."

"Trading what?"

"Books, of all things."

"And you? What did you give them?"

Luc shrugged. "Odds and sods. They pay a lot, but it's a dangerous trip. When I heard they were looking for a girl with your description, I knew I'd hit pay dirt, and I was right. They let me name my price."

Fury overtook my fear of punishment. He had sold me, sold my life away, all because he was too greedy to do honest work. Booted heels lashing out, I caught him in the knees and watched as he toppled over the edge of the rock and out of sight. Unfortunately, his grip on the rope did not slacken and I was dragged forward until my feet dangled over the edge.

"You just don't give up, do you." Luc sat about four feet below me in a pool of guck, and a rank stench rose up to assault my nostrils. He wasn't alone.

"Looks like you have a friend," I snapped, pointing at the skeleton lying on the floor next to Luc. "Shame you didn't meet a similar fate."

Luc looked down and grimaced. Then his curiosity got the better of him and he gave the body a closer examination. "Shine the lantern down this way, Cécile. I can't believe I've never noticed him before."

I obliged, but only because I had no other options. He'd just pull me over the edge if I didn't obey. Judging from the bareness of the bones, the man had been dead for some time. My skin broke out into a fresh set of goose bumps. "What is that slime?"

"I don't know – never seen it before." He sounded nervous, and his trepidation caught hold of me like a plague.

"How many times have you been this way?" I asked, my mind turning to the real fear that we might be lost and he just didn't know it.

There was no chance to respond before the cavern thundered with a strange roaring noise. *BAROOOM!* The echoes faded, replaced by the wet swish of something slithering in our direction. Something large.

Luc's terrified eyes met mine and he whispered, "Run!"

CHAPTER 3
Cécile

Terror may have given us wings, but the labyrinth of Forsaken Mountain kept us to a crawl. We wriggled across boulders, boots slipping on the loose rock and ears peeled for the tell-tale swish, swish of the sluag hunting at our heels. If it was fast enough to catch us, it was choosing not to. But whenever I thought we'd escaped, we'd round a corner and the swish, swish of slithering would accost our ears, forcing us to backtrack or take another way – almost as though it was toying with us. If not for the etched directions, we'd have certainly lost our way. Exhaustion was catching up with us, and when it did, so would the sluag.

Luc examined the markers, both of us panting and gasping for breath. We stood at the convergence of three tunnels. "This way," he whispered. "Just a bit further and we'll come to a narrow hole. You'll have to get down and crawl, but once you're through, we'll be into Trollus. The sluag won't be able to follow."

BAROOOM!

I started in the direction he pointed, but Luc shoved me aside and went first. Reaching the tight bit, he fell to his stomach and squirmed his way in. His small pack caught on the edge, forcing him to back up, take it off, and shove it ahead of him.

Swish, swish, swish. *BAROOOM!* Triumph thundered in the creature's voice as it drew closer.

"Hurry, hurry, hurry," I whispered, and turned to look back the way we'd come.

Swish, swish, swish.

Only Luc's feet stuck out of the tunnel now. I dropped to my knees, ready to dive in the second he made room.

Swish, swish, swish.

Luc's heels disappeared. I glanced behind me one last time, the light of the lantern catching the monster rounding the corner. The sluag reared, white and glistening like a giant slug, and out of its mouth shot a long, whip-like tongue. The lantern smashed at my feet, guttering out. I screamed and scrambled into the hole.

I could see nothing – only hear Luc cursing ahead of me, and the swish of the sluag coming up from behind. I crawled faster, uncertain how far into the tunnel I had progressed or if my ankles still protruded enough for the monster to catch hold.

BAROOOM!

I screamed, and something smacked into the heel of my boot, the force driving me onto the back of Luc's legs. "Hurry! It's coming!"

BAROOOM!

We clawed our way forward, and the tunnel shuddered as the creature slammed into the rock. I shrieked, snot and tears coating my face as I shoved against Luc's feet, trying to get through the tight hole. Even after he reached the other side and pulled me out of the tunnel, it took a long time for my panic to recede enough for me to think. I was not safe. Not only was I kidnapped, my kidnapper was too stupid to get us safely to those he intended to sell me to. It was all for nothing. I was going to die for nothing.

"I hate you," I croaked. I swallowed hard and repeated myself. "I hate you." The sentiment still wasn't enough, so I howled the words. "I hate you, Luc!"

"Where's the lamp?" His voice held no emotion, but I felt him pick up the end of the rope still attached to my ankle.

"At the end of the tunnel with the sluag – feel free to go get it." Except the thought of the creature wolfing him down didn't make me feel much better. I would be alone in the dark, with no sense of time or direction. The chances of finding my way out were nonexistent – I'd starve to death down here and no one would ever suspect what had happened.

Luc groaned. "Idiot! Now what are we supposed to do?"

I listened to the sound of him fumbling in his pack and looked around, if such a thing is possible in complete darkness.

Or perhaps not so complete after all.

In the distance, a silvery glow beckoned that could only be one thing: moonlight. And moonlight meant my escape.

"Drop the rope," I whispered, my prayers somehow finding their way into my voice, hope giving them power that fear had not.

"What?"

"I said, drop the rope."

Water dripped. Luc's breathing grew still and even. A draft chilled my skin and the rope around my ankle grew slack.

But before I got the chance to run, the light was upon us. Someone else was in the tunnel.

"What the…" Luc started to say, and then with a grunt, he tackled me from behind.

"Help!" I gasped, but I couldn't draw breath beneath his bulk. Squeezing an elbow underneath me, I pushed up, gasped in a mouthful of air and screamed. Luc's fist connected with the back of my head, driving my face into the rocky floor, but my voice echoed through the tunnel. *Help… help… help…*

I tried to turn over to fight, but Luc pummeled my skull, sending a wave of dizziness through me. Light flashed in my eyes, and abruptly his weight disappeared. With a muffled "Ooofff" and a groan of pain, Luc fell to the ground next to me. Every inch of me ached, but I didn't think anything was broken. I could still run.

"I don't believe this was part of the arrangement, Monsieur Luc."

Rising to my knees, I gazed up at the man standing in front of us, his figure outlined by moonlight. "Help me," I pleaded, tugging on the silken fabric of his cloak. "Please help me! He's kidnapped me from my family and intends to sell me to the trolls."

"Is that so?" His voice had the lyrical cadence of the court, although I was surprised to find a nobleman stooping to treasure hunting. I was in no position to judge, though. I'd take assistance where I could find it. I crawled on hands and knees, putting the man between Luc and me. Anyone had to be better than Luc.

My eyes fixed on the glowing lamp dancing behind his head. No, not a lamp – an orb that seemed to be floating through the air of its own accord. It swung round, hanging near my face, dazzling me with brightness but exuding only a little warmth.

"How badly are you injured, Mademoiselle de Troyes?"

I reached up to touch the light, then, thinking better of it, withdrew my hand. Only then did I realize he'd called me by name. I met his eyes. Or eye, rather. He stood peculiarly and kept his face turned to one side, revealing only his profile. He was perhaps my brother's age, and particularly handsome. The light of the orb reflected in his silvery grey eye as though the glow came from within. I'd never met anyone in my life with eyes like his.

"I'm afraid you have the advantage, monsieur, for while you know my name, I don't know yours." My heart beat faster. Something was dreadfully amiss. Apprehension made my hackles rise like a dog's as I eyed the man up and down. Who was he and what was he doing beneath the rubble of Forsaken Mountain?

"I should beg your pardon, mademoiselle, for failing to introduce myself. I am Marc de Biron, Comte de Courville." His attention moved to Luc. "You were to bring her unharmed."

"You're lucky she's still alive – we nearly got ate by that sluag," Luc retorted.

"You're lucky you didn't bring half a dozen of them down upon you the way you two carried on. I wouldn't be surprised if they could account your argument word for word in Trollus, you were so infernally loud!"

"No," I whispered. "No, no, no." Every instinct said to run, but which way? I had no light, and the sluag blocked the way we'd come from. But forward was where he'd come from and he was... Rising to my feet, I cowered against the wall. "You're a... He's a..."

"Aye, Cécile," Luc said, finally taking notice of my yammering. "He's a troll all right."

"But you said they were monst..." The troll abruptly turned and faced me straight on, and the word died on my lips, replaced by a scream. Luc had been telling the truth.

CHAPTER 4
Cécile

The two sides of his face, so flawless on their own, were like halves of a fractured sculpture put back together askew. The lack of symmetry was more than unsettling – it was shocking, gruesome even. One eye higher than the other. One ear lower than the other. A mouth marred by a permanently sardonic twist. I leapt back and into Luc, who clamped a filthy hand over my lips, silencing the scream.

"Not a wise idea," he whispered in my ear before dropping his hand.

"I'm sorry," I said, and repeated myself again because my mind didn't seem able to come up with any more words. "I'm sorry."

The silence stretched. When I raised my head, the light had retreated behind him, casting his face in shadows once more.

"Come," he said. "They are expecting you."

Abruptly, he turned, cloak flaring out as he strode down the tunnel. Then he hesitated, and to my dismay, extended his elbow. "Mademoiselle."

I didn't want to take his arm, because doing so meant agreeing to go with him. I stared back the way we came – towards the surface, where my father and our neighbors were frantically searching for me. But they'd never suspect where Luc had taken me. I'd have to rely on my own gumption to get free, but now was not the time – not when they expected an escape attempt.

"You have my word, mademoiselle. I will not harm you in any way."

Something about the way he said the words made me believe him. Taking a deep breath, I walked towards the troll and rested my hand on his arm. The brocade of his coat felt warm and rich beneath my cold fingers. There was strength, too – caged like the tiger in the circus my father had once taken me to see. But that wasn't what sent a shiver down my spine. Like the prickle of a sand-filled wind, or the charge in the air during a thunderstorm, power washed over me. Though I never thought such a thing was possible, magic existed here with the force to lift a man and light the darkness. Perhaps my ready belief was naive, but I knew in my gut that the trolls possessed magic.

My tongue ran over dry lips. For now, I would play along. "Then we shouldn't keep them waiting."

He escorted us through the maze of tunnels, always confident of which way to turn, though to my eyes, nothing distinguished one tunnel from another. A labyrinth designed to lure a man in, but never allow him out again. Despite my best efforts, I shivered.

The troll glanced down at me. Silently, he disengaged his arm from mine and unclasped his cloak, draping warmth on my shoulders. "Thank you," I said, wrapping the silken fabric around me. One silver eye met mine, his face tilted to restrict my view to his profile. I wondered if he always carried himself this way, or whether he concealed his deformity for my benefit. "It is nothing," he said. "I've been instructed to ensure you are well treated."

Behind us, Luc gave a soft snort. I ignored him and took the troll's arm again.

The ground grew more even, rubbed smooth in a manner suggesting countless feet had trod this path over the years. Eventually the bare rock gave way to paving tiles set in flowing mosaics of black, grey, and white. On the walls of the tunnel, a clear, horizontal line delineated the break between mountain and a rubble of man-made, or perhaps troll-made, structures. The line rose as we walked, as though an invisible force held the fallen mountain up higher and higher the further we went, a city street rising from the rubble. I reached out to trail my fingertips along the seemingly empty space and jerked back.

It was warm.

Tentatively, I raised my hand again and slid my fingers into the gap. Liquid heat enveloped my skin, tangible, but somehow not. I tried to scoop some out, but the magic flowed through and around my hand, bound to its place. The break rose until it was beyond my reach.

"The magic holds the mountain up," I murmured, examining the walls of stonework between which we now passed.

"It does," the troll agreed. "It is part of the tree."

Tree?

Glancing up, I realized he had been watching me. The look in his eye was considering, appraising, even. But it was the pity I saw there that revived my fear. Why was I here? What deal had Luc negotiated with the trolls and what part did I play?

We rounded a turn and ahead metal gates barred our path. Beyond shone a silver glow that I knew better than to mistake for moonlight. A faint gust of air blew down the corridor, dampening my cheeks with mist, accompanied by the sound of falling water. Curiosity warred with fear. Dropping the troll's arm, I stepped through the gate and out on a ledge. The cavern was enormous and what lay in the valley below drew me to my knees.

The lost city of Trollus.

"Stones and sky," I whispered.

"Just stones here," Luc commented from behind us. The troll's hand balled up into an angry fist, but Luc spoke the truth. Darkness cloaked the cavern and solid rock formed the ceiling. No stars shone through, no moon.

"This way, mademoiselle." He took my arm, and pulled me to my feet. The three of us started down a flight of granite steps lit periodically with crystal lampposts glowing silver. The sides of the valley were terraced, the white stone buildings lining each level. Most impressive, though, was the waterfall cascading out of the blackness to form the churning river below. The roar of water echoed ceaselessly through the cavern. It was enough to drive one to madness, and I wondered how the trolls abided the constant din.

Realization struck me. "That's the Devil's Cauldron!"

"We call it Heaven's Gates," the troll murmured, and I did not miss the irony in his voice. I had heard the legend of the Cauldron. It was said that the Brûlé river flowed between Forsaken Mountain and its southern neighbor, but where it met the rock fall, it disappeared into a hole in the ground. It was said that a past duke had paid a beggar man to brave the Cauldron in a wooden barrel, and that a dozen years afterward, he had appeared in Trianon hale and healthy, but unable to account where he had been.

"Good evening to you, Lord Marc."

The approaching voice startled me and I jumped, then peered into the darkness. A glowing orb moved steadily towards us – a faintly visible shape moving awkwardly across the ground. The troll rolled into our pool of light, and I had to bite my lip to keep from gasping at the shrunken, useless limbs attached to the creature's torso. Rolling to its crippled feet, it reached out to touch a crystal lamppost, the light flaring brighter.

"Good evening, Clarence," the Comte said, his voice soft as he tugged me towards the next set of steps.

"Is she the one?"

"We'll soon find out, I suppose," Marc replied. His tone indicated that no further questions would be appreciated.

The thing called Clarence looked me over with glowing silver irises, as if wondering whether I was good enough to eat. I turned away, cringing. When I found the nerve to glance back, the troll had resumed its rolling progress.

"Am I the one for what?" I asked, darting a look at his face. But the Comte did not answer. My mind raced with possibilities, but none seemed to justify the effort that had gone into procuring me.

An impeccably clean cobbled street snaked down the side of the valley, but the Comte led us instead down the long flights of stone stairs towards the river below. The masonry was unlike anything I had ever seen, no surface left unadorned. It would have required centuries of work, but I supposed that centuries they'd had. Fountains and statues graced every corner. In place of greenery stood gardens of glassworks sculpted into trees, bushes, and flowers. The delicate displays would not have lasted more than a month exposed to the elements above ground. Then again, hailstorms likely did not trouble Trollus.

But it was an empty beauty. With the exception of ourselves and Clarence, I had not seen a single sign of life within the city. "Where is everyone?" I asked in a low voice.

"It is past curfew," the Comte replied. "They are inside." He gestured towards a building, and I noticed a set of curtains twitch shut, but not before I'd glimpsed a set of luminescent eyes staring out at me.

"That's new," Luc muttered, and I looked around with unease at the dark windows lining the streets. Now that I knew they were there, I could feel eyes on me. The Comte gripped the hilt of his sword with one leather clad hand, tension cloaking his shadowed form as he scanned our surroundings. "We should not linger," he said, lengthening his stride so that I had to trot to keep up.

He relaxed only when we reached the palace rising up next to the misting river. Although the darkness prevented me from ascertaining its total magnitude, I suspected it was enormous. Passing through gilded gates guarded by armored trolls, we walked up a long drive flanked with marble statues and glasswork. The entrance to the palace loomed ahead of us, white and glittering gold in the Comte's approaching light. It was more opulent than even the Regent's palace in Trianon, but it was the silence that struck me most. No horses' hooves, no barking dogs, no voices. Only falling water and the ever-present silver glow of troll-light.

"This way, please," the Comte said, leading us through an unguarded entrance into the palace.

It was much darker within than without, illumination limited to the small orb dogging the troll's steps. "Do you all have one of those lights?" I asked. "How do they work?"

He glanced up at the orb and it flared brighter and larger, split into three little orbs, and then reformed into one. "Magic," he replied, "defies explanation."

And I had no chance to ask for one as we reached a set of doors guarded by one troll. No... two? I tried not to stare at the troll as we walked by, but I'd never seen a man with two heads before. Both heads saluted and said, "My lord," to the Comte, so I settled on two.

"I'd advise you to speak only when spoken to," he murmured as we marched down the long hall. Looking over his shoulder at Luc, he added, "You as well."

Our boots thudded against the tiled floor, the sound echoing throughout the cavernous room. Mirrors lined the walls, reflecting my terrified expression back at me. Next to each of the columns supporting the roof stood a golden floor lamp carved into a fantastical creature, troll-light glowing from its eyes. The ceiling above was painted in a fresco, but the details were obscured by the dimness.

The two trolls on the far dais drew my gaze, for they could not have been more different. The male troll sat on the throne, or rather perched, for his enormous, silk-encased rolls did not fit between the arms of the chair. He stared intently at me, his glittering eyes shrewd. At his side stood an exceptionally lovely troll, long black curls cascading over her jeweled velvet clothing. Her expression was vacant and unseeing, and I shivered as a dreamy smile crossed over her lips.

The Comte stopped and bowed deeply. I curtsied awkwardly next to him.

"Your Majesty, may I present Mademoiselle Cécile de Troyes."

The corpulent King peered down at me and then made a flapping gesture next to his head. The Comte hastily pulled back the hood of my cloak.

"Hmmm," the King said, making a face. "I'm not sure this is what we bargained for, boy. We expected the girl to be attractive."

If I hadn't been so terrified, I would have been insulted.

The Comte came to my rescue. "She's been through quite the ordeal, Your Majesty. They had a near encounter with a sluag, and she's been ill treated by her guide. I'm certain once she's cleaned up and properly attired, she will be a fair beauty."

Whether the trolls found me attractive or not was the least of my concerns, but I was grateful for Lord Marc's defense. There was something about the tone of his voice that suggested he did not support what was being done to me. And he had given his word that he would never harm me. Between Luc and the King, I was beginning to think that Marc was the closest thing I had to an ally in this place.

"Hmmm." The King looked me up and down, silver eyes narrow. "I suppose there might be something beneath all the filth."

"Let me see her," said a shrill voice, and I searched the room for its source. "Turn around!" the voice demanded, and so I did.

"Not you, girl," said the King.

Turning back to face the throne, I felt a wave of dizziness hit me. "Oh my," I said. "Oh my, oh my." It had been the Queen whom the voice had ordered to turn, and from her back sprouted a doll-sized woman who gestured for me to step closer.

"Come here, girl."

Stiff-kneed and frozen in place, my heart pounded so hard it rivaled the waterfall for noise. The Queen began an awkward backwards shuffle towards me, her skirts tangling up her feet and threatening to send both of them toppling. Marc rushed forward to grasp her arm and prevent disaster, while I remained rooted still.

The little troll scowled. "You'd think after all these years you'd have learned to walk backwards, Matilde."

"Thank you, Marc," the Queen trilled, ignoring her twin. She shuffled until her miniature attachment and I stood face to face. "I am Sylvie Gaudin, Duchesse de Feltre." She clamped child-sized hands on my cheeks. I squeaked, fighting the urge to slap her away. Her silver gaze bore into me, and I swear she delved into the depths of my soul. "This is the one."

"Are you certain?" the King asked from his perch on the throne. "She rather smells."

"She meets the criteria given to us by the foretelling. You do sing, don't you?" the troll woman asked.

"Yes," I croaked, not knowing why it mattered. "What do you intend to do with me?"

"Why, to bond you to our dear Tristan," the troll said, smiling at me. "You are to be a princess of Trollus and mother of his children; and in doing so, you will set us all free."

The world spun and I jerked away from her grip. Behind me, a small group of trolls had silently gathered and they watched me stumble down the steps towards them. Not all of them were deformed, but they were monsters still, every one of them. And I was to wed one. To be bedded by one. To bear its children. This wasn't how it was supposed to go. I was supposed to be on my way to Trianon to get everything I had ever wanted. Now, not only had I lost everything – my family, my friends, my dreams – I had just been informed that what life I had left would be spent in an endless nightmare.

I heard motion behind me, and Luc bent to pass me a handkerchief. "At least you'll be rich," he murmured into my ear. "Just close your eyes and think of gold."

I spat at him, the glob of vomit-tinged spit dribbling down his cheek. He raised a hand to slap me, but it froze in place.

"There will be none of that, Monsieur Luc." The tiny troll's face grew cold and expressionless.

"You can't make me do this," I said to her, climbing to my feet. "I want to go home."

Her brow crinkled, but whether from sympathy or anger, I couldn't tell. "This is your home now, Cécile."

"No." I shook my head rapidly, heedless of the tears running down my face. "I'd rather die."

She tilted her head. "Making statements like that will do you no good, girl. We will only have you watched day and night to ensure you do not harm yourself."

I bolted down the steps, but barely got halfway before bands of warm power lashed around my waist, lifting me up into the air. I screamed, but the sound abruptly cut off as a ball of what could only be magic shoved its way between my teeth. I struggled to breathe as invisible cords dragged me through the air and dropped me in front of the troll queen's conjoined twin.

"You are only making things more difficult for yourself."

Hovering in the air with my arms bound and my mouth gagged, it was hard to put up much of a show of resistance, but I threw venom into my glare. The tiny troll chuckled. "You've got spirit, I'll grant you that."

The King abruptly rose to his feet. "We are of a mind to let Tristan have a look at her first. Perhaps she won't be to his taste."

"How could she be?" a dry voice chimed in from behind me. "She's human."

I craned my neck around to look at the troll who had spoken. He was older, black hair streaked with grey. My eyes searched for whatever defect marked him like the other trolls, but there was none. He was shaped as well as any human, but there was no mistaking what he was. Otherness radiated from him, and the malice in his metallic gaze made me look away.

"The human part isn't negotiable," the King snapped. "And if I wanted your opinion, Angoulême, I would have asked." He turned back to the little troll woman. "You are certain this will work?"

"If we've interpreted the foretelling correctly, then yes," she said.

"Ironic, don't you think, that Tristan was the only one to bear witness to this foretelling," the troll called Angoulême said. "Unless you can remember the details, Sylvie?"

The Duchesse shook her head.

"I was there," the Queen chimed in. "Of course my memory isn't what it used to be."

No one paid her any attention except me. I desperately wanted to know more about the circumstances that had brought me here. What did the foretelling say and what did it have to do with me? Was it just because I was a convenient human girl, or was there something more? Why, if they loathed humans so much, could they possibly want to wed me to a prince? Only that wasn't the word she'd used – she'd said I'd be bonded to him. What did that even mean?

"I questioned Tristan myself," the King snapped. "For all his faults, the boy has excellent attention to detail. He made no mistakes."

"I didn't say he had," Angoulême said. "My concern is rather for what he might have done on purpose."

"Enough!" The King gestured to the doors. "Let him see her. If he is content, we will proceed."

"He will be." The Duchesse's voice was so quiet, only I heard. "She will shake the foundations of Trollus to the core. Mark my words."

We walked in a procession through the corridors. Or rather, they walked and I floated along behind them. While I might normally have been keen to experience the weightlessness of flying, the knowledge that I flew towards an unwanted fate ruined the effect. The Queen marched in front of me, leaving me to face her tiny sister for the journey. My mind spun with the possibilities awaiting me, each more horrible than the next. Would he be dimwitted like the Queen? Deformed like Marc? Enormously fat as his father, the King? He could be all of them together, or more terrible than my wildest imagination.

I made little note of the palace corridors as we passed through them. I couldn't make out anything clearly, anyway. A tiny ball of light floated in front of every member of our small entourage, though the gloom troubled the trolls not in the slightest. Their metallic eyes pierced the darkness, and I marked how they watched me, finding it impossible to decipher what they were thinking. Did their cold hearts pity me? Were the women glad it was I, and not they, floating towards this forced match? A fresh crop of tears stung the cuts on my cheeks. I tried to wipe them away, but of course, I could not. My body was bound in place as surely as if I'd been tied head to foot with rope.

Ahead of the procession, I heard the tinkling laugh of a girl and the sound of a door slamming against a wall.

"His Majesty, the King!" the two-headed troll guard announced.

Afraid, I squeezed my eyes shut. When I finally found the nerve to open them, I hovered in a room richly decorated with tapestries and thick carpets. At its center stood a table and two high-backed chairs. Above the table floated half a dozen boards littered with tiny figurines. A young woman stood next to a chair, her face lowered and knees bent into a deep curtsy. Little of who sat in the other seat was visible to me, for his back was to us: only the bend of a black-clad elbow, the curve of a pale-skinned hand resting on the arm of the chair.

My head swam and I gasped for air, having unconsciously been holding my breath. The girl rose, and her eyes latched onto me. She was beautiful, for an instant, and then her expression twisted with rage. The game boards fell to the table with a clatter. I jerked my gaze away from hers, fixing it instead on the tiny figures spilled across the carpet.

"You can't be serious?" she hissed. "Her? This, this thing?"

The Duchesse spoke. "Leave us, Anaïs."

She didn't move.

"Now, Anaïs. This is no business of yours."

The girl remained fixed on the spot, jaw clenched in obvious anger.

"Anaïs." The King spoke softly, but the girl reacted to the sound of her name as though she'd been slapped, recoiling backward. I watched in amazement as a red, hand-shaped mark rose briefly on her cheek, then faded away. Eyes filled with real terror, the troll girl cowered in front of us.

"Get. Out."

"Your Majesties. Your Grace," the girl whispered as she bolted out of the rooms. If the thick carpets managed to muffle the hurried thump of her heeled shoes, they did nothing to hide the slam of the door shutting behind us.

The King cleared his throat. "Tristan, we have the human."

The Prince said nothing at first, but the boards rose once again into the air, invisible fingers plucking the pieces off the carpet, pausing in consideration, and then returning them to their places on the board. "We'd been at this round for nigh on three months now."

His voice was quiet, marked with the faint accent all the trolls had, and showed no concern for the female companion his father had just slapped. I shuddered, wishing he would turn around and, at the same time, hoping he wouldn't.

"I'm certain Anaïs will regret dropping the game," the King said.

The Prince laughed softly, but he didn't sound the least bit amused to me. "Unlikely, given that she was losing. She hates to lose."

The King frowned. "Tristan, I thought you'd want to have a look at the girl before we…" he glanced over at me, "finalized the contract."

The Prince's hand flexed, fingers digging ever so slightly into the upholstery. I might not even have noticed if not for the fact my eyes had been fixated on that one glimpse of flesh, trying to judge his proportion and failing mightily.

"Why?" The irritation in his voice cut across the room. "My opinion of this venture has counted for nothing up to this point."

"Well, it matters now," the King snapped. "Look at her. Decide."

The Prince didn't move. "And if I say no?"

"Then we'll procure another."

"And if I don't like her," the Prince asked, "will you procure another? Will you empty your vaults searching for a human girl who meets the criteria and whom I find tolerable? Will the river run red with the blood of my discards?" Not waiting for an answer, he said, "This one will do as well as any."

He rose suddenly from the chair, and before I had the chance to take a breath, he turned. All my preparations were for naught, for despite the magic gagging me, I still managed to gasp aloud.

He was nothing like what I'd expected.

CHAPTER 5
Cécile

Prince Tristan was tall and lean, and a fierce intellect gleamed in his silver troll eyes. He couldn't have been much older than I was – that is, if trolls aged the same way humans do. Dressed impeccably, he wore a black frock coat with a single-breasted vest and fine linen shirt beneath. Black breeches were tucked into black riding boots that I doubted had ever seen the sides of a horse.

He also had the most exquisite face of any boy I'd ever seen. Inky black hair, sculpted cheekbones and jaw, and a full but unsmiling mouth. He looked like Prince Charming from the fairytales, except for one thing: Prince Charming was human, and the boy standing in front of me was decidedly not. His pale skin was too flawless, his motions too smooth and controlled. My skin prickled with a sense of wrongness.

He crossed his arms. "You know, it is exceedingly rude to stare."

I flinched and began an intent examination of the carpet at my feet. Apparently I could scratch the charming bit as well.

"Be pleasant, Tristan," the Duchesse said.

He sniffed. "She's the rude one, Aunty. First she stares and now she refuses to look at me. I'm quite convinced I have greens or something worse stuck between my teeth."

I glanced up, hoping to catch a glimpse of said teeth. He caught me and grinned. "Were you expecting them to be pointed?"

My face burned and I fixed my eyes back on the carpet, determined never to look up again. I immediately caught myself glancing through my eyelashes at him once more.

"Pointed teeth would give one an appearance of ferocity," he said, tapping a straight white tooth. "Although that might require one to follow through with biting someone from time to time, and the thought is enough to make one feel ill. I don't even like my meat cooked rare."

"You bit Vincent once," Marc said from behind me. "So you can't be entirely opposed to the idea."

Tristan shot a vitriolic glare in his direction. "Curse you for bringing up such vile memories, Marc, and in the presence of a girl. In my defense, lady, I was only three and Vincent was sitting on my head. I rather thought I was about to meet my end suffocated between his bum cheeks. Anyone would have done the same. Wouldn't you agree, mademoiselle... what did you say her name was again?"

Even if I hadn't a gag of magic in my mouth, I wouldn't have dared spoken.

Tristan peered at me as though I were a curious insect. "She isn't mute, is she? That would be dreadful." He leaned back against the chair, his strange eyes fixed on me. "On second thought, perhaps it wouldn't be dreadful at all. I hardly need another woman in my life telling me what to do, and it would mean I could do all the talking and she the listening."

"Perhaps our mistake was in not finding you a deaf one," Marc said. "And her name is Cécile de Troyes, which you very well know, so quit pretending otherwise."

"Thank you, cousin. It was on the tip of my tongue. Now Mademoiselle de Troyes, tell us your thoughts. Astound us with your wit."

"Mmmmm hmmmm," I mumbled around the gag.

"Could you repeat that?" he said, coming closer. "Afraid I didn't quite catch the punch line." A slender finger caught me under the chin, lifting my face. He frowned. "Release her, Aunty."

"She tried to run."

A noise of exasperation passed his lips. "To where? There is nowhere for her to go, nowhere to hide. Binding her is unnecessary."

His flippancy made my heart sink – the very idea of my escape was so improbable to him that it was little more than a jest.

I felt power brush over my skin, and I dropped to numb feet. If not for Marc taking hold of my arm, I'd have sprawled across the carpets in front of them all.

"Now that your speech impediment has been rectified, perhaps you might say something. It would be best if it were humorous. I enjoy a good jest."

"You are dreadfully rude," I said to him.

He sighed. "That wasn't the slightest bit funny."

"Nor are you in any way a gentleman."

"Cruel truths, mademoiselle, but tell me, did you expect otherwise?" His eyes gleamed, not with humor, but something else.

"I confess my expectations were low," I snapped.

"I'm a firm believer in low expectations, myself," he said cheerfully. "Makes for less disappointment in life. For instance, I expected you to arrive fully clothed, but here you are in little more than a scrap of fabric that might once have been a shift." His eyes raked over my body, and I jerked the edges of Marc's cloak around me.

"Watch your tongue, Tristan," the Duchesse snapped.

"Ridiculous expression, that," Tristan said. "I can't very well observe my own tongue unless I am to sit in front of a mirror, and I can't tolerate such vanity. Now tell me, Cécile – you don't mind if I call you by your given name, do you? Considering we are about to become as close as a dog to his fleas, the familiarity seems appropriate, don't you think?"

I glared at him.

"Splendid! As I was saying then, Cécile, what became of your clothing? Or is this the latest fashion on the Isle, and I am merely behind the times?"

I scowled at him. "I was deprived of my dress."

"Really?" One eyebrow rose. "That sounds most salacious – perhaps you'll regale us with the details later?"

"Perhaps not." I crossed my arms tightly, trying to hide my mortification.

"More's the pity," Tristan sighed rather melodramatically. "It would have been the first interesting thing you've said."

"Are you very nearly finished, Tristan?" the King asked wearily. "We are somewhat pressed for time."

"Nearly," Tristan agreed. "I have only one question."

"Which is?"

"Who damaged her? Granted, I don't spend much time in the company of humans, but in my experience, they don't generally drip blood without cause. I was under the impression I'd be getting a whole and healthy human."

Out of the corner of my eye, I watched Marc jerk his chin in Luc's direction. Tristan's gaze turned to my kidnapper, whose arm remained frozen up in the air where the Duchesse had left it, perpetually poised to strike. The Prince's jaw tightened, and the temperature in the room rose, driving the chill from my fingers.

"Tristan." The King stood behind me, but I heard the warning note in his voice. "He upheld his end of the bargain. We shall uphold ours."

The troll prince rubbed a hand across his face, his countenance turning to indifference. "Of course. We agreed to her weight in gold, did we not?"

I gasped, as horrified as I was astonished by the amount.

"Aye, Your Highness," Luc replied.

"You see, Mademoiselle de Troyes, another instance where low expectations have served me well. Given the contract your dear friend Luc made with us, I half expected him to deliver me a girl of prodigious girth to tip the scales in his favor. Imagine what a pleasant surprise it was for me to discover you were just a little bit of a thing."

"Tristan." The King's voice oozed admonition.

Tristan's mouth twisted up at the corner. "Well then, best of luck in your travels through the labyrinth with all your gold, Monsieur Luc. I hope you have a strong back."

He gave Luc a companionable slap on the shoulder that sent him staggering, but also released his frozen arm.

Luc shot him a black glare and rubbed his shoulder. "Aye, my lord. Best wishes on your forthcoming nuptials."

To this, Tristan said nothing, only strode out of the room. I cringed, though; for as much as I did not want to marry a troll, I was just as certain the troll didn't want to marry me.

The bargain truly was for my weight in gold. Our procession continued through the hallways and into enormous rooms piled high with treasure of every sort. Gold and silver in heavy chests, amethysts and opals spilling across tables or adorning priceless jewelry. Stacks of precious plates and beautiful glassworks sat on tables or the floor. In the center stood a giant copper scale, and a warm coil of power gently lifted and deposited me on one side. Luc leapt to sort through the treasure, piling up select pieces on the other side of the scale, a grin plastered on his face. Gold coins, gold plates, gold jewelry, and even a golden duck statuette, but when he tossed up a jeweled necklace, the King snapped his fingers.

"Gold only, boy!"

Marc plucked the offending jewels off the scale (I don't think the King moved if he could help it) and tossed the necklace back into the piles of treasure.

Then they dithered. A coin here, a coin there, all in an attempt to secure a perfect alignment. My incessant shivering set the scale to trembling and did not speed along the process. They had deprived me of my cloak and boots, leaving me in only a shift and my mother's necklace. The

King certainly would have stripped me naked if not for the intervention of the Queen and her sister. As it was, I was frozen and hungry and I desperately had to pee. No doubt the King would have sent me to the privy to rid myself of the extra weight, but I wasn't about to share my discomfort.

And I was done with crying – tears accomplished nothing but exhausting me further and I needed my wits about me if I were going to escape this place. Perhaps not today, tomorrow, or even the next day, but I would stand beneath the sun again. I swore it to myself.

My scowl deepened as I brooded on the various ways I would see Luc punished for his actions. I did not realize the weighing process had concluded until I was abruptly lifted off the scale and set next to Marc. He wrapped the cloak around my shoulders and pulled the hood up, obscuring my face.

"Your mien is of one who is plotting murder," he said in a quiet voice, handing over my battered boots.

"More than one," I replied, struggling with numb fingers to tie the laces.

To my shock, he knelt at my feet and tied them for me, black hair falling forward to hide his face from me. "Your feelings are understandable, Cécile," he said, "but for your sake, it would be best if you kept them to yourself. Tristan is my cousin and closest friend. I assure you that he will allow no harm to come to you. Although you did not choose this life, perhaps, over time, you might come to find it satisfactory." He stood up.

I met his gaze. "Is that what you aim for in life, my lord? Satisfactory?" He was being kind, I knew, but I had never had a good grasp over my temper. "For I have always aimed for something more. Happiness, for instance."

"I aim to live, my lady," he replied, turning to the shadows. "You should do the same."

The King's voice silenced us. "You needn't take payment all at once, boy. No doubt it would be easier to make several trips."

Luc snorted. "You think I trust you to give me the rest if I leave my gold here? Stones and sky, you must take me for a fool." He continued shoving the treasure into his pack.

I was convinced his rudeness would garner the King's ire, but His Majesty seemed only amused. "As you wish." He gestured in our direction. "Get her cleaned up and dressed, Marc. The moon reaches its zenith in only a few hours."

"What happens then?" I asked, feeling my hands turn colder still.

Marc took hold of my arm and led me from the room. "You'll be bonded."

CHAPTER 6
Cécile

The chambers Marc led me to were lit by the light of two lovely troll girls dressed in drab grey dresses belted with black and white sashes. They dropped into deep curtsies at our entrance. The room itself was lushly appointed: tapestries and paintings covered the walls and thick carpets muffled my footsteps. In the center stood a giant copper bathtub filled with water and next to it was a small dining table set with a feast fit for a queen. It made me think of the dinner I had missed tonight – the one my grandmother had been preparing for my going away party. My father would have set up a pig turning on a spit over the open flames, and I could imagine our dogs watching with wistful eyes, begging whoever walked near for scraps. Gran would have made some potato mash, along with last year's carrots and beets drenched with butter. And her famous apple cinnamon cake. Cake that couldn't be made without eggs. I squeezed my eyes shut, remembering the way the yellow yolks had mixed into the mud. I had gone away, but there would have been no cake, no dinner, no party. Only a fruitless search in the growing dark.

"Quit being a sentimental fool," I muttered to myself. "It's just food." The three trolls look at me askance, and I gave them a weak smile. "That's quite the spread."

"Have as much as you like," Marc said. "If there is anything in particular you want, let the girls know and they will arrange for it." He then turned to the servants. "You have three hours."

"Yes, my lord," the girls responded in unison, curtsying again as he strode from the room.

"You must be hungry, my lady," one of them said.

"Mostly, I have to pee."

The girls giggled and pointed to a side door. "Over there, my lady."

After I had rid myself of a few gold coins' worth of extra weight, I came back and surveyed my options: bath or food. My growling stomach decided for me. I set into a bowl of thick stew as if I hadn't seen food all day, which I hadn't, and then gobbled down handfuls of berries and an apple, their juices running down my chin to add stains to my already destroyed shift. The girls watched me with wide eyes. "What are your names?" I asked between bites.

Both of them jerked as though slapped. I stopped chewing, and watched them exchange meaningful glances. "I don't think that is what she means," one whispered to the other.

"I'm called Élise," the elder said to me after an uncomfortable pause. "Call her Zoé."

"Cécile," I said around a mouthful of bread, deciding to ignore the awkwardness. I was acting like I'd never met a manner in my life, but stones and sky, I was hungry.

"We know, my lady. We've been expecting you."

The bread stuck in my throat, and I set aside the rest of the loaf, my hunger vanished. "I'm not anyone's lady. I'm just Cécile."

"You are betrothed to Prince Tristan, my lady. After tonight, you will be a princess of Trollus," Zoé said, her wide eyes growing even wider. "You are so fortunate, my lady – His Highness is exceptionally handsome."

"And brave," Élise chimed in. The girls clutched each other's arms and pretended to swoon.

"And dreadfully rude," I grumbled, getting to my feet and walking over to the tub. I'd never bathed in front of anyone other than my gran or my sister before, but I knew that this was how the nobility did things. Making a fuss over their presence would only draw attention to my common upbringing. Pride was armor, and I wouldn't let them take it from me. My scant clothing discarded, I climbed hurriedly in, wincing as my collection of abrasions stung.

"Is the water warm enough, my lady?" Élise asked, passing me a sponge.

"It's…" I glanced towards the cold fireplace on the one wall. Clearly the grate hadn't known a fire in a long time. After a moment's contemplation, I realized I hadn't seen an open flame since Luc's lantern. "I'd like it a bit warmer," I said, curious as to how she'd manage such a feat.

The troll set aside the bottle of bath salts she had been pouring in and touched the water with a fingertip. It swirled around me, glowing faintly silver, and almost instantaneously the temperature rose. She withdrew her hand, and the steaming contents settled. "Warm enough?"

I soaked for a good hour in the tub, the trolls ignoring my

protests and setting to scrubbing, trimming, washing, and filing with an intensity never before directed at my body.

With the dirt washed away, my injuries stood out in stark reds and purples on my pale skin. Élise dispatched Zoé to get some ice – something I learned their magic could not create –and I spent the rest of my bath holding a silk-wrapped block against my swollen eye while I sipped a cup of mulled wine.

Élise and Zoé were quite beautiful, but something set them apart from the broken beauty of the troll nobility. Their hair, for one, was not jet black but dark brown, and a faint flush warmed their faces that did not mark the cheeks of the other trolls. "You two are sisters?" I asked.

"Yes, my lady," Zoé replied from where she sat at my feet. Her eyes scrutinized my face as though searching for something. "Our mother was human – like you."

So the legends were true. The trolls had been at the business of stealing, or perhaps purchasing, young women for some time. "Is she here in Trollus?" Maybe they let them go once they'd fulfilled their duties.

"No, my lady." Sorrow crossed her face. "She died when we were quite young."

"I'm sorry," I said, wishing there was some way to ask how the woman had died. Part of me was still convinced I'd come across a case of a human roasting in a cooking pot.

"Such a beautiful color," Élise said, interrupting my thoughts. "When they told us you had red hair, I scarcely believed their words. Is such a shade common under the sun?"

"Not really," I admitted.

"Then it must be prized."

I thought about how often I'd wished I'd been born with my sister's blonde hair, or even my brother's plain brown mop. "Red hair isn't prized at all. Everyone teases me all the time, and being a redhead means I get loads of freckles in the summer. My mother tells me I should stay out of the sun, which is hardly possible on a farm."

"Why would anyone choose to stay out of the sun?"

I bit my lip, realizing that obviously the sun would be a sensitive issue for the trolls. I shrugged and set the cup aside. "My mother is vain. Besides," I said, in an attempt to change the subject, "I'd rather have dark hair like you trolls." A compliment never hurt.

Élise shook her head. "Nothing common is prized, my lady. One might as well value a stone in a sea of rock as value black hair in Trollus. Now come," she said, motioning for me to follow. "Time for you to dress."

Walking stiffly over to the privacy screen, I ran a hand down a heavy, dark green silk dress, which felt warm, almost alive, under my fingertips. Onyx beads decorated the cuffs and tiny jet buttons marched up the back to the high lace collar.

My wedding dress.

"Why isn't it white?" I couldn't think of anything else to say. In the Hollow, we had a tradition where every girl's dress included something from a wedding dress of a family member or friend. Sometimes it was just a bit of lace or some fancy buttons, but often gowns were entirely created out of dresses from weddings past. Gran said that the tradition brought love and good fortune into the union. I had always seen myself in the dress in which she had married my grandfather, with its handmade lace overlay. Not this unworn, unloved... thing.

Sweat broke out on my hands and I grew cold beneath the thick robes. A haze of black crept over my vision of the dress. My knees trembled and my body swayed. "I think I'm going to be sick." A basin appeared in front of me, and I proceeded to retch up everything I'd just consumed. I couldn't do this; couldn't go through with what they were asking of me. If I stayed, my virtue would be the price, and that was something I could never win back. No one would care whether it was against my wishes or not – my reputation, such as it was, would be ruined. I had to escape now.

Avoiding the concerned gazes of the girls, I held up my hand. "I need some time alone." My eyes latched on the adjoining bedchamber. "I'll lie down for a few moments." Walking into the other room, I shut the door firmly behind me and then dashed on silent feet to the one leading to the hallway. The lock was bolted.

With one of my hairpins, I set to work on the lock, grateful, not for the first time, to my brother for teaching me how. When the catch was sprung, I turned the knob, and with a backward glance at the empty room, stepped into the hall. I immediately collided with something solid.

"Fancy meeting you here, Cécile."

My heart sunk. "It's you."

"The one, the only, as they like to say," Tristan said affably, brushing off his coat where I'd bumped into him.

"Which 'they' would that be?" I asked.

"Oh, you know. Them." He waved a hand in the air, dismissing the question. Then he frowned. "Have you recently vomited? How vile. It wasn't because you indulged in too much wine, was it? I can certainly tolerate drunkenness in myself, but not in a woman. It's quite unladylike."

Raising my chin, I tightened the cord holding my robe in place. "I'll have you know that I've never been drunk."

He smirked. "You needn't act like that is such a grand accomplishment. I've heard the continent is full of a similar sort – teetotalers, they call them. I understand they can reduce even the liveliest party to a dull affair in no time at all."

"Don't act like you know the first thing about the continent," I snapped. "It isn't as though you've ever visited."

He flinched, silent for a moment. "Have you?"

"No," I admitted. "But I very likely would have if you hadn't kidnapped me."

"I didn't kidnap you," Tristan said, his voice filled with irritation. "Your friend Luc did."

"He wouldn't have done so, if not for you. And he isn't my friend."

"That might be the case, but I don't doubt that he'd have substituted an equivalently dastardly deed in its place." He pointed a finger at me. "Mark my words, the boy was of a vile sort."

"Then you are two of a kind," I snapped.

"Ha ha," Tristan snorted. "How dreadfully clever. And speaking of clever, is this to be your bid for escape?" He contemplated my clothing. "In a dressing gown and bare feet? Now tell me, if I go put on nightclothes and slippers, might I join you, or is this a solo adventure?"

My eyes stung. "You think this is all exceedingly funny, don't you? I'm nothing but a joke to you."

His brow creased in a frown. "If you're a joke, it isn't an especially humorous one."

I threw up my hands in frustration. "You are the most intolerable individual I've ever met."

He bowed. "Why, thank you, Cécile. Always a pleasure to have one's accomplishments recognized."

"You are the last person in the world I'd choose to marry," I hissed.

"I don't entirely relish the idea myself," Tristan said, "but sometimes we must do the unthinkable."

"Why must I?"

Tristan tipped his head slightly, expression considering. "Because you have no choice," he finally said. "Just as I have no choice. There is no way for you to escape Trollus, Cécile, and if you were caught in the attempt..." His eyes closed, black lashes resting against his cheeks. "My father's anger is a formidable thing, and I do not wish to see you harmed for aggravating him."

His eyes flickered back open. "Now let's return you to your maids – you can't very well marry me wearing such a tasteless outfit."

Élise worked a small miracle with her cosmetics. While my eye was still swollen nearly shut, at least it was returned to a normal flesh tone. The dress covered the worst of my injuries. Tight lace sleeves concealed the scrapes on my arms and the bruise purpling my right shoulder. The bodice could not have been tighter if it had been painted on, and the fabric stretched sleekly down my torso, loosening at the hip and cascading out behind me like a waterfall pouring into a river of green silk. A knock came from the door, and I wobbled as I turned, unsteady on my green and gold brocaded heels. Marc entered, carrying a gilded box and half a dozen sparkling tiaras hooked haphazardly around his arm. Setting the box down with an unceremonious thud, he unhooked the various jeweled bands and let them clatter to the table, showing as much care for their value as if they'd been glass and tin. "Take your pick."

I picked up a masterpiece of gold, black diamonds, and emeralds, marveling at how the gems glittered in the troll-light. The tiara alone would be worth a small fortune. The box of jewels Zoé was sorting through was worth enough to buy whole estates. Yet she showed less reverence for gems than she had the shoes I wore on my feet.

"That one is gaudy," she said, plucking the tiara from my hands. "This is better. And these." She handed me a simple coronet of gold and onyx and a pair of matching earrings. "You'll need to take that off," she said, gesturing to my necklace.

I touched it with one hand. "I never take this off – it was a gift from my mother."

"You aren't a farm girl any more, Cécile," she said softly. "There are expectations regarding your appearance."

I closed my hand over the pendant, loath to part with it. It was the last thing that was mine – the last bit of my identity that would be stripped away if I gave it up.

"I'll give it back to you as soon as the ceremony is over," Zoé said, and though I could see pity in her expression, she still held out her hand. This was not a choice – and the last thing I needed was her tearing it from my neck and breaking it.

Sighing, I undid the clasp and handed it over. "Put it somewhere safe."

Nodding, she put the necklace in her pocket and began fastening my new jewelry. Once these were in place, she turned me to face the full-length mirror in the corner. In the eerie glow, I scarcely recognized myself: I appeared older and, if one ignored my swollen injuries, pretty.

"Are you ready, Mademoiselle de Troyes?"

If a thousand years came and went, I still wouldn't be ready, but I gave a weak nod.

"Be brave," Marc said, the half of his face I could see filled with sympathy. "Just do as His Majesty requests and this will all be over quickly."

On Marc's arm, I walked through the hallways of the palace. The only sound beyond the ever-present roar of falling water was the click of my heels and the rustle of my dress. He said nothing. I said nothing; although I was desperate to know what to expect. I contented myself with examining the artwork lining the hallways. No surface was left unadorned, walls and alcoves filled with sculptures so detailed I half expected them to spring to life, and paintings so vivid it was like looking out a window. Never in my life had I seen such a wealth of beauty, and it seemed such a shame that it was forever consigned to shadow.

As though sensing my thoughts, Marc's light grew brighter. "I think we take the artistic talents of our people for granted sometimes," he murmured.

He paused and pushed open a door. I quickly recognized the mirrored hall from earlier, when I'd been brought to meet the King. Light flew up to the ceiling, illuminating the paintings I had caught but a glimpse of earlier. "The life's work of one of my ancestors, Charlotte Le Brun," he said.

"It's beautiful," I said, forgetting my apprehension for a moment. Winged sprites flitted among flowers, serpents soared across skies, and men and women with jewel-like eyes and hair in every color of the rainbow stared down from the ceiling.

The sound of a bell being rung echoed through the hallways. "The release of curfew," Marc explained, but his attention wasn't on me. He stood frozen, head cocked slightly as though listening for something. All I could hear was the sound of my heart pounding louder and louder. It was a long moment before he relaxed.

"Trollus isn't all bad," he said, pulling me out into the hallway. I wasn't certain whether he was trying to convince me or himself.

Despite the release of curfew, we met no one on our way. The palace seemed to be devoid of life until we reached the vaulted front entrance. The King and Queen stood waiting, surrounded by a handful of grey-clad, black- and white-sashed attendants. Tristan sat on a bench near them, head in his hands. At the sound of my heels, he leapt abruptly to his feet, but I found I could not meet his gaze. Instead I approached his parents and dropped into a deep curtsey.

"Your Majesties." Turning in Tristan's direction, but keeping my eyes lowered, I added, "Your Highness."

"Let me see her!"

I had forgotten about the Duchesse.

The Queen dutifully turned about, and her sapphire-bedecked sister peered at me, her orb of troll-light dancing so close that my eyes watered from the brightness. "See, Thibault, I told you she would clean up quite nicely."

"Hmmm," the King said, looking over me much as my father did a cow at auction. "Smells better, at least." He flapped his hand in the Queen's direction. "Let's get this over with. I don't want to wait another month for a moon to find out if this will work." With the Queen at his side, the King swiftly departed through the enormous front entry, servants fluttering ahead of them. Marc had disappeared while I had been making my courtesies, and now only Tristan and I stood in the cold entrance. He watched me with those inhuman eyes, expression bland, perhaps even a bit bored.

"You look exceptionally... colorful."

My cheeks and chest flushed a blotchy red. "I didn't choose the dress, my lord," I replied stiffly.

"I wasn't talking about the dress. I've only seen human hair that color in paintings, and I was certain the artists were being fanciful. It's more noticeable now that you've cleaned up..." He paused, shifting his weight from one leg to the other. "And it's somewhat brighter in here. See the lamps?" He broke off. "Of course you see them. I just meant... Your hair is very red."

Mortified, my skin flared so hot I thought it might burn clear off my bones. I fought the urge to wipe my sweaty palms on the gown and muttered, "I didn't get to choose the color of my hair, either."

He opened his mouth, no doubt to add further insult to injury, but I shot him a dark look and he wisely shut it again.

A young troll stepped through the entrance. "Your Highness." He held out a tray with two crystal glasses filled with a glowing blue liquid. Tristan examined them. "Do you suppose it would be inappropriate," he asked the servant, "for me to top them up a bit with some whiskey?"

The servant stared at him, expression horrified, tray trembling in his hand. "I suppose you're right," Tristan said glumly, although the man hadn't spoken a word. He took the two glasses and handed me one of them. "Cheers!"

I took it and eyed the contents with suspicion. "What is it? Not some sort of poison, I hope?"

"I call it Liquid Shackles. It has another name, but I prefer to use my own inventions. As to its nature, well…" He shrugged. "I wouldn't say it isn't harmful, but it certainly won't kill you. At least it shouldn't – we've never had a human drink any before."

"Why do you call it Liquid Shackles?" I asked, pursing my lips. I did not like the sound of *that* one bit.

"Because it is a clever metaphor," he replied, holding the glass up to examine it more closely. I waited for him to explain further, but it was clear he had no intention of elaborating.

"And if I refuse?" I asked.

He cocked one eyebrow and gave me a dour look.

"I suppose you'll just force it down my throat," I muttered.

"Certainly not," he said, lowering the glass. "It is always better to delegate nefarious tasks. You know, to keep one's reputation intact."

I scowled, but all my dark look garnered was a grin from him. "Keep in mind that I have to drink it too."

"What does it taste like?" I asked.

"Having never been bonded before, I haven't the foggiest idea. But I expect quite vile." He clinked his glass against mine. "Bottoms up!" He drowned the liquid in one mouthful.

Resigned, I sipped mine carefully. It tasted a bit like honey, only sweeter. A slow, but not unpleasant, warmth swept down my throat and into my stomach, spreading out from there. I took another small sip and then another until the glass was drained. "Quite lovely, really," I murmured. The room seemed brighter, and I swayed slowly from foot to foot as though caught in some unheard rhythm. The pain of all my injuries faded away and I felt languid, blissful. "Are you certain there was no liquor in that?" I asked, my voice dreamy.

"Quite." Tristan's eyes had grown so dilated that only a thin rim of silver remained around them. "Though I see it has made you rather punch-drunk."

"You mean it hasn't affected you at all?"

"I expect I have a more resilient constitution."

The side of his throat fluttered with the rapidness of his pulse, belying his words. A strange urge to reach up and touch him filled me, if only to prove that he was in fact alive, not some vision my mind had conjured. I didn't remember moving, but suddenly my fingers brushed that very spot, his skin hot against mine. He shuddered beneath my touch, eyelids drifting shut. Then his hand shot up, faster than anyone had the right to move, and caught my wrist, gently pulling it away. "I think, Mademoiselle de Troyes," he said, sucking in a ragged breath, "that you are not yourself." He let go of me, my skin burning from his touch.

"This all seems like a dream now, but like every dream, eventually you must wake." He raised a hand to brush back a tendril of hair that had fallen across my face, careful, I thought, not to touch my skin.

"My lord?"

We both jumped, turning to look at the servant standing at the door.

"The moon rises."

Tristan sighed. "And she waits on no one, not even me." He offered his arm and I took it, feeling muscles flexed hard with tension beneath his coat. We descended down the marble steps and through the empty courtyard filled with glass trees and carved statues. Beyond the gates, light glowed; and as we passed under the iron portcullis and out into the city, I gasped. Thousands of trolls lined the path leading down to the river, and above each danced a glowing orb of troll-light.

I stepped on the hem of my dress and stumbled, clutching Tristan's arm for support as my eyes scanned the crowd massed on either side of us. They were young and old, some badly malformed and some nearly as lovely to behold as the one holding my arm. The vast majority of them were wearing shades of grey, and pockets of those dressed in vibrant colors stood out like jewels in a bed of ash. One thing linked them all, though: their expressions of desperate hope. Dozens of them dropped to their knees, fingers brushing the train of my dress as we passed, which should have been unnerving, but wasn't. Not one of them said a word. There was only the sound of the waterfall: water that thundered as it hit the pool and echoed over and over again in a wild cacophony, piercing through the veil the strange liquid had cast over my mind. I shook my head, trying to clear my thoughts, but to no avail. My body shuddered as panic crept in, every instinct telling me to run.

The King and Queen waited with the rest of the troll nobility at the water's edge. Their eyes were not on us, but rather on a marble platform sitting in the middle of the river. At its center stood a glass altar glittering not with the eerie light of the trolls, but one with which I was much more familiar. "The moon," I whispered, and raised my eyes to the tiny hole in the rock ceiling far above.

"The moon," Tristan agreed. "It took fifty years after the fall for my ancestors to make that opening, and for those fifty years, no one could be properly bonded. Lucky bastards."

"How sad," I murmured, my panic receding as I watched the beam of light grow in strength. If only I had wings, then I might fly up and through that hole to escape. My heart fluttered in my chest, and everything around me seemed unreal, as though I was walking in a dream. "Can you fly, my lord?" I asked, my voice sounding distant even in my own ears. "Can your magic take you to the sky?"

"No," he said, and I swore I heard regret. "Our magic can do a great many things, but not that."

I was distantly aware of passing through the ranks of trolls and of the heat beneath my feet as we stepped up on a bridge of power forming magically ahead of us. It was transparent and faintly glowing. I'd never have dreamed it would hold our weight, but Tristan drew me resolutely across. My heels clicked against the surface as though it were made of glass. My eyes remained locked on the opening above us. Then abruptly, the edge of the moon appeared. My gasp was drowned by the collective murmurs of the thousands of trolls lining the banks of the river.

Tristan moved to the far side of the altar from me. "Cécile," he said, and I tore my eyes from the sight of the growing moon to meet his gaze. "Give me your hand."

Without hesitation, I reached across the glass surface and let him interlock his warm fingers with my own. His face betrayed no emotion, if he felt anything at all. Do trolls feel the same way a person does? I wondered. Does a troll know sadness, anger, or happiness? Can a troll love another troll? Or are they as cold inside as the rocks they were buried beneath? The dreamlike euphoria the drink had induced began to fade, and I cast my gaze skyward again just as the lights of all the trolls winked out. Countless pairs of eyes watched silently as the moon grew full over Trollus. As it reached its zenith, a cool tingling swept over my knuckles, almost as though a damp paintbrush was tracing across my fingers, but I dared not look down. I was afraid if I looked down, my moon would disappear forever. Mist from the river dampened my skin, and my hair clung to the sides of my face, but the chill did not touch me.

I could not say how much time had passed, but slowly, inch by inch, the moon crept across the opening in the rock until only a sliver was visible, and then nothing.

Trollus fell into darkness and the dream fractured, breaking into a million pieces of black glass. Emotions that were not mine bombarded me, and my knees buckled. I collapsed on the platform and pressed my forehead against the damp stone.

I was no longer alone in my mind.

CHAPTER 7
Cécile

Light flared and I looked over my shoulder. Tristan knelt on the far side of the altar, one hand gripping the edge for support. "What have you done to me?" I choked out. There was something invading my thoughts. He was in my mind – his emotions, burning hotter and brighter than my own.

His eyes met mine. Misery and shame built in the back of my skull until I half forgot my own fear. "Stop!" I screamed, my voice rising above the thunder of the river. "Get out!"

Tristan turned away from me.

"Did it work?" More troll-lights blazed and the King was next to me, his thick fingers digging into my wrist. He examined my hand, which now bore a mysterious silver lace pattern, and then let go of me, the corners of his mouth creeping up. His attention turned to Tristan, who was watching him much as a mouse does a snake. "Did you bond her?"

"Yes." The word was flat, emotionless.

Triumph flashed across the King's face. "Check the River Road!" he bellowed, charging over the invisible bridge, his son forgotten.

"What have you done to me?" I repeated. "What did he mean about you bonding me?"

Tristan rested his forehead against the altar. "I didn't do anything more to you than you did to me."

"What does that mean?" I asked precisely, with venom.

Tristan looked up, a faint smile on his face. "Old magic, neither troll nor human, although we've made use of it over the years. It bonded us, or linked our minds, if you prefer."

"I would prefer the bond ended," I hissed. "Or better yet, never happened at all."

"In this, we are of an accord, dearest wife. However, it is something we must both learn to live with."

"For how long?"

He grimaced and climbed to his feet. "Until one of us ceases to draw breath, one heart stills, one body is consigned to dust. Or in less poetic terms, a bloody long time." Leaving me to scramble to my own feet, he fixed his attention on the mob of trolls making their way to the far end of the valley. "Unless, of course, this doesn't work," he said softly and half to himself. "Then we may not have long to wait at all."

"If what doesn't work?" I shouted, seizing hold of his arm. "Quit talking in circles and explain what is going on and what any of it has to do with me."

Tristan ignored both tugging and words, his eyes fixed down the valley. His anticipation grew in my mind. Anticipation and fear. My own anxiety growing, I turned my attention to the hoard of trolls standing in front of the wall of rock at the end of the city.

We waited for what seemed like an eternity, then, abruptly, a collective groan of disappointment passed through the throng of trolls. Tristan did not echo them. His face was expressionless, but I sensed his relief and elation.

"Did it work?" I asked, heartily wishing someone would explain what it was.

"No," Tristan said. "It didn't." He tore his gaze away from the mass of trolls and took my arm. "We should probably hide you out of the way – he isn't going to be best pleased." In the faint light I could see that fights were beginning to break out in the crowd, but instead of fists, the trolls struck invisible blows with magic. Screams echoed through the cavern and the air grew blisteringly hot.

"Not that it will matter if they kill you first," Tristan growled over the noise. "Establish curfew," he shouted at the guards surrounding us. "Get the half-bloods back under control!"

"We need to get out of here." Tristan bolted across the invisible bridge, but when I tried to follow, my feet got tangled in the damp fabric of my skirts, slowing me down. I thought he would keep going and leave me to the crowd, but he was back in an instant. Snatching up the train of my skirt, he tore the thick fabric as easily as if it were paper and tossed it into the river. Then he grabbed hold of my wrist. "Run!"

We stopped running once we reached the safety of the palace walls; then Tristan dropped my arm and stepped ahead of me. I scurried after him through the maze of palace corridors with no small amount of difficulty. Even without the train, the skirts on my dress were heavy and prone to tangling up my feet. Pride kept me from asking him to slow down and fear kept me from falling behind. It was made all the worse by Tristan's anxiety pressing hard in my skull. If he was afraid, what did that mean for me?

Once I was thoroughly turned about, Tristan finally opened a door and pulled me into a room I recognized as the one where we had first met. He went immediately to the sideboard and, to my surprise, bypassed the decanter of wine and poured himself a glass of water instead. He guzzled the liquid down and poured another. "Wine?" he asked.

"I'd prefer an explanation."

He gave me a curious look. "I suppose there is no way you could know."

I shook my head.

Passing a tired hand across his face, he nodded. "Fine. We are cursed, and by we, I mean trolls, not you and me; although perhaps you might consider yourself so. Nearly five centuries ago, a human witch broke the mountain in two, burying Trollus in rock. Through magic, we were able to keep the city from being crushed; but suffice it to say, it took a significant length of time to dig a way out, only for the trolls to discover that the witch had cursed them to the confines of Trollus for as long as she drew breath."

"If your ancestors were half as irritating as you are, I can understand why."

Tristan glowered. "This is no laughing matter, Cécile."

"Why not?" I said. "You think everything else is."

"We've known each other the space of three hours and already she thinks she knows me," Tristan muttered. "Do you want the rest of the story, or not?"

"Please."

"As I was saying, all of those trolls and their descendants have been trapped within the confines of the city for the past five hundred years, while you humans carried on your merry way above. Three weeks ago, my aunt – you may remember her, tiny woman, practically inseparable from my mother – anyway, she has the gift of foresight. She foretold that when a prince of night bonded a daughter of the sun, the curse would be broken."

"I'm the daughter of the sun," I said, my mind racing.

"Far cleverer than you appear." Tristan stuck his head out into the hallway and looked both ways before slamming the door shut.

"But the magic didn't work. You bonded me and the curse is still in place."

"Correct again. Remind me to choose you for my team if we ever play charades. I like a stacked team."

"But how does the curse work?" I envisioned trolls turning into stone and crumbling to dust once they passed out of the darkness and into the sun.

Tristan went to a drawer, removed something, and handed it to me. It was a small sphere of glass and, inside, what appeared to be a highly detailed miniature version of the city of Trollus. "It is like being enclosed in an impenetrable glass bubble," he said. "One that humans and animals and water can pass through, but which we cannot. As if pulling a mountain down on our heads wasn't enough." He muttered the last bit under his breath.

The sound of boots coming down the hall caught both our attentions.

"Hide in here." Tristan pushed me into a small closet. "Be silent – your life may depend on your discretion." The lock clicked shut. Kneeling down, I peered through the keyhole and waited.

I didn't wait long. The door slammed open, the King's bulk filling the frame as he passed through. Tristan's anxiety spiked, but to his credit, he didn't even flinch. I wished desperately that the bond would allow me to read his mind, but despite my best efforts, all I felt were his emotions. And even then, it was hard for me to decipher what was mine and what was his.

"Where is she?"

"Never mind her," Tristan said, "I've got her locked up safe."

"Good, good," his father replied, rubbing his hands together. He was breathing hard, and big drops of sweat beaded and ran down his fleshy jowls. I half expected his heart to blow out of his chest, and I didn't feel at all bad for wishing it would.

Tristan poured his father a glass of wine. "From what I gather, all did not go as planned."

An understatement, if I had ever heard one.

The King took a long swallow of the red liquid. "No."

Tristan hung his head. "You are disappointed, I expect."

"Aren't you?"

"I've gone through a great deal today and still the curse remains. How do you think I feel?" Tristan answered without hesitation.

The King eyed his son with critical interest, considering his words. The glass drained, he motioned for Tristan to pour him another. "What do you propose?"

"I propose," Tristan said, pouring the wine nearly to the rim, "that we bind her with oaths swearing her to secrecy and send her on her merry way."

"Or we could just cut off her head. The dead, as they say, tell no tales."

My blood ran cold and I had to clamp a hand over my mouth to keep from gasping aloud. Tristan's apprehension rose, but the shrug he gave his father told another story. "You could, although given that I've just been bonded to her, the process would cause me no small amount of discomfort."

"Attached to the little thing already?" the King smirked, the chair he settled into groaning beneath his weight.

"She was brought here to serve a purpose," Tristan scoffed. "What I am attached to is my life. You know the risks."

The King chortled at this and his son laughed along with him. Tristan's words were surprisingly painful to me – not that I had any reason to expect anything different. I'd been brought to Trollus to lift the curse – and I'd failed. Why should he care what happened to me now? But why would my death jeopardize his life?

"As it turns out," the King said, laughter cutting off abruptly, "she'll be neither leaving nor dying."

Tristan froze, and this time the shock on his face matched that in his mind. "Pardon?"

"Your aunt believes it premature for me to give up on her fulfilling the prophesy. She proposes we keep her around for a while longer, and that you should treat her as any man does his wife. We need to give the people some form of hope or who knows what sort of trouble they'll cause."

Tristan blanched. "You can't be serious?"

The King raised one eyebrow.

"She's a human."

"I noticed." The King took another mouthful of wine, leaving a red stain on his upper lip.

"You want me to…"

"Yes. You've bonded her, and now you shall bed her. I can't say I relish the idea of a bunch of half-bloods running about the royal nursery, but quite frankly, I'd breed you to a sheep if that is what it took to break the witch's blasted malediction. You're seventeen years old, time to man-up."

"I don't care for mutton." Tristan crossed his arms. "It's too tough."

"Well then count your lucky stars that your dear Cécile isn't a sheep," the King said, climbing to his feet. "I'm certain you'll find her markedly more tender."

I pressed back against the closet, bile rising in my throat. They were discussing me as though I had no more value than a side of meat, and… My mind refused to delve any further into what else they were discussing.

"This isn't a debate, Tristan. This is an order – do you understand?"

"Yes, sir," Tristan said, plainly out of glib retorts.

His father patted him on the shoulder. "It will be worth the cost once you are outside in the sun – just imagine, eventually you'll rule lands wider than the eyes can see."

"Who wouldn't want that?"

The King nodded, satisfied. "Good lad."

As the door shut behind him, I let out a huge gust of breath that I hadn't noticed I'd been holding. "Tristan," I whispered. "Get me out of here."

He didn't move from where he sat on the arm of a chair. "Tristan!"

He looked up, his troll-light casting eerie shadows on his face. "I'll send someone to let you out," he said. "I need to..." He got to his feet and, ignoring my pleas, left the room.

The knot of emotion residing in my mind did not depart with him. Resting my head against the closet door, I attempted to thrust aside my own feelings to better focus on his. Which was an exercise of frustration. He was unhappy, that much I could say, but it was hard to pick specifics out of the seething stew of emotion. And what good was knowing specifics anyway? What good was knowing how he felt? What possible advantage could such a connection give me?

Tired, sore, and more than a little scared, I settled on the floor. My skirts rustled as I arranged them to make myself comfortable. I could probably have picked the lock, but there seemed no point. The closet was darker than the darkest of nights and the room no better. I could not escape without light, and that would be hard to come by in this place.

I needed to get away. Any hope the trolls would let me go had been dashed by the conversation I had just overheard. The King intended to keep me in Trollus indefinitely, and he had expectations of what I would do while I was here.

At best, I was an instrument for breaking a curse, and at worst, a broodmare for what they called half-bloods. The very idea made me shiver. It wasn't Tristan who repulsed me – despite the fact he wasn't human, he was handsome, and if I were being honest with myself, the strange drink they'd given me had drawn out stirrings of desire I would gladly do without. Clearly the same had not occurred for him. To him, I was little better than a sheep. And the idea of spending the rest of my life with someone who was disgusted by me made me cringe. Because I would never be able to escape it – even standing on far sides of the city, I would still be able to feel it.

I leaned my head against the shelves, exhaustion starting to take hold of me. Only as I started to drift off to sleep did it occur to me: if the trolls had been trying to break the curse for five hundred years, why had Tristan been so happy when we failed?

CHAPTER 8
Tristan

"Bloody stones and sky, Marc," I hissed as he walked through the door, "where have you been?" I glanced at the clock on the wall. "I've been waiting a good hour for you."

"So sorry, cousin," he replied, tossing his cloak in the corner and pouring himself a drink. "I am at your beck and call, but it did take a bit of time to reestablish curfew."

I pushed aside my books and leaned my elbows on the table, only now noticing the drying blood on Marc's black sleeve. "Casualties?"

"Twelve dead, all miners except for one street worker, but I believe he got caught in the crossfire, such as it was."

I grimaced. "Perpetrators?"

Marc shrugged. "Hard to prove, but it sounds like guild members. They did not report any injuries."

"They wouldn't." I rubbed my temples, trying to push aside the knot of emotion residing in the back of my skull that most decidedly did not belong to me. The emotions belonging to the girl. Cécile.

"Do we know who instigated?" I asked.

Marc's expression was grim and told me all I needed to know. Sliding my arms across the table I rested my forehead against the smooth surface and then banged it against the wood twice for good measure. "I can't think," I said. "Can you deal with it until I have more time?"

"I suppose."

Marc sat down in a chair across from me and said nothing else, which allowed me to turn my attention back to the girl. She was fading. I straightened abruptly. "It's diminishing! The bond, it's fading away." The triumphant grin on my face vanished at the sight of Marc's slowly shaking head.

"She's sleeping. You'll notice her a lot less when she's asleep, unless she dreams – that can get interesting."

I motioned for him to fill my glass. "It isn't interesting at all," I said. "It's a problem. She's a problem – one that needs dealing with."

Marc's face darkened. "*Cécile*," he said, emphasizing her name, "isn't a problem. She's an innocent girl who has been dragged into this situation entirely against her will. Your father had her violently kidnapped, dragged through the labyrinth, and then bonded to a *troll* using a magic that I am certain she didn't know existed. She is not *our* problem – we are hers."

Leaning back in my chair, I watched my orb of light circling above us. "You make a valid point."

"The poor girl is probably terrified," Marc added. "How could she not be?"

"Well, she isn't," I said. "What she is, is blasted inquisitive. I'd rather the fear – fear doesn't think, it just reacts."

Marc snorted. "Tristan, the bond changes everything," he said. "Whether you like her or not, keeping her safe will become your ultimate priority. The last thing you are going to want is for her to be afraid – especially of you." He took a sip of wine, watching my face. "For the rest of your lives, you will feel what the other is feeling every waking moment. Sometimes in your dreams."

I covered my eyes with a hand, a heavy feeling in my chest. I was the one that was afraid.

"Where did you leave her?" Marc asked. "Is she safe?"

"She's safe enough," I said, hesitating for a moment before adding, "She's locked in the closet of my sitting room."

Marc's face twisted – which for him, was saying something. "Are you quite serious?"

"It was the only place I could hide her." I quickly explained the conversation I'd had with my father.

"And you left her there? After she had to listen to that?"

I nodded, starting to feel somewhat ashamed.

Marc got to his feet, left the room, and was back moments later. "I sent a message to Élise. She'll take care of it."

I bit my lip hard, considering all my options, none of which were good. "Is it always going to be this invasive?" I finally asked, realizing how strange my lack of knowledge was about something so common to my people. A mystery that was kept a secret by those who had experienced it. "Explain it to me."

Marc sighed. "You'll get used to it, but in your case, that might not be such a good thing. In a few days, you will only notice extreme emotions. Fear, happiness, anger, sadness, or pain."

"And physical distance?" I had noticed walking over here that I could feel the distance, like a lengthening cord, growing between us.

"Only if it changes dramatically. Or if you concentrate." He smiled. "You'll always be able to find her."

"And she will be able to find me, I suppose?" I drained my glass. "And therein lies the crux of our problem." I held up a hand to keep him from interrupting. "It is not that I know what she feels – it's that she feels what I feel. She's going to know when I'm being the deceitful, manipulative... *troll* that I am. If she betrays that information for an instant, it could be my undoing."

Marc opened his mouth to speak, then closed it again and nodded.

I could feel the pressure in the room building as my magic responded to my frustration, the air growing hotter by the second. "So, what you're telling me is," I shouted, my words directed more at myself than my cousin, "that on top of controlling every word I say, every relationship I have, every twitch, tick, and gesture that I make, that I must also now control how I *feel?*" I slammed my fists down on the table, the wood groaning beneath the impact.

"No, Tristan," Marc said, ignoring my anger. "You're the one who thinks you can control every aspect of your life. But you're wrong. You can't control this. You'll have to find another way."

"What other way?" I demanded.

"Win her over," he said. "Make her your ally – you're bonded, be what you are supposed to be to each other."

The world spun around me and I grabbed the edge of the

table for support, feeling my aunt's prophesy driving me towards what seemed like an inevitable and unavoidable goal. "No," I said under my breath. "I'll do what it takes, but it won't be that. The cost is far too high."

CHAPTER 9
Cécile

If Zoé and Élise were surprised to find me locked in a closet, they didn't say so. My hands in theirs, they led me to an adjoining room, and I immediately fixated on the large four-poster bed dominating the space. Under other circumstances, its thick blankets and mounds of pillows might have been inviting. Tonight they held all the appeal of a torturer's rack.

The maids removed my gown and jewels, and at my request, clasped my mother's necklace back around my neck. They proceeded to dress me in a white lace nightgown and a thick velvet wrap. "We'll bring your breakfast in the morning," Élise said, then motioned for her sister to leave. Their troll-lights followed along behind them, the room already growing dim.

"Wait," I called out. "I have no light."

Zoé hurried back over to me. "Our mother had this problem when she was alive," she said. "I remember my father leaving lights about our home for her."

"Your father," I asked tentatively, "did he care for your mother?"

Her eyes widened. "Of course he did, my lady. Very much so. They were not bonded, though. It was forbidden." Her gaze flickered down to the silver marks on my hand. "Perhaps that will change now."

A second ball of light appeared next to us. "I'll leave this with you, my lady. Though I'm not certain how long it will last," she added, cheeks flushing faintly. "My magic has a tendency to wander. I'm sure His Highness will think of a better solution – he is exceedingly clever about such things."

Alone, with only Zoé's diminishing ball of light for company, I wandered through Tristan's cluttered room. Not an inch of wall space had been left bare, and I examined the assorted collection of artwork, tapestries, and maps in an attempt to find insight into the mind of the creature I'd just married. There were landscapes, seascapes, and cityscapes I recognized as Trianon. He had a great many paintings of men on horseback galloping after foxes, boars, and deer. Unlike the other rooms in the palace, no prevailing theme dominated, only a wild and random representation of the world outside of Trollus. The normal, unmagical, Isle of Light.

A mantle took up one wall, and I saw with amusement that he'd nailed a painting of burning logs in the empty space where a real fire ought to have been. A small sitting area surrounded the fireplace, reminding me for a moment of home. But only briefly: this room was cold, unfamiliar, and empty, which our farmhouse never was. I settled down in one of the chairs, pulling my cold feet underneath me, and began to sort through the large stack of books on the table. They were novels: adventures of pirates on the high seas, tales of knights slaying dragons, mysteries set in the underworld of cities on the continent.

The door opened and I leapt to my feet.

"I see you've made yourself comfortable," Tristan said, tossing his hat on the desk.

"No thanks to you, sir," I replied, wrapping my arms tightly around my body. "You left me locked in a closet."

"And you came to no harm, which leads me to believe the closet might be a good place to keep you in the future."

"You wouldn't dare," I gasped.

"I've warned you about expectations before, Cécile," he said, pulling off his coat and draping it on the back of a chair. "Be gone!" He swiped at Zoé's fading ball of light and it winked out.

"I heard everything you two said! I know your plans for me." I watched him cross the room towards me, not realizing I was backing up until my shoulders hit the wall. He kept walking until we were only inches apart. The top of my head barely came up to his chest and the outlines of muscle were visible through his shirt.

"Good," he said. "Saves me from having to explain what is expected of you."

Terror flooded me. If I screamed, no one would come to my rescue. He could do whatever he wanted to me and no one would question him. Every instinct told me to grovel and beg for mercy beneath the weight of his determination, but my knees didn't buckle. I met his piercing metallic gaze, knowing that a defiant expression would mean little when he felt my terror as though it were his own.

His face twisted in disgust that matched the emotion pounding in the back of my head. "You can take the bed," he said, spinning away from me. "I'll have none of this."

Crossing the room, he threw himself down on a chaise and pulled off his boots. I stood in silence as he sorted through a stack of books, opened one and stared at the first page longer than it would take to read. With a sigh, he tossed it back on the pile, and without looking at me even once, said, "Goodnight." His troll-light winked out, leaving me standing in absolute blackness.

One hand pressed against the wall, I waited for my eyes to adjust to the darkness so I might make my way over to the bed, but it never happened. Swallowing hard, I rubbed my hands briskly over my arms, trying to ward off tears as much as the cold. *He'll hear you if you cry, I thought.* Bad enough that he knows what I feel without giving him the satisfaction of hearing me break. But it was hard not to. Tristan's melancholy magnified my own, and my weary and aching shoulders slumped beneath the burden.

This was not how my marriage was supposed to happen. A drop of blood rose on my lip as I bit it in an attempt to force away visions of what might have been. Gran's dress, my friends and family feasting on a warm summer's day. A young man from a good family who loved me as fiercely as the sun shone at noon. My wedding night... A fat tear ran down my cheek before I could wipe it away. The older girls living in the Hollow often whispered about what passed between two people who'd just been wed, and I'd wanted those things. But I also knew enough to recognize that I'd been lucky tonight.

Taking a couple of tentative steps in the direction of the bed, I gained confidence walking blind and promptly collided with a table. The furniture and I both went down with a thump, accompanied by the sound of smashing glass.

"Stones and sky, girl!" Tristan snapped. "Have you not made things hard enough without destroying everything I own?"

"I can't see," I shouted back at him, trying to climb to my feet and banging my head against another table in the process. "Ouch!"

A ball of light appeared above me as I rubbed the growing lump on my skull. I was starting to get quite the collection.

"Are you all right?"

"Fine," I snapped, getting up.

"Watch out for the…"

I winced as a sharp pain lanced into my heel.

"Glass," Tristan finished, and sympathy filled his corner of my mind.

I hopped on one leg towards the bed, making it halfway before warm ropes of power lifted me up and deposited me on the covers. "I didn't need help," I grumbled, pulling on my ankle in a vain attempt to examine the bottom of my foot.

"Sorry." He came closer. "I'd forgotten you had no light."

The way he spoke made me feel like I lacked something as fundamental as a heart or a brain.

"Here." He handed me the wineglass I'd brought in with me. As I touched the stem, the bowl lit up with bright silver light. "It will glow at your touch, and," he took it again, "dim when set down."

I snatched the precious item from him like a greedy child.

"You're welcome," he said, and I flushed at my rudeness. "Let me have a look at your foot."

With one hand, he took hold of my ankle, his brow furrowing as he examined the shard embedded in my heel. I clutched my glowing wineglass and held my breath.

"Ready?" He met my gaze.

I gave a quick nod, hoping my feet didn't smell.

A sharp sting and the pink-tinged glass floated through the air to drop on the bedside table.

"Don't you ever do anything with your hands?" I asked. "I mean, without magic?"

A ghost of a smile touched his lips, and he pulled a handkerchief out of his pocket, wrapping the silk around my foot. "Sometimes."

I grew aware of the warmth of said hands on my ankle and jerked out of his grip. Avoiding his gaze, I pulled up the covers and carefully set my glass on the table, watching its light dim. He did not light another to replace it, and soon we were surrounded by darkness once again.

"Cécile?"

"Yes?"

He hesitated, the sound of him swallowing loud against the silence. "In the morning, they'll ask... They'll want to know if we..."

I listened to him breathing, and I waited.

"I'll need you to lie convincingly, or I'm afraid there will be consequences for both of us."

"If you're so concerned about my abilities to tell tall tales, why don't you do it?" I snapped.

I felt his irritation mount. "Because I can't."

"What do you mean, you can't?" I grabbed hold of my wineglass so I could see him.

"Because I can't tell a lie. No troll can tell a lie." He pointed to a cushion. "I couldn't so much as claim this cushion was any color other than red."

My brow furrowed. "I don't believe you."

"Of all the things that you have discovered today, this is what you choose to disbelieve?" He passed a weary hand over his face. "It doesn't matter if you believe me or not. Lie about it. If you don't, and my father discovers I have disobeyed him in this, we will both suffer for it."

"Afraid of your father?" I asked.

"I'm not…" he started, then broke off, silent for several deafening moments. "I will take his punishment before I compromise my standards in this. Of that, you can rest assured."

I set my glass on the table, extinguishing the light. My cheeks burned and I pulled the covers up higher, hoping he couldn't see in the dark. Knowing he would not willingly force himself upon me was a relief, but there was also a part of me stung by his words. I'd never been the girl the boys fought to dance with at festivals; that was my sister with her golden hair and sunny disposition. But neither had anyone been so blunt as to tell me I did not meet their standards. "Fine," I finally mumbled.

I listened to him walk slowly across the dark room and settle down on the chaise, shifting back and forth several times before he lay still. His emotions were as confusing as those swirling through me. I searched for my anger, but it had abandoned me when needed most. My legs tucked close to my stomach, I stared at the blackness where my wineglass stood. My precious source of light.

"Thank you," I whispered, and sensed him relax and slowly drift off to sleep. Let him think I was grateful for him giving me light, granting me respite, or even for bandaging my foot. He could think anything he liked, but only I knew the true reason for the hope rising in my heart. I smiled into the darkness.

He had given me the first thing I needed to escape.

CHAPTER 10
Cécile

"Where are all my clothes?"

I jerked awake, knocking my elbow against the headboard. Any hopes of it all being a dream were dashed by the sight of Tristan, his arms full of colorful silk dresses, storming about the room. Both my maids and a grey-clad manservant stood in a row, their heads lowered. Covers tucked up around my shoulders, I watched Tristan dash into the closet and emerge with another armload of dresses. He threw them in a pile on the floor. "Why is my closet full of dresses?"

"Are they mine?" I asked with interest.

Silver eyes fixed on me. "Well, they certainly are not mine. Unless you imagine that I dress up in ladies' clothing and prance about the palace when the mood strikes me?"

A giggle slipped out of Élise, which she promptly smothered with a hand over her mouth.

"You consider this a laughing matter?" Tristan glowered at the girl.

"Sorry, my lord," she said. "Your clothes are in the other closet."

"Why?"

"Her Grace thought the larger closet more appropriate for her ladyship's gowns, my lord."

"She did, did she?" He stormed back into the closet, returning with another armload. "That's the last of them."

"You are wrinkling my dresses," I said. "Zoé and Élise will waste their entire day pressing them."

"And then they can hang them somewhere else," he snapped.

"You're creating an enormous amount of unnecessary work."

"It is the role of the aristocracy to create work," he said, kicking the pile of gowns. "Necessary or otherwise. Without us, who knows what would happen to productivity."

I rolled my eyes and climbed out of bed. Catching the corner of a sheet, I set to making the bed.

"What are you doing?" Tristan shouted.

"What does it look like I'm doing?"

"Ladies do not make their own beds! It shows initiative, which is broadly considered most unladylike!"

My temper rising, I whirled about. "Dear me," I shouted. "I must have forgotten that my new purpose in life is to create work." Jerking all the blankets off the bed, I threw them on the floor. The pillows followed next, and I proceeded to run around the room taking all the cushions off the chairs and tossing them about the room. The last I deliberately aimed at Tristan's head. It froze midair. "You are making quite the mess of my room."

"Our room!" I shouted back.

"What is going on in here?" The Queen strode into the room, but it was her sister who had spoken. The Queen turned, as though out of habit, so that her sister was facing us.

"Explain to me why she must stay in my rooms," Tristan demanded. "Surely we have the space to put her somewhere else?"

"She is your wife, Tristan. Keeping her in here with you will help remind you of your duties."

"I am unlikely to forget them," Tristan replied acidly. "And I would be willing to bet a great deal of gold that most men require only five, perhaps ten minutes maximum, to conduct their duties. Any longer is the business of romantics; and I dare say, I haven't given you a reason to believe I have a single romantic bone in my body."

"She'll stay until I say otherwise, young man," the Duchesse barked, crossing her arms. "And you'll quit acting like a spoiled brat and start acting like a man."

"I'll act how I please!"

I smiled as I watched him storm out of the room. Only a heartbeat later, I realized his satisfaction mirrored my own. Which made no sense at all. I took in the room, which looked much as if a hurricane had passed through. In hindsight, it occurred to me that throughout his apparent tantrum, I'd never felt a bit of anger from him. An act, then. But to what purpose?

The Duchesse turned her attention to me. "Well? Is it done?"

Lie.

"Yes," I mumbled, not having to fake my mortification.

"Good. You humans are as fertile as rabbits – perhaps a child is the key."

Magic jerked my chin up. "*They've* predicted a large number of events in my day, girl," she said. "*They've* never been wrong before. Do you understand what I'm saying?"

I nodded, although I didn't. Who were they? Wasn't it the Duchesse who predicted the future?

"Good. Now why don't you get dressed and go into the city. Buy yourself something pretty."

"Is it safe, Your Grace?" Élise asked. "The riots…"

"Perfectly safe," the Duchesse snapped. "The King has decreed that anyone who harms her will suffer the most extreme of punishments. The law secures her well-being. Besides, presenting her as a princess will demonstrate our continued faith in the accuracy of the prophesy. Help keep the mob quiet for a time."

"I haven't got any coin," I mumbled. Nor did I think a new pair of shoes would compensate for the risk of a mob of angry trolls tearing me limb from limb. My gran always said it was the nature of people to resent those who had more than them. Parading me around in fancy clothes didn't seem like the best way to earn me popularity.

The Duchesse smiled. "You are a princess now, Cécile. You have unlimited credit everywhere in the city. One of the girls will show you the best shops."

"Yes, Your Grace," Élise murmured. "I heard a shipment of fine fabrics arrived this morning – perhaps her ladyship would like a new gown made."

I glanced at the rainbow of dresses Tristan had scattered

through the room. Why I'd need another was beyond me. Looking pretty would not keep me safe. A frown creased my brow, and I traced the silver tattoo lacing my fingers. At least I would be a well-dressed corpse.

"An excellent idea." The Duchesse snapped her fingers. "Now leave us alone for a moment." The girls darted out of the room.

"You've spirit in you, Cécile, just as I knew you would. No doubt you've put a substantial amount of thought towards how you might escape. Let me save you the effort – escape from Trollus is an impossibility. In my opinion, there are two ways this can go for you: either you curl up on the floor and wait to die, or you live each day for all it can give you. Little will be denied you here. Clothing, jewels, delicacies from the continent, are all yours for the taking." She tilted her head. "An education, if you desire. Perhaps further training in the arts. You can become a great woman, Cécile. Or you can remain a prisoner. The choice is yours."

"I understand," I said, and watched as the Queen glided from the room. I could have everything in the world but the one thing I wanted. The Duchesse was wrong about my having only two options. I wouldn't lie down and die, but neither would I give up on obtaining my liberty. I would live each day and fight for what mattered most: my freedom.

The city was marred with innumerable signs of the prior night's riots. Everywhere I looked, there were grey-clad trolls collecting piles of shattered glass or loading chunks of broken rock into wagons that others pushed down the streets. Although the telltale troll-light hung over each troll's head, they were all doing the work manually with brooms and shovels. "Wouldn't it be faster to use magic?" I asked, clutching my glowing wineglass to my chest. No amount of cajoling on Élise's part could have convinced me to leave it behind.

Élise glanced at the workers. "Certainly. If they had enough power to manage it. Which they don't."

"Oh," I replied, trying not to stare at their downturned heads as we passed.

Dust motes hung in the light of the multitude of lamps, and the small amount of sun that peered in through the hole in the rock above was made all the more faint by the haze. The trolls in the streets hurried about in twos and threes, expressions alert and wary. There were not many of them considering the size of the city, but to me, Trollus seemed overcrowded and stifling, as though each individual needed ten times his physical space. It was a corked bottle ready to blow at any moment – the witch's curse must be powerful indeed to keep it all contained.

The worst of it all, though, was the way the trolls reacted to my presence. I had expected dark looks, nasty comments, or even the odd rotten fruit tossed my direction. But after a few near collisions that required me to leap out of the way or risk being knocked down, I realized the trolls were content to pretend I did not exist. I was flanked by two hulking guardsmen whom Élise called Guillaume and Albert, but they ignored me as well, seemingly content to discuss what they'd eaten the prior evening and what they hoped would be served at tonight's dinner hour. Even the dressmakers ignored me, directing all their questions to Élise. Which seemed to be going right to her head, because as time passed, she grew more and more bold and less deferential, until I started to doubt which of us was the servant.

"They are acting as though it's all my fault," I grumbled as we exited the shop where yet another troll had refused to acknowledge my existence. "It isn't as though *I* was the one who cursed you lot to an eternity stuck in a hole."

Élise made a face. "Don't be ignorant – they are well aware of how powerless you are."

"How powerless you are, *my lady*," I corrected, giving her a sweet smile.

"You are very flippant for someone in your position, *my lady*," she replied wryly. "I could hang you upside down from your ankles if I were so inclined."

"Be my guest. No one would notice, and my feet feel like raw meat in these blasted shoes."

"Oh, they'd notice," she muttered. She began to speak very quietly, keeping an eye on our trailing guards, who seemed far more interested in the pink-frosted cakes they had purchased than in what we were saying. "The Montignys – the royal family," she began, "they shocked everyone by bonding His Highness to you. Everyone expected them to lock you up in a closet when the bonding failed to break the curse, but instead they have you parading about in front of everyone as though you actually *are* a princess." She chuckled softly. "Now they're all waiting to see how the great houses react – whether they will support your existence or not." She gestured discreetly at the passing trolls. "They aren't ignoring you – they are merely waiting to see what side of the table those they are sworn to will sit at."

"When will that be?" I asked, looking over my shoulder at the women who had just walked by.

"Soon," Élise said. "Though you might find yourself wishing they had taken their time. Now enough questions. Put your head up. Walk like you belong here."

Ignoring my complaints, Élise paraded me up and down the streets and in and out of shops until my blisters popped. The only advantage the excursion provided was that it allowed me to quickly gain my bearings within the city. The labyrinth gate was on the northwest side of the river, as was the palace and what looked to be the homes of wealthier citizens. While it was too dark for me to see where the crest of the valley met the rock above, Élise explained that the rubble of destroyed homes had been cleared in centuries past, and any openings to the labyrinth sealed up with stone and mortar.

"Why?" I asked, curious as to why they would isolate themselves any further than necessary.

"To keep the sluag out," she said. "But they are always trying to find ways into the city, and sometimes they break through. Their venom is deadly – even to one of us."

I shivered, remembering the massive white bulk of the monster rearing up in the dark.

"You needn't worry yourself... *my lady*. It is a rare occurrence, and every household keeps a steel sluag spear, just in case. There is one in the corner of His Highness's room, if you are interested in examining one of them."

"Doesn't the magic that holds the rocks up keep them out?" I asked.

"The tree?" Élise glanced at me sharply. "No. It doesn't."

"Why is it called a tree?"

"A legacy from what it used to look like," she gestured upwards. "Single trunk with branches spreading out."

"Oh." I frowned at the black cavernous space looming above our heads. "What does it look like now?"

"Not like a tree. It is a far more complicated structure in its current form."

"Where does the magic come from?"

"You mean who," she replied, and I blinked. "Magic comes from within," she explained. "So what you should have asked is who the magic comes from."

I opened my mouth to ask just that question when Élise interrupted me. "This is Artisan's Row," she said. "Perhaps you would like to go in to view some of their work?" She gestured towards the entrance to one of the shops.

I nodded, although her tone implied it was more of an order than a question. I didn't want to waste my time inside any of the stores –I wanted to go to the base of the valley. There had to be a way for the river to flow out of the city and to the ocean, and if there was a way for water to escape, perhaps there was a way for me to get out as well. But Élise seemed intent on my seeing the contents of the shop, and it was probably better if she believed that I was aimlessly following her through the city with no purpose of my own.

A bell chimed as I pushed open the door and stepped into the well-lit shop. The proprietor curtseyed deeply, but I focused on the woman who did not. Brown eyes regarded me with curiosity.

"You aren't a troll!" I blurted out.

"Neither," the woman replied, "are you."

The proprietor of the store grimaced but interestingly, didn't ignore me. "My lady, this is Esmeralda Montoya. She is a trader of fine goods."

One of the woman's eyebrows arched upwards. "My lady? I must say, I've heard the trolls call us humans any number of things, but generally speaking, none of them are so polite. You must be the girl they bonded to His Royal Highness."

I gave a faint nod.

"By choice?"

"No."

Esmeralda shook her head, her brow furrowing. Although she was dressed in men's clothing, the fabrics looked expensive and she wore no small amount of jewelry. Her business with the trolls was clearly a lucrative one. "And now you are caught in the midst of the rival politics of a place you probably didn't even know existed," she said.

"I was supposed to break the curse," I said. "Otherwise, I know nothing of the politics involved."

"When it comes to the curse, there are no politics, no sides," she said. "It is the one thing that unites all trolls – their desire to be free of this place."

I frowned, remembering Tristan's reaction to our failure to break the curse, and how it had been decidedly contrary to the sentiment of the crowd. "If they are united," I said, "then I fail to see how I can be caught in the middle."

Esmeralda opened her mouth to speak, but the proprietor interrupted. "You overstep yourself, Montoya. One would have thought you'd have learned to keep your mouth shut by now."

"So report me to the trade magister," Esmeralda replied, not looking overly concerned about the prospect. "Though of what you'd accuse me is a mystery to me."

"Meddling." The troll planted her hands on her hips.

"I hadn't realized that was a crime." One corner of Esmeralda's mouth quirked up. "Why don't you do me a favor, Reagan, and leave us to our conversation."

"A favor?" The troll's face perked up. "In exchange for what?"

"Ill-nurtured harpy!" Esmeralda swore. "The pox on you lot and your favors. What do you want?"

Reagan grinned. "The pox is of little concern to me, Montoya." She rubbed her hands together. "A promise that you will grant me a moderate-sized favor of my choosing."

"A small favor."

The troll shook her head. "She is the wife of the heir to the throne. This is no small thing." A dark smile touched her lips. "His Majesty has hanged you humans for less."

I gasped, but Esmeralda didn't blink. "A quick enough death, in the scheme of things."

"For you, perhaps," Reagan said, rubbing her hands together. "You are a fragile creature, human." Her gaze flickered past me to Élise. "Tell me, girl, how long did it take for the last half-breed to die? How long did he hang from the noose, his better half clinging to life while his human half dragged him towards death?"

The silence grew and I shuddered.

"Six days," Reagan said, answering her own question. "And I rather think one of his fellow sympathizers put him out of his misery." She chuckled. "In fact, I think I've reconsidered. It will take a large favor for me to excuse myself from this conversation."

Esmeralda's voice was grim. "And buy your silence that a conversation took place at all."

The troll considered the arrangement and nodded. "Done."

A prickle of power ran across my skin and, without another word, she hobbled awkwardly towards the back room, bright yellow skirts brushing against the cane she used.

"You should have negotiated specifics," Élise said tonelessly. "Leaving it open-ended was a large concession."

The whole exchange was disturbing and bizarre to me, which must have been apparent to the others by the expression on my face. "Trolls value favors even more than they value gold," Esmeralda explained. "When they make a promise to do something, they must fulfill it, no matter what the cost to them, which is why they almost never promise anything for nothing."

"You cannot break a promise to a troll, Aunty," Élise warned. "She will extract her pound of flesh when you least expect it, mark my words."

I blinked. "You're related?" And what could be so important to tell me that was worth the bargain that had just taken place?

"Aye," Esmeralda admitted. "My fool of a sister fell in love with one of them. Only good thing to come of it was the girls."

"She married a troll willingly?" I could not keep the astonishment from my voice. She'd told me trolls couldn't marry humans, but how else...

"Not married," she replied. "It is forbidden for a troll to bond a human. What goes on behind closed doors, though, that is more difficult for them to monitor." She winked, and I looked away, uncomfortable.

"If it is forbidden, then why did Tristan bond me?"

"As I said, they will stop at nothing to break the curse."

"I would marry you to a sheep if it would set us free" the King's words echoed in my mind. "They don't have much regard for humans, do they?"

"Much?" demanded Esmeralda. "Try none. They see us as little more than animals; see the children of troll-human unions as abominations that deserve nothing more than abject slavery. They hate humans. They tolerate us only because they need our trade to survive."

"Not all trolls think that," Élise said softly.

"The ones who matter do. The aristocracy." Esmeralda spat on the floor. "Twisted creatures, as no doubt you've seen. They won't even lower themselves to bonding a troll commoner. Instead, they insist on picking and choosing amongst each other and the result is a palace full of inbred monsters. Deformed, sickly, insane – but powerful."

I thought of Marc's twisted face, constantly shrouded in darkness, and a shudder ran through me.

"Aunty, you're scaring her," Élise said.

"Good – she should be terrified. This is her reality now, and she needs to understand the politics if she is to be of any help."

"Aunt Esmeralda!"

The tension between the two was palpable. I was no fool – it had become clear that Élise had brought me here to speak to her aunt, but it seemed the conversation had gone beyond what she had intended.

"Help with what?" I demanded.

"You're supposed to keep her out of things, not involve her more!" Élise hissed angrily.

"Quit talking about me as though I'm not even here," I snapped. "You've clearly brought me here to tell me something, so get on with it."

Esmeralda and Élise glared at each other, but eventually the younger woman conceded. "Do as you want. You always do."

Her aunt nodded and leaned closer to me, her voice barely above a whisper. "There is a small faction within Trollus pushing for better treatment of those with mixed blood – equality, even. As it stands, any child less than pure blood is born into servitude. They are owned by the noble or the guild who owns the mother – or in the rare instance one of the parents is a full-blooded troll, they are auctioned to the highest bidder when they turn fifteen, and the money goes to the crown. They are traded like animals until they have grown too old to be useful and then they are left in the labyrinth as fodder for the sluag."

I shivered, the memory of my own flight from the sluag fresh in my mind. I had always had the hope of getting out – I could not even fathom what it would feel like to know that no matter how fast you ran or how well you might hide, escape was futile. For trolls, there was no way out.

"Some don't even last that long," Esmeralda said softly. "I've heard of girls as young as fifteen sent to their deaths for spilling soup on their lady's skirts." She pointed a finger at me. "The Montoya family is wealthy and powerful. I will not stand by and watch while my sister's daughters are relegated to the servant class, or worse, food for an overgrown slug, because of antiquated perceptions."

"I can understand that," I said, crossing my arms against the chill. "But I don't understand what you expect me to do about it. I have no power here."

"The very fact that the trolls have allowed one of their own to bond a human – and a Montigny prince at that – is coup enough in itself. Not for five centuries has a human held any position of power with them. And you, you will be queen one day – your half-blood children will be the heirs to the throne." Her eyes glittered with excitement.

I had precisely zero intention of letting matters get that far, but Esmeralda was the first person I'd met in Trollus willing to give me straight answers, so I was more than willing to hear her out.

"I don't see how you have any hope of changing things," I said, hoping my dismissal of her plans might force her to reveal more. "What can a handful of mixed bloods and a few humans do against that kind of magic?"

"Not just a handful," she replied. "There are more sympathizers to the cause than you can imagine."

"But do any of them have any power?"

Esmeralda opened her mouth to speak but then snapped it shut again.

"Just as I thought," I said, my frustration growing. "I am sympathetic to your troubles, but I have just been *bonded* to one of those you want to overthrow. I'd be a fool to conspire against him." I bit my lip after the words came out, realizing that I was perhaps being too hasty. If this force of sympathizers was actually a force to be reckoned with, there was a chance they might be willing to help me. Maybe they would be able to send word to my family. I chewed the inside of my cheeks, considering the risks. If I got caught, the King would have me watched more closely and I would lose any chance of escape. And who knew what sort of punishment I would receive for conspiring with those who plotted against him. Or what he would do to them, if he discovered they were trying to help me. As much as I might pretend otherwise, what Esmeralda had told me about the half-bloods' situation in Trollus had roused a great deal of indignation in me. I hated the King and so did they: it seemed a good enough reason for me to ally myself with their side.

"I am under a great deal of scrutiny right now," I said, choosing my words carefully. "But I will consider what you have told me. And if there is a way I can help…"

The bell on the door jingled and we all jumped. Albert leaned inside. When he saw Esmeralda, his expression darkened. "What are you doing here?"

"Negotiating with Reagan," Esmeralda said.

"Where is she, then?"

"I'm here." The troll appeared from the back, limping slowly across the room.

"I need you to come outside, my lady," he said. "You aren't supposed to consort with humans."

Reluctantly, I followed him out of the shop, Élise trailing at my heels. The city streets were as they had been before, filled with trolls going about their business, but

I began to see them with a whole new set of eyes. Those dressed in grey were marked with the small differences I'd first seen in Zoé and Élise: lighter hair; flushed skin; and, most importantly, human eyes. Where only a half hour past I had felt invisible, now I caught furtive glances from the downcast faces of those cleaning the streets and from those carrying parcels behind the brightly clad ladies. A great and entirely unwanted burden descended on my shoulders. They were expecting me to help them.

"My lady?" Albert had stopped eating and was watching me with the first bit of interest he'd shown all day. I realized I was standing in the middle of the intersection, forcing traffic to go around me.

"One moment," I whispered. Closing my eyes, I turned slowly like a compass searching for north. When I opened them, I was staring across the river valley. A tall figure dressed in black stood staring back across at me, hand resting on his sword hilt. There was nothing that greatly distinguished him from all the rest, but I knew instinctively it was Tristan.

"Élise?" My voice sounded hoarse.

"Yes, my lady?"

"Who... owns you?"

A long pause. "His Highness does." Her fingers plucked at the black and white sash at her waist, and for the first time, I noticed the letters embroidered on it: TdM. She was monogrammed just like Tristan's shirts. A possession.

"And Zoé too?" I asked.

"Yes. The Montigny family owns three hundred and twenty-one individuals, at present."

"At present," I repeated. A steady pounding grew in my ears, and my fingers twitched with the urge to lash out, at anything or anyone. "Does that figure include me?"

Élise's hand flew to her chest. "No," she stammered. "Of course not!"

"Spare me the lies!" I hissed, my grip tightening around the stem of my wineglass. Whirling around, I opened my mouth to scream my hatred across the valley. Tristan was gone. My head jerked back and forth spasmodically as I searched the opposite shore for his tall form, but he had blended into the crowd.

Laughter caught my attention, and I spun around to see crumbs falling from Albert and Guillaume's frosting smeared lips as they chortled at me. "Where is he? Where is he?" they pantomimed me, spinning in circles.

No one on the street ignored us now. Every which way I looked, trolls were exchanging amused smirks with each other.

Élise reached for me. "You're making a fool of yourself!"

Something inside me snapped.

I threw my wineglass against the paving stones. It smashed, and the magic sent bits of glass flying up into the air. Élise jumped back and collided hard with the two guards. Despite knowing there was no chance of escape, I bolted.

No one stopped me.

I wove through the alleyways and streets, making my way steadily down the hill towards the river. I concentrated on the sound of the water – the river had to flow out somewhere. I was a strong swimmer. If I could just make it to the water, there was a chance of escape.

I kicked off my shoes and ran barefoot down a back lane, swung right, and cursed as I came up against a stone wall. Wheeling around, I backtracked the way I'd come. A dark shadow stood at the entrance to the street, ball of troll-light hanging ominously behind him. His chuckle reached my ears, seeming to bounce off the walls, assaulting me from all directions. I ran back to the wall and jumped, my fingers just catching the edge. Legs tangling in my skirts, I heaved an ankle over the edge and slipped over the other side.

"Run, run, run, little girl." Laughter chased my footsteps as I staggered forward.

"Do you really think you can get away?" The question came from above. I looked up and saw Guillaume sitting on the edge of a roof, leaning back on his hands with ankles crossed. A shudder ran through me. They were toying with me, like a pair of cats with a mouse.

But I was no mouse.

Kicking in the backdoor of a house, I felt my way through the dark until I found the front entrance, which I flung open but didn't exit. Instead, I concealed myself behind a curtain near the opening. Boots thudded against the paving stones near the door.

"You see which way she went?"

"Through the house," came the muffled reply. "She didn't come out."

I held my breath as steps came closer, into the house, and past the curtain where I was hidden.

"Must be hiding. Check upstairs."

I waited a few moments more and then slunk out from behind the curtain. A gleam of light came from the other room. Stepping softly, I crept towards the front door. Through the doorway, I had seen the bridge stretching over the river only a few yards away. I could make it if I was quick.

Feet slapping against the cold ground, I darted across the street, ran up the curved arch of the bridge and clambered up on the railing. Water surged beneath me, icy spray rising up from where the river smashed against the buttresses. I took a deep breath. I could do this.

"Cécile, no!"

As I leapt into the air, I saw Élise standing on a footpath near the river's edge. Then I was falling, and the realization that I had made a grave error filled me with terror as the water approached. A scream tore from my throat, but cut off abruptly as something lashed around my waist and hurled me upwards. I landed on my back in the center of the bridge to the sound of a splash from below.

Using the bridge railing for support, I hauled myself upwards in time to see a grey-clad figure being swept downstream.

"There she is!" My guards had apparently realized I was no longer in the house.

"Help her!" I screamed, pointing at the water. "Élise fell in the river!"

Guillaume's face twisted with indecision, but in a heartbeat, he was running towards the water.

Albert started up the bridge. Snatching up my skirts, I ran down the other side and into the crowded marketplace.

Trolls and half-bloods grudgingly made way as I pushed through, not certain where I was going, but knowing I couldn't stop. Then a familiar voice caught my attention.

"Be another week or two, I expect. Thaw was late this year."

I started walking faster, my eyes searching until I found what I was looking for. A blond head amongst a crowd of black-haired trolls. Next to him was a mule I'd seen countless times before. But the shock of seeing him in Trollus was overwhelmed by the hope that he might somehow be my salvation. Snatching my skirts up, I broke into a run. "Christophe!" I shouted. "Chris!"

The blond-haired boy turned and his eyes widened in shock at seeing me. "Cécile?" I flung my arms around his neck. He smelled like horses and hay and sunshine – like everything I knew.

"God in heaven!" he gasped. "What are you doing here? Everyone is looking for you – we found your horse in our fields and signs of a struggle in the woods."

"Luc took me," I choked out, burying my face in his neck and inhaling the smell of home. "He sold me to them. You need to help me. You need to tell my brother. You need to take me home." I was babbling, I knew, but I couldn't seem to stop myself. "Help me, Chris. Please!"

He grew still, his arms tight around my waist. Raising my face, I saw that all around us trolls were watching with angry faces. Albert pushed his way through the crowd, his face twisted with a dark scowl. Everyone backed away, giving him room.

"Get away from her, human," he snarled.

Chris set me down between him and the wagon. "I don't think so."

"It wasn't a request, stupid boy." Albert stalked towards us, his smooth movement at odds with his bulk.

There was a commotion in the crowd and a soaking wet Élise stepped through. She darted around Albert and hurried over to me.

"You must stop this madness, Cécile," she gasped out, wet strands of hair clinging to her face. "You are going to get people killed!"

"Stay away from her, you nasty creature!" Chris swatted at Élise. She ducked under his hand easily, but the damage was done.

Albert roared an inhuman word and Chris was launched up in the air, then slammed against the ground.

Shrieking, I grabbed hold of him, trying to stop the invisible force, but I was powerless against it. Both of us were shaken in the air like rag dolls in the mouth of a maniacal hellhound.

"Don't hurt her!" Élise shouted.

Abruptly, I was torn away from Chris and landed in a heap next to the wagon.

Chris remained locked in Albert's magic, which now had him pressed hard against the paving stones.

"Let me go!" he bellowed, squirming ineffectually against his invisible bonds.

"Kill him!" someone in the crowd shouted. "He broke the laws!"

"Kill the human," another chimed in. "Slit his throat!"

Chris's oaths abruptly broke off, his face turning red. "I prefer smothering," Albert said to the crowd with a smile. "Less mess."

"It is the duty of the trade magister to pass sentence!"
Élise's voice was strong. "You overstep your authority."

"Stay out of this, Élise," Albert said. "I would not want
to see you hurt."

"What is going on here?" The crowd parted and Tristan
sauntered over, pausing to pat the mule on the nose.

I flung myself at his feet. "Make them stop – they're
killing him."

"I see that," he said. "I assume he did something to
deserve it. Guillaume?"

"Took a swipe at Miss Élise, and," he added, raising his
voice, "he disrespected me."

"Is that so?" Tristan raised one eyebrow. "One can
hardly imagine why."

"He…" the guard started to respond, but Tristan
interrupted.

"Yes, yes, Albert. I believe you. Now would you mind…"
He brushed at his mouth.

"Oh!" Albert dragged a sleeve across his face, removing
most of the pink frosting. "Sorry, my lord."

"Much better," Tristan said. "It is always important to
look the part when you are about to do something nefarious.
You were really ruining the effect." He ignored my attempts
to get his attention. My eyes searched the crowd for
someone, anyone, who might help. But all the half-bloods
had retreated. I saw Chris's father, hands balled into fists and
eyes wide with fear. He stood at the edge of the crowd, but
he wasn't watching his dying son. He was watching Tristan.

"Who wants to see the human boy killed for his
insolence?" Tristan shouted.

"Kill him!" the crowd shouted.

I reached for the dagger at his waist, intent on burying it in his gut if that's what it took. He caught my wrist, holding it still.

"Who wants to see his blood run through the streets?" he shouted over their cheering voices.

"Kill the human!" they screamed.

"Who wants to suffer through another famine?"

Silence.

"Just as I thought," Tristan said, his voice carrying through the crowd. The hand holding my wrist twitched and I heard Chris gasp behind me, Albert's magic vanquished.

I jerked out of Tristan's grasp and scrambled on hands and knees to Chris's side. "Are you all right?" I whispered.

"Yes." His voice was raspy, but the redness was fading from his face. "He's a devil, that one," he whispered. "The worst of them – you should hear the things he says. The rumors of what he does to those who cross him."

I frowned. "He just saved your life."

Chris's lip curled back, his teeth showing. "Listen."

"These humans are our tools," Tristan lectured to the crowd. "Until someone can teach the mule to grow crops and load his own wagon, we must rely on creatures with at least a modicum more intelligence to do the work."

"I'll get you out," Chris said, hand rising to grip my shoulder. "Whatever it takes, I promise I'll get you out of here."

"You all know my feelings about humanity," Tristan shouted. "But that does not mean I do not recognize their usefulness. If I cut my finger on a good blade, I don't melt it down out of spite!"

"Listen to him prattle on," Chris hissed. "Treating us like animals!"

"Shut your fool mouth!" His father had pushed his way to our sides. I flinched as he cuffed Chris across the head. "I swear your mother must have dallied with another man because I'll never understand how I fathered a boy as daft as you."

Jérôme caught my wrist, eyes running over the silver marks tracing my fingers. "Lord in heaven, I never believed I would see the day." He gripped my hand tightly. "Listen to me, Cécile, and listen well. You've landed yourself in a pit of vipers, each one slyer and deadlier than the next. They are incapable of lying, but that does not mean they cannot deceive." He pulled me closer and I could smell the sweat of hard labor on his skin. "Actions speak louder than words – remember that!"

"I don't understand," I whispered. They were leaving me here – I could see it in Jérôme's eyes.

"You're a smart girl, Cécile. You'll figure it out."

Fingers closed around my arm, heat burning through the sleeve of my dress. Tristan unceremoniously hauled me to my feet. "Jérôme, it would be best if you left as soon as possible. I trust your next visit will be less eventful. And you." He glared at me. "You and I are going to have words about this."

I sensed his agitation and prudence warned me against dragging my feet. With his hand latched on my arm, I followed him through the streets. The guards and the dripping Élise came too, but I did not fail to notice the distance they kept.

"There," Tristan snapped. "That is the River Road. I assume that was your intended destination with that idiotic stunt?"

At the end of the valley was an almost sheer rock face that rose up into the darkness above. Two tunnels bisected the river, water flowing down each. The tunnel on the right was open, but had only a narrow footpath leading off into the darkness. The tunnel on the left was lit with troll-light, but thick steel bars stood as a barricade. In front of the gate stood four trolls, two facing the tunnel and two facing away. They were heavily armored, faces stern and unyielding.

But what stole my attention, and my breath, were the heavy steel bars through which the river flowed. They were so tightly spaced that only a fish might pass through, and the river slammed against them with deafening force. If I had made it into the river, running up against those would almost surely have killed me instantly. Élise had saved my life, and risked her own in the process.

Tristan carried on, seemingly oblivious to my thoughts. "The River Road tunnel and the gated entrance to the labyrinth are the only ways in and out of Trollus. Only oath-sworn and thrice-proven traders may use the River Road. One oath prevents them from speaking about Trollus outside the witch's boundaries. The other oath prevents them from undertaking any action that might jeopardize Trollus or its citizens. These are magic oaths, utterly and completely binding. Do you understand?"

"Yes." My voice was weak, because I understood. What he was saying was that there was no way for Chris or any other human to rescue me or bring me aid from outside. Even though countless farmers in the surrounding area might know I was here, not one of them could tell my family where I was. "Why wasn't I brought this way?"

"Because your friend Luc is a greedy bastard who will never earn the right to walk that road," Tristan replied, his eyes darkening.

"There are four rules that all traders must follow while they are in Trollus, but they are not magically binding. The first is that they are subservient to any and all trolls. The second is that no human male may touch a troll woman, whether it is against her will or not. And, as my wife, that includes you, in case you were curious. Three, all humans are forbidden to lie while they are in Trollus, so I suggest you don't get caught at it; and four, no human may charge more than market rate for any good or service. The punishment for violating any of these rules can be, and often is, death."

"Why aren't they magically binding?" I asked in a whisper.

"Because my father is a sadistic villain with a taste for blood, human or otherwise!" Tristan exploded. He cast a backward glance at our followers and added more quietly, "The oaths used to be magically binding, but that didn't provide much sport, if you understand my meaning."

"God in heaven," I whispered.

"I cannot say whether your God exists or not, Cécile, but if he does, he has turned his back on this place. Darker powers rule Trollus." He stared at the water rushing through the rock. "To be bound is a burden, but it is the actions we freely take that cause us the most pain." He said the last nearly under his breath, but it was impossible to miss the sudden jolt of anguish.

My eyes widened and I shuddered. If what Tristan was saying was true, Chris had broken two rules, both of them unwittingly and both because of me. Almost as though he could read my mind, Tristan said, "What happened today was your doing, Cécile. If you value the lives of your fellow humans, I suggest you don't let it happen again."

Abruptly, he let go of me and walked down the street. He paused in front of Albert and Guillaume. "I know what you did to her today." His voice was monotone and steady, making his words far more ominous than if he had shouted. "It was ill-considered."

The two guards exchanged uneasy looks.

"She is bound to me," Tristan continued. "Which means that what she feels, I feel." His fingers rested on the hilt of his sword. "When you hurt her, you hurt me. Why the hell else do you think my father passed a law against harming her?"

The two trolls fell to their knees. "We did not think, my lord."

"No," Tristan said. "But then, you rarely do." He looked over his shoulder. "Élise, take her back to the palace and keep her there for the rest of the day. I don't want any more incidents."

"Yes, Your Highness." Élise curtsied.

"And Élise," he added. "When lifting something heavy, with magic or otherwise, it is best to ensure one has good footing. Nevertheless, it was well done."

A gold coin flipped through the air, and she snagged it with one hand and took hold of my arm with the other. "Come with me."

"What is he going to do to them?" I asked once we were out of earshot.

"Nothing they don't deserve."

"I hate him," I said, my voice sounding hollow and distant in my ears. "He's evil and wicked, just like his father."

Élise leaned closer to me, close enough that I could feel her breath on my ear. "If that were true, your friend would be dead."

Everything snapped back into focus.

Taking my arm, Élise pulled me along with more strength than someone her size should possess. "We need to go back to the palace."

I went with her, but her comment unnerved me. Only moments ago, I was certain that how I'd seen Tristan behave was proof of what Esmeralda had told me about the troll nobility – that he was human-hating and evil. Now I wasn't so sure. He'd shown no regard for Chris' life, but Élise was correct – Chris was still alive. Alive, even though he'd broken rules that carried a death sentence.

And then there were Jérôme's actions to consider. I tried to focus and replay the events in my mind, but everything had happened so quickly. Jérôme had looked afraid, but not as panicked as a father about to lose his son should be. It was obvious Albert was the one smothering Chris, but Jérôme's eyes had been fixed on Tristan. Why? Was it merely because he knew enough about the trolls to know that Tristan had the power to pass sentence, or was it because he knew that Tristan would save his son?

Actions speak louder than words.

A common enough saying, to be sure, but what had Jérôme meant by it? Had he meant that Tristan's sparing Chris' life meant more than the human-hating drivel that he had been spouting? But Tristan was a troll – he had to tell the truth, so I couldn't discount his words. He had to mean what he said, didn't he? Otherwise, wasn't he telling a lie?

I spent the rest of the afternoon alone in Tristan's rooms with Élise's fading light, which gave me time to think and, more importantly, time to snoop. I was looking for something that would give me some insight into the Prince's mind, whatever that might be. There was something about him that didn't add up. My hands hesitated on the stack of old invitations through which I was rifling as I tried to recollect his precise words.

"You all know my feelings about humanity…"

Or at least thought they knew. His words were hardly a declaration – merely an affirmation of everyone's conceptions about him. Or misconceptions?

"You're grasping, Cécile," I muttered. I set the stack of cards back where I'd found them and pushed the drawer closed. It jammed. "Darn it!" I pulled the drawer back open and bent down to see what had caught. It was another card. Careful not to tear it, I extracted the thick red paper and skimmed the black cursive script. It was an invitation to the eighth birthday of His Royal Highness, Prince Roland de Montigny. Tristan had a younger brother.

"Looking for something?"

Jerking upright, I unsuccessfully tried to wipe the guilty expression from my face. Zoé stood in the doorway, her arms crossed. "You didn't eat your dinner."

My eyes flickered to the untouched tray sitting on the table. "I wasn't hungry."

"He won't appreciate you rooting about in his things. His Highness is very private."

"I wasn't rooting about in his things," I said quickly. "I was only looking for some paper."

"They just roll off your tongue don't they," she said bitterly. "The lies. The worthless promises. How anyone would dare trust a human is beyond me."

My back stiffened. "A bit of the pot calling the kettle black, wouldn't you say? You lot are the deceitful ones, all vying for control over your little cage. What was your sister even thinking, bringing me to meet your aunt and trying to get me mixed up in your schemes? I didn't choose to be here. In case you need reminding, I was kidnapped. The last thing I need is to make my circumstances worse!" I stopped talking when I realized the room had gone eerily silent – even the ever present sound of the waterfall was absent.

"A ward against eavesdroppers," Zoé snapped. "You nearly got my sister killed once today – I don't want her sent into the labyrinth because you can't keep your fool mouth shut."

"No one can hear us," I snapped back. "Besides, who would want to listen in on me anyway."

She strode over to the wall, pulled aside a tapestry and pointed at a hole neatly drilled in the wall. "This wasn't here yesterday."

My skin prickled and I had to fight the urge to rip everything off the walls to find any other peepholes that might exist.

"Élise shouldn't have trusted you – she's delusional, blinded by hope." To my amazement, Zoé slid down the wall and sat on the floor. "There is no hope," she whispered. "You didn't break the curse. Any hope we might have had of breaking free of our bondage is gone."

"I don't understand," I said.

"You don't understand anything." She closed her eyes. "They will never condescend to release us from slavery, and as long as we are cursed, we dare not attempt to force them. Magic holds the mountain up – magic of a strength that only the most powerful of the great families possess. If we destroy them, we gain our freedom only for the length of time it takes all that rock to fall down upon our heads."

CHAPTER 11
Cécile

"There is always hope." Even as I said the words, I knew how hollow they sounded. The half-bloods were trapped like rats on a sinking ship. "Maybe they'll change."

"Not in this lifetime."

Silence hung between us, then abruptly, she climbed to her feet. "I'm sorry, my lady. I should not have burdened you." Looking around the room, she crinkled her nose. "I need to straighten things up before he returns."

Now that she had mentioned it, it was more than a little obvious what I had been about.

"Have the guard take you to the glass gardens. They're walled in – no one will trouble you there."

And there was no way for me to get into trouble, either.

"And here, I meant to give this to you straight away." She handed me a dark green envelope. Inside was a green and gold invitation. "Lord Marc is throwing me a party," I said slowly, once I had read and reread the inscription.

Zoé nodded. "Then it begins." She pointed towards the door and the sound of the waterfall returned, making me jump. "Go for a walk," she said. "It will help clear your head."

I was no small amount surprised to discover Albert standing guard outside the door.

"I didn't expect to see you again," I said, tilting my head back so I could look him in the eye.

He frowned. "Why is that?"

Perhaps because you chased me through the city and then almost killed one of my dearest friends. And put a bee in the bonnet of His Royal Crankiness in the process. "Never mind," I grumbled. "Take me to the glass gardens."

He led me through the maze of quiet palace corridors and out an entrance in the rear.

"The paths are lit," he said. "Don't wander off them."

I set off, the white gravel on the pathway crunching beneath my feet. On either side rose glass hedgerows, each branch and leaf blown with exquisite attention to detail, guiding me towards the center of the garden. I paused from time to time to examine delicate flowers, bushes, and even trees that soared beyond the pools of light cast by the widely spaced lampposts. There was beauty all around me, but it was like walking in any garden in the darkness of night – I had no sense of the whole, only the little pieces revealed by too few circles of light.

The garden was like the whole city of Trollus – shrouded in mystery but for the few snippets of information revealed by those seeking to use me. Part of me wanted to turn my back on their problems – I wasn't the one cursed to this place.

But another part of me was drawn to the half-blood's conundrum. It seemed unsolvable: on one hand, they had abject slavery, and on the other, almost certain death. What would I choose, if the choice were mine?

Out of habit, I began to sing to relieve my frustration. Softly at first, but my voice was drowned out by the endless roar of the waterfall, so I sang louder. I could sing over a full orchestra, but tonight I fought the waterfall for supremacy. I walked until I found a gazebo, and it became my stage. I chose the powerful pieces belonging to heroic women, my heart hammering and my lungs aching from the sustained effort. It made me feel alive, stronger than the elements and more powerful than the seas. I sang with my eyes closed and imagined I was in faraway places, free to roam and love as I pleased. When I opened them, it seemed I had been transported far away, to a place not of darkness, but of light. All around me, the garden was glowing with an impossible brilliance. Nothing on this earth could be so beautiful.

"Heavens," I gasped, clutching the gazebo railing and blinking at the brilliant light.

"More like hell, really, but the Artisans' Guild has done a good job disguising it." I whirled around. Tristan was standing at the foot of the gazebo steps. "You've a lovely voice. I can't say I've ever heard anything like it."

"That's the first nice thing you've said to me," I said, my mind reeling. How long had he been standing there listening?

"Don't get used to it," he laughed snidely, turning to go.

"Wait!" The word was out of my mouth before I knew

what I was saying. Tristan froze, then turned slowly back around to look at me. I hurried down the steps and stopped in front of him. "I wanted to thank you for saving my friend's life today."

He tipped his head to one side, eyes searching my face. "Is that what you think happened?"

"Yes." I hesitated. His face was smooth, but his unease was a growing knot in the back of my mind. "Albert would have killed him if you hadn't made him stop."

"Albert's an idiot," he shrugged. "Christophe didn't deserve to die just because you foolishly decided to throw yourself on him in public."

"You know his name?" I asked, surprised.

"I know all their names. What of it? I'm sure you know the names of all your pigs."

I rolled my eyes at the comparison. "I'm just surprised you bother, given that you supposedly hate us so much."

One eyebrow rose. "Supposedly?"

"It's what I've been told," I said. "Although if you do hate humans, then you wouldn't have cared if it was my fault or not. You'd have killed him anyway. And don't give me any of that nonsense about humans being tools."

"Nonsense?" A faint smile drifted across his face.

"Quit parroting my words back at me," I snapped, "and answer my question."

"But you haven't asked one." He tapped his chin with an index finger and waited.

He was right, I hadn't. It was sitting on the tip of my tongue: why were you happy when we failed to break the curse? The cynical, logical side of me wondered if he was even more extreme than his father – that he would rather stay in a cage forever than give up an ounce of power – but my gut told me otherwise. He had a reason he was desperate to keep secret. I opened my mouth to ask, but nerves kept the words from coming out.

Tristan cleared his throat. "When I was a young boy, Jérôme used to let me ride around on his mule. He would tell me stories about what it was like outside, and I would imagine that I was a knight on his horse riding off to save the world. That the curse was broken and we'd escaped Trollus."

Was that an answer to my unasked question? I wasn't certain. "Do you still dream of escape?"

He closed his eyes and his misery rushed over me. "Yes, but I don't call them dreams anymore."

"What do you call them?"

"Nightmares," he said, so softly I barely heard him. He was shaken, visibly so, but I didn't understand why. What about coming out into the world above terrified him so much?

"My lady?" Zoé's voice made me jump and I turned, half expecting to see her right behind me, but her dancing orb of light was still over by the hedgerows.

"She probably thinks I'm lost," I started to explain, but when I turned around, Tristan was already some distance away and walking quickly.

"My lady?" Zoé called again, and I could hear the concern in her voice.

"Over here," I called and she hurried over. Albert, I noticed, was with her. "You should come in now, my lady. It is getting quite late."

"Quite late," I echoed, my eyes searching for Tristan's light.

"Was there someone out here with you, my lady? I thought I heard voices." Albert was watching me intently, and I felt a shiver run through me like ants marching down my spine.

Zoé gave an almost imperceptible shake of her head. *Don't tell.*

"No," I lied, not knowing exactly why. "I was just talking to myself."

He frowned. "Who lit up the garden then?"

I tensed.

"Oh don't be such a boor, Albert," Zoé said, smiling winsomely at him. "The poor thing is miserable – I thought the gardens would cheer her up a bit."

"Only royals or members of the Artisans' Guild are allowed to light the garden, Zoé," he chided, but I could see he wasn't immune to her charms, half-blood or not.

"I know." She lowered her head. "You won't tell, will you?"

"I suppose not," he said, motioning for us to start towards the palace. "Not unless I'm asked, at least. I would not care to see you punished."

The girl smiled at the hulking troll, but said nothing.

I kept my mouth shut, but my mind was whirling about like some great machine. Zoé had just lied. Not overtly, of course, but the effect was the same. But why was she covering for Tristan's presence when the whole city knew that we were bonded? Why was she covering for him at all when by all accounts she should hate his noble guts?

What were they trying to hide?

CHAPTER 12
Tristan

"Idiot, idiot, idiot," I muttered to myself as I navigated through the gardens away from Cécile, hoping Zoé would be quick-thinking enough to conceal my presence. I needed my association with Cécile kept at a minimum, or I'd risk questions arising over why I had suddenly changed my tune about her. What had I been thinking? If anyone knew I had followed her into the gardens like a lovesick puppy and then lit them up in a moronic attempt to impress her, it would undermine the purpose of my performance in the market today.

It had been a risky move to intervene and save Jérôme's son's life. I'd thought I'd played the circumstances well enough to hide my true motivations, but if Cécile, who'd only known me for the space of a day and knew nothing about politics, suspected me, then a savvy bastard like Angoulême was bound to have seen through my act.

Sure enough, I caught motion out of the corner of my eye as I crossed the bridge into the city proper. Plastering a smile on my face, I tipped my hat to Angoulême's man, who at least had the decency to look embarrassed. Not that it mattered. I never bothered trying to lose them anyway.

Keeping Christophe alive hadn't been up for debate, but following Cécile into the gardens and telling her the truth? Inexcusable. For one, I couldn't trust her, and two, the more she knew the greater danger she was in. If everyone believed her to be nothing more than a failed experiment in my father's quest to break the curse, they'd let her be. But the minute anyone thought she could be used against me...

I ground my teeth in frustration. I hadn't thought it would be this hard, even though Marc had warned me. "The bond changes everything," he'd said. "Whether you like her or not, keeping her safe will become your ultimate priority." Lo and behold, I'd been awake all of last night fretting about the tiny cut on her foot and whether the cold damp of the city would cause her to catch a chill. She'd shivered uncontrollably in her sleep until I'd warmed up the room, forcing me to spend the rest of the night dripping sweat.

And that voice. The strange acoustics of Trollus had filled the city with her song, luring me to her. And when I'd seen her standing in the dark, so fierce and defiant with hair like flames trailing loose down her back... If I wasn't careful, she would be my undoing.

I turned into the Dregs, negotiating the narrow streets until I came to a ramshackle house leaning against a tavern. Anaïs stood in the shadowy doorway, a smile touching the corners of her lips when she saw me. "You're late."

"My most sincere apologies."

She slid her arms around my neck and leaned in for a kiss, but I turned my face at the last minute so that her lips landed on my cheek. For me, this was a ruse – a valid reason to be skulking around the Dregs in the middle of the night; but for Anaïs, it was something more. Nudging the door open with my foot, I swung her across the threshold, her giggles filling the street until I shut the door behind her.

She clung to me even after I'd dropped my hands from her sides, dangling from my neck like a child. "Let go, Anaïs."

"What if I don't want to?" she purred into my ear, holding on easily without assistance. I walked from room to room with her feet banging against my knees, ensuring we were alone in the house, setting barriers against eavesdroppers and whispering to my magic to set off firecrackers if anyone came in.

I looked down at Anaïs. "Please?"

She made a pouty face, but let go of my neck. It was one of the things Angoulême never seemed to understand about his daughter. No one made Anaïs do anything. All you could do was ask and pray she was in an amicable mood. I didn't thank her though. That would imply she'd done me a favor, and I already owed her enough as it was.

"You're in a foul temper," she said, watching as I tossed my hat across the room before flopping face down on the bed.

"Tired," I mumbled into the dank-smelling pillow. "And I missed dinner."

"New little wife keep you up all night?"

I glared at her with one eye. "Don't start."

She shrugged. "There's already a rumor going about the city that your first-born son will reach out and shatter the barrier with his little fist."

"They may have a long wait."

"That isn't what I heard," Anaïs said, examining the contents of a basket sitting on the floor. "I heard two of my maids talking. They heard from the kitchen staff, who heard from one of the groundsmen, who heard from one of your wife's maids that you are a vile wheezing hog. The lady Cécile reckons she's never been so mistreated in all her life, and she'll never read another romance novel because the knowledge of what she's missing breaks her heart." She plucked a pastry from the basket. "Éclair?"

I munched on one of the pastries and counted the cracks in the ceiling. *Well played, Cécile*, I thought, if perhaps a tad overacted.

"I assume she's lying?" Anaïs nibbled on an éclair, expression mild, but I wasn't fooled.

"Assume what you want – it's none of your business."

She laughed. "My business or not, I told my father what I'd heard and added in a bit about how you were never ever cruel to me. Given that he finally thought he'd found a way to discover where your loyalties truly lie, he was furious. He was certain you'd be sweet to her in private."

"Of course," I murmured. Several months ago, Angoulême ordered his daughter to seduce me and spy on my activities to see if she could discover any sympathetic leanings. Anaïs had promptly told me everything. It was she who concocted the plan to pretend to do her father's bidding, but actually feed him useless information. It had also been her idea, although I was against it, to continue the ruse of her seduction so that I might have a way to meet with the revolutionaries. I hadn't wanted to damage her reputation, but in the end, her argument had won out. "What does my reputation matter?" she'd said. "I'm afflicted in the worst sort of way, and everyone knows it. There isn't a man in Trollus who'd risk the odds, even if my reputation were pure as the driven snow."

And to my shame, I'd had to agree with her.

"How is Roland?" I asked. Anaïs hesitated and my heart sunk. "Worse?"

"Yes and no. His rages in themselves are no worse, but he's stronger. When he learned you'd bonded the human, he quite lost himself. The servants couldn't control him and I had to step in."

"He's eight, how strong could he be?"

"He's your brother, a Montigny descended from the most powerful trolls to ever walk this earth. Another few years and only a handful of us will have the power to hold him. By the time he's grown, he'll be nearly unstoppable. My father believes he can control him, but he's a fool. The boy's insane, Tristan." She coiled a finger around a lock of hair and nibbled on the ends – a nervous habit she'd never been able to break. "I know it's a hard thing to consider, but…"

"No."

She threw up her hands. "Tristan, not only is he a danger to everyone around him, as long as he lives, he also puts everything you've worked for at risk. A steel knife in the heart would solve all our problems."

"No!"

The air in the room grew hot, but Anaïs didn't flinch. "You're being a sentimental fool, which is something a king cannot afford to be."

"Perhaps, but neither should he be a murderer. Not even my father murders trolls." Though he'd torture them to the point that they wished they were dead...

"And here I thought you were against discrimination... but it would appear that even you, with your lofty morals, value troll lives over those of your precious humans."

I shot her a dark look. "That wasn't what I meant."

"Are you certain?" Her eyes searched mine. "I know some of them are precious little pets to you, but is it possible you weigh our lives equally with theirs?" Anaïs sighed. "I, myself, do not. Oh, I recognize the need to treat them well or risk another embargo, but within reason. We are better, a higher level of being. It is like comparing dragons to mice."

"There are no dragons here any longer, Anaïs," I chided.

"I know." There was longing on her face. "But when the curse is broken, perhaps they will come back. All the others, too."

The witch had been more than savvy in her cursing. My people were not the only ones who looked for her death. "All things are possible," I said, and Anaïs was too lost in her own thoughts to notice my non-committal response.

The silence stretched. "We have little power to control such things," Anaïs finally said. "But we can resolve the matter of your brother."

"Leave the matter be, Anaïs. I'm no murderer, and I'm certainly not going to kill an inno... a child." My voice caught on the word. Innocent, Roland was not.

She tilted her head to one side. "Of course you're not, that's why I'd do it for you."

Leaping to my feet, I leveled a shaking finger at her. "Anaïstromeria, you will not…" I broke off before giving the order, and slowly turned away. I could hear the sound of her ragged breathing. A bead of sweat dripped down my neck as the temperature rose, her magic responding to her fury.

"I gave you my true name as a token of trust, Tristan. To demonstrate my loyalty to you and you alone. Not so that you could use it to compel me whenever we disagreed."

Her voice was bitter, and I had to fight down the wave of guilt it inspired. Not only because of what I'd nearly done to Anaïs, but because it occurred to me that I'd lost count of the number of true names I possessed, the number of trolls I had the complete power to compel. It was a power I never intended to use – it was enough that they knew I could, but chose not to.

"It's time," she said, handing over my hat. "They'll be waiting for you now. You've only got about another half-hour until curfew."

Glad to have a reason to drop the conversation, I pushed the bed aside, lifted the trapdoor, and jumped into the tunnel leading to the cellar of the tavern next door. When I emerged, they were all there waiting for me. Hair more brown than black, eyes more grey than silver, I could feel the weakness of their magic, could tell even with my eyes closed that everyone in the room was half-blood. Except for the one human. I frowned at Esmeralda, who leaned against the wall. Her patience with my timeline was growing thin. I would have to find an excuse to get her out of Trollus before she caused any more trouble.

Walking to the front of the room, I silently regarded my followers. I would be their champion, lead the revolution to tear down the autocracy that valued only power and bloodlines, even if it meant starting a war against my father. I would risk my own life and those of my friends to accomplish these goals, but there was one thing I'd never do: break the curse.

Some creatures were best kept in their cages.

CHAPTER 13
Cécile

I hadn't heard Tristan come in during the night, but when I awoke the following morning, there was something sitting on the pillows next to me. At one end was a clear glass ball that was attached to a pommel-like handle wrapped with soft white leather. The handle had a thin leather wrist-strap hanging from the end of it. Next to it was a short note written in the flowing script I recognized as Tristan's.

You looked ridiculous walking around the city carrying an empty wineglass. I don't care to be associated with a drunk. Particularly one who damages glassware. Touch the diamond with your finger to turn it on.

TdM

Examining the item more closely, I saw that there was a formidable diamond embedded in the handle. Tapping it with my finger, I smiled in delight as the bulb at the end lit up. Tapping the diamond again extinguished it. "Clever, clever," I whispered, climbing out of bed and dragging the covers with me.

The door flung open. "Good morning, Cécile!" The Queen smiled at me, but as usual, it was the Duchesse who had spoken.

Even though my ankles were tangled in the pile of linens, I managed a passable curtsey, wondering if they intended to intrude on me every morning. "Your Majesty. Your Grace."

"Where is Tristan?" The tiny troll demanded. "Matilde, turn around so that I can see."

"He isn't here," I said. "But he was here," I added when she frowned. "Briefly." It wasn't entirely a lie – he must have come in at some point to leave the light.

"Briefly." The Duchesse's eyebrow rose.

"He gave me this," I said, hoping to forestall any other questions.

The Duchesse examined the light stick and then read the note. "Ha ha!" she cackled.

"What is it! Let me see! Is it a love note?" the Queen demanded, reaching over her shoulder.

"I suppose some people might call it a love note." The Duchess winked at me.

Tristan's mother read the note and sighed. "Oh dear. It isn't very good, is it?"

"It's his first time, Matilde," the Duchesse replied. "I'm sure he'll improve with practice."

I stifled a laugh at the thought of His Royal Highness putting any effort into love notes. Especially ones addressed to me.

The Duchesse clapped her hands together. "Now let us get down to business. Yesterday was a disaster, to say the least. I don't want anything similar to occur at the party this evening." She gestured for me to come closer. "How much longer do you suppose it will take your face to heal?"

I glanced at the mirror across the room, my black eye prominent even in the dim light. "Another week," I ventured. My gran had the knack for herbs and healing, and she'd taught a lot of it to my sister, but I'd never paid much attention. I hadn't needed to.

"Mercy!" The Duchesse shouted the word, making me jump. "So long? It amazes me you survive a trip to the privy, you humans are so fragile. Élise!" she hollered, rather unnecessarily, given the girl was already in the room.

"Yes, Your Grace?"

"Is your aunt in the city?"

I saw the nearly imperceptible tightening around Élise's eyes at the mention of Esmeralda. "She is, Your Grace."

"Go see if she has anything that might speed up the girl's healing. I'm tired of her looking like one of those dreadful drawings my eight year-old nephew is always sending to me."

"He uses a lot of color, I take it," I said, examining the virulent bruises on my arms.

"He uses a lot of gore," the Duchesse corrected. "Now tell me, do you know how to dance?"

It turned out that I did not know how to dance, at least not by troll standards, and my aching toes did not let me forget it as I stood in the ballroom of Marc's manor, watching trolls glide across the floor.

Esmeralda had been all too truthful in her description of them. Seen like this, en masse, with only me and a handful of half-blood servants to color the mix with human blood, it was like watching a circus freak show while being locked in a madhouse. At least half of them were marked with physical deformities or were clearly not sound of mind, but power crawled through the room, making it hot. I watched them with wide eyes, half afraid and half entranced by the bizarre display.

A prickle ran down my spine.

"They are all here," said a deep voice. "Even now, none of them dare test the limits of my power."

I stiffened before dropping into a curtsey. "Your Majesty." The King stood beside me, arms crossed, though how he had gotten his bulk there without me noticing was a mystery.

"They are all here to prove their support for our continued reign, but my son, my heir, is notably absent."

I swallowed hard, fighting the urge to run. Something about Tristan's father filled me with dread. It was like having a shark circle you in the water, knowing it intended to strike, but not when.

"I cannot even begin to describe what it is like to spend one's life trapped. To be the most powerful being in this world, but reduced to ruling a dark, dank cavern. To be forced to rely on the greed of lesser creatures for sustenance. For life." He sighed, shifting his massive bulk. "It violates the order of the universe."

Stones and sky! If I hadn't been so darned terrified, I would have rolled my eyes at his arrogance. Order of the universe?

"You're afraid of me, aren't you." There was no inflection in his voice, and his eyes remained passively on the dancers.

I was afraid of him. Horribly afraid, but somehow I managed to keep my voice level. "I know that if you hurt me, it hurts him in some fashion." I straightened my shoulders. "And he's the heir to your precious Montigny line."

A faint smile grew on the King's face. "True. But he is not my *only* heir. A fact you might remind him of when you next see him."

A sour taste appeared in the back of my throat as I watched Tristan's father stroll away, nodding his head at those he passed as though he had not just threatened his own son's life. And mine. Ignoring curious glances, I hurried through the ballroom, desperate to be away from the stifling heat.

The hallways were cool and I walked for some time looking for a way outside. The sounds of shouting and laughter reached my ears, and I followed them onto a balcony overlooking a courtyard filled with racks of weapons. Dominating the space were two enormous trolls – I judged them to be at least eight feet apiece – leaping back and forth across the yard on one foot and shouting insults at each other.

"Those are the twins, otherwise known as the Baron and Baroness, and individually known as Vincent and Victoria."

I clapped a hand over my mouth to keep from squeaking in surprise and spun around. "You trolls make a fine habit of sneaking up on people," I accused Marc, who was leaning against the building, cloak pulled up to obscure his face. "And what are you doing out here anyway? Isn't this your party?"

"I don't like parties."

"Oh," I said, my brow creasing as I tried to make out his face in the darkness. "Then why did you throw one?"

"I owed someone a favor." Marc shrugged one shoulder and came over to stand next to me. "It was not the worst thing he could have asked for."

I quietly wondered who *he* was. I had thought the party had come as a request from the Duchesse, but apparently that was not the case. And it wasn't the King – *he* wouldn't have needed to use a favor to get Marc to throw a party. Which left Tristan. But why? The point of the party was to see whether all the troll aristocrats would give their support to the King's decision to install me as a princess, which seemed decidedly contrary to what Tristan seemed to want. So why ask his cousin to throw a party that would speed along the process? I bit my lip, realizing with a surety that Tristan was not the passive victim of circumstance that he was playing himself off to be. What remained unknown was the nature of his end goal. As we stood watching the two giant trolls leap around the courtyard, I considered putting the question to Marc but eventually decided against it. "What are they doing?" I asked instead, gesturing to the courtyard.

"Victoria and Vincent are continually having contests to determine which one of them is head of their household," Marc replied. "Sprinting, rock throwing, javelin tossing, breath holding, handstands... You'll get the picture soon enough. They'll probably want you to judge."

"But Victoria's a girl," I protested. Although not like any girl I knew. She was dressed in a coat and trousers like her brother, and only the long braid hanging down her back and her slightly more refined features gave her away as female. "Even if she was born minutes before him, wouldn't he still inherit his father's title?"

Marc started laughing. "Best you not ever mention such an idea to Vic," he said, his shoulders shaking. "She has no time for the limitations of what she terms 'ridiculous human ideologies'. And besides, their barony was actually passed down to them from their mother. For trolls, the child with the most formidable magic inherits – regardless of whether the troll is male or female, or who was born first."

"Oh," I breathed, liking the idea very much.

"The twins, however, are equal in all things, including magic," Marc continued. "I expect they will be content to share their title for the rest of their lives."

"Sort of share," I giggled as the two giants collided with each other, hopping wildly to keep from toppling over.

Both trolls looked up at us.

"Hello there, Marc!" Vincent bellowed. His eyes fixed on me and he set his foot down.

"Disqualification!" Victoria shouted, but her brother wasn't listening.

He barreled over to us and fell on his knees in front of me. "My lady! You are even more beautiful up close!"

I thanked him and let him kiss my hand, until his sister elbowed him out of the way. "Vincent, you are entirely unoriginal. I am Victoria de Gand, Baroness de Louvois, my lady." Vincent scowled at her, but he was ignored. "Allow me to say," she continued, "you are as lovely as a flower in bloom. Especially now that your face is less scabby."

"Thank you," I said, smiling at them. "Are you by any chance the Vincent that sat on His Highness's face when he was a child?"

He shook with laugher. "Yes, indeed, my lady. Though I couldn't manage the same feat now. Tristan would toss me across the city."

"True," Victoria agreed. "No one out-magics Tristan, except for his Majesty. And Anaïs." They said the last bit together with an eye roll. "She's a looker, our Anaïs," Vincent said. "But she's got the personality of one of those prickly fellers. You know, the ones with the quills."

"Porcupines?" I guessed.

Vincent pointed at me. "That's the one. Personality of a porcupine." He sighed happily. "I do love alliteration."

"I trust you two can manage to keep the lady entertained for the time being?" Marc asked. "I suppose I should make an appearance at my own party."

"Would be our pleasure," Victoria said. "Could we interest you in a contest, my lady?"

After eliminating such options as rock tossing and jumping to see who could touch the highest point on the wall, we settled on archery. Victoria and Vincent easily hit the bull's-eye on the target. Mine landed right between theirs.

"Perhaps if we back up a few paces," I suggested. We did so, but still, all three of us easily hit the bull's-eye.

"There's no sport in this," Victoria complained.

"I agree," I muttered. "We need a moving target."

The twins looked at me with interest.

"Not me," I clarified.

"That would be a bit more of a challenge," Vincent muttered. Then his eyes brightened. "I'll be right back." He dashed through an open door and returned moments later carrying a moose head, horns and all. "This creature is a moose, isn't it?"

I examined the dusty old thing. "Perhaps a few centuries ago."

"'Twill do," Vincent muttered. The moose head flew out of his hands and began to dance around the yard. I laughed, noticing that several other trolls had come out to watch our game.

"You there, boy!" he shouted at a page. "Make this thing dance about while we shoot arrows at it. Be sure to make it erratic."

It didn't take long for the contest to be modified so that we all were standing on one leg with our right eyes closed shooting arrows at a flying moose head. I was laughing so hard tears ran down my cheeks and my ribs ached beneath the tight stays of my corset. Then out of nowhere, a steel spear as thick as my arm shot through the air and pinned our moose against the wall. The three of us spun around. Tristan was brushing his hands off, looking exceedingly pleased with himself. Anaïs stood next to him in a brilliant red gown. Smiling, she rested a hand possessively on Tristan's arm.

I felt my temperature rise, anger and perhaps... jealousy? Surely not. What did I care about how he spent his time?

"No one likes a show-off, Tristan," Victoria shouted.

The two of them strolled towards us and I became acutely aware that I was sweaty, dusty, and my hair had come loose from jumping about. "How do you know it wasn't Anaïs?" Tristan asked, looking fondly at the beautiful girl on his arm.

"She'd burst out of her dress if she even tried," Victoria sniffed.

"That a challenge?" Anaïs's voice was sultry and low.

Victoria pointed a finger at her. "Always."

We all watched as she hoisted one of the spears off the rack. "If you wouldn't mind, Tristan."

He shrugged and the moose pulled away from the spear, which clattered onto the stone floor. With a surprisingly unladylike grunt, Anaïs launched her spear, piniong it to the wall. "What do I win, Victoria? Do I get to be Baroness for the day?"

The twins rolled their eyes as if to say I told you so. I raised a hand to get their attention and recited: "The perfectly pretty porcupine perfumed the palace with the putrescence of a porky pig." They both fell to the ground in hysterics.

Anaïs crossed her arms. "What is she going on about?"

"Inside jest," Victoria laughed, wiping tears from her face. "Had to be there."

She sniffed. "Perhaps you'd like to give it a go, my lady." Picking up a spear, she tossed it my direction. I caught it, but the weight of the metal spear sent me stumbling backwards. I wasn't strong enough to throw it more than a couple of feet much less hit a target. "It's what we use to hunt sluag for sport," she said. "Afraid your little arrows wouldn't do you any good."

There wasn't much I could say to that – she was right.

"I'm surprised you use weapons against them at all," I snapped. "Why not just use magic like you do for everything else?"

Anaïs rolled her eyes. "Magic doesn't work against sluag – they nullify it. I've killed five of them," she boasted.

I clapped my hands loudly, doing my best to be patronizing. "And here I thought your sole purpose was to walk around looking pretty."

"Jealous?" she sneered.

"Not hardly," I lied.

"You're lying – I can tell."

I smirked. "Jealous?"

Her face darkened. "Unfortunate the sluag didn't gobble you up."

I looked at Tristan to see how his growing irritation would manifest, but he said nothing, seemingly absorbed in polishing one of the buttons on his coat. "Why don't you go back to the party, Cécile?" he said, flicking at an invisible bit of lint on his coat. "I'm sure they have all manner of entertainments concocted to keep you busy."

"Speaking of the party," I snapped. "Your father has taken notice of your absence and isn't best pleased. He asked that I remind you that you are not his *only* heir."

Tristan's finger froze in the process of flicking another bit of lint, and I felt the stab of his unease. "Did he ask you to relay any other message to me?"

"He did not." He hadn't needed to.

"Well then," Tristan smiled a patronizing little smile. "Unless you care to speculate why he might have felt the need to remind me of my younger brother's existence –

a fact I could hardly forget – then perhaps you might consider finding your way back to the party."

My skin burned hot with anger. "Excuse me," I muttered and hurried back into the house.

The last thing I wanted was to rejoin the party, so instead I wandered through the empty corridors until I found a staircase that led to what appeared to be a basement. Holding my light up so that it shone ahead of me, I made my way down. The corridor was lined with doors, which I opened one by one. They were all filled with wine bottles and casks, but nothing else of interest. Above me, I could hear the footfalls of dancers, the faint thrum of music, and the occasional burst of laughter. They clearly were not missing their guest of honor.

Rounding a corner, I reached for the handle of yet another door. It was locked. Curious, I pulled out a hairpin and set to work on the complex mechanism. When it finally clicked open, I cautiously shone my light through the entrance before stepping inside and turning the handle lock behind me.

The room was dominated by a large table surrounded by a dozen chairs. Its surface was littered with books, paperweights, and a large abacus. I perused the titles as I circled round the table: *The Cathedrals of Castile*, *Trianon's Bridges*, and *The Great Palaces of the Sea of Sand*. A black coat was tossed over the back of one of the chairs, and the white embroidered TdM on the cuff glimmered in my troll-light. "What have you been doing lurking in Marc's basement?" I wondered aloud, settling myself in the chair. Several empty glasses and a plate of half eaten cucumber sandwiches sat on the table in front of me, but no clues as to why Tristan was reading books in the cold comfort of a wine cellar.

The handle of the door jiggled. I gasped and clambered out of the chair, diving behind a tea service trolley and extinguishing my light just as the door opened.

Tristan hurried into the room, with Marc, Victoria, Vincent, and Anaïs hot on his heels. I swore silently, certain he would notice my presence the second he walked in.

But he seemed oblivious. I could see him talking to the other trolls, but magic prevented any sound from reaching me. Which meant they had something to hide. Through stacks of teacups, I watched him wave his arms around, a wide grin stretching across his face as he spoke to his friends. I could feel his excitement as he rounded the table to where I had been sitting only seconds before. Leaning down, he pulled a lever on the bottom of the table, and a secret compartment popped open. He reached inside, extracted several large rolls of paper, and proceeded to spread them out on the table. I tried to stay calm so as not to draw his attention as he explained whatever it was he was showing them. Soon they all looked equally excited, except for Anaïs, who frowned and wagged a finger at Tristan. Tristan only shrugged.

A loud knock came at the door. Tristan quickly shoved the papers back in the secret compartment and slammed it shut. "Yes?" he said, his voice loud after the enforced silence.

A grey-clad servant hurried through the door. He was visibly shaken, wiping his sweating palms against his trousers. "My lord! Your brother, His Royal Highness, he..." he stammered.

"What about Roland?" Tristan snapped, good mood vanished.

"He's in the city."

Anaïs gasped and clapped a hand over her mouth.

"Doing what?" Tristan demanded.

"Hunting, my lord," the servant croaked.

Tristan bolted to the door. "Marc, find Cécile," he shouted over his shoulder. "It will be on your life if anything happens to her."

Seconds later, I was alone in the dark once more. My chest felt tight and it was several long moments before I could relax enough to take a proper breath of air. I could feel the distance between Tristan and me growing as he moved towards the city. I hurried over to the table, and feeling along the lower edge, I popped the catch holding the secret compartment. Pulling out the rolled parchments, I quickly scanned the diagrams of columns and arches, and read through lists of materials and costs. None of it meant anything to me, but they had to be important if Tristan was hiding them.

The handle of the door shook.

"Drat!" I hissed. Slamming the compartment shut, I hid under the table.

The door opened and shut, and the faint glow of troll-light illuminated the room. I stared at the shoes coming across the floor. Far too small for either of the twins, and both Tristan and Marc wore boots. And they certainly didn't belong to Anaïs. Who then?

Books thudded open and shut above me as the troll circled the table. I bit my lip as I watched a pale hand slip under the lip of the table, clearly looking for the catch to the compartment. Please don't look down, I prayed, my neck swiveling to watch his progress.

The troll reached the chair with all the used dishes in front of it and paused.

Click.

The compartment popped open and I heard a sharp intake of the troll's breath. "Damn you, Montigny!"

Angoulême's voice. And I knew the source of his ire. There was nothing in the compartment because Tristan's papers were clutched in my hot little hands.

Abruptly, he stormed towards the door, slamming it shut behind him.

I stayed frozen where I was for a long time, nervous he would come back. But eventually, I had to move. Marc was looking for me and I didn't want him to find me here. I briefly debated putting the papers back where I found them, but decided against it, instead hiding them in my underclothes. The bustle of the dress would hide any suspicious lumps. I wanted another chance to look at the diagrams to try to puzzle out what they were, but more importantly, I felt to my core that it would be wrong to let Angoulême have them. There was a darkness to the troll – worse in its own way than that of the King, although I could not have said why.

My light on, I left the room, careful to lock it behind me. Then I made my way through the meandering hallway and up the stairs. Just when I thought I was beyond discovery, magic locked around my throat and slammed me against a wall.

"What is he planning?"

Angoulême stepped out of the shadows, his arms crossed. I dug my fingers into the magic wrapped around my neck, but it slipped around my hands like water. "Who?" I wheezed. "I don't know what you're talking about."

One black eyebrow arched up. "For a human, you are a poor liar, my dear." The magic around my throat loosened fractionally. "But I'll humor you. What is Tristan planning?"

A hoarse laugh pushed through my lips. "How should I know? He doesn't confide in me – he doesn't even like me. After all, I'm human."

Angoulême watched me with unblinking eyes, a snake: coldblooded and cruel. "We can help each other," he said softly. "If you tell me what he plans, after I dispose of him, I promise not to stand in your way when you try to leave Trollus." His head cocked slightly to one side. "I would even help you do so."

Everything stilled. Not for a minute did I believe that he was offering my freedom out of the goodness of his heart. He was only doing it because he thought I could help him. But did that matter? If I helped him, I would be free. I could hand over Tristan's papers and let Angoulême do the rest of the work. I could trust that he would do so – trolls were bound to keep their word.

"What do you mean by dispose?" I asked.

A smile slithered onto his face. "I think you know."

My fingers curled against the sudden chill that racked me to the core. He'd kill Tristan.

"Your Grace. Your Highness." Marc's voice sliced through the tension, and the magic fell away from my throat.

"I'm surprised to find you here, given your ward is currently on a rampage through the city," Marc said, examining a fingernail.

I could all but hear the sound of Angoulême's teeth grinding together. "Your Highness," he said, inclining his head. "Please do stay off the streets – I would hate to see anything happen to you."

Marc waited until the Duke was around the corner before he said, "Did he hurt you?"

I shook my head.

Marc's shoulders slumped. "Small mercies. Cécile, he's a very dangerous man. You must stay away from him."

"I didn't exactly seek him out," I muttered, prying my shoulders away from the wall. "He found me."

Marc's troll-light hung behind him, as it always did. Although I could not see his face in the shadows, I imagined his eyes narrowed.

"What did he want from you?" His voice shook with anger.

I kept silent. Anything I told Marc he was sure to tell Tristan, and I didn't want to limit my options just yet.

"Do not trust him, Cécile," Marc warned. "He holds no love for your kind."

My kind…

My temper flared. "Oh, but I should trust you – you, who always hides in the shadows and refuses to let anyone look upon your face."

"Is that what you want?" he hissed. "To look the monster in the eye? Is it easier for you to understand the danger when it comes from the mouth of something ugly and strange?"

"I'm not afraid of you, Marc."

"Then you're a fool," he snapped. "You should be terrified of every last one of us."

I shook my head. "Not you. You promised you'd never hurt me."

A short bark of laughter filled the hallway. "You do not know how easy it is to get around words." He turned away, pressing a pale skinned hand against the wall as though to balance himself. I frowned at the black lacework tattooing his skin. "I didn't know you were bonded."

In a blink of an eye, his hand disappeared into a pocket. "I'm not. She's dead."

My whole body jerked in surprise, and I wiped my hands against my skirts, horrified that I'd brought it up.

He turned back to me, face still shadowed. "What did Angoulême want?"

"He thinks Tristan is up to something," I said slowly, considering just how much I wanted to reveal. "He wants me to help him find out what."

"Don't help him, Cécile." I could hear the plea in his voice. I had bargaining power here, and I was damn well going to use it.

"Give me one good reason why I shouldn't," I said. "Better yet, give me one good reason why I should side with Tristan at all."

"Because it is in his best interest to keep you alive."

"Why?" I asked. "What difference does it make to him? I didn't break the curse – you would think he'd be happy to see me dead."

Marc shook his head. "He is bonded to you. If you die, he dies."

Realization slowly sunk in. "And if he dies?"

"Your heart may just stop. And if it doesn't, you'll do everything in your power to stop it yourself."

"I see," I whispered. If Angoulême killed Tristan, I would die. I closed my eyes, barely noticing as Marc steadied my arm. In my naiveté, I had nearly handed away my life. That was why the King had instituted a law forbidding anyone from harming me – not because Tristan could feel my pain, but because if I died, so did his son.

"But you're alive." I met Marc's gaze. "Even though she died."

"Only because stronger powers wouldn't let me die." Marc's voice was grim. The light drifted around him, and in a rare moment, his twisted face was illuminated. But it held no horror for me now. "Don't help him, Cécile. Stay out of the politics and trust that Tristan will keep you alive."

I thought of the parchments tucked safely against my backside and of the excitement on Tristan's face as he showed them to his friends. Thought about how he had saved Chris's life and the words he had said to me in the garden. What side are you on, Tristan?

Hours later, long after I had drifted off to sleep surrounded by the sumptuous silks of Tristan's bed – my bed now, it would seem – I snapped awake, panic-stricken. Not my panic, no, it was his. Tristan had discovered his papers were missing, I sensed it. In the blackness of the room, my eyes fixed on the drapes where I had undone the stitching and hidden the documents between heavy layers of fabric. I had done the work in the darkness, afraid that someone might be watching me through one of the hidden peepholes into the room. Years of needlework under my grandmother's watchful eyes had allowed me to restitch the hem by feel alone. No one would guess they were there.

Lying back against the pillows, I tried to calm my pounding heart. I had the leverage I needed to confront Tristan tomorrow – to demand the truth. I just needed the courage to do it.

CHAPTER 14
Cécile

Sleep eluded me the rest of the night and, in the wee hours, I rose and went in search of Tristan. I found him in the palace stable yard, still dressed in the finery he had worn the night before. Resting my elbows on the smooth stone railing of the balcony, I watched him from afar. He sat on a square of stone that may have once served as a mounting block, elbows resting on his knees. His face was still and drawn and dark shadows from lack of sleep lurked under his eyes. With one finger, he slowly traced the gold marks lacing his other hand.

I wanted to storm down to confront him, but my feet seemed frozen in place. I was scared of what he would say, how he would react. I was afraid of what it would mean for me to get involved with troll politics.

"Spying on me so that you have something to report back to your new friend?" Tristan's voice floated up to me.

My fingers twitched against the railing. "No."

I made my way down the steps. He didn't look up, or even move, until I was standing in front of him. "I wanted

166

to speak to you about something." My voice shook, despite my best efforts.

"Then speak."

I opened my mouth, but nothing came out.

He frowned. "I'm waiting."

"In private," I managed to blurt out.

He looked around the empty yard. "There isn't anyone here."

I gritted my teeth against each other. "Please."

"Fine." He motioned for me to follow him through a pair of doors, which I shut firmly behind us. We were inside a set of stables, rows of pristine horse stalls stretching out in either direction. "A waste of space, don't you think?" I gestured at the empty building.

Tristan unlatched one of the stall doors and hung off the edge, swinging slowly back and forth. "Wishful thinking, I suppose. Now what is it you want?"

"Make it so no one can hear us."

"It's considered rude to tell a troll what to do with his magic."

I jammed the toe of my shoe against the stall door to stop the swinging. "Well, I can't very well do it myself. Besides, it's your secret I'm trying to protect."

Magic brushed my skin, wrapping silence around us like a cloak. "What secret would that be?"

A drop of sweat trickled down my spine. "That you're a sympathizer."

He laughed, but the flash of unease gave him away. "You can quit trying to hide the way you feel," I added. "You can't fool me the way you do everyone else."

The smile slid from his face. "Works both ways, Cécile."

I held my ground. "I'll ask the questions. Do you hate humans?"

He snorted softly. "I thought you had all the answers."

"I want to hear it from your lips."

"What difference does it make to you? Knowing won't change anything."

His anxiety fed mine and my breath came in short little gasps. "Yes or no."

"That's awfully limiting," he said, licking his lips. "I prefer to qualify my answers."

"Yes or no, Tristan."

Silence.

He didn't trust me. I didn't blame him. But I had to know. There had to be a way to convince him without resorting to blackmail. I was good at persuading people – all it took was a bit of concentration and the right words. I focused. "We both have a vested interest in each other's survival," I said. "No one else in this cursed city needs you alive more than I do. But in order for me to help, I need to know the truth. Please tell me the truth." I leaned into the words, putting every ounce of willpower I had into them.

The sound of my heart was loud in my ears, the rocks solid beneath my feet. One of the unlatched stall doors swung against the wall. Tristan's attention jerked in the direction of the sound. He frowned and looked back at me. Worried. Curious. But unconvinced and unmoved by my force of will, which was something that had never happened to me before. There was only one way to get him to cave.

"I believe you have recently been deprived of certain documents," I said softly. "Documents that certain individuals are eager to possess."

Fury burned through the back of my skull. Tristan became unearthly still, unblinking. "Where are they?"

I fought the urge to step back. "Safe. Hidden."

"You surprise me, Cécile," he said, voice frigid. "I didn't figure you for the backstabbing type."

I scowled at him. "I only want the truth – you are the one who is so damnably secretive. And besides, I didn't take them to use against you. I took them to protect you."

His eyes widened fractionally, but I felt his surprise.

"I think you had better explain yourself," he said.

In short, terse sentences, I explained how I had wandered into the cellar and what had happened afterwards. "If I hadn't taken them, Angoulême would have," I said. "And I had them hidden in my skirts when he made his offer. I could have given them to him then, but I didn't."

"To protect yourself."

I shook my head. "I didn't know about... that until after. Marc told me what happens if one of us..."

"Dies." He finished my sentence. "You didn't know?"

"How could I know?" I scuffed the toe of my shoe against the floor. "You trolls have taken away everything that matters to me. There is no way for me to escape on my own – I need help. Angoulême offered that to me, but I know he doesn't mean it. He hates me and means to see me dead, I can feel it." My hand balled into a fist and I hesitated. "But I think you would help me, if you could."

He didn't react. I closed my eyes and tried to read his emotions, but they were tumultuous and confusing.

"Is that your bargain, then?" he asked. "My promise to help you escape Trollus in exchange for my papers?"

"No," I said. "I want something else."

Silence. I didn't bother opening my eyes to look for clues on his face. They wouldn't be there – he had been at this game for far too long. All the clues I needed resided in my own head. Tristan was nervous. He had thought he could predict me, control me, but I'd just demonstrated otherwise.

"What?"

"I want you to tell me what those papers contain. I want to know why they are so important to you. Why they are so important to Angoulême."

He laughed. "Of all the things in the world you could ask for, *that* is what you want?"

I nodded, not fooled by his flippancy. I had taken a chance and struck gold. Of all the things I could have asked for, this was the one he wanted to give up the least, which meant it was valuable. Within his answer lay the truth, the heart of his politics. Yes, I could have asked for him to help me escape, but I'd seen how easy it would be to get around that promise. A bird in hand was worth two on the fly, and if he gave me what I wanted, I was certain I would have something valuable indeed.

"Just because I can't kill you doesn't mean I can't hurt you," he said, stepping forward.

I shook my head. "I'm not afraid of you."

"You should be." His hand slid around my throat,

thumb resting against my fluttering pulse. "I could hurt you in ways that might make you wish for death."

"You won't."

Breath hissed between his teeth. "How can you be so sure?"

"Because if it was in you to torture the information out of me," I said, "you'd have done it already." I leaned towards him, and his hand slipped from my throat to cup the back of my head, his fingers tangling in my curls. "You hate the way your father is, how he treats the half-bloods. I heard it in your voice yesterday, but more than that, I felt it." I pressed a hand against his chest and for the first time ever, he did not recoil at my touch. "You aren't like him."

His heart thudded rapidly, the heat of his skin warming my hand through his shirt.

"Life would be much easier if I were," he said softly. Sighing, he moved back, putting an arm's length of distance between us. "You drive a hard bargain, but I suppose I have no choice."

"You do have a choice," I said. "That's what makes this difficult."

A faint smile brushed his lips.

"Tell me," I urged.

He rested his head against the bars above my head and I felt the great burden of his misery press down on my shoulders, words bursting out of him in a wild torrent: "I didn't want you brought here. I fought my father's decision at every turn, but he wouldn't listen. All he cares about is breaking the curse. He will stop at nothing to get free."

"I could help you," I said, watching the rapid rise and

fall of his chest. "If I broke the curse, your father would have no reason not to let me go." I knew his feelings about the curse were complex, and it was high time I got to the bottom of them.

"No!" Tristan jerked away from me, eyes wide. "I mean…" He held up one hand. "Breaking the curse has consequences."

"You don't say." I crossed my arms.

Tristan grimaced. "Do you want my father released on the world?"

"Hardly," I snapped. "I'd like to see him dead, but fat as he is, I don't suspect he intends on keeling over for a long time."

"What he intends may not matter," he replied softly. "If everything goes according to plan. *My* plan."

An odd sense of relief went through me at his admission. "You're a sympathizer. You're their leader, aren't you?"

He nodded and took hold of my shoulders, giving me a gentle shake. "If you betray me to Angoulême, he'll tell my father. And my father won't just kill me. He'll kill Zoé and Élise, and countless others you haven't even met. And even if by some miracle you survive my death, he'll make sure it isn't for long."

"I understand," I said. "You have my word that I won't say anything."

Still gripping my shoulders, he said, "In a year, I'll be eighteen, which is when troll magic matures and reaches its full strength. I'm…" He hesitated. "I'm already a match for him now. By then, I'll be stronger. Stronger than any troll alive; and in Trollus, power is king."

I gasped. "You intend to depose your own father?"

He squeezed his eyes shut and let go of me. "In a manner of speaking."

Coldness swept over me. "You plan to kill him."

"Sometimes," he said, so quietly I could barely hear him, "one must do the unthinkable."

"It's treason." Worse than treason, what he was contemplating was patricide. The murder of his own father.

"Yes."

"What about your mother? If you kill your father, won't she die too?" I thought about it for a minute. "And your aunt?"

Tristan looked sick and felt worse. "It's a possibility, but my aunt believes she can keep my mother alive."

"She knows then? What about your mother?"

He gave a slight nod. "Only my aunt – it is easy enough to muffle our conversations with magic. My mother isn't the suspicious sort." He rolled his shoulders, the movement reflecting his discomfort. "It was my aunt's plan from the beginning. She despises him and how he rules Trollus."

There had to be more to it than that. "Why?"

"She had a… a friend. He was a half-blood and they were very close." Tristan grimaced in discomfort. "Because of the conjoined nature of my mother and aunt, my father has a tendency to consider them both his. When he found out about my aunt's… friendship, he had the man flayed in public. Twice." He closed his eyes. "Even a half-blood can survive a great deal of torture. I believe the executioner deliberately sliced the artery in the man's leg for fear that if he survived, my father would order him flayed a third time. And a fourth."

My knees wobbled at thought of enduring so much torture – if there was a downside to the troll's near-invincibility, this was surely it.

Tristan continued. "He's never ordered the execution of a full-blooded troll – there are too few of us left – but he orders the deaths of half-bloods for the slightest offence. And they are never clean deaths."

Gruesome, horrible deeds, but such is the nature of kings – human or troll. I could understand the Duchesse wanting to see him dead because of what had been done to her friend, but what had pushed Tristan over the edge so that he would consider killing his own father?

As though anticipating the question, Tristan said, "I had a human friend, once. He was old and wore funny clothes. He always brought me candy and told me stories. He never treated me like I was a prince or even like I was a troll – he treated me like I was just a boy. My father killed him to punish me." He lowered his head. "I couldn't do anything to stop him. I was young and helpless against him. But I'm not anymore."

Closing my eyes, I shuffled through his emotions. Fear. Shame. Doubt. And how did I feel about becoming an accomplice in a murder plot? I hated his father – he'd arranged for my kidnapping, ruined my life. To him, I was a tool here to serve a purpose, and ultimately, disposable. But could I stand by and see a man killed? I didn't need to think long or hard. In this case, not only would I willingly stand by, I'd stick the knife in myself. If that made me a bad person, then so be it. But even with the King dead, one fundamental problem remained.

"The sympathizers," I said. "They don't just want to be rid of your father – they want to be rid of all the troll nobility so that there's no one powerful enough left to lord over them. What's to stop them from killing all your friends, all your family, other than the fact they need you to keep Forsaken Mountain off their heads?" Then the realization dawned on me: he was waiting until *he* was in power before breaking the curse. Not only would he be king, he'd be a hero to his people. I opened my mouth to say as much, but then snapped it shut again. Withholding freedom from a city full of people was certainly a dangerous secret, but knowing he was doing so did nothing to explain the purpose of his diagrams. "Well?" I finally asked.

He took a deep breath. "Are we in agreement then? You will tell me the location of all my papers in exchange for me explaining their contents?"

"Yes," I said. What could be more important than the knowledge he was purposefully keeping the curse in place? "I agree."

"You must understand: Marc, Anaïs, and the twins are the only ones who know. And I only trust them because I have their true…" He broke off. "Why I trust them is irrelevant. My point is, I have no such assurance from you."

I said nothing. Telling him he could trust me wouldn't make a difference. I could lie.

Tristan took a deep breath. "The documents contain the plans for building a structure that would support the rock."

"No magic required," I whispered.

"Not after I finish building it."

"But to what purpose?" I demanded. "Once you are king, won't you just do what is necessary to break the curse? With it gone, couldn't you fling off all the rock, or… or, leave this place?"

"That is a possibility." There was no emotion in his voice, but I could see the forced rise and fall of his chest. He was controlling his breathing, trying to control his emotions so that I couldn't read him. But why? What more was he hiding?

I bit my lip. "You don't think the curse can be broken, do you?"

He sucked in a deep breath and sighed. "It may be too much to ask for."

"Low expectations, right?"

"You've a good memory," he said. "I know I can build. I have no such certainty about how to end our imprisonment."

Which was just as well for me. Once I escaped this place, I'd sleep far better at night knowing the trolls could not get out. Pushing aside those thoughts, I turned my attention back to his plans.

"But if you build this for the half-bloods, they wouldn't need you anymore," I said. "What's to stop them from killing you? Get you out of the way rather than risk future enslavement?"

"Goodwill?" he said, a faint smile touching his lips. "They could call me Tristan the Liberator and compose songs in my honor."

"My question was serious, Tristan," I replied. "And what of all the full-blooded trolls? Will they kill them all?"

"Hardly," he said. "I've negotiated the safety of most. There is a list of names they have sworn not to harm."

I shook my head. "I can't see all of them thanking you for freeing their servants. For diminishing their power."

"And there lies the rub," he said softly. "In freeing thousands from servitude, I will be gaining many powerful enemies. I have no doubt the attempts on my life will come often and regularly. But the benefits of the many are worth the risks to myself."

I bit my lip. "You don't seem as concerned as you should."

The corner of his mouth turned up. "I'm exceedingly difficult to kill."

"But I'm not."

Tristan's smirk fell away. "No," he said. "You are not. Which is why I didn't want you brought here. I am very sorry for that."

I'd saved him from one death only to allow him to walk freely towards the promise of another. And not just his death, mine too. Sharp tears stung in my eyes, blurring my vision so that I did not see him reach over until he tucked a stray strand of hair behind my ear. "It will take years to build, Cécile, and I promise, the instant I have control over Trollus, I will send you away and pay as many humans as I must to keep you safe. To go and live how and where you might wish."

Forever fearing the assassin that would come for me in order to kill him.

"I know this is a great deal to take in, and likely not the answer you were expecting," he said in a low voice. "But don't focus on what might happen years down the road –

focus on the now. If I am discovered before I am ready to strike, we will both be dead. I must keep up the ruse that I am loyal to my father and, in order to do that, I must make people continue to believe that I view humanity with contempt."

My chin jerked up and down with understanding.

"I will ignore you. Be cruel to you. And you must play along. Act sad and unhappy. Never give anyone a reason to think I've shown you a moment's kindness or that I've confided in you in any way. And above all, never let anyone suspect that I care one way or another whether you live or die, beyond how it might impact me."

"Do you?" I asked, stepping towards him before I knew what I was doing. We were nearly touching now, and he smelled clean, of soap, with a faint hint of leather and steel – like a boy should.

"So many questions," he said, smoothing my disheveled hair back from my face, his hand running down the length of it until it rested at the small of my back. I trembled beneath his touch: not from fear, but something else. Something that made the blood in my veins boil while raising goose bumps along my skin. His hand tightened around my waist. My lips parted slightly and the overwhelming need to have him pull me closer flooded over me like an ocean wave. My eyes drifted up his chest, past his throat, coming to rest on his face. He was watching me through long black lashes, his eyes half closed; and in them, I thought I saw something, knew I felt something…

Abruptly a veil fell over his eyes, hiding whatever it was I thought I'd seen, if it had ever been there at all. His face resumed the mask of indifference he always wore, callous and arrogant. And he was angry. "Where did you hide my plans, Cécile?"

"Sewn into the draperies in your bedroom." The words came out without my bidding them to do so, as though I had no control over my own tongue. *Be careful making promises to a troll.*

I blinked once and he was gone, the thunder of the waterfall deafening my ears once more.

CHAPTER 15
Cécile

I did not let the momentum that came from my encounter with Tristan go to waste. I had hope now – and something to look forward to. Most of all, I had an ally, and a powerful one at that. But Tristan's plan would take time to enact – time that I had no intention of wasting by moping around in my bedroom.

"Élise," I said, having found her making the bed. "If I wanted to speak with the Duchesse, how would I go about doing so?"

Élise smoothed a hand over the blankets. "You could send her a card requesting an audience."

I frowned, not at all fond of the idea of waiting around for a response to an invitation.

"Or I could take you to see her now," she said, a smile touching the corner of her lips. "The Duchesse is not a stickler for formality – or of anything she considers an inefficient use of time. She'll not mind you dropping by unannounced."

"You seem to know a great deal about her," I murmured as we walked through the corridors. Now that I had my own light, I was able to pause and examine the artwork lining the endless corridors of the palace. I tried to find little details to remember to help mark my way.

"She was my first charge, when I turned fifteen."

"Really?" I stopped in my tracks and turned to her in surprise, accidentally blinding her with my light in the process. "I wouldn't have thought someone so young would…" I trailed off.

"Have the privileged position to empty the chamber pots of the Duchesse and the Queen?"

I flushed, because that was precisely what I'd been thinking.

"She knew my mother," Élise continued. "She purchased the rights to Zoé and me when we were quite young, so we had many years to prepare for serving royalty."

There was an edge to her voice that I could not help but notice. "Sorry," I muttered, certain that I had offended her.

"Why?" she asked, knocking firmly on a door. "It wasn't any of your doing, and besides, there are worse things than being a lady's maid. I could be dredging sewers or working in the mines."

Choice. The word came swiftly to my mind although I did not speak it aloud. Until these last few days, I had not truly appreciated what it meant to have control over one's own life. The right to *choose* mattered – and it was a right none of the half-bloods had.

"What do you want?" shrieked a voice from inside the room.

"It's me!" I shouted back. "Cécile!" Squaring my shoulders, I turned the handle and went inside.

"Cécile!" the Queen exclaimed as she caught sight of me. Rising to her feet, she hurried over and kissed me on both cheeks while I was still mid-curtsey. I wheezed as she pulled me into a hug that made my ribs creak.

"Don't break her, Matilde," the Duchesse shouted over her shoulder. "She's positively fragile."

"I'm not really," I said, smiling awkwardly at the Queen as she led me towards a sitting area surrounded by mirrors. "I did grow up on a farm, you know."

"These things, as is often the case, are relative," the Duchesse replied.

"Your hair is positively tangles," the Queen declared, seemingly oblivious to our conversation. Picking up a hairbrush, she pushed me down on a stool in the middle of the circle of benches and began to work the snags out of my hair.

"Just let her," the Duchesse said, the soft tone of her voice out of character. "She is better when she has someone to mother."

I nodded into the reflection of the mirrors, which had clearly been set up for this purpose.

"Why are you here?"

Élise had been right – Tristan's aunt was not one for wasting time.

I cleared my throat. "Before, you said there were opportunities for me here in Trollus – that little would be denied me. I'd... I'd like to take advantage of that."

She took a mouthful of tea and watched me in the mirror. I waited for her to ask me what had changed, but she only nodded. "Is there something in particular you wish to pursue?"

Knowledge. "I'm not sure," I replied.

"Music?"

"No," I said quickly. "Not that." My singing was my own – the thing I was best at, that I cared about most. I did not want them interfering in that.

"Art? Literature? History? Language?" She rattled off a series of topics.

"All of those things," I agreed.

The Duchesse bit her lower lip and then smiled. "Things to pass the time."

I realized then that she didn't need to ask what had changed – somehow, she already knew. And it became just as clear to me that the matter of Tristan's politics and plans was not something that would be overtly discussed between us.

"The game you play," I pointed towards the boards hovering in the corner. "Will you teach it to me?"

"Guerre," she mused. "Yes, perhaps that is an appropriate place to begin. With strategy."

"Tristan. He…" I hesitated, watching the Queen in the mirror. She had ceased with brushing my hair, and her eyes seemed glazed over and unseeing. "He likes this game?"

The Duchesse shook her head. "He does not like it – he lives it. Now, shall we begin?"

The following two days were filled from dawn till dusk with a wide assortment of activities. I learned the basics of Guerre from the Duchesse, practiced with a dancing master, learned how to blow glass, wrote bad alliterative poetry with the twins, and followed Marc about on tours of various parts of the city. Not once did I so much as catch a glimpse of Tristan, which is why, on the third day, his abrupt arrival at my painting lesson caught me off guard.

"That," said a voice from behind me, "is without a doubt one of the ugliest combinations of color I have ever seen. Please do not tell me you call that art!"

I turned slowly from the brown and green mixture I had been idly smearing across the canvas to find Tristan standing behind me, arms crossed and a frown on his face. "How long have you been at this?"

"All afternoon." I scowled and got to my feet.

"If this is what an afternoon of lessons by the finest artists of Trollus can accomplish, I can only imagine what you were like when you started." He glanced towards my teachers. "You're wasting your time."

"The Duchesse asked us to give Lady Cécile instruction, Your Highness," one of the artists said, looking like she would rather be anywhere but here.

"Well, I am telling you to cease and desist immediately," Tristan snapped. "This," he gestured vaguely towards my painting, "is not worthy of your attention."

"Excuse me, Your Highness." I grabbed handfuls of my skirt and squeezed the fabric, feeling the hot flush of anger and embarrassment on my cheeks. "But I was led to believe I could pursue whatever activities I wished, so I do not see what right you have to stand in my way!"

"Royal prerogative!"

I snorted. "More like royal need to interfere with everyone else's business because you have nothing better to do with your time!"

His eyes widened with apparent outrage and he stepped towards me. Out of the corner of my eye, I could see the other trolls trying to discreetly retreat. "What do you know about how I spend my time, *human?*"

The way he said the word made it seem like something disgusting and foul. I squeezed my eyes shut for an instant to control the sting. This is a fake fight, Cécile, I reminded myself. It's just acting, don't take it personally. But it was hard.

Perhaps he sensed that he was pushing me too far, because Tristan stepped back. "What is this bit of *art* supposed to be, anyway?" he asked, gesturing at the smears of paint.

I squared my shoulders. "A representation of feelings through color."

"Oh? And what feelings, pray tell, does this represent?"

I lifted my chin and looked him straight in the eye. "My feelings for you, dear husband."

One of the trolls gasped and clapped a hand over her mouth, but I barely noticed over the sharp jab of shock in the back of my head. Good, I thought spitefully. If we were going to fake fight, he'd better get used to taking his fair share of the blows.

Abruptly, Tristan began to laugh. "I suppose," he said, after his fit of laughter subsided, "that you aren't wasting your time after all." He gestured at the wide-eyed trolls hiding in the shadowed corners. "Get back to it, then."

He spun on his heel and left the studio without another word.

"Are you well, my lady?" One of the trolls came forward, touching my arm. I realized that I was trembling then, my breath coming in little hiccupy gasps.

"Yes. No." I pressed a hand against my stomach and took several deep breaths. "Please have my painting framed and delivered to me at the palace."

Ignoring her slack-jawed look of horror, I hurried out of the studio, my guards following at my heels.

The painting was waiting for me when I returned to my rooms late that evening after a rousing game of three-legged tennis with the twins. Sweaty and more than a little disheveled, I stood staring at the silk wrapped package sitting on Tristan's desk, wondering if I had made a mistake by having it brought here.

The door swung open, and Tristan strode into the room. As it shut behind him, the sound of the waterfall disappeared and a faint haze appeared, obscuring the walls from view.

"Hungry?" Without waiting for my answer, he tossed an apple in my direction. I snagged it out of the air without thinking.

"Nice catch. Influence of your older brother?"

I nodded warily. "What do you know about my brother?"

Tristan took a bite of the other apple he was holding, chewing and swallowing before answering. "Frédéric de Troyes. Nineteen years old, brown hair and blue eyes. He is second-lieutenant in that imposter-you-call-a-regent's standing army. He is rumored to be an excellent shot with a pistol. He is also known to have a particular fondness for strong drink and tavern wenches, the combination of which is likely to yield several illegitimate children, if it has not already."

I set the apple down. "How do you know all this?" It was true, but it was not how I knew my brother. The Fred I knew was a boy who took his younger sister hunting and on weeklong treks through the wilderness. Who never treated her like she was incapable just because she was a girl. To see my brother reduced to a womanizing drunk troubled me.

"Spies," Tristan replied. "I sent dozens of them out to learn what they could about your life and family after your friend Luc delivered you to us."

"He isn't my friend," I said coldly, hating the idea of a bunch of strangers spying on my family.

"I suppose not," Tristan said, tossing his apple core onto a tray.

A thought occurred to me. "Are they still watching them? Your spies?"

He stiffened almost imperceptibly – I might not have noticed if it were not for the tension growing in my mind. "Yes."

"And?" It was hard to ask the question, because I knew whatever he said would hurt.

"Most of the town has given up hope you will ever be found alive," he said, gesturing for me to take a seat and waiting until I did before he settled across from me. "They think you fell victim to a bear or mountain cat. But your father and brother continue to search, as does the innkeeper's daughter, Sabine. She refuses to hear any talk that you might be dead – has ridden out every day to look for you."

"But she's terrified of horses," I managed to choke out between my fingers. "She never rides."

"Then I suppose that she chooses to do so now is a testament of her devotion to you," Tristan said quietly.

It was too much – it was bad enough missing them as much as I did, but bearing the burden of their grief as well? I broke down into heavy gasping sobs, tears running down to soak my skirts until Tristan handed me a handkerchief. It was the only move he made. He offered no comfort or words; only assumed that strange preternatural stillness that reminded me of how different we were.

"I should not have told you," he said when my tears subsided.

"No," I said, hugging my arms around my body. "Thank you for telling me. I want to know. Need to know." I paused, searching my mind for the words to convey what I was feeling. I looked at him in mute appeal.

"I know how you feel," he said, and then shook his head, rejecting the statement. "I feel how you feel." His voice was raw.

Having him admit it was oddly comforting. "It's just that I hate knowing that they're suffering and there's nothing I can do about it," I said. "If only I could send them word…"

"You can't," Tristan said, eyes darkening. "That is not a possibility."

"I know!" I snapped at him. "But that doesn't stop me from wishing there was some way to make them stop searching. To get on with their lives."

Tristan's brow furrowed. "There is one way," he said reluctantly. "I could arrange for… remains to be found."

A sour taste filled my mouth. "My remains."

"In a manner of speaking. Bones showing signs you were killed by an animal. We'd have to include some sort of token easily identified as yours. It will be devastating to them at first, of course, but it will give them closure. If that is what you want."

But was that what I wanted? Did I want my family and friends to think I was dead? To bury some stranger's bones thinking it was me, when in truth I was living and breathing only a few leagues away? Or did I want them to keep hoping I was alive, just as I kept hoping I would one day be free of this place?

"Is it better that way?" I whispered. "Will they be happier?"

Tristan shook his head. "That isn't my choice to make."

Lifting my hair, I reluctantly unclasped the golden chain from around my neck. "Here. This is my mother's necklace – I always wore it before. Everyone will recognize it."

He silently took it from me.

"Don't tell me the details," I said. "Just take care of it."

"As you wish," he replied, and I felt his pity as he slipped the necklace into his pocket.

I took a deep breath and my gaze fell on the package on the desk. "I have something for you," I said, glad to change the subject. "A gift."

One black eyebrow arched. "You do?"

I gestured to the object in question, and, looking somewhat puzzled, Tristan pulled off the wrappings.

Silence.

"I meant it as a joke," I explained. "You know, ha ha?"

He nodded slowly. "You did well today. Talk of our little argument has spread like wildfire through the city.

Everyone is convinced we despise each other."

"You were very convincing," I said.

He raised his head to look at me. "As were you. I almost believed…" He trailed off and then waved his hand, as though what he had been about to say was no matter. "This really is dreadfully ugly."

"I know." I broke out into a grin. "You should have seen the looks on their faces when I told them to frame it."

Tristan laughed, and I felt the tension flow out of me in a welcome release. I realized that I had been half-afraid that he'd meant what he said earlier – that the argument had been real. Our allegiance was tenuous at best, and his anger towards me today had been so convincing that part of me thought he'd changed his mind. Or worse, that it had been all my imagination that he was on my side in the first place.

"You should sign it," he said. "Artists always put their mark on their work."

As I set down his tear-stained handkerchief to pick up a pen and ink, I noticed the monogram on it. For reasons I could not explain, I scrawled *Cécile de Montigny* on the bottom of the painting.

Tristan went still. "I suppose that's true," he said, softly as though to himself. He straightened abruptly. "But the Cécile you presented today would not make such a concession, would she?"

The ink rose off the painting, coalescing into a blob before dropping back into the pot. "I suppose not," I muttered, letting my hair fall forward so he wouldn't be able to see the embarrassment written all over my face. Not that he wouldn't be able to feel it. Re-dipping the pen,

I scrawled a *C* in the bottom corner. "Better?"

He made a noncommittal noise, and pulled something from his pocket. "As it turns out, I have something for you as well."

My mouth made a small "o" as he held up a necklace glittering with tiny diamonds, wrought to look like a cascade of snowflakes. "It's beautiful."

"Try it on," he said.

He took hold of my shoulders and turned me towards a mirror. I stood frozen as he brushed my hair aside, his expression fixed with concentration as he undid the clasp and fastened it around my neck. My senses seemed magnified, and I felt everything keenly: the brush of his wrist against my shoulder, the warmth of his breath on my hair, the faint scent of apples on his hands.

When he was finished, he eyed our reflection. "The Jewelers' Guild had it made expressly for you – they sent it to you at dinner, but you weren't there."

It was like ice water had been poured through my veins. "Oh," I said. "How kind of *them*."

He frowned. "You don't like it."

"It's… cold." I moved, needing to put distance between us. I could sense his confusion and it made my own thoughts seem scattered. "Everything here is beautiful!" I said, my voice bordering on a shout. "Everything. But it doesn't mean anything because I'm always alone."

"You're rarely alone," he replied warily.

"That's not what I mean!" I pressed my hands to my temple as I struggled to articulate myself. "Everyone around me is there because they've been told they have to be. By you, your father, your aunt! No one cares about me except for what they think I can do for them. And now," I clenched my teeth. "Now, I'm about to send you off to ensure that the only people who *do* care about me think I'm dead. Soon I'll be nothing, no one to anyone."

"I see." His voice was toneless.

Suddenly the necklace broke away from my neck. I watched helplessly as it rose up into the air and rent into countless pieces before dropping into a heap on the carpet.

"Why did you do that?" I shouted.

"It was ill-considered."

I dropped to my knees and touched the scattered bits of jewels and metal. "You didn't consider it at all," I said bitterly. "Someone else did."

Tristan turned his back on me and I watched him grip the edge of the desk so hard the wood groaned in protest. "I can't do this," he muttered.

"Do what?" I asked.

Silence.

"Victoria and Vincent," he finally said, not turning around. "They are more than passing fond of you. And Marc, well, I didn't think there was anything that could breathe life back into him, but you seem to have managed. And given the amount of time you spend with all three, I can only assume the fondness is mutual. Avail yourself of them, and perhaps you will find the *warmth* you're lacking."

Before I could think of anything to say to that, he was gone, the door left swinging from the force of his departure.

CHAPTER 16
Cécile

"Cécile, I thought you said this would be fun."

I glanced up from my contemplation of the swirling water of the river. "I said no such thing, Vincent. You asked how 'we human folk went about catching fish' and I said that I would show you. *You* said that it sounded like fun."

"That's true," Victoria declared, looking up from the worms she had lined up on a rock in an attempt to get them to race. "Although I must say, Cécile, this technique of fish-catching seems flawed, as we have caught none. What we have done is sit in a row for nearly an hour, listening to Marc's dreadful conversation and watching you stare pensively at the water."

"Sorry," I said. "Fishing is better done at dawn and dusk." I squinted up at rock above. "Although I'm not certain that matters as much here."

"I find it rather relaxing," Marc said from where he lounged across a rock on my right. "It would be the perfect activity if you two could stand to be quiet for more than a minute."

"I expect no more from you, Marc," Victoria replied. "But Cécile is usually far more entertaining than this." She poked me in the ribs. "What's wrong with you?"

"Tristan and I quarreled at breakfast," I muttered. "I'm afraid he put me in a poor mood."

"About what?"

"Apparently I chew too loudly."

"That is a very annoying habit," Victoria said. "So is this." She threw a handful of worms at me. I tried to dodge, but the wriggling mass landed square on my skirts.

"What happened to the farm girl I once knew?" she teased. In response, I picked one up and pretended to eat it. Then I tossed it on Marc's sleeve.

"Can a day go by without you and Tristan shouting at each other across the dinner table?" Marc asked, picking the offending worm off his sleeve and setting it in a crevice between two rocks. "Do you ever have a civil conversation?"

"No." I pushed away the worms, then reached down to the water to rinse my hands. It had been weeks since the necklace debacle, but I had not once seen Tristan alone. We were together often enough in public – at parties and dinners, sometimes in audiences with his father – but he always treated me with either cold civility or picked cruel little arguments that sent rumors swirling through the city. I had no choice but to play along – and I played my part well – but every argument left a sour taste in my mouth and a cold emptiness in my heart. I slept alone in our rooms every night, although he kept up the pretense that he was making at least some attempt at fathering a child by ensuring he was seen stopping in at odd hours of the night. But he arrived when I was sleeping, was gone again by the time I awoke. The only evidence that he had been there at all would be a rumpled shirt tossed over a chair back or objects rearranged on a table – enough that I would notice and know to come up with another version of the same lie about what passed between us in the night.

Marc knew me well enough now to know this wasn't a topic I cared to belabor, and he changed the subject. "Did you fish much before?"

"When I was younger," I said. "My father used to take my brother and me, and my friend Sabine would come as well – not because of the fishing, but because she fancies my brother. Sometimes she and I would go, but instead of fishing, we would lie by the banks of the stream and tell stories to each other. And once I learned to read, I would sometimes bring books and read them to her. But I had less time at that point."

"You learnt to read late," Marc commented, winding up his fishing line.

I shrugged. "That is a matter of perspective, I suppose. Most Hollow folk can't read much – there isn't a need. I wouldn't have learnt if my mother hadn't insisted. She started sending tutors to teach me when I was thirteen. I was the only one who received more than a cursory education." I paused for a minute, then I glanced at Marc, who was silent. "I feel as though that misrepresents them, though. They are very practical folk – everyone knows how to *do* things. They are a very self-sufficient lot. Just because they can't read, doesn't mean they are stupid."

"I never said it did," Marc replied.

"I know. But it seems as though you value a different sort of knowledge."

Marc chuckled softly. "By *you* do you mean Tristan? Because I have certainly never given you cause to think such a thing."

I made a non-committal noise. While we had been talking, Victoria and Vincent had decided to wade into the river and were attempting to catch fish with their bare hands. A smile slipped onto my face as I watched their antics. "This city is too small for them," I said. "I think they are stifled here."

"The world might be too small for them," Marc replied, and we both laughed as Victoria threw a fish at Vincent's head. He promptly grabbed her braid and dunked her under the water.

"When you spoke about your village," Marc said, "I noticed that you said 'they' and not 'we'. It seemed as though you saw yourself as separate."

I frowned and plucked at the ribbon on my dress. "I was. My mother and her tutors ensured that. They didn't just educate me – they changed the way I spoke, the way I moved, the way I acted. At first I tried to be two different people so that I wouldn't seem strange to everyone, but that didn't last." I swallowed hard. "They changed the way I thought – once I could read, especially, it seemed the world grew in leaps and bounds with every passing day. There was so much I wanted to talk about, but no one wanted to listen." I felt my cheeks flush. "I wanted to leave so badly, and the second I was gone, all I wanted was to go back."

"Do you still? Want to go back to your village, that is?"

"I…" Such a simple question demanded a simple answer, but I found I had none. Shoving my hands into my pockets, I felt a piece of paper crinkle: the most recent of Tristan's notes.

His love notes, as his mother insisted on calling them, had not improved in quality. If anything, they had grown snider, but I found myself treasuring each one more than the last. With the notes had come fur-lined cloaks and heavy blankets to ward off the endless chill. The high-heeled shoes I detested all but disappeared from my wardrobe, replaced by practical flats that did not pinch my feet or cause me to "limp about like an old lady". Sheets of music and collections of famous operas appeared on tables, chairs, and the pillows of the bed. A lute was the first instrument to arrive, and was followed in short order by a harp with a note stating his hope that I would "show more talent if given more strings to pluck". Everything he sent seemed for the express purpose of making me happy. But all the gifts in the world meant nothing, because all my heart wanted was the one person it shouldn't.

"I don't think my absence has changed much," I said, not liking the direction of my thoughts. "Life goes on, with or without me."

"How do you know?"

"He keeps me appraised," I said under my breath. Within the pages of my books, I'd often discover programs from my mother's performances in Trianon, news clippings from the papers, and, once, a lengthy report written by one of Tristan's agents describing how my family fared. I cried when I read those pages, and cried harder when they disappeared from my possession a day later.

The sound of rushing water dropped away, and Marc's light drifted behind us so that our faces were cloaked in shadows. The twins reacted to some discreet signal and increased their antics, drawing attention away from us. "He isn't supposed to be telling you anything about the outside," Marc said. "None of us are. The King gave very specific orders that you were to be kept isolated from the human world as much as possible – that's why we keep you away from the market."

I kept still, my face smooth, so no one watching would suspect we were talking about anything out of the ordinary. "Why? Is it some sort of cruel punishment?"

"I do not know," Marc replied. "He did not explain why."

"His Majesty does nothing without purpose," I mused. But what did he hope to prevent by keeping me isolated? Or was it something he intended to accomplish?

"Agreed," Marc replied. "Which is all the more reason not to let Tristan get caught."

"I won't." I chewed my lower lip, my mind grappling with why Tristan took the risks at all. It would be easier, and certainly wiser, to be constant in his cruelty, but he seemed intent on countering every argument we had with some act of kindness. Which should have made my life easier, but which managed to do the exact opposite. To receive thoughtful bits of kindness and then face the cold cruel persona he wore in public was more than just confusing, it was painful. It made every word he said against me hurt all the more.

"Even if I went back to the Hollow," I said softly, "nothing would ever be the same."

It was no answer, but Marc did not press me further and the sounds of the city returned to my ears. "You're meant to be having tea with Duchesse Sylvie this afternoon, are you not?"

I nodded. "She is teaching me to play Guerre."

"She will teach you well," he said. Rising to his feet, he reached down a hand to help me up. "Get out of the water, you oafs," he shouted at the twins. They waded out, heedless of their dripping clothes.

"Who won?" I asked, taking Marc's arm.

The twins exchanged frowns. "You mean you weren't counting the fish?"

I winced. "Sorry."

They both heaved deafening sighs. "Poor form, Your Highness, poor form," Victoria said, giving my shoulder a gentle shove. "I think we can attribute your failure to a distinct lack of focus."

"I second that," her brother announced, the two coming around to walk on either side of Marc and me. "Too many hours spent in too many lessons on too many subjects."

I grinned, because it was true. The trolls knew so much about so many things, both past and present. Every day I spent with someone new, trying my hand at their trades, learning new languages, or listening to them lecture about some historical event. All my instructors were kind and eager to exchange their knowledge for what I could tell them of the outside world.

"We may have to crown you champion of knowing the least about the greatest number of topics," Victoria said. "Well done."

I dropped into a deep curtsey. "It is an honor and a privilege."

The four of us meandered up the stairs, my guards keeping their distance for fear of becoming victim of one of the twins' pranks. In truth, I hardly noticed them anymore. They never spoke to me, only followed me everywhere I went. But I did not like how they listened to all my conversations, and so I encouraged any sort of behavior that caused them to keep their distance. Marc and the twins were far more powerful and capable anyway, and I didn't worry about them blabbing my words to the King.

"Lady Victoria! Lord Vincent!" We all looked over our shoulders to see a young troll woman wearing a bright red dress running up the stairs after us.

"Drat," Victoria muttered, exchanging a worried look with her brother. "It's her again."

"Who is she?" I asked.

"A sculptor we commissioned a while back."

The woman slid to a stop in front of us, bobbed a quick curtsey at Marc and me, then turned a chastising finger on the twins. "When are you going to arrange to pick up your sculptures? And more importantly, when do you intend to pay for them?"

"Done so soon?" Vincent asked, stepping between the sculptor and his sister. "Are you certain they are properly finished?"

The woman glared at them. "You question me?"

Vincent shook his head rapidly. "No, no. Are they very large, then?"

"You ordered life size!" she shouted at them. "You two are large, thus are the sculptures."

Victoria flinched, and looked at her feet. I had always thought she appreciated her size because of the advantages it gave her in fighting. But perhaps I was wrong.

"That is true," Vincent said glumly. "I had thought it might take you longer to finish them."

"Lady Anaïs insisted the work be my first priority." The troll placed hands on her hips and scowled.

"She would," Vincent muttered. Victoria tucked a lock of hair that had come loose from her braid back behind her ear.

"This might take a while," Marc whispered in my ear. "Let's go."

I was reluctant to leave my friends in the company of the sculptor, but Victoria gave a faint nod indicating I should leave.

"What was that all about?" I asked, watching the exchange over my shoulder as I walked.

"They lost a bet to Anaïs," Marc said. "So they had to order life-sized sculptures that were to be placed in front of their house for no less than one month."

"That isn't so bad," I said, raising an eyebrow.

"Nude sculptures," Marc added, his brows coming together in a frown. "She was being cruel – she knows that Victoria is… shy."

I scowled. "Why is she so blasted nasty all the time – Victoria is her friend. Friends don't do that to each other."

"They shouldn't," Marc agreed. "But, I suspect Anaïs is angry at Victoria for how much time she spends with you."

"Maybe if she was more pleasant, Victoria would enjoy her company more," I snapped.

Marc sighed. "Anaïs is very unhappy, Cécile. And you don't know her well enough to judge her."

I know enough, I thought angrily, but I kept my mouth shut. Next time I talked to Victoria, I would suggest she dress her statue in clothes and let Anaïs try that on for size.

We entered a square dominated by a fountain with a giant winged serpent spouting water from its mouth, its emerald eyes gleaming malevolently. On the far side of the square, two trolls were shouting at each other. One shoved the other, and the argument quickly turned to blows.

Marc sighed. "Wait here a moment."

I watched as he strode over to the fighting men. Raising one hand, invisible magic jerked the two apart, leaving them to dangle in the air while he questioned them on their grievance.

I went over to the fountain to examine the serpent more closely. It had been carved in great detail, from its overlapping scales to its sharp golden-tipped claws. The plaque on the base read *The Dragon Called Melusina*. "A dragon," I muttered, eyeing up the creature, wondering if such creatures existed somewhere, or if they were merely a figment of some sculptor's imagination.

Turning my back on the dragon, I leaned against the fountain, nodding at the trolls who offered bows and curtseys with their greetings as they passed. The sight of an older, but statuesque, woman walking across the square caught my attention. She was dressed all in black, which was unusual, and though I didn't recognize her, I marked her easily as an aristocrat. Her gown was elaborate, the taffeta rustling across the cobbles, and she wore a wealth of jewels that glittered in the lamplight. But what made me certain was the air of authority in her walk, and the way all the other trolls made way for her as she passed. A slender servant woman walked a few steps behind her, head downcast and arms loaded with packages.

Straightening, I prepared myself to receive and deliver the expected courtesies, but the troll only glanced my direction and kept walking. Her servant shot me a wide-eyed look of dismay and dropped into sort of an awkward moving curtsey. "Your Highness," she whispered, looking back over her shoulder.

I opened my mouth to warn her, but I was too late. The servant woman collided with her mistress and the packages in her arms dropped to the ground with the distinct sound of breaking glass. I winced.

"You idiot!" shrieked the troll. She rounded on the servant, and I watched in horror as magical blows fell across the woman's face, blood splattering against the pale grey paving stones.

"I'm sorry, mistress," the servant begged, cringing against the blows as they fell. Wounds opened and closed on her face, the red gore dripping onto her dress the only permanent mark.

"Stop," I said, but the troll didn't hear me. "Stop!" I shouted louder. She glanced my direction, but ignored the command.

In two strides, I was next to her. "I order you to stop this abuse immediately."

The troll turned her head to look at me, eyes dark and menacing. "You have no right." She raised her hand to strike another blow, and I moved without thinking. Reaching out both hands, I shoved the troll woman hard.

"Cécile, stop!"

Magic lashed around my waist, jerking me back, and Marc stepped between the troll and me.

"Your Grace," he said. "I don't believe you have met Her Highness. May I introduce Her Royal Highness, Cécile de Montigny." He glanced over his shoulder at me. "Your Highness, the Lady Damia, Dowager Duchesse d'Angoulême."

I blinked. The troll was Angoulême's mother. "Your Grace," I muttered, and reluctantly curtseyed. This was not a random meeting, I was sure of it.

The woman snorted. "It is a bit late for courtesies, girl." Grabbing hold of her servant's hair, she dragged the half-blood away from us.

Marc held up a warning hand to keep me from going after them, but it was unnecessary. I knew the troll was trying to provoke me, but it was still infuriating to stand by and watch her treat the half-blood woman so. There had to be something I could do. I couldn't just walk away.

"My Lord Comte." The sound of Damia's voice jerked me to attention. I could feel tension radiating from Marc as he acknowledged the other troll. "Yes, Your Grace?"

Damia's eyes glittered. "Make arrangements to have the labyrinth opened this evening. This one's actions merit disposal." She jerked her chin towards the half-blood cowering at her feet. "I do not care to have my household's reputation tarnished by such behavior."

Marc's hands tightened into fists. "Surely such an extreme reaction is not warranted."

"I did not ask for your opinion," she snapped. "She is my property, and I can do with her as I wish."

The twins came up on either side of me, but I scarcely noticed. I felt the blood drain from my face and my hands turn cold. How far was she willing to take this? Would she really send her servant into the labyrinth to die just to elicit a reaction from me? Because I was positive now that that was exactly what she was trying to do. She was baiting me in an attempt to get at Tristan. If I went to him appealing for help in saving the half-blood, it would not only undercut the carefully crafted ruse defining our relationship, it would also put him in the position of having to choose between sacrificing the servant's life or revealing his true sentiments towards half-bloods.

"If you are so eager to get rid of her, I'll take her off your hands," Victoria suddenly said. "Five hundred is fair, I think."

"She isn't for sale," Angoulême's mother snapped.

"A thousand, then."

"No."

"If you value her so much, I fail to see why you want to see her killed," Vincent said, closing a hand over my shoulder. He was warning me not to take the bait, but what would be the consequences of me walking away? Could I stomach the guilt of letting the half-blood go to her death? But what could I possibly do to stop it? The law was clear – the servant was her property to do with as she willed. Only a royal decree from either Tristan or the King could stop her from sending the half-blood to her death. I did not see the King being forthcoming in that regard and asking Tristan would feel like I was passing the problem to him. I had to think of another way.

"Ten thousand."

Damia shot the twins a look of distain. "She is not for sale to you two for any price. You hardly need another in that menagerie you call a household."

"Sell her to me," I blurted out. She could refuse the others – she outranked them. But she did not outrank me.

A slow smile made its way onto the woman's face. "With what coin?"

I glared at her. "I am hardly destitute."

Her smile broadened. "That may be so, but it would still be Montigny gold doing the purchasing, and I'm afraid that would be breaking the law."

"How so?" I demanded.

The troll chuckled. "This one," she gestured towards the cowering servant, "is a Montigny bastard. And the law forbids the purchase of one's own blood." She laughed again.

I clenched my jaw, wondering how much thought and preparation had gone into this moment. The law stood in my way at every turn, driving me towards only one possible option: asking Tristan to save the servant. I gritted my teeth, my mind searching desperately for a solution. And I found one.

Forcing a dejected expression onto my face, I stepped backwards. "I'm afraid there is nothing I can do. Neither His Majesty or my husband are likely to take my side in this." I glanced at Marc. "Make her arrangements."

Silence greeted my words, surprise written across all their faces. None of them had expected me to let this go.

"Mercy, Highness, mercy!" the servant shrieked, throwing herself at me and clutching my skirts. "Don't let her kill me," she pleaded, the fabric of my dress tearing beneath her grip.

"I'm sorry." I let my lip tremble and tears rise in my eyes. "The law is the law." I stumbled back and my dress tore.

"Lessa, you fool!" shouted Damia. "Must you give me more reason to rid myself of you?"

Magic slapped against the half-blood over and over again in a sickening rhythm.

"Stop!" I screamed, but Damia only shot me a dark smile, baiting me to take the step that would end this violence. She thought me a fool – thought she could use the laws against me. But two could play at that game – and there was one law in particular that I knew would work in my favor. Bracing myself, I leapt between the two women, the sound of the magic lash falling loud in my ears.

CHAPTER 17
Tristan

The sharp stab of pain made me jump in surprise, the motion noticeable enough that my father looked up from the reports the Miners' Guild had delivered that morning. "What?" he demanded, fixing me with a piercing stare. "Cécile?"

I gave a slight nod, and rose to my feet. Judging from Cécile's mood, the injury did not seem grievous, but I wanted to go make sure. "By your leave..." I started to say, when the door swung in, interrupting me.

"Your Majesty. Your Highness." The troll bowed low, and I recognized him as one of my father's men.

My father grunted and leaned forward on his desk, fingers interlocked in front of him. "What has she done this time?"

The troll cleared his throat. "The lady Cécile is currently quarreling with Dowager Duchesse d'Angoulême, Your Grace."

Rubbing one eye, my father glanced my direction. "That's new. I thought she only quarreled with you."

I shrugged. "We are all wrong from time to time, Father. Even you." Looking to the messenger, I asked, "What was the nature of the argument; and importantly, who instigated it?"

"It was regarding Her Grace's abuse of a servant, my lord. And it is a matter of opinion as to who instigated the confrontation."

My father leaned back in his chair. "Explain."

By the time the messenger finished his tale of the events with "...and the Dowager Duchesse requested the Comte open the labyrinth so she could dispose of the servant," sweat was trickling down my spine. It was made all the worse by the knowledge that Cécile was coming in our direction. Which meant she intended to ask me to thwart the blasted old woman's plans to dispose of her servant, no doubt entirely unaware that she had been set up. And by falling for the ploy, had set me up.

"Cécile is coming this way," I said abruptly. There was no point in hiding the knowledge.

My father shook his head wryly. "If she intends to ask me to make an exception, she will be sorely disappointed. I don't make laws for the purposes of breaking them at the whim of a human girl." He turned in his chair to look at me. "Unless, perhaps, you are feeling benevolent today."

I kept my face still. "I don't make a practice of countering your decrees unnecessarily." Picking up my glass of water, I stared into its depths and contemplated how best this situation might be resolved. "Did you happen to notice," I said to the messenger, "the identity of the servant in question?"

The messenger coughed uncomfortably and I instantly knew. "It was Miss Lessa," he said, voice hoarse.

The desk exploded away from my father, smashing against the far wall. He was on his feet in the blink of an eye. "That bloody manipulative old hag!" he shouted, the air growing hot and the pressure of the room building until my ears popped.

"Get out," I said to the messenger, and breaking courtesy, he turned and bolted.

I remained still, watching my father storm around the room. Lessa, Lessa, Lessa, I thought. Her mother had been three-quarters troll, making Lessa almost a full-blood. And a powerful one at that – she was reckoned to be the strongest mixed blood alive in Trollus, and she was worth an absolute fortune on the markets. The Dowager Duchesse kept her more as a companion than as a servant. A certain element of prestige came from owning Montigny blood. This was a multi-angled scheme intended to get at not only me, via Cécile, but at my father. Angoulême was growing bold.

"What do you intend to do?" I asked. My father didn't respond. His eyes were distant, deep in thought. If he protected Lessa, he would be seen as not only willing to circumvent our own laws, but as willing to do it for his own benefit. But if he didn't protect her, he would be allowing his rival to send one of our blood to her death, and we would be seen as weak. There were no good options.

A knock sounded at the door.

"Come," my father snarled.

Cécile entered, but to my surprise, she was not alone. Trailing at her heels was the Dowager Duchesse herself, along with Lessa, Marc, and the twins. Cécile's expression was cross, but despite whatever injury she had sustained, she felt oddly eager. Everyone else was unreadable. Which made me worried.

Her eyes took in the smashed desk and she paled slightly.

"We heard about your exploits," my father said darkly. "I assume you are here to make a request of me?" His fingers twitched ever so slightly as he anticipated Cécile's appeal. The Dowager Duchesse was strangely quiet. What was going on here?

She glanced in my direction. Please don't ask me, I prayed, then cursed my own cowardice. I watched her reach up with one hand and rub her arm, obviously the source of her injury, her eyes fixed on me for a long moment before she turned her attention back to my father. A message.

"You really ought to arrange for the girl to be educated in our laws and customs, Your Majesty," the Dowager Duchesse said, obviously deciding to take advantage of Cécile's silence. She glanced Cécile's direction, and their eyes met for a long moment. Cécile said nothing. Damia looked away first. Interesting.

"Unfortunate circumstances such as those that occurred between us," Damia gestured at Cécile, "would not happen if she knew better. If Her Highness were aware of the laws governing the relationship between a troll and her servant, she would have known not to interfere. It is my right to treat my servants in any way I see fit. To dispose of them how and when I choose, if I no longer care to keep them in my household." Her eyes flicked from Cécile, to my father, to me. She was visibly flustered, and the Dowager Duchesse was never flustered.

Cécile said nothing, only scuffed the toe of her shoe against the marble floor.

Sweat broke out on Damia's brow. "The silly girl went so far as to try to purchase Lessa from me, which everyone knows is against the law because…" She broke off as my father shifted his weight. "If she had only known…" she stammered.

Cécile coughed and Damia's face twitched. "The law does not account for your refusal to sell Lessa to Lady Victoria." She lifted her chin, meeting my father's gaze. "The Lady Damia's assault against her servant was malicious and unjust, and an obvious abuse of the power granted her by Your Majesty's laws."

My father cocked one eyebrow.

"I was rash," Damia blurted out. "Lessa did not deserve punishment, and I find that I have reconsidered my request that Lord Marc arrange for her disposal. She is a favored servant, and Her Highness's interference has prevented a loss I most undoubtedly would have regretted."

Cécile inclined her head. "I am glad to have been of assistance."

Damia's lips tightened with suppressed fury. "Then we can consider the matter closed."

"I can't see why not."

Damia curtseyed deeply. "By your leave, Your Majesty?"

I cleared my throat. "One question before you leave, Damia." Rising from my chair, I walked towards Cécile, took her by the wrist, and pushed up her sleeve. Her forearm was marred with an angry red welt. Fury surged through me, and it was an effort to keep from showing it on my face.

"I don't suppose you would know anything about this… Your Grace?" I asked.

"It was not intentional," she snapped. "The fool of a girl got between Lessa and me. The blow was not intended for her."

"I'm quite certain I don't give a damn about your intentions," I said quietly, raising Cécile's arm so my father could see the mark.

"It seems *you* are the one needing an education in our laws, Lady Damia," he said, settling his bulk down on a chair. "Allow me to bring you up to date. Following my decision to bond my dearest son and heir to this fragile human girl, I decreed that anyone found to have directly or indirectly harmed her in any way would be subject to severe punishment."

Damia looked ill. "It was not my intention to harm her," she repeated.

My father leaned forward, his eyes glittering. "Intentions mean little when the results are the same. Your actions jeopardized the welfare of my heir and, as such, they cannot go unpunished."

The Dowager Duchesse dropped to her knees. "Mercy, Your Majesty. I am but an old woman."

My father snorted at her pitiful display and opened his mouth to say something, when Cécile interrupted. "Your Majesty, if I may?"

I winced, but my father only nodded, brow curling with curiosity. I wasn't curious – I was nervous. Cécile had managed to keep control of this entire exchange through silence, but she clearly intended to have her say.

"I do not care to see any more violence – I have had my fill today," she said, turning to Lessa who had remained kneeling on the floor this entire time. "If you insist on punishing the Lady Damia for her actions, I would prefer that it came in the form of compensation."

My father rested an elbow on the arm of his chair and propped his chin up. "I'm listening."

"I have been led to believe that the laws prohibit the purchase of one's own relations, regardless of whether they are related by blood or marriage. Is that correct?"

I grew very still. She was treading on dangerous territory. "You are correct."

"Illegal to purchase, but what about to own? Say, if one received the individual as a gift?"

A faint smile rose on my father's lips. "A loophole, I believe. Is that what you want then?"

Cécile nodded.

My father rose to his feet. "There you have it Damia. You will give us Lessa." He paused, tilting his head in thought. "Or you will give us your head. Your choice."

The Dowager Duchesse made no attempt to hide her fury. She had gambled heavily and lost. To a human. I smiled inwardly.

"I'll have her papers delivered in the morning," she hissed, then stormed out of the room.

Lessa straightened, turning to watch her former mistress leave. She did not, I noticed, look particularly pleased with this turn of events. Cécile may have thought she was doing her a favor, but Lessa seemed to think otherwise.

My father flicked his fingers in Cécile's direction. "You

can go." She hurried out, Marc and the twins trailing after her. I started to follow them, but my father held up his hand. "You stay."

I waited silently as my father contemplated Lessa, but as to what he was thinking, I could not say. Sighing deeply, he raised a hand and a dark sphere encircled her, blocking off both sight and sound.

"I've always hated that manipulative old bat," he muttered. "It was high time one of her plots turned back around to bite her on the ass. Although I didn't expect Cécile to be the one doing the biting."

I made a non-committal sound.

"I hate that whole bloody family," he continued, pouring a glass of wine.

"Then why did you foster Roland with them?" The words were out before I could think.

A glass floated my direction and I snatched it out of the air, drinking deeply.

"You know why," he said. "I didn't want your aunt whispering in his ear like she did to you."

"But why them?" I persisted. "Why a family that has been our enemy for centuries? Our most powerful enemy."

"Ah." He stared into the depths of his glass. "It was because they are our enemies." He cleared his throat. "I wanted the girl Anaïs for you – she had all the makings of a good queen, and uniting the two of you would have done much to reduce tension between the houses. Angoulême was of an accord, with the exception of one aspect of the contract: he would not allow her to be bonded. And I could not risk such a union – there would be too much chance that she'd stab you in your sleep."

I nodded slowly. Those of that family did not bond – they considered it a weakness. Anaïs's mother had died mysteriously a few years ago, and there were whispers that her husband had murdered her. It was to his advantage – he had only two daughters, one of them now dead – and a new young wife gave him another chance at a son. Though in my opinion, anyone who married him was a fool.

"I gave them your brother to sweeten the pot, so to speak. The Duke agreed, and the contract was finalized." He drank deeply. "Later, of course, we discovered that Anaïs and her sister were afflicted, and I broke off the engagement. She was unfit – something your cousin did a fine job of demonstrating when he made the mistake of bonding Pénélope."

I was glad Marc was gone – he did not consider Pénélope a mistake.

"I did not know there was a contract," I said.

"I know," he said, regarding me with an unreadable expression. "Despite what you might think, there are a great many things you do not yet know."

I shrugged. "Then enlighten me: why not take Roland back? It would be in your right."

"And do what with him?" He drained his glass. "Your brother is a bloody menace, and the Duke's family is the only one other than us with the mettle to control him. And I can't very well bring Roland to the palace with Cécile wandering about. He'd slaughter her on sight. And that," he inclined his head to me, "would be most unfortunate."

That was an understatement.

"Anaïs knew about the contract," he said, almost as an afterthought. "I've always been surprised she didn't tell you."

I wasn't surprised – my friend did not suffer shame well. "Anaïs is loyal to me," I said, "not to her father."

"As you say," my father replied, waving away the conversation. His eyes settled on the swirling black orb obscuring Lessa from view. "Go," he said abruptly. "I need to deal with this."

I quickly removed myself from his presence, sensing his mood was about to take a turn for the worse. Part of me wondered what he intended to say to Lessa – I had no fear he would harm her – but, oh, to be a fly on that wall. Having been hidden away under Damia's wing most of her life, Lessa was something of an unknown commodity. I didn't know anything about what she was like, only that she was powerful. And, I suspected, loyal to Angoulême.

Walking blindly through the corridors, I pushed the matter of Lessa to the back of my mind and turned instead to my father's behavior. It was not like him to be forthcoming. And why, after all these years, bring up that I had been contracted to Anaïs? I chewed the inside of my lip as I considered what he would gain from telling me the information. Not, certainly, to provide more proof that the Duke was a deceptive bastard – that was obvious. This was to do with Anaïs – the fact she had known about the contract, but never told me. An attempt, then, to undercut my faith in her loyalty? To drive a wedge between us? It seemed counterproductive given that our friendship promised to do much in smoothing over the discord between our families.

Not friends, lovers.

"Ah," I muttered, everything becoming clear. He must believe that it was at least partially Anaïs's doing that I continually avoided or fought with Cécile. He was trying to drive me away from Anaïs and towards my human wife.

Pushing open a door, I trotted down a set of steps, then froze, realizing I stood at the entrance to the glass gardens. The sound of Cécile's voice was thick in my ears, a fiercely defiant song of a warrior woman in some distant civilization. Apparently my meandering through the halls had had more purpose than I thought.

It was almost habit now for me to seek her out whenever I heard her singing – her voice was my only respite. The one moment in the day when I allowed myself to forget the growing pressures of my life. The one moment when I allowed myself to forget who I was.

Extinguishing my light, I started into the garden towards her voice, but not before pausing to break a single rose from the glass bushes lining the gates.

CHAPTER 18
Cécile

There was only one way to lure Tristan into my company, and that was to sing. As often as I could, I would go out into the glass gardens and do battle with the thunder of the waterfall, my voice echoing through the cavernous hall of Trollus, knowing that no matter where Tristan was in the city or what he was doing, he would come to listen.

He never said anything to me in those moments, always keeping his distance. Sometimes he stood on the edge of the gardens or sat on one of the many benches, staring at his feet. If I walked while I sang, he'd trail after me, careful to keep a glass hedgerow between us. I always pretended not to see him, even though I was keenly aware of his presence. And even more keenly aware of the gap between us that he would not breach.

Today was no different. I sang. He listened. And when my voice grew too tired to carry on, he hesitated in the silence for only a heartbeat before departing. But today, I decided I could not leave it at that. Holding up skirts stained with Lessa's blood, I strode through the winding pathways, taking the steps into the palace two at a time. Servants bowed and curtseyed as I passed, but I hardly noticed, my attention all for tracking Tristan's progress through the palace. He was heading towards our rooms, but I knew he wouldn't linger. He never did. It took every ounce of control I had not to run – running garnered attention, and I needed some time alone to speak with him.

Our rooms were dark and empty when I finally reached them. But I sensed he was here. Holding up my light, I walked from room to room, searching. Then I noticed one of the doors to the courtyard was slightly ajar. Pushing it open, I stepped outside and shone my light down the stairs. In the center of the space stood a black piano, my light gleaming off its shiny surface.

Closing the door behind me, I made my way down the stairs and over to the instrument. The wood felt strangely warm to my touch, but perhaps that was only because I spent my days surrounded by glass and stone. I pressed a finger against one key, and then another, listening to notes ring out. Then my eyes caught sight of a single glass rose resting against the music rack. Tentatively, I reached out to pick it up. At my touch, it blossomed with a warm pink glow.

"Can you play?"

I didn't answer, but instead sat on the bench and began a quiet little piece I knew by heart. When the last note trailed off into the darkness, I rose and walked over to where Tristan sat in the dark. The only light was the one dangling from my wrist, but it was enough for me to see fatigue written in the shadows of his face.

"She set you up," he said. "But you knew that already, didn't you?"

"Once I found who she was, I figured it out."

Tristan tilted his head. "And if you had known from the beginning, what would you have done differently?"

I chewed my lip as I thought. Even if I had known it was a ploy, would I have been able to walk away from a woman being whipped? The blood was real, and so was the pain. "I would have done the same thing," I admitted. "Which is probably pretty stupid."

Tristan's mouth quirked. "I've found that bravery and wise judgment rarely go hand-in-hand."

"What would you have done?" I asked.

His smile faded. "I'd have walked away."

"Oh." I shifted my weight from foot to foot.

He rose, coming within an arm's length. His coat was unbuttoned, and he seemed far more disheveled than usual. "But I'd have wanted to do what you did," he said. "I suppose that makes you the brave one."

"And you the smart one," I replied, raising an eyebrow.

"I'm not so sure about that." He shoved his hands in his pockets. "I've never seen Damia squirm. Ever. You made her confess everything without saying hardly a word. It was a clever bit of work. Reckless, mind you, but clever. I think my father was impressed."

Pulling his hands out of his pockets, he took hold of my hand and pushed back my sleeve. A ball of light blossomed, and he examined the growing bruises surrounding the welt. "How fearless must you be to step in front of a blow, knowing you would have to live with the injury for days, weeks, even. That you could die?"

I remained quiet, sensing the question was not for me, but rather for Tristan himself.

Carefully, he pulled down my sleeve and then adjusted my cloak so that it covered my shoulders more fully. Then he stepped back. "I need to go."

"Where?" I asked. It was past the dinner hour, and curfew would fall in another hour. Not that such things restricted him.

"Here and there," he replied, stopping at the base of the stairs. "I like to walk."

He would not tell me where, so I did not ask. What I did know was that Tristan paced the city throughout the days and into the nights, only resting when exhaustion pushed him to the brink of collapse. He walked, plagued by melancholy, anxiety, fear, and guilt. Except when I sang and he came to listen. I thought those were the only times he felt any peace.

"Tristan," I said quickly, before he had the chance to move. "Who is Lessa?"

He exhaled softly and looked up at the blackness overhead. "Lessa is my half-sister. My father had an affair with a servant when he was a little older than I am now." He hesitated. "Do not trust her – she is loyal to Angoulême."

I pressed a hand against my throat, shocked. "But your father despises half-bloods."

Tristan nodded slowly. "Perhaps he did not then. Perhaps Lessa's mother was the exception. Perhaps he was drunk. Perhaps…" He shrugged one shoulder. "It is an event cloaked in a great deal of mystery." He met my gaze.

"Resist the temptation to simplify my father's motivations. He is ruthless, but he is also complex and clever – one needs to be in order to rule this city for long." He inclined his head to me. "Good night, Cécile."

I sat and played at my piano for a long time after he left. For weeks, I had spent my days learning about a myriad of topics, but perhaps my attention had been misplaced. I was starting to realize just how complex Trollus's politics were, and how little I understood them. There were not two sides, there were countless. Not all the half-bloods were sympathizers looking to overthrow their oppressors. Nor were the full-bloods united against them – many were far more interested in their squabbles with each other. I had thought I knew whom I was fighting against, and whom I was fighting for, but now I wasn't so sure.

What I did know was that I needed to rectify this lack of knowledge, and soon. For there was no peace in Trollus. Beneath the cultured and austere surface, there was a battle brewing, and it was my greatest fear that I had aligned myself with the losing side.

"This is a terrible idea," Zoé moaned.

"The worst," Élise agreed. "If we get caught, we are sluag-fodder for certain."

"Nonsense," I said softly, pulling my hood further forward to ensure my face was concealed. "We won't get caught, and even if we do, I'd hardly let them feed you to the sluag."

"Because *you'd* be able to do anything to stop them?" Zoé asked, looking at me sideways.

I didn't answer – there wasn't any point in arguing about it now. They'd already sneaked me out of the palace and we were halfway to the Dregs. It had taken days for the girls to set up this excursion, and another chance would not be forthcoming.

We hurried through the side streets of the poorest area of Trollus, stopping in front of a home that blended in with all the other unadorned stone buildings. Zoé knocked firmly on the door, and after several long, nerve-racking moments, it opened.

"Ah, there you are. I was starting to wonder if Her Highness had turned craven on us at the last moment." The half-blood man who had opened the door winked at me, but my attention focused on the jagged scar running across the empty socket where his left eye had been.

"Don't call her that!" hissed Élise, pushing me through the threshold. "Do you want us to get caught?"

"Ain't no one in these parts that would turn on old Tips," the man said, gesturing for me to start down the hallway.

I glanced back at him, taking his measure. Behind the scar – and what seemed to be permanently embedded grime – was a young man. I'd eat my left shoe if he was more than twenty-five. "Old?" I remarked.

He grinned. "For a miner, I'm practically a relic, m'lady. But you'll learn about that soon enough."

The room we entered seemed to be a common eating area. It was filled with grey-clad half-bloods, mostly boys and girls around my own age. They all looked up when I entered, their expressions curious. "You all know who she is," Tips said. "So I won't bother with introductions."

"What is this place?" I asked, looking around.

"It's a dormitory owned by the Miners' Guild," Zoé explained quietly. "It houses two mining gangs. There are fifteen half-bloods in each gang."

"Thirty people live here?" The house seemed barely large enough to contain the fifteen miners in front of me.

"Day and night shifts," Tips explained around a mouthful of porridge. "We only cross paths to and from work."

"What about your days off?" I asked.

The whole room erupted into laughter.

Wiping porridge off his chin, Tips said, "If you get a day off from mining, you're likely to spend it trying to outrun the sluag in the labyrinth."

"I see," I said.

"Sure you do," Tips said. "Now tell me, what's His Royal Highness thinking putting you up to this?"

"He doesn't know I'm here," I said. "He's sleeping." Which wasn't precisely true… I didn't know where he was or what he was doing.

Tips's eyebrows rose. "And you think when he wakes up to find you missing from his bed, he won't wonder where you got to?"

I refused to meet his gaze. "That's not your concern."

"Oh ho!" Tips cackled. "That's how it is. Separate sleeping for the royal lovebirds."

"He has business to take care of," I snapped. "And you should keep your nose out of other people's bedrooms."

"Perhaps the King should have found Tristan a boy songbird to fulfill the Duchesse's prophesy!" one of the other miners said, and the room echoed with their laughter.

I glowered at them.

"Just jokes." Tips gave me a companionable swat against the shoulder. "Ain't nobody more loyal to Tristan than Tips's gang." He motioned for the girls and me to follow him into another room. "You sure you wanting to be doing this?" he asked.

"I wouldn't be here if I wasn't sure."

Tips's remaining eye narrowed. "I need you to be sure, cause once we're lowered into the mines, we're down there for twelve hours, no matter what happens. If one of us gets hurt, we tend to it down there. If *you* get hurt, we'll help you the best we can, but understand, there is no way out before our shift is over." He waited to see if I would react before he continued. "We'll be going further down into the deeps than you probably ever thought possible. The air will taste foul, and there will be times you'll feel short of breath. And you'll feel it, the weight of all that rock and earth piled above you. There's some who can't handle it – some who'd rather be dead than spend five minutes at the bottom of those shafts."

Élise squirmed uncomfortably next to me. She'd already told me that it would be Zoé who would come with me into the mines. She hated tight spaces.

I swallowed hard. "I can do it." I met the miner's gaze. "I need to know what I'm fighting for... who I'm fighting for." I squared my shoulders. "I need you to give me a reason why I should risk everything for you." This was part of the speech I'd used to convince Zoé and Élise to help me: I needed something worse than coddled lady's maids or even forlorn street sweepers to motivate me. I needed to see the worst in order to understand why Tristan had chosen to lead a revolution against his father. The mines were the worst.

"I reckon we can do that," Tips said softly, then watched silently as the girls tucked a miner's cap over the braids binding my hair to my head. They smeared black grease over the parts that showed and rubbed a bit of grime over my cheeks. I was already dressed in the grey trousers and tunic the miners wore.

"Will do," he said when they finished. "Mind you keep your face down – those pretty blue eyes of yours will give you away."

I walked in the center of Tips's gang, doing my best to imitate their unconcerned amble while keeping my head down. Zoé walked next to me, providing a second ball of light as part of my disguise.

"Has he noticed yet?" she asked under her breath.

"No," I whispered back. "It's too early – he probably just thinks I'm at one of my lessons." It was the one flaw, albeit a major one, in our plan. Tips's gang's shift ran from seven in the evening until seven in the morning. There was only another hour until curfew fell, and although I wasn't subject to punishment for breaking it, he would wonder what business kept me out of the palace. And that was only if he didn't notice that I was suddenly a league below Trollus. I had no doubt he would figure out what I was doing – the only question was whether he would interfere or not.

The entrance to the mines was at the opposite end of the valley from the River Road. It looked innocuous enough –

a wide set of white stone steps leading underground. The groups of exhausted and filthy miners coming up the stairs and making their way into the city were all that marked it for what it was.

All that changed the moment I took my first step down the stairs. A cacophony of sound assaulted my ears: the clanging of metal against metal, the dull roar of explosions, and the din of countless half-bloods crammed into a too-small space. Dust filled my nostrils and it was a struggle to keep from coughing and choking.

"There's a barrier to keep the dust and sound from getting out," Zoé said into my ear.

"I noticed." Wiping my nose on my sleeve, I tried to look around while still keeping my head lowered. I could see several half-bloods arguing with a guild member, gesturing wildly, their expressions angry. "What are they fighting about?"

"Quotas," one of the gang members answered. "Now keep quiet until we get out of sight of the guild."

We took a corridor leading to the left and joined a long line of miners standing on the right hand side. Every few minutes a gang of tired-looking day-shifters would pass us on the left, burdened with large crates of rock laced with yellow metal.

"Next!" I heard someone shout. The line surged ahead. It wasn't long until I could see what we were lined up for. A large shaft girded with gleaming troll-light lay in the center of a chamber. Two uniformed guild members stood on either side of the shaft, looking bored. Another stood at the head of the line with sheaves of parchment in his hand – it was he who kept calling, "Next."

I watched the shaft with nervous anticipation. A dull roar of wind rose out of it, and moments later, a platform loaded with miners and crates rose into view. The miners climbed off the platform, carrying their crates with a combination of magic and physical strength. The group at the front of the line grabbed empty crates from a pile against the wall and hopped on the platform. They dropped out of sight into the shaft.

"Next!"

There was only one group ahead of us. Tips abruptly appeared beside me. "Last chance to back out," he said into my ear.

I shook my head.

When Tips's gang rushed forward to grab their crates, I went with them and grabbed my own. They kept me in the middle of their pack as we ran over to the platform. The guild members paid only enough attention to note we were aboard before letting the platform drop.

I gasped aloud, my stomach rising into my throat. Zoé grabbed my hand and smiled reassuringly as we hurtled downwards, rock and glowing girders flashing by on all sides. "Amazing," I shouted over the rushing air. It was like nothing I'd ever experienced before. My excitement only faded a bit when I looked up and realized the top of the shaft had faded from view.

"Is this the only way in and out?" I shouted.

"The only way, Princess!" Tips shouted back.

We fell and fell, then the platform slowed and we ground to a halt. Picking up my crate, I followed the others, keeping my head down so the half-bloods waiting to go up wouldn't notice me. The air felt tight and close, so dusty it seemed like my lungs were choking on grit. I coughed softly as we walked through one of the narrow tunnels that branched away from the shaft, noticing with great relief that the tunnels were well lit by all the magic beams and girders that supported them.

"You can relax now," Tips said. "Ain't no one but us down here. Guild only comes down when there's a problem."

His words, I noticed, were not meant just for me. Everyone relaxed out of their postures of forced submissiveness. Where there had previously been slumped shoulders and lowered heads, I now saw straight backs and raised faces. I wondered if tension always ran high when they were around the guild or if it was only a function of my presence, hidden in their midst.

We left the crates in a pile and walked over to a long row of metal carts sitting idle on rails that led off down the tunnels. "Get in," Tips said.

"I can walk." I hadn't grown *that* soft.

He grinned. "No one walks. Not when we can ride. Now get in."

Zoé and I got into the dusty cart. "Hold on," Tips laughed. Grabbing the handles of the cart, he gave it a hard shove. We started slowly, then picked up speed until Tips was sprinting. Then he leapt on the back of the cart and it surged forward. "Woo hoo!" he shouted, and shouts from the rest of the gang echoed after us as we all flew through the tunnels.

At first I was terrified. The cart seemed out of control, and with every turn I was convinced we'd all meet our dooms, but my fear soon turned to euphoria. I was having fun. The miners shouted rude jokes over the squeal of the metal wheels, and Zoé and I screamed and clutched each other every time we surged down a decline.

The ride ended all too soon. Tips pulled a lever on the side of the cart, and with the piercing wail of metal against metal, we ground to a halt. "Fun part's over. Now it's time to get to work. You ready to pick up the slack, Zoé?"

"I need to stay with Cécile," the girl said, shooting me an apprehensive look. Clearly this had not been part of the agreement.

"And we need to make quota," Tips said. His voice was conversational, cheerful, even; but the expression on his face was not. "Two of my gang are having the first and only days off of their lives so that her Highness can undertake this little excursion. She can't help, but *you* can. Prissy as you are, Zoé, and I mean that in the most affectionate way, you're still stronger than three of my boys combined. Might be we even get ahead of the game with you down here today. Cogs!" he shouted. "Get Zoé started on detonations."

"What sort of quotas?" I asked, watching Zoé and the rest of the miners turn down another tunnel.

"Production quotas are what we live and die for down here," Tips said, settling down on the floor of the tunnel. "It's the amount of product each gang is expected to deliver each month. Lean against the magic girding the tunnel, girl, it will keep you warmer."

I did as he said, and when we were both comfortable, he continued. "Product is mostly gold down this way, but there's all manner of glittery things hidden in the mountain. The guild keeps track of where each gang is at and gives us the numbers at the beginning of each shift. If we make monthly quota, all's good. If we don't..." He shrugged. "Not so good."

"What happens if you don't?"

"If we don't, then someone from the gang gets sent into the labyrinth as sluag-fodder."

I hugged my arms around my middle. "They kill one of you just because you didn't mine enough gold? How do they decide who goes?"

Tips chuckled. "They don't. Those maggot-gobbling guild members are too clever for that. They make us choose who has to go."

Clever indeed. And cruel. "How do you choose?"

Tips picked up a rock, tossing it from one hand to another. Which struck me as an oddly human gesture, although I couldn't pinpoint why. "If we're lucky, someone will volunteer. There's those who have had enough of the never-ending toil, the fear of cave-ins... Those who'd rather meet their end now than go on another day in the mines. And if we're not fortunate enough to have one of those optimists in our mix, then we choose whoever is holding the gang back."

"How often do gangs miss quota?"

Tips set the rock down. "Rare for more than a few months to pass where at least one gang doesn't have to send someone."

So frequent. I stirred a finger in the bits of rock by my feet, trying to imagine having to choose which one of my friends to send to their death. Not just once, but having to choose on a regular basis. The guilt would be overwhelming.

"Cover your ears," Tips said abruptly.

I barely managed to clap my hands over my ears as the tunnels echoed with a loud boom. Dust coughed over us, but Tips didn't look the slightest bit concerned. "We're going to get all sorts of work done with Zoé here," he said with a smile.

"If she's so powerful, why isn't she a miner?" I mused.

"You really don't know anything, do you?"

Tristan's words echoed through my mind. *In Trollus, power is king.* "It's because she's powerful that she isn't down here."

Tips nodded. "They know when we're children how powerful we are likely to be, and when we get auctioned off, those like Élise and Zoé get picked up to be servants. Having more magic makes your presence…" he searched for the word, "desirable to the full-bloods. Then there's those with little or no magic. All they tend to be good for is street cleaning and sewers. Dirty jobs that can be done by hand rather than magic. Everyone else goes to the mines."

Down in the mines where death lurked at every corner.

"So, if you are half-blood, and you aren't powerful, it's better to have almost no magic," I said, picking up Tips's discarded rock.

"You'd think so," Tips replied, raising one eyebrow. "Polishing sewer grates is lots easier than mining gold and a whole lot less dangerous. 'Cept if you were one to be noticing such things, it would have dawned on you that while plenty of half-bloods are born with little or no magic, there aren't too many of them that live long enough to make it to the auctions." He blinked. "Accidents happen."

"I see," I breathed. If you were at the bottom of the pack of miners, in regards to magic, then you would be first on the chopping block if your gang didn't meet quota. It was better to be top of the pack of sewer workers, except that in order for there to be positions available, it meant eliminating the very weakest of them all. "The full-bloods don't even need to dirty their hands," I whispered. "You kill off your own weak."

"When it's your life, or someone else's..." Tips shrugged. "Maybe you understand better now why we're fighting for change. Cover your ears."

The ground shuddered and another cloud of dust rolled over us. "How do you know when the explosions are going to happen?" I asked when the noise subsided.

"Been doing this a long time. I know the rhythms."

I leaned forward. "And how have *you* survived down here this long?"

His face darkened, confirming my suspicions. He acted too human: trolls did everything they possibly could with magic. Even idly tossing around a rock. And I'd noticed that he was the only one that let his troll-light fade when we entered the mines. The man sitting across from me looked almost human, with his badly healed scar and eye more grey than silver. Tips was one of those with weak magic.

"I can smell the gold," he said, voice chilly. "I always know where to dig. And since I joined this gang, not once have we missed quota." He pointed a finger at me. "Despite what *they* think, a man's value ain't just determined by his magic."

"Or a woman's." I met his glare calmly until he blinked.

"Or a woman's," he agreed. "Right you are about that, Princess. Now how about we go see what sort of progress our friends are making. If I leave them alone too long, they'll dig in the wrong direction."

We walked through the tunnels until we found Zoé and the rest of the gang sorting through rubble. I hadn't missed Tips's choice of words: "our friends". Before tonight, helping Tristan had been primarily about securing my own freedom, but now I realized that my own freedom wasn't enough. I wanted to help bring down the laws that forced the half-bloods to kill each other to save themselves. The half-bloods weren't just my friends – they were my comrades. "You're risking a lot telling me these things," I said. "And bringing me down here – if we get caught…"

"The sluag would feast for days," Tips said. "But it's worth it."

"Why?" The ground shuddered from a distant detonation.

Tips slowed his pace. "We are slaves caught in a cage within a cage, Princess. And for the first time in history, a future king is willing to put the lowest but largest caste of his people ahead of his own interests. Tristan's willing to risk his own life to save ours, and there is nothing most of us wouldn't do for him. But unless the curse can be broken…" He shook his head. "Power breeds power, and it ain't going to cede to morality or what's right for long. We need to be able to put physical distance between us and the full-bloods, it's our only chance at being truly free. And that's not something Tristan can accomplish on his own. It's human magic that binds us, and it will be a human that sets us free. And we don't need a stinking prophesy to tell us that." He stopped and inclined his head to me. "We need your help."

Put that way, the request was daunting. "I'll do what I can," I said.

"I know," Tips replied. "Now cover your ears."

Hours later, Zoé came over to where I was sorting through bits of rock. "Has he noticed?" she asked, wiping sweat off her brow and leaving a streak of grime. She'd been working tirelessly the entire time.

I sat back on my haunches, closed my eyes, and focused on Tristan. He was awake, but he wasn't coming any closer. "I think he knows what I'm doing," I said. "But I think he's decided not to interfere." I tried to smother a yawn. "He knows I'm all right."

"We'll start loading up soon," Tips called over. "It's a long walk back to the lift, and we've got a big haul today." The gang all cheered, clapping each other on the back, but they were cut short by the roar of falling rock. I'd heard the sound on and off all night – both from Zoé's efforts and from those of other gangs working nearby, but this sounded much larger. And it was coming from behind us.

"What was that?" Zoé asked, her eyes wide.

"I suppose we'll find out soon enough," Tips replied, but I caught the warning glance he gave to the other miners. "Load the trolleys, it's time we got moving."

Walking back took hours and, within the first hour, all I wanted to do was lie down and sleep. And I wasn't even carrying anything. Through a combination of physical strength and magic, Zoé and the other miners pushed the rock-filled trolleys back through the tunnels. With the exception of a few muttered oaths, the only sounds they made were grunts of effort and panting breaths. It was no small amount of relief when we could finally hear the ruckus of miners loading rock into crates at the lift.

I helped the best I could with the unloading – more because I didn't want the other gangs to notice us than because I was any help. We were next to ride up when Tips hissed, "Guild members!" Everyone dropped their heads, shoulders slumping. I mimicked their posture and tried to conceal myself behind the other miners.

Two of the guild members got on the lift with the group ahead of us, but one remained behind. He leaned against the far wall, eyes closed and face slack with weariness as we waited for the lift to come back down. I could feel the tension in each member of Tips's gang as we set to loading the lift, and it only escalated when the troll got on board with us.

"Cave-in?" Tips asked as the lift began to rise, moving much more slowly than when it had brought us down.

"Yes," the troll replied. "Finn's gang was working the south tunnel and brought the whole thing down. The one we'd closed over concerns about stability," he added pointedly.

"Survivors?"

"None." The troll scrubbed a hand through his hair, making it stand on end. "No idea what the blasted fools were doing down that way."

"Heard they were looking short on quota," Tips replied, tone neutral. "That tunnel was known to be rich pickings."

The guild member straightened and glared at Tips. "And now Finn and all his gang are dead because they couldn't accept the loss of one."

"Easy for you to say," Tips muttered.

All murmurs of conversation ceased. It was fair to say none of us even breathed as we watched to see what would happen. The troll's uniform rustled as he straightened his shoulders, then in a flash, he shoved Tips hard against a stack of crates and the whole platform rocked. "Easy for me to say? I just spent the past four hours digging up fifty yards' worth of tunnel to find only blood and unrecognizable raw meat!"

The two of them were practically on top of me. I tried to squeeze away, but there was no room. The troll had Tips by the shoulders, but he didn't seem to be hurting him. I felt the tremble of his arm where it rested against me and realized that the guild member was genuinely upset about the death of the miners. "Half you miserable lot don't have the power to keep the dust off your heads and you insist on going into tunnels a bloody Montigny would avoid. And when the rocks come down, I have to dig you out."

"So don't," Tips said. "It's not as though you care whether we live or die."

Several of the gang members groaned in dismay, but Tips showed no sign of backing down. "Just be careful you don't kill us all, or you lot might find yourselves having to do an honest day's work."

"Stupid half-breed!" The troll punched him in the face and I winced at the sound of cracking bone. "Every time those tunnels cave, I will dig out your miserable hide, even if there isn't enough left to fill a bucket. That's a promise."

My skin prickled with the charge of magic, and several of the miners gasped aloud in surprise at a troll uttering those binding words. As I tried to struggle away from the two, the troll looked up and our eyes met. His widened in shock. My chest rose and fell in short little jerks as I waited for him to react to my presence. I was caught. He was sure to turn me in and I couldn't even begin to think of an explanation for what I was doing down here. He opened his mouth to speak, and I held my breath.

"They aren't my laws," he said, his voice rough with emotion. "But I have to live by them too."

My head jerked up and down in understanding. The half-bloods were not the only malcontents in Trollus. I wondered how many more full-bloods were secret sympathizers and whether Tristan knew about them. Or whether they knew about him?

The lift lurched to a halt, and the guild member clambered off Tips and hurried through the crowd. Stunned, the gang and I set to unloading our crates and taking the gold down to where it would be sorted. All I could do was pray that the guild member wouldn't tell anyone he'd seen me in the mines, because if he did, I would have some serious explaining to do.

CHAPTER 19
Cécile

For days after my visit to the mines I laid low, afraid that the Miners' Guild member would reveal my little excursion and that word would get back to the King. Before sneaking out of the palace to go to the mines, I hadn't been too concerned about getting caught, because how bad could the ramifications be? Just more guards, or better ones at any rate. Sneaking me in and out of the palace had been surprisingly easy. Restrictions on my freedom? That was certainly possible, but not the end of the world. But now that I'd had time to think about it and stew in a pot of worry, I realized that while getting caught might not hurt me, it would hurt those with whom I'd gotten involved.

Tristan had explained the half-bloods' situation, but I hadn't really understood until I'd spent a night in their shoes. It was Tips and his gang who had made me *feel* just how little those in power valued the lives of the half-bloods, and how one small transgression could cost them their lives – lives that were already at risk every time they stepped into the mines. I realized how much they were risking by even considering a rebellion, and what failure would cost them. And knowing what I did now, being able to close my eyes and remember faces and names... it made me willing to risk my own life to help them. But to help, I needed to know more.

I had only seen the library from the outside. In fact, I had never been inside a library before, and nothing could have prepared me for the magnitude of the place. Rows and rows of shelves stretched through the building, some so tall that their tops were obscured by darkness. I would have been at a loss about where to begin, but fortunately, the library was not empty.

Leaving my guards at the front, Élise and I walked towards the telltale glow of troll-light until I came upon a man bent over a large book, quill in hand. He leapt up at our approach, and I noticed he had an ink stain smeared across the bridge of his nose.

"My lady." He bowed awkwardly and pushed his thick spectacles back up his nose. They promptly slipped back down again.

"Are you a librarian, sir?" I asked politely.

"Fourth librarian, if it please you, my lady."

I didn't overly care if he was fourth or fortieth, so long as he could help me find what I needed. "I am hoping you can help me with some... er..." I glanced at Élise, who was examining the titles on one of the shelves, "research."

"On what subject, my lady?"

I took the librarian's arm and led him deeper into the stacks. Élise seemed content to stay where she was, which was fine with me. I didn't want to involve her unnecessarily. "Is there anything written on the Duchesse Sylvie's prophesy?"

His eyes widened. "No, my lady. She would not consent to being questioned about the details. But His Highness was present – he knows precisely the words she spoke."

I frowned. "What about the Fall, then? Or... the witch?"

"Anushka." His expression was grim – this was not a topic the trolls liked to discuss.

"Was that her name?" I had never heard her called anything but "the witch".

"Indeed, my lady. She was foreign-born, obviously, from the northern part of the continent. A favored courtesan and entertainer of the court of King Alexis III."

We reached a pedestal with a glass case sitting on it. Inside there was a book, which the librarian removed: *Chronicles of the Fall.* He flipped carefully through the heavily illustrated pages and then paused. "This is her."

I leaned over to get a better look and gasped. The redheaded woman on the page stared out at me with brilliant blue eyes.

"A few years older, but the resemblance is uncanny," the librarian agreed.

"It is indeed," I breathed. "Tell me sir, what is your name?"

"Martin, my lady."

"Martin, will you leave me with this book and seek out others that might be of assistance to me?"

"Gladly, my lady."

Before he went, he set the ponderous book on a table for me. I started at the beginning, the morning of the Fall. *Just before noon, all of Trollus was alerted of their impending doom by the echoing crack of thunder. As countless tons of rock spilled down the valley, tens of thousands of trolls lifted their hands and magic to protect themselves and, in doing so, created a collective shield that protected the city as the rock blocked out the sky.*

I pored over the illustrations showing beautiful, terrified troll faces with their arms thrown skyward as the mountain poured down on them. The drawings showed humans, too, all of them crouched in terror at the feet of the trolls. Helpless.

The city was organized into shifts of trolls holding up the rock and trolls digging a way out. Bodies of those killed by falling rocks rotted in the streets and the human population was quickly stricken by plague, which was exacerbated by famine and lack of clean water. The humans began to die out, and only the favored few were given what they needed to survive.

Drawings showed emaciated humans on their knees begging, corpses littering the streets around them. And in the midst of them stood the trolls, their eyes focused on the rocks overhead, not on the misery surrounding them. I shuddered to think of what it must have been like: to be starving in the dark, to be shown no mercy because my life was considered worthless.

It took them four weeks to dig through the rock. King Alexis was the first to cross into the sunlight with his human mistress, Anushka, at his side. But as he turned to welcome his people to freedom, Anushka slit his throat and uttered the malediction binding the trolls to the confines of Trollus for as long as she drew breath. All the surviving humans walked into the sun, but no troll could pass the boundaries of the rock fall.

But why? Was it because she'd grown bitter over the way her fellow humans were treated during the crisis? That didn't make sense – by breaking the mountain, she was the one who'd put both races in such dire straits in the first place. A personal vendetta, then? Revenge against the trolls for something that had happened to her? By all descriptions, she was treated even better than the Queen. What could Alexis have done to inspire such an enormous act of evil?

Martin reappeared and set a stack of books down next to me. "You may find these interesting," he said.

I nodded and pointed to the enormous portraits lining the library walls. "Which is King Alexis?"

"The Third?"

"Yes. The one Anushka killed."

Martin's light flew along the portraits until he found the one he was looking for. I rose and made my way over to it. King Alexis was handsome, with strong, straight features, and black hair that fell to his shoulders, but his good looks were marred by his haughty expression.

"His son, King Xavier II, also known as the Savior." Martin's light moved over to reveal a grim-faced troll with the eyes of a man who has seen too much. "He ascended to the throne at age sixteen, but it was his genius that designed a way in for the river. Trollus would not have survived if not for the fish.

"He was succeeded by King Tristan I, also known as Tristan the Builder. He was the architect of the original structure of the tree. His work reduced the number of trolls required to maintain the ceiling by more than half. He was also responsible for the construction of the moon hole."

Tristan the Builder was as grim-faced as his father, but as Martin continued his description of the Montigny line, I noticed a return of the haughty expression that Alexis had worn. Even King Marcel III, known to all as Marcel the Dimwit, had a look of self-entitlement.

"What do you suppose they will call His Majesty?" I asked, looking up at Tristan's father's portrait. Either it was from many years ago, or the artist had taken a great deal of liberty, because the Thibault in the painting was not the enormously fat man I knew. In fact, he looked eerily like a somewhat older version of Tristan.

"I don't make a habit of speculating on such things, my lady," Martin said, but I saw the corners of his mouth creep up.

My vote was for Thibault the Corpulent.

I turned back to the book and flipped to the portrait of Anushka. "Martin, why would she have broken the mountain while she was still in the city? Why risk her own death?"

"No one knows for certain, my lady."

"And if she was powerful enough to break a mountain, why didn't she break herself out? Why did she suffer through everything that went on down here for the four weeks it took to dig out, and then curse the trolls?"

Martin shrugged. "It is not in my nature to– "

"Speculate, I know." I frowned at the book. It simply did not make sense for her to have broken the mountain while she was in the city unless it was some act of suicide.

"Could a troll break a mountain?"

"One troll?" He shook his head. "No. Not possible."

"What about several working together?"

"It's feasible, I suppose." He didn't look very happy at the direction I was going. "But that isn't what happened. The witch broke the mountain, waited until safety was in our grasp, and then uttered the curse."

"Are curses anything like troll magic?" I scratched my head. "How is it possible for her to still be alive after so many years? Are you even certain that she is?"

Martin's face pinched together – apparently I'd offended him. "Troll magic is not the same as human magic, which is to say witchcraft. Not the same in the least. And we know she is alive because the curse is still in place."

"But how?" I persisted.

"Blood magic, my lady. The dark arts."

"What do you know about it?"

"Little. It is human magic that draws power from the spilt blood of sacrifice."

I frowned. "Is all human magic dark? Is blood the only source of power?"

He cleared his throat. "No. My understanding – which, I must reiterate, is limited – is that blood magic is not the norm. Most witches draw power from the earth by tapping into the power of the four elements."

"What can they do with their power?" I persisted. "Other than curse trolls."

Martin looked uncomfortable. "A witch can affect the world with the words she speaks. Heal other humans. Convince them to do things."

My whole body jerked. "What do you mean, 'convince them to do things'?"

He shrugged. "I mean what I say."

What he was telling me was alarmingly familiar. "The ability to convince..." Did that mean? The countless times I'd been able to convince the inconvincible scrolled through my mind. Could it be that what I had always attributed to willpower was something else entirely? Sweat broke out on my palms. "Where does troll magic come from?"

"The fifth element: spirit." He tapped his own chest. "Our magic comes from within. Witches are merely conduits of the earth's power."

"How do you know all this?" I asked.

Martin shrugged one shoulder. "Our ancestors were curious about such things. Foolishly, it turned out, believing that human magic was no danger to our kind. They kept records of what they learned, and we also have documents written by witches themselves."

He tapped the spine of one of the books he'd brought me. "This is a witch's grimoire. It was found in Anushka's rooms after she fled Trollus."

Tentatively, I reached out and plucked the book from the pile, half-afraid the thing would burst into flames at my touch. It was in surprisingly good condition considering it was over five centuries old. I touched the runes engraved on the cover, which was made of a strange sort of leather that I'd never seen before.

"Human skin," Martin said helpfully.

I dropped the book.

"Try to open it, my lady," he said.

Reluctantly, I retrieved the book from where it had fallen. The smooth feel of it beneath my fingers disgusted me. This wasn't something, it was someone. I tugged on the clasp, gently at first, and then harder. It refused to budge.

Martin sighed. "No one has been able to open it. I thought perhaps because you are human it might…" He sighed again.

"Perhaps one needs to be a witch," I said. "And do I look like a witch to you?"

Martin laughed nervously.

"Do you know where she is now?" I asked.

"No one knows, my lady."

"She could be anywhere, then. Pretending to be anybody?"

"Don't ask him to speculate, Cécile. Martin only deals in facts."

I leapt off my chair, spinning around. "Tristan! I mean, my lord."

"Your Highness." Martin bowed. He eyed the two of us as though wondering what sort of destruction we would wreak upon his library. "If you could please keep your voices down." Then he walked hurriedly away.

Tristan gave a soft snort of laughter as he warded our conversation against eavesdroppers, but I could tell he wasn't feeling very amused. "I suppose I should consider this an improvement over the mines."

I eyed him nervously, wondering if this would be the moment of reckoning. "It was something I thought I needed to do. Thank you for not interfering."

He cocked one of his eyebrows. "Once I realized where you'd gone, there wasn't much I could do without making a scene and raising more questions than I've a mind to be answering. It was reckless of you, though. And dangerous. I have noticed that there is a certain pattern to your behavior, and it makes me nervous."

"I didn't get caught," I said. "At least, not really."

His jaw tightened.

"A guild member saw me," I admitted. "But I think he was a sympathizer."

Tristan went very still. "Tell me what happened."

I explained, and when I finished, he nodded thoughtfully. "I don't think we need to worry about him."

"I don't either," I said. "Do you know who he is?"

"Yes."

I had hoped he would elaborate, but as usual, he was unwilling to divulge any more information than necessary.

Silence hung between us, but I felt his anxiety mount. Though he knew we were allies, he did not trust me. Not completely. Not in the way I found myself trusting him.

"Why are you in the library, Cécile?"

I stepped away from him and back to my table full of books. I cleared my throat. "I was brought to Trollus for one reason, Tristan, and that was to fulfill the prophesy that came from your aunt's foretelling."

"I'm not sure anyone actually believes you will," Tristan started to say, but I interrupted him.

"Oh, they believe," I said softly, thinking of the faces of the half-bloods in the mine. "Not everyone is as pessimistic as you."

I rested my elbows on the table and stared at the grimoire. "Clearly it wasn't the two of us being bonded under moonlight. It must be something we need to do. What exactly did your aunt say?"

He stared at me, his reluctance palpable.

"I've a right to know, don't you think?"

"Fine. It was in verse. They always are, but don't ask me why, because I don't know."

I shrugged. "I like poems."

"Eyes of blue and hair of fire
Are the keys to your desire.
Angel's voice and will of steel
Shall force the dark witch to kneel.
Death to bind and bind to break
Sun and moon for all our sake.
Prince of night, daughter of day,
Bound as one the witch they'll slay.
Same hour they their first breath drew,
On her last, the witch will rue.
Join the two named in this verse
And see the end of the curse."

He recited the words quickly. "It isn't very good, as far as poems go. But it is clear."

Clear on the surface, maybe, but binding the two of us obviously wasn't all it would take.

Tristan settled down in the chair across from me, nibbling on a fingernail. "Any ideas?" He seemed oddly nervous given that we sat alone in a library.

I brooded on it for a moment, not liking the only idea that came to mind. "I think we need to track her down and kill her."

Tristan rubbed his hands across his eyes. "Do you think we haven't tried?"

"I don't know what you have or haven't done," I snapped, annoyed that he was fighting me on this. "No one has bothered to tell me."

"Then let me tell you now. For years after the Fall, humanity avoided Trollus like the plague, which wasn't surprising given the way they'd been treated. But eventually, greed drove them back."

"Gold?" I asked.

"Always the gold. Trollus had plenty of wealth, but no food. When the first men found their way back in, do you think that is what Xavier asked them for? No. First, he sent them after her. Wealth beyond their wildest dreams if they could produce the corpse of the witch. Countless women resembling her were slaughtered, but never the right one. His people were dying of starvation, but his entire focus was on hunting her down. Only when his own larders grew lean did he turn his resources to establishing trade for food. And they called him the Savior for it."

"If there was ever a chance of finding her, it was then. Her face was well known. But the humans were not unhappy with the results of what she had done." He tapped the book in front of me. "This doesn't tell the whole story – not even half of it. There are things we did that no king would allow to be written, because that would mean they could never be forgotten."

"Such as?"

"Such as feeding humans the flesh of their own dead while troll aristocracy feasted in their palaces. Sending humans like rats into the labyrinth with promises of riches if they found a way out. Slaughtering human babies and using their mothers like milk cows for troll infants. And once the humans had all fled, doing the same to half-blood women."

I held up a hand to make him stop, his words making me feel breathless and unwell. What he was telling me was shocking, but looking at the expressions of the kings above us, I could well imagine them giving the orders.

"But human memories are short, it seems," Tristan continued. "They soon forgot the atrocities of Trollus, or perhaps their greed overwhelmed their fear. They agreed to continue the hunt for the promise of gold. When it became clear she would not be found through her physical description, the hunt turned on women who followed her practices."

"The witch trials?" He had my attention now. The trials happened once a generation, at least. I'd been ten the last time a mob of men swept through the Hollow looking for women who were uncannily skilled with herbs or predicting the weather. Calling them trials wasn't even the truth, because anyone the mob accused was burned to death.

Tristan nodded. "Hundreds of years and thousands of women slaughtered and for what? We're still trapped like rats in this hole. She's still alive and no doubt has a good daily chuckle about our worsening predicament. And my father continues to send men out hunting for her, when he knows that it's useless. It is like trying to thread a needle with a battering ram. It's a waste of time."

"It isn't a waste of time," I argued. "Your aunt told me the prophecies always come true."

The anxiety in him rose to a fevered pitch. "I want you to drop this, Cécile. I don't want you to spend another second thinking about it."

"What is wrong with you?" I demanded.

"Leave it," he shouted, jumping to his feet. "Do not pursue this any further!"

I realized then that he had duped me. "It isn't that you don't think the curse can be broken," I said, snatching hold of his arm. "It's that you don't want it broken at all. Not even once you are king. Not ever."

"And if you had any sense, you'd be thankful for it!" He jerked away from me hard enough that I almost fell off the chair.

"Perhaps I would be if you'd give me half the chance," I said, rubbing my strained fingers. "But it's difficult given you seem intent on deceiving me. Why not try the truth for once. If you're even capable of it."

He flinched and was quiet for a moment before speaking. "Cécile, consider this: my ancestors did not just rule Trollus, they ruled all of the Isle of Light and much of the western half of the continent. Do you honestly believe if we are set free that my people will settle for anything less?"

"I don't think what happened in the past dictates what will happen in the future," I said. "It doesn't have to be that way."

"I don't agree," Tristan said coldly. "And I think if you knew more about what you speak, you would be singing a different tune."

He gestured at the table and three books toppled sideways off my stack, revealing a huge tome underneath.

"Some light reading on our prior conquests." Then he turned and walked out.

Reluctantly, I opened the book and shone my light stick on the page so I could read. Before long, I wished I hadn't. For the centuries prior to the Fall, the trolls had been a conquering force like no other in the world. They had ruled lands that reached far beyond the shores of the Isle. Foreign nations had either bent a knee and paid tribute in slaves and goods, or their people were slaughtered. A lone troll had the power to wipe out hundreds of men, and the troll kings had armies in the thousands. The artists illustrated the history in graphic detail. My stomach turned at the sight of it.

Was this what I should expect if I set the trolls free? King Thibault's army might be a mere echo of the trolls' strength in prior days, but what could armies of men do in the face of a magic with the strength to blast rock and tear metal asunder? The Regent of Trianon would not willingly give up power – he would ride against the trolls and learn his lesson the hard way. And I did not see Thibault showing any mercy against an enemy army – an army that included my very own brother. I swallowed hard at the images running through my head.

But what about after Tristan was king? Then it would be within his power to ensure peace. He wasn't like his father or like those other kings. And what's more, with only a few exceptions, the trolls I knew were not evil marauders intent on domination. The half-bloods were fighting against oppression, and I knew there were full-bloods who were like-minded. The past did not have to repeat itself.

Rising, I smoothed out the wrinkles in my skirt, and the grimoire caught my attention. I stared at it, thinking. For all the trolls' magic and strength, it had been a human who broke the mountain and trapped Trollus for eternity, or at least near enough to it. Humans had magic too, at least some of us. I'd be a fool to not learn what I could about it.

I picked up the book, hating the feel of the strange leather cover. "What answers do you hold?" I whispered, examining the strange lettering on the cover. Probably the language of the north, where the witch had come from. It was all gibberish to me.

I examined the clasp again, but there was no catch or release trigger that I could see. I tugged on it, but the clasp wouldn't budge. "Stones and sky!" I swore. "Open!" I pulled hard and my hand slipped, the catch slicing painfully across my finger.

Click.

The book fell out of my hands and landed with a thud on the table, pages open. I quickly looked over my shoulder to ensure I was alone, then shone my light on the pages. The language looked the same as that on the cover, written in a tiny but neat hand. The open pages were thick with words and little drawings, but I understood none of it. Tentatively, I reached down to flip the page.

Dizziness washed through me and I closed my eyes, focused on keeping the contents of my stomach where they were. When I opened them again, I gasped aloud. The words were as clear to me as if they were my native tongue.

"Love potion," I read aloud. The ingredients were plants and herbs that I'd never heard of – the only thing that was familiar was stallion's urine. Three drops of the potion were to be served in red wine to the man in question, and it would be at its most potent at the stroke of midnight. "Yuck." I flipped to the previous page: "Infliction of Boils." Vile. I turned the pages, and my disappointment grew. The spells were petty and trivial – the sorts of things a silly village girl would use to improve her fortune or embarrass her enemies. There was nothing as grand as how to break a mountain, curse a troll, or live forever. The only spell that looked useful was one for healing, but judging from the lack of wear on that page, healing arts were not where Anushka's interests had lain.

The spells started to grow darker. I read page after page of recipes that weren't spells at all, but poisons designed to inflict great pain and even death. There were many that would end a pregnancy – of the witch herself or of her chosen victim. It was here that she began to use sacrifices in the rituals. Chickens, sheep, cattle – it seemed the more difficult and ugly the spell the greater the sacrifice required.

Trolls.

My eyes took in the chapter heading, and then a hand closed on my shoulder.

CHAPTER 20
Cécile

"Find anything interesting?"

Twisting in my chair, I looked up at Élise. She didn't seem to recognize the grimoire for what it was. "It's all very interesting," I said, trying to keep my voice steady. The last thing I needed was the trolls finding out I'd opened Anushka's diary – with my luck, they'd take it away before I got the chance to finish reading it. "None of it was very helpful, though."

"Oh." Her shoulders slumped, and I felt instantly guilty. She and all the other half-bloods were relying on me, and so far I had done nothing to prove my worth. But at least I was trying, which was more than I could say for Tristan, their leader. There was no way they knew his true feelings about breaking the curse – they'd have turned on him in an instant if they did. And I had no intention of letting that happen.

"If the answers lay in books, I'm sure scholars would have found them by now," I said gently. "But at least I know what... happened, now."

Élise nodded. "We should go back – you are supposed to be dining with the King this evening."

I made a face. "Watching *him* dine, you mean."

Élise giggled and then clapped a hand over her mouth. "You're fearless in the things you say, sometimes."

I shrugged. "Foolish is probably a better word. But you're right, we should go."

As she turned, I shoved Anushka's grimoire into the deep pocket of my dress. "What did you get up to while I was reading?"

A faint smile touched the corner of the girl's lips. "Once he was finished helping you, Martin, the librarian, that is, he showed me how they keep track of all the books."

Which sounded terribly boring to me, but I kept my mouth shut as I watched her trail a finger longingly along the spines of books on the shelves.

"Can half-bloods work in the library?" I asked.

"If by work, you mean clean the floors," she said, looking at me out of the corner of her eye. I gave a slight nod of understanding, but in truth, my thoughts were all for the book burning a hole in my pocket. All I could think of was the grimoire and how for five centuries it had refused to open, only to release its clasp at the touch of my blood. And of that tantalizing chapter title: *Trolls.*

I walked through the streets of Trollus as quickly as I could without attracting notice. Not once did I even bother to glance up at the moon hole to assuage my sense of endless night like I usually did. When we made it back to my rooms, I made a beeline to the garderobe. It was the only place I was certain I could look at the book without worrying about someone walking in on me.

Sitting down on the seat, I pulled the book out of my pocket and, nipping at my fingertip, I allowed a drop of blood to fall on the clasp. It clicked open. I flipped to the page where I left off.

It was all blood magic. In tiny letters in one of the margins, I read why: *The earth holds no power over these creatures who are not her children. No illness, infection, or poison can harm them.* Nor would the blood of animals or even of a human suffice; only troll blood, sometimes a little and sometimes a lot. I wondered how she would obtain their blood. Certainly they would not volunteer it for anything that might be used against them. Then it occurred to me that perhaps she wasn't performing these spells for herself, but rather for other trolls.

I squeezed my eyes shut, trying to remember what I knew about Anushka herself. She'd been a courtesan. In other words, a high-priced prostitute. There was a spell for muting the connection between two bonded trolls – the advantages of that for someone in her line of work were clear enough: it would allow a troll to be unfaithful to his spouse without her suspecting. Other spells were for deception, delving into another's thoughts, influencing moods. The worst were for murder: *the easiest method for killing a troll is to separate him from his magic... accomplished with a pint of troll blood mixed with iron.* When the mixture was thrown on another troll, he was blocked from his magic until the mixture was washed off. Strike immediately, Anushka advised. *Their physical strength is formidable and they are exceedingly swift.*

The loss of their magic will provide only a moment of distraction.

Flipping to the last page of writing, my heart skipped a beat.

Curses.

The writing was cramped and far messier than anywhere else in the book. Water stains marked the page and made the ink run. Most of the writing described remembered bits of lore from her homeland. Four words were underlined so roughly that the paper had nearly torn. Death, Desire, and True Name.

Which wasn't particularly helpful. The death – King Alexis's – made enough sense. And she obviously knew his name. But desire? Was it his desire for her? Or her desire for the trolls to be cursed? Something else? Anushka wrote nothing about specific incantations required to make the curse take effect, or about how long it would last, as she had with the other spells. And there was nothing about breaking a mountain. Instead of answers, all I had were more questions.

"Are you feeling unwell, my lady?" Élise called through the door.

"I'm fine!" I answered back. Shoving the grimoire into a set of drawers, I exited the garderobe. I'd need to find a better hiding place for it later.

"Blue or red?" Élise asked, holding up two gowns.

"Blue," I said. It was Tristan's favorite color. Not that he was likely to attend dinner. And not that it *mattered* if he liked what I was wearing.

Our argument in the library today hadn't been a fake one. He did not want the curse broken. I understood his argument – he was afraid the trolls would wreak havoc on the world and enslave humanity all over again. I was just surprised to hear it coming from him, because it meant he was putting humanity ahead of his own people. But what surprised me more was that I didn't agree with him. When I had first arrived, the trolls had seemed dangerous and evil – and a few still did – but I'd come to realize that such was not the nature of the majority. The half-bloods were clearly against oppression, and I knew there had to be more full-bloods like the Miners' Guild member who were of a similar mind. Keeping everyone captive forever because of a few seemed... unfair. Especially once the King was dead and unable to harm anyone. But Tristan was no fool, and he clearly saw things differently. What did he know that made him so sure history would repeat itself? And was I an overly optimistic idiot to think otherwise? Surely there had to be a solution.

Like a binding promise.

My fingers twitched as a glimmer of an idea came to mind. Trolls were bound to keep their word. Wouldn't it be possible to make every one of them promise not to do violence against humans in exchange for their freedom? It seemed like a fair enough exchange to me. It would have to be a carefully worded oath, but surely something could be crafted that would serve?

"Ready," Élise said, stepping back and interrupting my thoughts.

I got to my feet, and impulsively, I wrapped my arms around my maid and hugged her tightly. "I'm trying," I whispered into her ear.

"Thank you," she whispered, squeezing me back. "I have faith in you."

At least someone did, I thought, as I rushed through the palace to the King's private dining room.

"Your Majesties," I said, dropping into a deep curtsey. "Your Grace."

Only the three of them, plus a dozen servants, were in the room. Lessa stood behind the King with a wine pitcher, her face expressionless. Tristan, as I had suspected, was absent.

"You're late," the King snapped around a mouthful of food.

"My apologies," I replied, sitting down in my usual seat. "Thank you for waiting for me to arrive before you began."

The Duchesse cackled merrily, the wine in her glass sloshing over the rim. "The glutton's gut eats all day and lechers all night. Such a thoroughfare of vice has no time to waste waiting on manners."

The King paused mid-chew and gave a baleful glare. "Where is Tristan?"

"How should I know?" I said, motioning for the servant to give me an extra portion of chicken. "He does not keep me appraised of his comings and goings." I was feeling somewhat bold – having read Anushka's spells, the trolls no longer seemed quite so invincible.

The King set down his fork and pushed his plate away, even though it was still laden with food. I felt my hands grow cold and it took a great deal of willpower to swallow my mouthful of chicken.

"I've had about enough of the way you two carry on," he said, his chair creaking as he leaned back. "Quarreling in public with no regard for how your behavior reflects on this household. How it reflects on *me*."

I forced myself to chew and swallow before answering. "I am not the one instigating our quarrels, Your Majesty. Forgive me, but perhaps your criticism would be better directed towards your son."

The Duchesse shot me a dark look from over the Queen's shoulder. She clearly did not appreciate me passing the blame to her nephew.

The King laughed. "Perhaps it would, but he isn't here, is he? Tell me, Cécile, why do you think he is so set against you?"

I hesitated. I considered pleading ignorance, but then decided against it. He would know I was lying. "Because I am human, Your Majesty. He dislikes my kind." I watched, barely able to breathe as he slowly shook his head.

"Excuses, Cécile. You were brought here to serve a purpose – a purpose you seem to have forgotten while you gallivant through *my* city pursuing every possible whimsy that this one," he gestured at the Duchesse, "can think up." He took a long sip of wine, eyeing me over the rim of the glass. Lessa leaned over his shoulder to refill it. "You are a splendid example of *your kind*, my dear, and for all his protests, Tristan is a seventeen year-old boy. Do you understand me?"

"Yes," I whispered.

"Good," he replied. "Because if I don't see an improvement in your conduct, not only will your gallivanting cease, I will lock you in a box with no room to move."

The fork slipped through my fingers, clattering against the plate.

"I'll leave you to rot in your own filth," he continued, "until you come to understand why there is no one alive who dares to disobey me." He smiled. "Now get out of my sight."

Knocking back my chair, I rushed from the room before he could see the pallor of my face. My bravado had long since fled. Being able to open Anushka's book and read spells that could separate a troll from his magic didn't mean anything unless I could use them. I needed to learn to do so.

"I hate him!" I announced loudly. "He's a vile, gluttonous, evil creature and I hope he chokes on a fishbone."

Élise stopped dusting and Zoé poked her head out of the closet. "What happened?"

Flinging myself down on a sofa, I waited for the girls to sit on either side of me before I explained in terse sentences what the King had said.

"Oh, he's a villain," Zoé said, her brow creased with indignation. "It isn't fair to threaten you – it's not your fault that His Highness is being…" She flung her hands up in the air. "I don't know, antagonistic?"

I nodded warily. To the best of my knowledge, the girls didn't know about our ruse – they thought our quarrels were real. It was all so complex and convoluted that I figured it was best to keep silent on it entirely. My head began to pound in frustration. "I don't know what to do." That much was honest.

The girls exchanged concerned glances. Zoé retrieved a hairbrush and began working on my hair while her sister set to filing my already perfectly filed nails. It was no hug – their training was too ingrained to instigate that degree of familiarity – but the sentiment was the same. It made me wish desperately that Sabine were here.

"I don't think you have any choice," Élise said, exchanging the file for a buffer. "You have to do what the King says – we all do."

"How?" I clenched my jaw. "I can't make Tristan be nice to me." Never mind that doing so would totally undermine the human-hating persona that he took such pains to cultivate.

"No," Élise said, "you can't. But you can be seen making an effort. It might buy you time."

"What do you suggest?" I asked, the growing gleam on their faces making me uneasy.

"We can lower the necklines on your dresses," she said. "Make them snugger in the right places."

"And there are certain fragrances that are said to stimulate ardor. I can procure some in the city and let it be known that you requested them. Word will spread like wildfire, and all gossip eventually gets back to the King."

"This all sounds humiliating," I said, slumping my shoulders. Élise shrugged. "It's better than ending up in a box."

She made a valid point, which is why I subjected myself to trying on gown after gown while the girls pinned, tucked, and altered, all the while thinking that this really wasn't the answer. I didn't want to buy time – I wanted to take action today. I wanted Tristan to get rid of his menace of a father now, not a year from now. The spells in Anushka's grimoire might just be the key to speeding along the process, if I could find a way to use them. And in order to do that, I needed to get my hands on the primary ingredient of all the spells: troll blood.

That would be no easy task.

"Too tight?" Zoé asked around the silver pins she had stuck between her lips. I realized I'd been frowning, and forced my face to relax and shook my head. She went back to work and I went back to my thoughts.

Marc was the most obvious person to ask, but he would want to know why, and I had no confidence that he wouldn't tell Tristan. Same with the twins. As much as they might like me, they were his kin, his closest friends, and they were fervently loyal to him. I glanced down at Zoé and Élise, their faces terse with concentration as they worked. They were my friends, but again, their loyalty was unquestionably to Tristan. There was no way they'd hand over something that might possibly be used against him, and besides, I had no way of knowing how their half-human blood would affect the spells. So that ruled out Tips and his gang as well.

All possible paths, it seemed, led back to Tristan. He was the only one I could ask, but I had a sinking feeling that that conversation wouldn't go well. He liked being in control of circumstances, and I was already something of a loose cannon running amok with his plans. He would not like giving me more power than I already had. He didn't trust me enough. He'd take the grimoire away from me, and with it, the only real leverage I had.

I sighed as deeply as I could in the tight dress. If only he would give me a chance to prove I was trustworthy and loyal, then maybe he would believe that I sought to harness Anushka's spells to help him, not to hurt him. I needed him to understand that he was the last person in the world that I would hurt; that I would do whatever it took to help him. That I... I bit my lip and forced the thought away. He didn't need to know *that*.

Clapping a hand over my mouth, I faked a yawn, then directed an apologetic look at my maids. "I think I'm about done for the night," I said. "I'd like to get ready for bed."

Once they had left me alone in my room, I crept out and retrieved the grimoire from the garderobe. The cover of the book felt vile and sinister in the darkness, and it was a relief to crawl back into bed and turn my light on. I made a tent of my blankets – in case anyone was watching – then I opened the book and flipped to the back. I slowly made my way through the pages, my mouth moving as I memorized the foreign words. It was easy enough for me – I was used to memorizing opera lyrics in other languages.

It was beginning to feel like fate that the librarian had found it for me; that after five hundred years, I'd been the one to open it. Maybe Tristan was right, and we shouldn't break the curse. But that didn't mean the knowledge that I could extract from Anushka's writing was useless. There had to be a way I could use it against the King. But first I needed to convince Tristan to help me, and to do that, I needed to lure him in. I glanced across the room at the shadowy form of an altered dress hanging on the closet door.

Maybe, I thought, just maybe, that might work.

CHAPTER 21
Cécile

"Well, you did a fine job of provoking him."

The sound of Tristan's voice pulled me out of deep sleep. Even after I'd hidden the grimoire away, I'd stayed up late trying to think of ways to get Tristan alone. And here he was. I rubbed the sleep from my eyes, blinking at the brilliance of his light, which hovered over the bed. I briefly wondered how long he'd been standing there watching me sleep. "Don't blame me. He was angry before I even got there. Where have you been all night?"

"If anyone asks, tell them I was here sleeping," he replied, turning away from me.

"I know the routine," I said. "It's just I don't think there's any point to it. He knows you're avoiding me. I think he thinks you're letting your dislike of humans interfere with finding a way to break the curse."

"That's better than the alternative." He studiously avoided looking at me and rifled through papers on the desk, but there was no missing the embarrassment growing in the back of my mind.

"True," I agreed, although I didn't understand why the alternative – his father knowing he didn't want to break the curse – had elicited his embarrassment. I frowned, mentally reviewing his words in my mind. He was acting strangely. I pulled the covers up around my chin and watched him unbuckle the sword at his waist, set it carefully on the desk, and then cross over to the closet. He took off his coat, hanging it carefully on a hanger, and brushed the fabric smooth. He untied his cravat with a quick jerk, but he folded it neatly and placed it on a shelf. There were dark circles under his eyes – all his sleepless nights were catching up with him.

"Do you ever sleep?"

"I try to, but I keep finding this girl in my bed." He meant it as a joke, I knew, but I still felt guilty.

"You can sleep in the bed if you want." As soon as the words were out my face turned bright red. "I mean, I can sleep on the chaise and you can sleep in the bed. It makes more sense – I'm smaller. You're really too tall to be sleeping on that thing. Besides, I get plenty of rest." I clamped my teeth shut to stop my babbling.

One corner of his mouth turned up. "It's all right, Cécile. You can have the bed – there are other places for me to sleep."

Which wasn't at all the answer I'd been looking for.

Silence stretched long beyond the point of awkwardness. He was incredibly nervous, which was making me nervous. I plucked at the blanket, folding it into tighter and tighter pleats. Think of something to say, I ordered myself, but everything I came up with sounded stupid or boring.

"I understand my father suggested you seduce me,"

he said abruptly, the words tumbling over each other. "Apparently he considers me susceptible to such things."

"Or overestimates my skills," I said, with a nervous laugh, glancing at the gown hanging across the room. "Perhaps your aunt can arrange for me to have lessons so that I can improve my chances of success."

"You don't need lessons," he replied. The light hanging above him flared brightly and he glanced up at it before mumbling, "I mean you don't... I don't know what I mean. I haven't slept all night. Forget I said anything. I'm only here for a change of clothes and then I'll be gone." Our combined mortification made my toes curl.

His fingers made small shadows on the wall as he unbuttoned his shirt, pulling it off and laying it across the back of a chair for one of the girls to launder. I stared at his naked back, the hard contours of muscle rippling as he reached into the closet for a clean shirt. A slow-burning warmth filled me that had nothing to do with the extra blankets he'd given me. He froze, sensing the direction my mind was going. Squeezing my eyes shut, I waited for him to make some snide comment that would make me look like a silly fool for admiring him.

He was silent and seconds later, his light winked out. Instead of confidence and conceit, I felt discomfort and a hint of embarrassment. I heard the faint rustle of fabric and the closet doors clicked shut. I tried to think about worms, sluag, even chamber pots, anything to distract me from the thought that the most handsome boy I'd ever met was undressing across the room from me. I was the one that was supposed to be seducing him, not the other way around.

There was a thud that sounded unmistakably like a collision between troll and furniture. "Bloody hell," he swore under his breath.

"Tristan?"

I could hear him breathing; feel the soft edge of apprehension. "Yes?"

"Can you see in the dark?"

He laughed softly. "Given I just walked into a table, I would suggest not. I'm not a bat, you know." His light winked back on.

I buried my face in a pillow, embarrassed. "Forget I said anything," I mumbled. He walked by the bed on his way to the door. "Wait. Where are you going?"

"I've things to see to."

"The tree?"

He was quiet for a moment. "What do you know about the tree?"

"That it's a magic version of what you plan to..." I broke off at the warning expression on his face. But if I was going to get him to trust me, I needed to spend time with him. "Will you show it to me?"

He bit his bottom lip and eyed me thoughtfully. "I suppose we would only be following His Majesty's orders."

"Only a fool would dare not to." Scrambling out of bed, I snatched up the altered gown and wriggled into it. "Let's go."

"So where is it?" I asked, peering down the cobbled lane while I hurried to keep up with his long stride. The dawn shone through the small hole above, but even the faint light was strangely comforting. It drove away the sense of never ending night that had afflicted me since my arrival.

"I'll show you soon enough, but first we must consult with Pierre." He hesitated, then reached down and fastened up my cloak. "You'll catch a chill showing that much skin."

Sighing, I followed him up a set of stairs and into a small home that was cluttered and in need of a good dusting.

"Morning, Pierre!" Tristan shouted as we entered. "Any movement since yesterday?"

"Quiet as a grave," a high-pitched voice shouted back, and moments later, a badly crippled troll flew into the room, seated on what appeared to be a stool with wheels. He was very small, his back contorted in a strange s-shape, but worst of all, he appeared to have no legs. Without the stool and his magic, I doubted he would have the ability to move very far at all.

"Or would have been," he continued, rolling to a stop, "if the Barons Dense and Denser hadn't gotten it into their skulls to have a rock-throwing contest outside my house last night."

Tristan sighed and looked at me as if it was my fault. "I'll speak to them about it later."

"Bah!" The troll threw up his hands. "They'll just think of another way to disturb the peace. Perhaps next time one of them will do us all a favor and drop a rock on the other's head. But who is this that you have with you?"

"This is the… I mean, this is my… Cécile."

"You mean, your lady wife, the Princess Cécile?" The odd-looking troll tsked and shook his head. His wire-rimmed glasses slid down his nose, and he absently pushed them up again as he inspected me. "And even lovelier than

I had heard. The poets will write songs about her beauty that will be sung for generations."

Feeling strangely shy, I let him take my hand, which he kissed and then patted warmly with his gnarled and bent one. "The young ones have no sense of romance," he said and winked. I giggled, despite myself.

Tristan coughed. "Pierre monitors the motions of the earth." He gestured around the room, and his orb brightened, revealing tables of equipment and charts.

"I didn't realize it moved," I said, walking over to examine a chart hanging on the wall. A list of dates ran across the bottom, with an erratic line running horizontally above them. There were numbers and notations written all over it, and I tried to puzzle it out with little success.

"Ah, but the earth, she is always moving," Pierre said, and with a theatrical gesture of his hand, dozens of glowing glass balls of various colors lifted into the air and began to rotate around the large yellow one at the center.

"The sun," Pierre said, and the yellow ball blazed brightly. "The planets and their moons." I watched with fascination as each glass ball lit up as he named it. "And here, this is us. Earth." The blue orb brightened. "Always moving, always moving. But what young Tristan here is concerned with is the times it moves like this." The blue ball shuddered violently.

"Earthshakes," I whispered, and I looked up, picturing the vast weight of the rock that hung over our heads.

"Just so, my lady," Pierre replied, and the glass balls settled gently back onto a table.

Shivering, I wrapped my cloak around me tightly. The earthshakes came often. Sometimes they were hardly noticeable, but there had been times when I'd been knocked off my feet or seen our house and barn shake so badly I was certain they would collapse. I had always been afraid of the quakes – any rational person was – but my fear took on another level as I considered the implications of having a half a mountain worth of rock dangling over my head.

"You shouldn't worry, Cécile," Tristan said from where he'd stood silently in the corner. "Not so much as a stone has fallen in my lifetime or even my father's."

"I'm not afraid. Much," I amended, seeing him roll his eyes. Blast this cursed connection between us. Nor did the sense of confidence radiating from him do much to chase away my fear. He hadn't said that rocks never fell; only that one hadn't fallen in a long time. That meant it was possible, and I didn't have troll magic to protect my head from falling objects.

With greater understanding, I examined the chart once again. "This line," I said, "it shows the motions then?" Pierre nodded. I traced my finger along the line, noting the dates where the line spiked. Many of them were burned into my memory. "Our barn nearly collapsed during this one," I murmured, tapping one of the spikes and remembering our panic as we ushered all the animals out. It was the highest one on the chart, which went back only thirty years, if I was reading it correctly. "Do you have one that goes back further?"

"I have charts going back nearly five centuries, my lady. It is an old craft, and one made exceedingly relevant by the Fall." Pierre's stool rolled across the floor and he extracted another chart from the cabinet and smoothed it out on the desk.

"How old is your father?" I asked, my heart skipping a beat at the sight of a spike in the line that eclipsed all the others.

Tristan cleared his throat. "Forty-three."

The spike was fifty years ago. "What happened?"

Tristan shrugged, but I could feel his discomfort. "We are better prepared, now."

"Did rocks fall?" I demanded. "Couldn't they catch them?"

"It happened in the middle of the night," Tristan replied. "A portion of the city was lost – you walked through it when you came through the labyrinth."

I blanched, remembering the crushed rubble of homes on either side of the tunnels. "Did trolls die?"

"Four hundred and thirty-six lives lost – crushed to death in their sleep."

A shiver ran down my spine. They wouldn't have even seen it coming.

"There are worse ways to go," Tristan muttered.

Uncomfortable silence stretched until Pierre broke it. "Perhaps she will feel better once you show her the tree."

"I somehow doubt that," I muttered.

Tristan smiled. "Have a little faith, Cécile."

We took our leave from Pierre's little house. "You come visit me when Tristan starts to bore you, my lady!" he called from behind us. I turned to wave goodbye and had to hurry to catch up to Tristan.

A laughing group of children carrying books ran by and we were treated to a chorus of "Good morning, my lord," along with many curious glances in my direction.

"Where are they going?" I asked, smiling at their antics.

"To school," Tristan replied. "We'll start here."

He stopped next to a low, circular stone wall that stood in the middle of the street.

I turned back around to watch the children, girls and boys, disappear into a stately building. "Truly? The girls, too?"

"Truly," Tristan replied, but his attention seemed elsewhere. "They all attend until they're ten, and then they start learning their respective trades. But look here, Cécile. This is the tree. Or part of it, rather."

With a wistful backwards glance, I turned to see Tristan standing on the stone wall, staring at empty space. "Where?" I asked, looking into the circle. There was nothing but stone.

"Here." He clasped my hand and pulled it forward. Immediately, it was enveloped in liquid warmth. I jerked my hand back. "I can feel something, but I can't see it." My eyes searched the empty air, trying to find a glimmer of what he was looking at. Reaching into the magic, I ran my hand up as high as I could reach, even on my tiptoes, but I could not grasp what was in front of me.

"No, I suppose as a human, you wouldn't."

"But trolls can see it?"

"See isn't precisely the correct word – we can sense it's there. Me better than most, because the magic is predominantly mine."

"Oh," I said, feeling more than a little let down. I'd thought he was going to show me something impressive, but all I'd done was warm my fingers in a column of magic. "I could see the magic girders in the mines – they were all lit up."

Frowning, he let go of my hand and cracked his knuckles. "Good idea." Reaching out, he touched the magic and it burst into silver light.

"God in heaven," I whispered, watching in awe as light flooded in a stick-straight column up and up. It reached the rocks above and bloomed outward into arches that canopied across the sky. Column after column lit up until all of Trollus glowed and I could see that the rock was supported much like the ceiling of the throne room, just on a larger scale.

My head tilted backwards, I turned in an awe-struck circle until the sound of shrieking children caught my attention.

The troll children poured back out of the school, running in circles around us yelling, "Light show!" over and over again. Tristan laughed at them, and suddenly bursts of light in all different colors exploded in the sky, like fireworks, raining bits of magic over the city. Fantastical creatures made of light soared through the air, diving down to circle the children, who screamed in delight, jumping for cover and then crowing for more. They made their own little flying beasts and sent them chasing after Tristan's red and gold serpent, which circled around and gobbled the children's creatures down.

He gave a flourishing bow to his little subjects and then, looking back at the glowing column, he snapped his fingers and the tree blinked out. I found myself clapping with delight along with the other children. "Bravo," I said. "Most impressive."

Grinning, he bowed deeply, then motioned for the children to get back to their studies. "Light requires little effort, and they are fond of parlor tricks."

"Who isn't?" Reaching out, I touched the magic again, allowing my hand to sink deep into the depths of the column. "How is it," I asked, "that I can pass my hand through it, but it can still hold up all that rock?"

"It knows the difference between the two."

"Knows?" I frowned. "Is it alive?"

Tristan stepped off the stone wall and I watched his brow furrow as he considered how to explain. It struck me that for once I was seeing the real Tristan, not an act designed to disguise his true feelings or a few kind words that accidentally slipped through. Gone was the cold callousness, and in its place was a young man content to let the little trolls pull at his sleeves with the irreverence only children can get away with.

"It isn't alive, precisely," Tristan finally said. "It is what I will it to be. I want it to hold up rock, but to let through the river and everything in it. The magic knows the difference, because I know the difference."

"I see," I said. "And what is it that you do to it every day?"

"Mostly, I fill it with power," he said, unconsciously offering me his arm and just as quickly pulling it back. "Magic fades," he added, sensing my confusion. "The tree constantly needs to be replenished. And when the earth shakes, it also needs to be adjusted to ensure the load is balanced correctly. That's what takes the most time."

"And you do this every day?" I asked. For all the grandness of the tree, it seemed a more monotonous task than milking cows or slopping pigs.

"Every day," he agreed.

"Can't someone else do it?"

He frowned at me. "Yes, but it is the duty of the king."

"But you aren't the king," I argued. Yet. "Why doesn't your father do it?"

"Because he entrusted me with it." I could feel Tristan's pride radiating through our bond. "When I was fifteen – the youngest ever to take on the task. It is a very great honor."

I nodded gravely, although in my opinion, King Thibault's delegating the task likely had more to do with him not wanting to drag his fat arse all around Trollus each day than trust in his son. "Is it hard?"

"It is tiring," he said, motioning for me to follow him down an empty side street. "It requires an immense amount of my power to maintain at the best of times. When it needs adjusting, I sometimes require assistance from the Builders' Guild – which is my guild, by the way. But not often."

"That wasn't what I meant."

He stopped in his tracks and looked back at me. "What, then?"

"I wondered," I started tentatively, "if it was hard knowing that everyone's lives depend on your magic; if you worry about an earthshake coming like the one that wrecked the city."

He started walking again. "I cannot stop the world from moving. All I can do is be prepared for when it does."

Looking around, I saw we were alone and closed the distance between us. "You didn't answer my question."

The only sound in the street was the roar of the waterfall. Finally, he spoke. "I used to have nightmares about it falling down. I'd wake up certain I'd heard rocks raining on the city streets. But not anymore."

"What do you dream of now?" I pressed, the desire to understand what went on in his mind like an itch I could not help but scratch.

"I dream of other things." Tristan's face was unreadable, but my mind filled with the same intense heat that had seared through me when I'd watched him change his shirt.

Desire. The word rippled through my thoughts, bringing a flush of heat to my cheeks.

"I was to leave to go live with my mother in Trianon the day that Luc brought me here," I blurted out, desperate to change the subject. "I was going to sing on stage, you see. It was my dream..." I broke off, expecting one of the many nasty comments he usually made to me in public.

Instead I saw curiosity on his face. "It was your dream..." he prompted.

"To sing on all the greatest stages," I said. "Not just in Trianon, but in the continental kingdoms as well. My mother... She's very famous, but she never leaves Trianon. Ever. She rarely even comes to visit us."

"They live apart, your mother and father." It wasn't a question – I knew that he knew all about me.

I flushed. "Yes. When my father was young, he left the farm to go live in the city. He met my mother, and they... well, she had my brother, my sister, and me. When my grandfather passed, my father went back to take over the farm and he brought us with him. She wouldn't leave Trianon."

"But she's his wife," Tristan said indignantly. "She is duty-bound to go wherever he wants her to go."

"Not according to her," I said. "And besides, *duty* has

got nothing to do with it. What matters is that she didn't *love* him or us enough to give up her career."

"You consider love more important than duty, then?"

I hesitated. "I suppose it depends on the circumstances."

Tristan slowly shook his head. "I think not. Otherwise individuals such as your mother, who clearly love themselves above all things, will use love as a defense of their actions. And who would be able to argue against them? Duty," he said, pointing a finger at me, "is what keeps selfishness from inheriting the earth."

"How bitterly pragmatic."

He glanced down at me. "I find a certain comfort in pragmatism."

"Cold comfort," I retorted.

"Is better than no comfort."

I rolled my eyes, irritated with his circular logic. But he had a point. Staring down at the paving stones, I remembered the silent sorrow on my father's face whenever my mother's name was mentioned. "He always gave her whatever she wanted," I said quietly.

"And at what cost to you and your siblings?" Tristan asked. "He sounds weak."

"He isn't!" I retorted, my indignation rising. "He's a good and strong man – it's only her to whom he always gives in. I love my father. I miss him." Sorrow shrouded me and I wrapped my cloak around me tighter. "I don't even know her. I can count on one hand the number of times I've seen her since I was small." My throat felt tight and I blinked rapidly against the sting in my eyes. "Not that it matters anymore."

"It matters." His voice was low, and even if we hadn't been alone on the street, no one would have heard but me. He slowed his pace, looking over his shoulder at me. The weight of the promise he'd made to me hung in his eyes – the promise for which he'd asked nothing in return. To set me free. I focused on filling my mind with gratitude, knowing he would feel it, and hoping he would understand what it was for. Almost too late did I see the beam of sunlight crossing his path.

"No!" I gasped, throwing my weight into Tristan, knocking him down sideways into a narrow alleyway.

He stared up at me in astonishment. "Have you lost your mind or is this some sort of retaliation?"

I eyed the beam of sunlight that was still too close for comfort. "The sun."

"What about it?"

"Everyone knows that trolls turn to stone in the sunlight," I said, although from the look on Tristan's face I was starting to doubt the "everyone knows" part.

His astonishment faded and to my horror, he started to laugh. Reaching out one arm, he waggled his fingers in the sun. "Oh, the stories you humans come up with," he gasped out, and my cheeks burned.

"I'm sorry," I mumbled. "This is what I get for putting stock in fables."

"Don't be sorry." He smiled up at me and my heart skipped a beat. "Are there any other myths I should know about?"

I felt breathless and acutely aware that I was indecently sprawled across him and he had made no move to push me away. My skin burned everywhere I was in contact with him: where my hipbone pressed against his, where my arm rested against the hard muscle of his chest, rising and falling with the rapidness of his breath. Most of all, where his hand pressed against my lower back, holding me against him.

"Well," I said, "trolls are supposed to have an enormous fondness for gold."

"Well, that is certainly true."

"And you're supposed to have great hoards of it." I thought about the half-bloods toiling day in and day out to extract the golden metal from the mountain. And they'd been at it for centuries.

"True," he laughed, "but I've also noticed in myself the tendency to hoard pocket lint and scraps of paper."

I smirked. "The stories don't mention pocket lint."

He sighed. "Dreadfully inaccurate, these tales. Perhaps I should write my own in order to clear up these misconceptions. Or create new ones?"

"Pointed teeth?" I asked, pretending to growl at him.

"Perhaps hoards of human bones."

I laughed. "I think that one already exists – trolls are supposed to boil human children in their cooking pots."

He grimaced. "That one came into existence after the Fall – I'm sure you can speculate as to why."

I blanched. "It's true?"

"Desperate times call for desperate measures," he said, solemn expression at odds with the amusement I knew he felt.

"You're horrible," I grumbled, then thought for a minute. "The stories also say that accepting troll gold will cost you more than you think, and that it can get you into a great deal of trouble."

"True. If the human is greedy, the trouble is far worse. Anything else?"

I hesitated and his brow crinkled. "Well?"

"Trolls," I finally said, "are supposed to be ugly."

He looked away, cheek pressed against the ground and eyes fixed on the wall of a house only a few inches from his face. "I suppose to you humans, many of us are."

My thoughts turned to Marc, who was always kind to me when no one else was. "They aren't ugly." I bit my lip, trying to find the right words. "More like beautiful things that have had the misfortune of being broken." Tristan turned his face back to me. I saw the sorrow in his eyes and felt it in my heart. "Why are you always so unhappy?" I asked.

"I think it is our nature to believe evil always has an ugly face," he said, ignoring my question. "Beauty is supposed to be good and kind, and to discover it otherwise is like a betrayal of trust. A violation of the nature of things."

"Do you think trolls are evil?" I asked.

"Do you?" His eyes searched mine as though he might find the answer there.

"No," I said. "I don't."

He exhaled softly, reaching up and stroking my cheek with one hand. "From your lips I can almost believe it's true."

My breath came in short little gasps. The desire for him to touch me, to kiss me, was so strong, it felt like another entity had taken over my mind. And maybe it had. Maybe he had. I could feel his need like it was my own. It was my own. Whatever boundaries existed between our minds fell away in that moment, making it impossible to differentiate between my emotions and his. But that didn't matter, because we both wanted the same thing.

"Cécile," he whispered, his fingers tangling in my hair, pulling my face closer. "I…"

"This is indecent behavior, even for you, Tristan. Especially for you," a dry voice said from behind us.

Tristan's shock mirrored my own, but while I was busy scrambling to my feet and smoothing my skirts, he merely folded an arm behind his head and crossed his booted ankles. "Afternoon, Your Grace. Cécile, this is the Duke d'Angoulême."

"I'm not interested in being introduced to your pet, Tristan." The Duke leaned on his golden-handled cane. "But I am interested to know why you are cavorting with it in the shadows."

"I had a pet mouse once," Tristan said. "I kept it in a box in my wardrobe and fed it cheese and bread crusts until one of the maids tattled on me to my mother. Not that she cared, of course, but when my father found out, he took my mouse away. He said to me, 'Tristan, if you are to ever have a pet anything, it will be a pet of my choosing, and it certainly won't be a mouse.'" Tristan smiled. "When my father gives me an order, I've always found it's in my best interest to listen."

"I'm well aware that the decision for you to bond this creature was your father's," the Duke said, his voice frigid. "I am also aware that you protested mightily against the union – I was one of the unfortunate few forced to listen to you go on at length." He smiled. "But you still haven't answered my question."

A flash of irritation seared through our bond, but Angoulême never would have guessed it. "Dreadfully funny reason, really." Tristan smirked. "Or it would be, if you had a sense of humor to speak of, Angoulême."

"Try me."

"I was walking along, listening to the girl prattle on about something she no doubt considered very important, when out of nowhere she shoved me clear off my feet."

"Something we've all wanted to do," the Duke said.

Tristan made a face. "What an awful thing to say. Anyway, when I inquired as to her motivation for the unexpected act of violence, I discovered that she was of the mistaken belief that trolls turned to stone when exposed to the sun's rays." He pointed at the beam of sunlight that had moved a few inches further away. "Dear thing thought she was saving my life."

"What reason have you given her to want to do that?"

"I asked myself the very same question," Tristan said, rising to his feet.

"Did you come to any conclusions?"

Tristan raised both his hands and shrugged. "Tale as old as time, I suppose. Human women throwing themselves at our feet, blinded by beauty, power, wealth. No matter how they are used and abused, they always come back for more. Like loyal dogs." He smirked. "Did you expect this one to be any different?"

In the past, his words had always been softened by the guilt he felt in saying them, but this time all I felt was vicious animosity. I tried to unravel his words – to see how I was different from those women – but I couldn't. He did treat me poorly, and what had I just done if not thrown myself at his feet. My skin crawled with the realization of how pathetic that made me, but reason still governed my mind enough to know that I needed to play along; needed to play my part. "Is that what you think I am? A dog? Some poor beast you can pat on the head or kick in the ribs as suits your pleasure?"

Tristan laughed. "Not literally, of course. I've yet to hear you bark."

It was too much.

I slapped him hard enough that my palm burned and my arm ached from the impact, but the pain was sweet. Raising my hand, I swung it again, but he caught my wrist, his motion so fast it seemed a blur. Fast enough that I knew he could have stopped my first blow if he'd wanted to.

"When a dog bites," the Duke said softly, "you put it down."

Tristan pulled me aside, stepping between me and the Duke. "You'd like that, wouldn't you, Your Grace? Kill her on the chance I wouldn't survive it? My brother – your ward – becomes heir to the throne. How long until my father suffers an untimely death and you become king of Trollus in all but name?"

"Big accusations, boy," the Duke hissed. "And I confess, I find it more than a little ironic that you of all people dare to accuse me of treason." He jabbed a long white finger against Tristan's chest. "I know what you are, Your Highness, and where your true sympathies lie. When I find proof, it will be the end of you."

"You'll be looking for a long time, Your Grace," Tristan said coolly, but I could feel the fury running through his veins. Fury and fear.

"Perhaps," the Duke replied. His eyes raked over me and he smiled. "Tell me, Tristan, how does your pet human feel about your ongoing affair with Anaïs? Or does she really hate you so much that she doesn't care?"

I staggered back, my veins filled with ice. "What do you mean ongoing?"

"Oh, you didn't know?" Angoulême wrinkled his lip. "Where did you think he was going every night, girl? In my experience, there is only one thing that drives a man from a warm bed and that's the bed of another."

"Tristan, what is he talking about?" I asked, but he wouldn't meet my eyes. Shame mixed with fury seeped into my mind.

"Can't even deny it, can you, boy?"

Tristan's hands balled into fists, but he didn't refute what Angoulême was saying. The pain of betrayal flooded through me. I'd trusted him. I'd put my fate in his hands thinking he was working to set me free, and the whole time he'd been sneaking off to meet with another girl. Worst of all, I'd thought he'd cared – that beneath the act necessitated by our circumstances he'd wanted things to be different. Wanted me.

Snatching up my skirts, I ran, my boots making faint slapping noises against the paving stones, the beam of my light bouncing as I raced through the winding back lanes of the city. Up and up the valley I went until I reached the waterfall, the spray dampening my dress as I stood staring up at the hole through which it fell. The Devil's Cauldron, and I was in hell itself. Misery doused my anger like a bucket of water on flames, and I clenched a hand against the sharp pain rising up beneath my ribs. And the worst of it was that I knew I'd brought this pain upon myself. I'd been a fool to care about Tristan and doubly a fool to hope that he might feel the same for me.

I stood with my eyes closed, waiting for someone to tell me to step back from the edge of the waterfall and go back to the palace that was my prison. Then it dawned on me – I was alone. My eyelids snapped opened and I took stock of my situation. Tristan had dismissed my guards, and they hadn't argued – why should they when Tristan was more than capable of controlling me? But Tristan hadn't moved from the spot where I'd left him. If there was ever a chance, this was it.

Taking a deep breath to calm my nerves, I stared up the flight of stone steps that led to the gate and the shadows beyond. Sweat trickled down my back as I gazed up into the darkness. Turning, I stared down the valley towards the glowing city. There was nothing for me there. But if I made it through... I thought of my grandmother and the rest of my family. Of Sabine. The wide open spaces of the countryside. I remembered the heat of the sun on my face and the sweet pleasure of freedom. The choice was obvious.

Moving as fast as I dared, I felt my way up the steps until I reached the narrow platform and reached out for the cold bars. Fumbling around in my hair, I pulled a metal pin from my coiled locks. "Please work," I whispered falling to my knees. Inserting the pin into the lock, I twisted it, waiting for the telltale click.

It stuck.

"Please, please, please," I chanted, trying again.

Nothing. I glanced back at the city, half-expecting to see someone running up the steps to prevent my escape, but I was alone. Unlike the gate to the River Road, this entrance was devoid of any troll soldiers. The labyrinth needed no guardian. Its very nature was deterrent enough.

Gritting my teeth together, I jammed the hairpin back inside the lock and closed my eyes, working by touch. Then, with a click, the lock sprung open.

CHAPTER 22
Tristan

I slumped against the wall, head in my hands, stone digging into my spine. Everything was falling apart – Angoulême would not have been so open with his threats unless he was certain. The man was a cold-hearted devil, but no fool. It wouldn't be long until he played his cards, and I was certain those cards would involve Cécile. If he thought the rewards worth it, he would not hesitate to break my father's laws. Most likely it would be a threat against her life that would force me to reveal my plots or watch her die. And risk dying along with her. Or, if he thought she knew anything, he might just take her and torture the information out of her. Once, I might have been able to see it through – to watch an innocent girl die for the greater good.

But no longer. Now I was certain that I'd sacrifice everything to save her.

The sound of footsteps caught my attention and I raised my head to see Marc coming towards me. A barrier of magic snapped up around us. "What the bloody hell is going on?" he asked. "I just saw Angoulême walking down the street looking like he'd been offered the keys to the treasure room."

I grimaced and stared at the tops of my boots. "More like the crown itself. He saw me with Cécile."

"What of it?" Marc retorted. "No one can expect you to avoid her completely."

"In a compromising position."

"Oh." Marc's voice softened. "I see."

"He knows, Marc," I said. "He's always suspected where my true sympathies lie, but now he knows the way to force my hand. He'll use her, mark my words."

"And if he does?"

I swallowed hard and looked up at my cousin, my best friend. The only person in this world I trusted, and even he did not know all my secrets. "I didn't think this would happen," I pleaded. "I didn't think I would care for her this way..." I broke off. "I'm sorry."

"You shouldn't be," Marc said. "If you didn't care about her life, then you wouldn't be the man I thought you were."

"It's more than that."

Marc chuckled. "Oh, I know. Trust me, I know. Now, where has she gotten off to?"

I raked my fingers through my hair. "She ran off. Angoulême told her I was having an affair with Anaïs."

"But you're not."

"I know!" I snapped, my frustration rising. "But I couldn't very well admit that in front of him."

"Well, go find her now and tell her the truth!"

I raised my head, eyes drawn north towards the falls, her misery a magnet to my own. She must have run without stopping to be so far away.

Too far away.

I leapt to my feet.

"What is it? Has something happened?" There was alarm in Marc's voice – he was fond of Cécile. He also knew better than most what would happen if she died.

My heart skittered and a wave of dizziness swept over me. "She's in the labyrinth."

CHAPTER 23
Cécile

I jerked the gate open, locked it behind me, and broke into a run down the twisting corridors. My only hope now was speed.

I wasn't afraid anymore, either. I was determined. The trolls would not catch me. The sound of the great waterfall faded in the distance and I was left with only the thud of my boots and the pant of my own breath. This was the easy part of my journey. These passages were the crumpled streets of abandoned Trollus, still smooth and easy to pass through. Once I reached the labyrinth proper, it would be a different story. It was with both relief and trepidation that I saw the narrow tunnel lying ahead, its opening black and menacing.

Dropping to my hands and knees, I shone my light inside, but it didn't reach far enough to give me much comfort. I bit my lip and remembered what Marc had told me about the sluag. Sluag were neither stealthy nor cunning – if you listen, you will always hear them coming. I sucked in a deep breath and held it, listening.

All I heard was the din of my heart. There was no telltale swish, swish and certainly not the thundering call of a sluag on the hunt.

I sat down on the cold stone floor, placing my light carefully on my lap, and I listened. To my mind, to my heart – call it what you will. I listened to Tristan's emotions and tried to understand what he intended.

Desperation.

He had not, as I thought he would, instantly rounded up guards to track me down. The sharp pain I had felt under my ribs returned and I drew my knees up to my chest to try to ward it off. Tristan wasn't coming. Disappointment chased away hope, and I forced myself to acknowledge the fact that I had hoped he would come after me. False hopes. Why shouldn't he abandon me to the labyrinth? Whether I escaped or died trying, the result was the same – he would be free of me, the repulsive human. He'd be free to be with Anaïs. Able to claim that his aunt's prophesy was nothing but ramblings and not worth taking seriously.

Fear.

That was there too, but of course it would be. His father would be angry that Tristan had allowed me to escape unbound by the oaths that kept Trollus secret from the outside world. But even the King's anger would fade when they realized there would be no retribution from me. I just wanted to forget ever being here. I wanted to leave and let time wipe away the memory of Trollus and its people, and most of all, of Tristan.

Misery.

This was nothing new.

"I don't care," I whispered. "I refuse to care any longer."

Sticking the leather handle of my light between my teeth, I got down on my belly and crawled into the tunnel.

CHAPTER 24
Tristan

"How?" Marc demanded. "It's locked, and I have the only key."

"She can pick locks," I said, remembering our encounter in the corridor the night we were bonded.

"We need to go after her." Marc turned to run, but I grabbed his arm, yanking him back. That had been my first instinct too, but was it the correct one?

"Wait."

Marc swore. "What do you mean, wait? If we go now, we'll catch her before anyone notices she's gone." His eyes widened as he realized what I was thinking. "You can't seriously be considering letting her make the attempt? She's unarmed and wearing a bloody gown and heels. She'll fall and break her neck."

I flinched, but kept my voice steady. "She's wearing boots and she isn't a silly parlor maid – she's strong and clever. She can do this."

Marc shoved me against a wall. "Have you lost your bloody mind? The labyrinth is deadly, even for one of us, and she's just a girl."

"No more deadly than it will be for her here." I closed my eyes and listened, Cécile's fear making my hands grow cold. Every inch of me yearned to go after her, to bring her back, keep her safe, and yet... "This is her chance, Marc. Her one chance to escape Trollus, and to escape me. If I stop her, she'll only hate me for it."

"Are you sure?"

I wasn't sure. Indecision racked me to the core, but there were no good options. If I interfered with her escape, not only would she hate me for it, I was certain Angoulême would make an attempt on her life. If I let her continue into the labyrinth, I risked her being killed by any number of things. But if she escaped, she'd be safe. Grinding my teeth, I forced myself to sit down on the ground and remain still. There was no good choice, because no matter the outcome, one thing was certain: I was going to lose her.

CHAPTER 25
Cécile

With no fear of imminent pursuit, I was able to move at a slower, and safer, pace. The stones scraped my hands and I felt bruises rising on my knees, but still I pressed forward. Though Tristan had not raised the alarm at my absence, it was inevitable Élise or Zoé would notice. And I had a long way to travel. The trolls could still catch me if I wasn't careful.

Reaching an intersection of rock, I scrambled my way up to consult the list of markers. Water ran across the etchings, and many were nearly washed away, but the one I had been following remained clear enough. Sitting on my heels, I gripped my light tightly and slid down the wet rock, landing with a splash in a pool of water that came nearly to my waist. This was new.

Cursing, I bent my head beneath the low ceiling and waded forward. The water grew deeper until it brushed my chin. I had never considered not being able to maintain my route. I was a fool for it – Marc had told me the labyrinth was always changing. I swam forward, my light unaffected by immersion in the water, and it was then I saw the source of the flooded passage. The way ahead was filled with rock. Cave-in.

My heart skipped a beat and I splashed backwards, eyes on the stone above me, which seemed deceptively solid. My way was blocked and I would need to find another. Wading back, I climbed onto the boulder and weighed up my options.

There were two: turn back or go upwards and to the right. I refused to consider the first – I had come too far for that. But next to the markers pointing to the right were ominous curved lines – sluag.

Even though the water was icy, I felt hot. I kept imagining the white bulk of the sluag rearing up in front of me, its poisonous stinger shooting out like a whip. My beam of light trembled as I pointed it into the passageway. I closed my eyes and listened.

Silence. And fear, both Tristan's and mine. His had grown considerably and that could only mean my absence had been noted and his father's wrath was at hand. The trolls would be after me now if they weren't already. I had to hurry.

The passage to the right soon opened up into a wider space. It was easier for me to pass through, but it also meant more room for even the largest of sluag. I could smell them. I stepped softly and tried to keep the rasping of my breath to a minimum. They hunted by sound. It was the sound of our shouting that had lured the sluag to Luc and me before. If I kept silent, I might pass unnoticed. From the stench, it seemed likely that at least one of them had fed recently and maybe it wouldn't be hungry enough to seek me out.

I pressed my hand against the damp wall to steady myself against the slippery drop ahead. Gripping the handle of my light, I navigated the sharp rocks, clinging to them with my free hand as I eased my way down.

I took a step forward and my heel slipped, sending me crashing down hard on my bottom. "Don't scream, don't scream!" My voice was a harsh whisper as I fought to stop my slide forward, but the surface was sheer and my clutching fingers found no purchase on the slick stone. I smashed up against a rock and bounced sideways, a sob escaping my throat before I managed to suppress it. All I could do was protect my light. It was possible I might survive a broken limb and battered ribs, but if I lost my light, it would be the end of me.

I slid faster and faster. The light shining between my feet showed only slick rock and never ending blackness, and then suddenly, there was nothing beneath me. I was flying out over nothingness. I screamed, my hands flailing to break my fall. The light-stick flew out of my grip and with dull horror, I heard it smash just before I splashed into a shallow pool of water and slime.

A vile stench filled my nostrils as I gasped for breath in the utter blackness. I was coated in foulness that even my panicked mind recognized as sluag shit, and I groaned when my fumbling hands brushed against the skeleton floating in the pool. My aimlessly searching fingers latched hold of something cold and smooth and I pulled it out of the slime. The heavy metal shape felt familiar in my hands and my fingers roamed over it. A duck. A golden duck.

This was Luc's corpse.

I shoved my filthy sleeve into my mouth to muffle the sobs that I could not suppress. There was no way out. A shower of pebbles rained down onto the pool, and my howls cut off abruptly as I held my breath to listen. But nothing else stirred. I huddled in terror in the cold wetness of water and offal next to Luc's bones. I had no sense of direction; not even of up or down or the size of the space around me. The darkness was unforgiving and my frozen body refused to reach out to discover the limits of my circumstances. I was terrified. It was not like the terror of running from a wolf, always knowing you can turn and fight. It was not like the sense of drowning, where there is a chance to flee to the surface. From this darkness and this place, there was no escape. I could neither run nor hide, and no one can fight the dark. All there was left for me to do was die.

But the very idea of ending it here, interned in a pool of offal with an idiot like Luc, struck fury in my heart. I wasn't injured or starving. There was hope yet. I began to move, feeling around in the pool in search of Luc's pack. The trolls must have given him a lantern to replace the one I'd lost, and I was certain his pack would contain a flint for lighting it.

My fingers brushed against rough fabric, and I hauled it upwards, knowing from the weight that it was the sack containing the rest of his gold. I felt around inside, pulling out smooth coins one after another until I determined there was nothing of use inside. I started sorting through the gold on the floor, but found nothing but metal and rock belonging to the mountain. No flint.

"Where did you put it?" I muttered, forcing myself to concentrate and remember the moment I had seen Luc first light the lantern. I remembered the desperation I'd felt at being deprived of sight, the splatter of water against my face as he'd climbed out of the pool, and the sound of steel striking against flint. And sight. In my mind's eye, I saw the glow of light, and the movement of him tucking the small rock into his coat pocket.

Grimly, I waded over towards the corpse, my fingers reaching reluctantly down to touch the bones and half-digested mush of fabric. Then I froze. From out in the blackness, I felt him. Like a silken cord strung between two points, one of them drawing ever closer. Tristan was coming.

CHAPTER 26
Cécile

I was running out of time. I dug my fingers into the fabric, my heart hammering as the moments ticked by. Tristan was moving many times faster than I had, and I was all but certain he was leading his father's soldiers towards me.

My skin brushed against a sharp edge, and I gleefully extracted the knife, sticking it between my teeth for safekeeping. "Flint, flint, where are you?" I hummed under my breath, trying to combat my panic. He was closer.

My fingernails grated across a stone stuck between two ribs, and I quickly pried it out, not allowing my mind to linger on how it became lodged there. Tristan wasn't far now. If I didn't get a source of light soon, he'd catch me.

I needed to find the lantern. Wary of the knife's sharp edge, I tentatively struck the two together. Nothing. "Quit being a ninny," I scolded myself, and smacked the two firmly together. A spark flew. I repeated the process, but the quick spark wasn't enough to help me locate the lantern. I'd have to do it by feel.

Clutching my precious objects, I continued my search. When my hand closed over the slim metal handle of the lantern, I very nearly crowed with delight. But I was too late. I heard the sound of boots, and then light blossomed from overhead.

"Cécile?"

I froze, the sound of Tristan's voice eliciting an unfortunate mix of emotion in my heart.

"Cécile? Where are you?"

My silence was only delaying the inevitable. "Here." My tight throat restricted the word to a croak. Coughing, I cleared it and called again. "I'm here."

"Are you hurt?"

I shook my head and then realized he couldn't see me. "No."

"I'm coming down."

With a recklessness I would never have dared, he scampered down the slick rocks and stopped on a ledge above me. He was alone. Brilliant light filled the chamber, and I looked around and saw in an instant that if my light hadn't broken, my passage out of the slime would have been easy. I stared at the open passage that led to freedom and struggled with my emotions. I should feel disappointment, devastation even. I had been so close. If I'd been better prepared, or bolder, I might be breathing open air. But part of me – a part that made me cringe – was glad that he had come.

A soft snort of annoyance caught my attention and I looked up. Tristan had his arms crossed and was glaring at me.

"Is it because you're a human or because you're a girl?"

"Is what because?" I retorted, infected by his irritation.

"Your blasted kaleidoscope of emotion!" he snapped. "One minute you're happy, the next you are sad. Then angry. Then ashamed. Every hour I'm forced to run the gamut of every emotion that ever existed and never know the cause of a single one of them."

I crossed my arms and scowled.

Tristan threw up his hands in exasperation. "I don't even know whether you want me to rescue you from this mess or to leave you here in the dark."

"Please," I snapped. "You aren't here to rescue me – you're here to stop my escape. And besides, I don't need any help from you."

"Oh?" His eyebrows rose along with his anger. "So I take it you are wallowing around in sluag shit because you enjoy the smell so much? And you thought it would be more entertaining to navigate the labyrinth in the dark? Perhaps," he whispered angrily, "we should stuff your ears with wool and tie one arm behind your back to make it truly entertaining for you!"

I held up the products of my search triumphantly. "See?"

"Yes, I do see," he snapped. "I see a broken lantern that has leaked oil everywhere and a fool of a girl about to set off sparks in the midst of it."

I looked down, only now seeing the rainbow of oil slicking across the pool of offal. "Then I suppose we should both be glad you finally decided to stop me," I said, not bothering to hide the bitterness in my voice.

Hurt stung through my mind, and I looked up at him in surprise.

"You think I'm here to save my own skin, don't you?" he demanded in a loud whisper. He looked away from me and shook his head.

I let the broken lantern slip from my fingers. "Why else?" I asked. "Duty?" I flung the word at him.

His eyes snapped back to meet mine. "To hell with duty. I came for you – I came because I was afraid you weren't going to make it. I came because I couldn't stand the thought of something happening to you."

A soft gasp filled my ears and I dimly realized it had come from my lips. This was not what I had expected. And even though I didn't know entirely why, I knew his statement changed everything.

The ropes of power that wrapped around me were blissfully warm as they lifted me out of the slime and settled me on the ledge next to Tristan, holding me steady until I had regained my balance. I looked down at the place where I'd almost met my end. The pool was murky and faintly green, but beneath the floating skeleton and scraps of fabric, there lay a carpet of glittering gold. "It's Luc." I gestured below. "My purchase price."

Tristan scowled. "Then he got what he deserved. The labyrinth always kills the greedy ones eventually."

"No one deserves this," I whispered, imagining what it would be like to be paralyzed and have the flesh stripped from your body. A shiver ran down my spine, and I wrapped my sodden cloak around me.

"He lied to you. He stole you from your family. He sold

308 *The Malediction Trilogy I*

you with no more regard than a trader sells a side of beef." Tristan's hands balled up, and my own teeth clenched from the fury emanating from him. "If any man deserved to die, it was him."

I regarded the bones that had once been Luc, finding it hard to hate a dead man, no matter what he had done. Besides, there was another side to the bargain. "And you purchased me, with as much regard as a nobleman buying a side of beef."

"I did not!" His silver eyes locked with mine and I shivered at the intensity in them. "I fought this arrangement at every turn. I've told you that."

"He gave you the choice. I was there." My lip trembled. "I heard you agree to me with my own ears. But the whole time, you wanted it to be her, didn't you?"

Tristan sighed and the heat left his eyes. He wiped a weary hand across his face and looked down at the glittering pool of gold. "Anaïs and I are only friends."

"Oh," I said, my voice weak.

"We have never been anything more and we never will be," Tristan continued, "but we pretend we are in order to give me the time and privacy I need to meet with my followers."

"Oh," I repeated. "I thought that maybe before I came that you and her…" I trailed off as he shook his head. "Did you ever consider it?" I asked, my mind having a difficult time coming to terms with what he was telling me.

Tristan frowned. "Do you really want to go down that path?"

"No," I said quickly, pressing the heel of my hand to my

forehead. "Anaïs is a sympathizer?"

"Not precisely," Tristan said. "But I trust her implicitly, so that isn't so much the issue. Her father, Angoulême, is head of those who wish to keep troll bloodlines pure. He wants to ban all human-troll interactions, ban any human from stepping foot within Trollus, and to conduct all trade at the mouth of the River Road. He also wants to purge the city of anyone with less than pure blood. He's suspected my leanings for a long time, and this isn't the first time he's tried to use Anaïs against me."

His lips clenched together in a bitter smile, and I could feel his hatred of the Duke sear through my mind. A hatred I was beginning to share.

"To make matters worse, he has my younger brother as his ward." Tristan swallowed hard. "Roland is… insane. Violently so. And Angoulême has directed his violent predilections towards his cause."

"Why did your father let Angoulême have him?" I asked, bewildered.

"Originally, it was part of a… a contract that he was negotiating. An alliance. But ultimately, I think it was because he didn't want him to turn out like me," Tristan said quietly. "So he placed him in a home where neither my aunt nor I are welcome."

"Anaïs' home," I said.

Tristan nodded. "Which is why I know some of his plans. Angoulême thinks he can control Roland and that he can get rid of me and put my brother on the throne of Trollus. And if he were to succeed he, Angoulême, would be king in all but name."

"So, why don't you tell your father about Angoulême's plot?" I demanded.

Tristan shook his head. "Because I don't have proof. And neither does he, so we exist in a sort of stalemate. Or at least we did," he added weakly.

I felt sick. "I played right into his hand, didn't I? If I hated you, like I was supposed to, I wouldn't have cared about Anaïs. I reacted just as he suspected I would. I've put everything at risk."

Tristan grimaced. "Yes, but it isn't your fault. It's mine. I should have told you everything when I had the chance. I thought you'd be safer if I kept you in the dark. But I was wrong."

But I hadn't been in the dark. I had known that Angoulême wanted Tristan dead, and yet still I had let myself believe him.

Tristan interrupted my thoughts. "It doesn't matter anymore. We are here now and very near the limits of the rock fall. I'll take you the rest of the way out." He hesitated and then added, "If that is what you want."

I opened my mouth, planning to say that I would like that very much indeed, but the words wouldn't come out. He was giving me the choice. Here he had the opportunity to be rid of me for good and he was letting me choose what I wanted to do.

"Won't you be in a great deal of trouble if you don't bring me back?"

"Very likely. But that's my problem, not yours."

The thought of anything happening to him terrified me, and knowing that it would be because of my actions made me ill. If only I'd thought things through, if only I'd trusted him and waited, in less than a year Tristan would have been king and I'd be free to go. Of course, he should have trusted me, too.

"You must decide, Cécile. My father's soldiers will catch up to us soon enough, and your moment to flee will have passed. After this, another chance will not be forthcoming."

Decide, decide. I closed my eyes and tried to muster up the courage to lay my cards on the table. I was afraid if I told him how I really felt that he would laugh at me; that maybe all these apparent confessions were part of a cruel game that I wasn't clever enough to discern. But I couldn't leave without knowing. I couldn't spend the rest of my life with his emotions hovering in the back of my mind without knowing why he was giving me this choice. Always wondering if maybe, just maybe, he had wanted me to stay.

I could feel his anticipation thick upon my mind, but that didn't help me know what answer he wanted.

"What do you want me to do?" I asked.

He shook his head. "This is your decision."

"I know." I dug my fingernails into the rock. "But before I make it, I need to know how you feel. About me."

His eyes met mine and I trembled at the intensity of his expression. "Don't you know?"

I shook my head.

From his pocket, he pulled out a necklace and handed it to me. It was my mother's pendant. "You didn't do it."

Tristan shook his head. "You asked what was better, closure or hope... And I think hope is better." His eyes grew distant. "Forcing your family to believe you were dead felt like admitting defeat – like we were conceding before the battle any hope they might see you again. I just couldn't do it."

I blinked back tears. "Are they still looking for me… or do they think…"

"Not every day; but as often as they can, they still search the hills. They haven't given up on you."

"Thank you," I whispered. Lifting the necklace, I watched the pendant turn, reflecting Tristan's light in little sparks. "You kept it in your pocket the whole time, then?"

"My hoarding tendencies manifest themselves in strange ways. It was the only thing that was yours." He smiled – not one of his false ones that didn't reach his eyes, but one that lit up my heart. "I noticed you wearing it when you arrived, and again that first night you sang. I watched you standing in the glass gardens, and I thought you were the most beautiful girl I'd ever seen. A flame in the long dark night."

"I'm not…" I started to argue, but stopped. Tristan couldn't lie. Reaching up, he fastened the pendant around my neck. The gold was warm.

"Most people would have given up a long time ago – just curled up in a corner and waited to die, but you've lived every day. I don't think I've ever met anyone so tenaciously optimistic." Carefully, as if he feared I might still swat his hand away, he reached out and brushed a slimy lock of hair away from my face. "I want you to stay, Cécile, but I'm afraid staying will only bring you misery."

My knees were trembling so badly that I had to reach out and rest a hand on his shoulder lest I topple off the edge and ruin the moment. I understood now why trolls bound themselves to each other, despite the risks it carried. To feel so much myself and have him feel the same – it was like drowning, only I had no desire to seek the surface. Tristan's hands circled my waist and I willingly let him pull me closer, lost in the moment. Then something over my shoulder caught his attention.

I saw his eyes widen in shock just before his light winked out.

Sluag.

Tristan jerked me round to the far side of him and pushed me backwards along the ledge, but it was too late. Something slammed into him and he fell backwards, knocking both of us off the ledge and into the pool below. The impact of hitting the slime knocked the wind out of me with a wicked slap that made every inch of me scream in pain. Out of range of the creature's ability to nullify magic, Tristan's light flickered back into existence long enough for me to see the white bulk of the sluag squeeze out from behind a rock and slide down the incline towards us.

BAROOOM!

"Cécile!"

Tristan dragged me backwards, but Luc's skeleton tangled in my skirts, holding me in place. The light went out and the soft bulk of the creature collided with me, driving me beneath the surface of the pool. Sharp pieces of gold dug into my back and the slimy body of the sluag pressed against my face, holding me down. I pummeled my fists against it, but they sunk deep into the monster's soft form with little effect. My lungs burned, and panic flooded my veins. Snatching up a piece of bone, I jammed it into the creature's soft hide.

The sluag shrieked and squirmed its bulk off me. Grasping hands caught hold of my cloak, helping me struggle upwards and pulling me back as I gasped in breaths of precious air. Tristan's light flickered faintly, growing in strength as we struggled out of the sluag's range. I kept my eyes fixed on it, watching it squirm its way onto a rocky perch where it sat, whip-like tongue flickering in and out. It had no more eyes or face than a garden slug, but I swore it watched us with the amused expression of a cat watching a mouse.

"Hurry, Cécile!" Tristan had me by the hand and was dragging me through the tunnels, but I kept my head turned back, watching the sluag as we rounded a corner. "Why isn't it attacking? What's it waiting for?"

"For me to die."

My head snapped back around and only then did I see the blood running down his hand, dripping onto the ground. "No," I whispered, and every inch of me grew cold as I remembered Élise's words: *their venom is deadly – even to one of us.* "You can't die."

"It can't be helped," he said. "There is nothing that can be done." I could see the tightness in his face, feel the fear and anguish in his heart, but I knew he'd never admit any of it. Anger at his fatalism drove away my terror. Trolls did little to help their injured, leaving it up to fate to determine whether the victim lived or died. But I wasn't a troll. I'd seen village wise women pull men back from the brink of death with herb-lore. More importantly, I'd seen my father save one of our neighbors from a viper bite that would surely have killed him untreated.

"Stop," I said, pulling Tristan to a halt.

"Have you lost your mind?" Tristan hissed.

I pulled up his sleeve, exposing the puncture wound. It was small, but already the skin around it was inflamed. Tearing a strip of fabric from my cloak, I tightly bound his arm beneath his elbow. "It's just like a snake-bite," I whispered. "Just like a snake-bite." Taking a deep breath, I raised his arm to my mouth and sucked on it hard like I'd seen my father do. The faintly metallic taste of blood filled my mouth, but it was foul with the bitterness of poison.

Tristan jerked his arm away, horror on his face. "Do you want to die too?"

I spat the noxious mixture onto the ground and gripped his arm again. "This is how it's done. It's just like a snakebite." I repeated the process until all I could taste was blood, but still the inflammation grew. "Knife," I ordered. He pulled one from his boot and handed it to me.

"This will hurt," I warned, and then made a series of cuts around the wound and left it to bleed freely. Tristan didn't flinch, but I could feel that he was in more pain than the knife cuts warranted. "You need to stay still now," I said. "Wait for them to find us."

On the tail of my words came the soft swish, swish from the tunnel behind us. The sluag was on the move, tracking its injured prey.

"I don't think that's advisable," Tristan said, and he pressed the palm of his hand against his forehead.

I felt his dizziness and pain like it was my own and rested a hand against the wet rock to keep my balance. "Perhaps not."

"We need to move," Tristan responded, refusing to look at me. "There isn't much time."

It did not take long for me to discover how Tristan had moved with such speed through the labyrinth. Magic flooded out ahead of us as we ran, making the uneven tunnels smooth as a marble corridor and springy as a grassy meadow. Where I had had to climb up and down piled boulders, he created glowing platforms that bridged the gaps. Even the spots where I had to drop to my hands and knees were made easier by the free-floating orbs that lit our path. He did not pause or even glance at the path markers, his knowledge of these tunnels ingrained through years of exploration, or perhaps by some knowledge innate to his kind. But Tristan was right: we did not have much time.

The venom was in his blood, coursing through his veins, and slowly, but surely, numbing his senses. He stumbled with greater frequency and his breath came in great heaving gasps whereas I was barely winded. And I could feel the haze in his mind, the growing confusion. He slowed to a walk, which quickly became a stagger. Then, to my horror, he fell to his knees.

"Tristan!" I swung his uninjured arm around my shoulder and tried to pull him to his feet, but he pushed me aside. His normally hot skin was cold and clammy to the touch, and his hand trembled in mine.

"Here." He beckoned to the orb of light and it floated close to us. "Take it," he said.

"I can't!" I said, but at the sight of his pained expression, I reached out and sunk my fingers into the warm power. To my amazement, it didn't flow away as it usually did, but maintained its form and followed my hand.

"Take it and go," he whispered, slumping against me.

I eased him down so that he lay with his head on my lap. "I'm not leaving you to be eaten by a giant slug," I said, hoping the false confidence in my voice would overpower the fear he must have known I felt.

"You have to go. The sluag will not stop until it finds us."

"Let it come."

"Cécile!" I could hear the frustration in his voice, weak as it was. "There is no sense in you staying. No one survives a sluag sting for long – I'm going to die. You need to get out of the labyrinth, past the barrier of the curse, and as far away as you can run. The distance will make it hurt less for you when my light goes out."

A sob tore its way out of my throat. "Marc will find us before the sluag."

"Even worse." Tristan's voice was barely audible now. "You will serve no purpose with me gone. My father will have you killed, and he won't be as quick about it as the sluag." He groaned in pain and a tear rolled down my filthy cheek. "Take the light and try to get out while you still can."

"I'm not leaving you for that thing to eat while you're still alive," I whispered. "If it costs me my life, then so be it."

"Stubborn until the end..." He sighed softly. "Stay until I'm dead then, but promise me when it's over, you'll find a way out. Promise me you'll live."

Feeling his panic and fear was hard enough, but seeing it written in hard lines across his face was even worse. His militant self-control was slipping, and I could see the true magnitude of his terror. And still he was thinking of me.

"No," I said. "I won't promise anything, because that would mean giving up. You won't die, you won't die."

For a moment, Tristan's fear turned to anger. "This wasn't how it was supposed to go!"

"Then don't let it end this way." Never before had I felt such a pure sense of helplessness. Why couldn't I have the power to help him, to make Tristan well again?

"Cécile!" He writhed in pain, his grip grinding the bones in my hand together. I closed my eyes and images of the sluag assaulted me. I would be powerless to stop it. It would sting me and then turn on Tristan. My mind recoiled at the thought of me lying there, paralyzed by venom, but still conscious enough to watch the monster strip the flesh from his face.

"No," I whispered. "I won't let it happen." Pushing up his sleeve, I examined the cuts I had made. Not only had they not healed over with the preternatural speed at which trolls usually healed, they were bleeding profusely. I pressed my hand against them, trying to slow the flow, but crimson liquid seeped through my fingers and coated my hands.

Troll blood... blood magic.

Hands shaking, I tried to remember Anushka's incantations, muttering the half-remembered phrases. But nothing happened.

"Please work!" Desperately, I called upon every ounce of will I had and used it to pull the foreign power filling the blood seeping from his veins. "Live, live, live," I chanted. A wind rose, whistling through the tunnels. Every sound grew sharper and everything near me clearer to the eye. "Stop bleeding," I shouted, and beneath my hands, I watched in amazement as Tristan's wounds ceased to bleed and sealed over, leaving pale white scars in their place. My breath caught. "Tristan?"

His eyes remained closed. The seething pulse of his pain and delirium remained. The healed wounds were meaningless – I had done nothing to stop the progress of the venom. Desperately, I pulled power from all around me: from the rocks beneath my knees; the stagnant air in my lungs; and the water dripping down onto my face. I felt full, flush, but it was all for naught, because the power refused to acknowledge Tristan. He did not belong to this world.

A racking sob tore through me – for a moment, it had seemed I had all the power in the world at my fingertips. But I could not help him, so it meant nothing. I was powerless.

Gently, I rested the ball of light on his chest, hopeful that the magic would warm him as it did me. I saw it then. Like blight on a grapevine, the silver leaves tattooed across my fingers were tarnishing at their edges.

Tristan was dying.

CHAPTER 27
Cécile

My tears dripped onto Tristan's face, and I wiped them away, exposing streaks of pale skin through the grime. I'd never touched him, not really, and now I realized that I might never have another chance. With one finger, I gently traced the solid line of his jaw, the slight dimple in his chin. His hair was soaked and plastered against his forehead and I pushed it back, the strands like fine silk. He looked younger, his dark brows relaxed from their usual furrow of concentration and his black lashes resting softly against his cheeks. And on my fingers, the silver vines grew progressively darker with every passing moment.

"I'm sorry," I whispered. But what good were my regrets? He was dying because of me. He had ventured into the labyrinth to save me, pulled me out of the way of the sluag's stinger and taken the blow himself. The anguish of regret was so strong, I very nearly groaned with the pain of it. Why had I let Angoulême goad me? Why hadn't I seen that Tristan was just putting on an act the way he always did? Why didn't I remember that I would have felt any indiscretion through our connection? He hadn't asked for this union any more than I had and still he'd placed my life above everything he'd worked for. I'd ruined everything and still he'd come for me when I'd needed him the most. I'd told myself to make the most of my life in Trollus, but instead I'd made the least of it. The worst of it! Because of me, the only other person fighting for my freedom was dying.

BAROOOM!

I shuddered at the noise, but the sound of the sluag approaching filled me with resolve. Tristan's life might be fading away, but he would have no chance at all if he ended up in the sluag's belly. I was all that stood between him and the worst of deaths, and I needed to think of a plan fast.

Carrying him was out of the question – he was nearly twice my size and even if I could lift him, there was no way I could outpace the monster. Gently easing Tristan's head down onto the stone, I pulled the knife out of his boot and examined it. If only he'd had his sword, or better yet, one of the long sluag spears. If I'd any skill at it, I might hit the sluag's little brain with a lucky shot. With a bow and arrow, I certainly could have managed it, but such speculation did me about as much good as spitting into a headwind.

I got to my feet and set about exploring my surroundings, Tristan's light clinging to my fingers. I couldn't kill the sluag or drive it off, but maybe I could hide from it long enough for Marc to find us.

Careful not to wander too far from Tristan, I searched through the fallen rocks. I quickly found what I was looking for: a tight sliver of space opening into a small chamber beyond. It was a dead end. The sluag wouldn't be able to sneak around behind me, but it also meant I would be trapped until the trolls found us. If they found us.

Running back to Tristan, I bent down to check his breathing. I was still flooded with the feel of him, but it made me feel better to check. His chest rose and fell and I could feel a faint pulse at his throat.

"Please don't go," I whispered to the light as I let go of it. Hooking my arms under his, I slowly dragged him in the direction of our hidey-hole. The light trailed after us.

BAROOOM!

It was closer now. Close enough that I could hear the swish-swish of its body sliding over the rocks. I had to hurry, but Tristan was both heavy and unwieldy.

Swish-swish.

Sweat dribbled down my back to join the filth soaking my dress. My heart hammered from terror and exertion, but with a final heave, I reached the mouth of the hole.

"Come on, Cécile!" I urged myself on.

Swish-swish.

My narrow shoulders fit easily enough, but Tristan's stuck and every muscle in my body screamed with the effort of turning him sideways and pulling him through.

BAROOOM!

It was nearly upon us. I pulled hard and we tumbled into the little chamber. I hurriedly dragged him to the far end and covered him with my cloak. Falling to my knees, I tucked the wet fabric around him and gently kissed his forehead. His breathing was ragged and though my own life was very much in jeopardy, my fear was for him.

"Please don't die," I whispered. "Don't leave me now, Tristan. Please, if you can hear me at all, fight this. Don't let this be the end." I pressed my mouth to his, feeling the softness of his lips beneath mine. "I love you," I whispered. "I know I shouldn't. I know I'm not supposed to, but I can't seem to help myself."

BAROOOM! The sluag slammed up against the mouth of the hole and I screamed, my voice echoing against the rock. Spinning around, I watched in terror as the creature's long stinger lashed into the chamber. It fell only an arm's length short, but I kept myself between the stinger and Tristan, for all the good I'd do.

The stinger whipped out again and again, always falling just short. The sluag shrieked in fury and I screamed back at it, angry and afraid.

"Go away," I shouted. "Get you gone, you filthy bugger!"

Picking up a loose rock, I hurled it out through the crack and was rewarded with a wet thud. I threw another rock and another and when there were none left at hand, I screamed every insult and curse word I had ever heard at the creature. It tossed its bulk against the rocks and shot out its stinger, but it could not reach us.

My supply of rocks and insults exhausted, I bent down to check on Tristan and noticed the fine layer of dust and bits of rock coating him and me both. I looked up nervously and watched a cloud of dust rain down every time the sluag slammed against the rock. They were mindless creatures. Bent on the sole purpose of catching its prey, it might pull the rocks down upon us all.

Then over the racket the sluag was making, I heard a voice: "Tristan! Cécile!" It was Marc.

"Here!" I screamed. "We're in here!"

"We've found them! Over here!" It was the sound of many voices and I breathed a sigh of relief. We were saved.

The sluag retreated from the entrance at the sound of the approaching trolls, but there was no chance for it to escape. The sound of its dying screams were deafening as dozens of long steel spears pierced its body. On hands and knees, I watched it collapse into a writhing heap before growing still. Marc's face appeared in the entrance to our hiding spot. "Cécile?"

"Marc," I croaked, my voice hoarse from yelling. "Tristan's hurt."

His eyes flickered past me to Tristan's still form and his face paled. Pushing his way in, Marc knelt next to the Prince. "What happened?"

"The sluag stung him. We were running from it and then he…" A sob choked off the rest of my words.

Marc leaned his head against the wall and I could see the sorrow written across his fractured face. "Then he's dead."

"He isn't!"

Angry eyes turned on me. "He will be soon enough. No one survives sluag venom."

I cupped Tristan's cheek and felt a whisper of breath against my hand. "You don't know that."

Marc grasped my arm and shoved me back. "He's dying because of you!"

There was murder in his eyes and I shrank away from the closest thing I'd had to a friend in Trollus.

"This is your fault, Cécile," he hissed. "He would have done anything for you, and this is how you repay him!" Power shoved me backwards like two hands pushing against my chest. "Get away from him."

"You have no right to keep me from him," I said. Immediately I knew I'd gone too far. Power pushed me out of the hole and I tripped, landing half on the body of the sluag. Marc came after me and I scrambled to my feet. He raised a hand to hit me, and I ducked my head under my arm and waited for the blow. It never came. I looked up and saw Marc standing frozen, his face twisted in fury. "I promised never to harm you," he choked out. His eyes flicked to Vincent. "But you didn't."

The big troll shook his head sadly. "If he lives, he won't forgive us for hurting her," he said. "And frankly, I couldn't forgive myself." Then he looked at me. "If he dies, her head won't stay on her shoulders for long."

"Take her back to Trollus," Marc snapped. He and several of the other trolls slid into the small chamber and moments later, they emerged with Tristan's limp form. Marc looked over at Vincent. "Mind she doesn't stab you in the back on the way."

I flinched, but said nothing.

I had dropped Tristan's ball of light when Marc pushed me, but it floated in my direction now. Grabbing hold of the magic, I held it up to my other hand and examined my tattoo. It was a dull grey now, but not black like those on Marc's hand. And I could feel Tristan, faintly, almost like when he was sleeping. He was still alive. I saw Vincent looking at my marks as well. "He won't die," I said.

Vincent nodded slowly. "For your sake, for all our sakes, I hope that is so." Then, with his iron fist locked around my arm, we made our way back to Trollus.

He left me alone with Zoé and Élise in the chambers where they had once prepared me for bonding. Neither spoke to me, but I could feel their anger and sorrow thick in the air. It suited my mood well.

It took three tubs full of bathwater to get the sluag stench off me, and I think they did it not for my comfort, but for their own. As they scrubbed my skin raw, I watched the grey marks on my hand grow darker, less metallic, and the feeling of Tristan in my mind grew fainter by the minute. Tears drizzled out of my eyes, but the girls wiped them away as though they were mere condensation from the bath.

I made no comment when they twisted my hair back into a severe knot or when they brought in a black silk mourning gown and laced the corset so tight I could barely breathe. They were acting like he was dead already, when I knew he wasn't. When they'd finished with me, I stood in front of the mirror. The woman looking back at me appeared haggard, a decade older than I was. Her blue eyes were dull and swollen red from tears and the corners of her mouth turned down. I turned away from my reflection and resumed my vigil, eyes fixed on my hand.

"You were supposed to be our salvation," Élise said. "We did everything we could to help you, and this is how you repay us? By trying to escape?"

I remained silent, refusing to look at her. There was nothing I could say.

"I can't decide if you're happy or sad that he's dead," Zoé said, and something inside me snapped.

"He's not dead!" I screamed, my hands balled into fists. "He's not dead," I repeated. Turning away from her, I fell to my knees and sobbed silently.

I was still on the floor when the guards came, and their rough hands lifted me and dragged my uncooperative form through the palace and into the open air. I looked up only when I felt the mist from the river hit my face and saw thousands of trolls standing all around, their eyes fixed on me. It was eerily similar to my wedding day, except this time I stood alone. And in place of an altar, there stood a guillotine.

Tristan's father walked away from the cluster of noblemen, managing to carry himself in a stately manner despite his bulk. His eyes were puffy and red, but when he stopped in front of me, I saw that his cheeks were dry.

He cleared his throat. "There is nothing to say other than I would kill you a thousand times for what you have done, were it possible." I said nothing. "Because of you," the King continued, "the house de Montigny is ended. We've ruled Trollus for nearly fourteen hundred years, and it is finished. Because of you!"

Anger rose up inside me. He cared nothing for Tristan his son, only for Tristan the heir. His dismay was not for the loss of his child, but for the loss of power and glory. I rose up to my full height and glared at the King. "If that's all you care about, then it's a good thing you have two heirs!"

"Roland isn't Tristan!" the King screamed at me.

"Kill her!" someone from the crowd shouted.

"She's a traitor!" It was the half-bloods who screamed this – accusing me not of treason against the king and crown, but against their leader and their cause.

"I'm sorry," I pleaded. "I didn't mean for this to happen."

A grime-coated miner spat in my direction. "Liar," he screamed. "Traitor! You killed him!"

My cheeks burned with fury. "Tristan isn't dead…" The word froze on my lips as a searing pain tore through me. I fell to my knees, retching, and heard the crowd moan, but it barely registered through the agony. It was as if my heart had been torn from my chest and all the rest of my body burned from its absence. I screamed and screamed, and then the pain fled. I was empty. There was nothing.

"He is now," the King whispered. "His death is written across you."

I couldn't respond. I couldn't speak. All I knew was that I could not live like this, with half of me missing. Raising my head, I stared up at the burning circle of light high above. The lone beam of sunlight that shone into Trollus. Then I leaned forward and lay my head in the guillotine, closed my eyes, and waited.

One heartbeat. Two. Three.

Life and emotion filled the void, the shock of its return nearly as great as its loss. My eyes snapped open. "Tristan," I gasped.

The guillotine clicked and the blade fell.

CHAPTER 28
Cécile

"Wait!"

A sharp sting burned at the base of my neck, but all did not go black, as I had expected. For a long moment, I was certain that my severed head had decided to live on for a few extra torturous seconds; but it soon became clear that my neck was still in one piece. I could feel the razor sharp edge of the guillotine cutting into my flesh and the hot trickle of blood running down my shoulder. Something had stopped the blade just in time.

"What is the meaning of this?" the King shouted.

"Her hand, look at her hand. The darkness is fading." It was Marc's voice shouting and I smiled, already knowing in my heart what had happened. He, along with several others, approached the dais to inspect my fingers.

"He's alive," I whispered, looking up at Marc. No one seemed inclined to move the blade and I was afraid if I moved much against the edge that I would do myself in.

Marc gave a half-nod. "Someone run to the palace. We need to be certain." He hesitated and then added, "Before we finish this."

"You'll be lucky if I don't take your head off for this interruption, Marc," the King shouted, but there was relief in his voice.

Marc turned. "If Tristan is still clinging to life, killing her will surely push him over the edge. He won't survive the shock."

"Wait, wait!" This time it was a woman's voice calling from a distance. "He's alive. Tristan's alive." The Queen's voice. The crowd parted, and she ran towards me with surprising speed, skirts pulled up to her knees. The blade rose, and a hand grabbed the back of my dress, pulling me down the steps and out of harm's way.

"Tristan's alive, and you will leave that girl alone if you know what's good for you, Thibault." The tiny Duchesse was speaking now and shaking her tiny fist at the King. "Leave her be!"

"Why should I?" the King said, his voice like ice.

"Kill her and you doom us all."

The crowd slowly grew silent as her words passed in a wave through their ranks.

"Kill her, and you lose the chance of ever seeing the light of day. Of ever regaining Trollus's previous glory."

The King grew still. The crowd fell silent.

"So be it," he said. "She lives." His eyes met mine, and he softly added, "For now."

A servant ran up. "Prince Tristan is asking for the lady Cécile."

"Then it is a good thing her head is still attached," the Duchesse muttered. "Come with me, girl."

I nodded and stayed close to her arm as we walked back towards the palace, though it took every ounce of self-control to keep from running to Tristan. It would certainly have been easier if I'd hurried, because our stately pace only gave me time to think; and with thinking came doubt. What if I had imagined it all? Not the sluag and Tristan nearly dying – I knew I wasn't delusional – but what about the emotions I'd felt from him in the moments before the sluag attacked? Had he really felt as strongly as I remembered, or were my feelings and desires coloring my memory?

I could feel his anger. What if that was the reason he'd asked for me? Not to profess his love as I might wish, but to tell me that he hated me for what I'd done and that he wanted me gone? Exiled from Trollus and his side forever.

We turned down the corridor leading to Tristan's rooms and, ahead of us, the door flung open. Anaïs stalked out of the room and slammed it shut. Turning up the corridor, she froze when she saw the three of us blocking her way. I noted her streaked cosmetics and the handkerchief clutched in her hand, but all of that was quite secondary to the fury written across her face. There was murder in those kohl-rimmed eyes, and I was certain that if I'd encountered her alone, she'd have killed me where I stood.

She dropped into a deep curtsey. "Your Graces. My lady."

"Anaïs." The Queen inclined her head.

"You'll be pleased to know that His Highness is recovering quite remarkably." Anaïs straightened, and I had to give her credit for regaining her composure so quickly. "By your leave." She hesitated only a moment and then spun around and strode off in the opposite direction.

"Wonderful news!" the Queen exclaimed, blissfully ignorant of the tension between Anaïs and me. It wasn't lost on the Duchesse, though she said nothing.

The three of us hurried into Tristan's room, where he lay in the center of his bed, propped up on a pile of cushions. The frown furrowing his brow disappeared at the sight of us. His eyes locked on me and I felt relief course through him and me both. He wasn't angry with me.

"Did they harm you?" He tried to push himself up on the pillows, but his mother scurried over and pushed him back down. "You must rest, Tristan." She set to fluffing the pillows and tucking the blankets tightly around him like a swaddled baby.

He seemed annoyed at being fussed over, but he smiled at her anyway. "Thank you, Mother."

Then he looked at me, taking in my severe hairstyle, the black dress, and, I realized far too late, the blood that dripped from the cut on the back of my neck. I should have cleaned it up before coming. "I'm quite well," I assured him. "Fit as a fiddle."

One of his eyebrows rose. "You are not suited to deception, my lady."

The light Tristan had left with me when he thought he was dying chose that moment to zip over to the bed, flying in dizzying circles around its patient twin hovering over Tristan's head. The result was a riot of light and shadows that caught everyone's attention.

"It stayed with you this whole time? It should have dissipated hours ago," Tristan said, clearly amazed. In truth, I hadn't even noticed.

"It isn't possible for a human to control troll magic," the Duchesse said, tapping her chin with her index finger and watching the lights reflected in the mirror on the wall.

"Oh, I don't control it," I said. "It's here because it wants to be."

"Wants to be! Bah!" She made a dismissive gesture with her hand.

Tristan didn't seem to be paying any attention to us. "Stop that!" he said firmly to my light. It ignored him and continued to fly madly around the room like a disobedient child. "You there," he said, pointing at it. "Come here." With obvious reluctance, the light slowly drifted over and landed on his outstretched hand. "It's a bit of my magic," he said. "But there's something changed about it." He stared into the depths of the light. "It seems content to maintain its purpose."

"What purpose?" I asked, confused.

"To light your path." The glowing ball lifted off his hand and floated over to me.

The Duchesse had a look of satisfaction on her face, but she made no comment.

Tristan cleared his throat. "I'd like to speak to Cécile. Alone."

After the Queen left, I walked over to stand next to the bed. My fingers played nervously with the blanket, while Tristan silently scrutinized my appearance.

"Never a dull moment since you arrived in my life."

"I'm sorry," I whispered. "I never meant for this to happen."

His hand closed over mine, our fingers interlocking. His skin was warm again, burning with the internal flame of magic. "It wasn't your fault. No matter what Marc said to you, it wasn't your fault."

I raised my head. "How do you know what he said? You were unconscious."

"No. I wasn't." He stared up at the ceiling, his thumb tracing circles over the back of my hand. "I couldn't move, couldn't open my eyes or speak, but I could hear. And I could feel."

"How horrible!"

"Not entirely." His mouth quirked up into a half-smile.

"Oh." I flushed down to the tips of my toes. "Oh, dear."

"And my repertoire of foul language is much increased."

I clapped my hand over my eyes, embarrassed to the core. Then realization dawned on me. "Then you know..."

He nodded gravely. "That you used magic to heal me."

"And failed," I said, trying to keep the bitterness out of my voice.

Tristan held his arm up to the light, revealing scars that looked years old. "You didn't fail." His eyes searched mine. "I'd suspected for some time that you might have magic in your blood. Why didn't you tell me?"

"I didn't know," I whispered. "That was the first time I tried, and I couldn't even get her spells right. The poison didn't leave."

"Her?"

I swallowed hard. Letting go of his hand, I retrieved the grimoire from its hiding place and handed it to him. It was clear from his expression that he recognized it. "You can open this?"

"Yes."

"Does it tell you anything about breaking the curse?"

"No, but there are spells to use on trolls," I admitted, watching as he relaxed fractionally at my answer.

Tristan nodded and handed the grimoire back to me. "Keep it hidden," he said. "No one must know about this."

I stored the book back in its spot in the garderobe, and came back over to the bed. I felt nervous. Would knowing I was a witch change the way Tristan felt about me? I could hardly blame him if it did, given what Anushka had done to them. "Are you angry?" I asked softly.

He shook his head. "You saved my life, Cécile. Not many people would have had the courage to do what you did." He sighed. "They brought me back to Trollus. I could hear them talking about what my father intended to do to you – they were acting as if I were already dead, even though they knew I wasn't. And there wasn't anything I could do about it. I could barely breathe and then..." He broke off, his eyes growing distant as though he were trying to remember something. "And then the venom's power over me lifted. It was a close thing." His gaze rested on my throat. "Too close."

I felt magic brush across my cheek and hairpins fell to the ground all around me. Magic teased my hair out of its knot and it cascaded down my back, still damp from my bath.

"You left a part out," I said, my voice shaking. "The part where you died."

Tristan's eyes closed. "I'm fine now."

"Now," I said, my whole body shaking. "But not before! I felt you die. It felt like my heart had been torn from my body. It felt like…" I struggled to keep calm. "You were gone," I said, misery filling me.

"But I'm fine now," he said, voice firm. He pulled on my hand, and I willingly clambered onto the huge bed and tucked myself into the crook of his arm, head on his chest. The spot I had wanted to be in for so long: I could scarcely believe I was there now, with Tristan, in his arms.

"How?"

"How what?"

"How did you come back to life? How is such a thing possible?"

He was quiet for so long, at first I thought he'd fallen asleep. "Someone with a great deal of power did me a favor," he said finally. "I owe her a very great debt."

I started to ask him who, but an icy wind smelling of frost blew through the room. A woman's voice whispered, "It is not for her to know. We have a bargain, you and I, Prince of the Accursed Ones."

My head went fuzzy, and I pulled a blanket up around us, pressing closer against Tristan to ward off the icy chill. What was it I had been thinking about? I couldn't remember.

Tristan gently stroked my back, and I listened to his heart beating strongly beneath my ear. But I couldn't relax. The King and most of the trolls hated me – the half-bloods most of all. I had jeopardized all of Tristan's plans and put lives at risk. I was supposed to be the key to the freedom of Trollus, but I was completely in the dark about what I was supposed to do. And to top it all off, I was fairly certain that Anaïs was plotting my murder for having stolen Tristan away from her.

I felt Tristan's exhaustion finally take over and he drifted off to sleep, but it was a long time before I was able to do the same. I could not hope for a long life if I remained a pawn constantly manipulated by those around me – learning to play Guerre had taught me that, if nothing else. I needed to take action, and soon. I began to form a plan, but eventually my mind grew heavy. I clung to Tristan as though it was our last moment together like this, which maybe it was. But there was nothing to be done about that now. Only the morning would bring answers.

When I woke many hours later, it was with a start. Dreams of sluag, darkness, and Tristan dying plagued my sleep. Again and again I'd relived the moment when death sliced through our bond like a scalpel through flesh. The loneliness, as though there was no one left in this world but me. I didn't know how anyone could survive it; what sort of strength it took to live on after the loss of the one you'd been bound to for years, decades even. I thought about the black lines tracing over Marc's hands, how he rarely removed the leather gloves hiding them and could not tolerate even the mention of her name.

My light had woken up with me, and it shone dimly as though it were still sleepy. In its glow, I gently traced a fingertip over the golden filigree inked across Tristan's left hand, more intricate and delicate than the finest lacework. Gold, because I was a child of the sun. The first human to ever be bonded to a troll, much less a troll prince.

Tristan sighed, his breath warm against my cheek. In his sleep, he'd curled around me, his arm tucked tight against my stomach. My perpetually cold feet were warm for once, tucked as they were against his shins. My body complained mightily as I extracted myself from his grip, but despite my attempts not to wake him, his eyes opened.

"You need to rest," I said. "You're exhausted."

"No time for it," he replied, crossing the room and quickly dressing. "I need to go make reassurances to a few individuals. And there is the tree."

"Can't it keep for one day?"

"Possibly, but I'd rather not risk it." He buckled on his sword. "Don't leave these rooms unless Marc accompanies you. Certain individuals misunderstand the cause of yesterday's events, and I don't want them going after you because of some misguided sense of loyalty." He kissed my cheek. "Try to stay out of trouble."

After he left, I tried to find ways to occupy myself in our rooms, but my mind wouldn't focus. So much had changed in so little time – going back to how things were before I'd fallen for Angoulême's trickery would be impossible.

Tristan was worried and upset, his uneasiness crawling down my spine like a spider. I wished I knew what was going on. What was he telling the half-bloods? Would they be able to forgive me for what had happened, or had I irreparably damaged my relationship with those who needed our help the most?

Tossing aside the novel I had been trying to read, I went through the doors and out onto the balcony, down the steps to the courtyard where my piano stood. The stack of music sat undisturbed on the bench, and after shuffling through it, I chose a lengthy piece and sat down. I had no great talent – my short fingers prevented that – but I played well within my limitations. I sat at the piano until my fingers ached, but I refused to sing. I would not call him. He would come to me when he was ready.

"You are a talented musician, but I must confess, I prefer to hear you sing."

The keys jangled harshly beneath my fingers and I froze. Slowly, I looked over my shoulder. The Duke d'Angoulême stood at the base of the stairs, his gold-tipped cane held horizontally between his hands. "Perhaps you'll sing for me, little bird."

I shook my head.

"Pity." He walked towards the piano, and I scrambled to my feet, wanting to keep some distance between us. Not that it would matter. If he'd come here to kill me, there wasn't much I could do to stop him.

"These are my private gardens," I said. "You have no right to be here."

"True." He ran a finger down the shiny surface of the piano. "But there isn't much you can do about it, is there?"

"What do you want?"

The corners of his mouth twisted up in a cold parody of a smile. "A great many things, Cécile, and I fully intend to have them." He picked up the delicate glass rose Tristan had given me, turning it over in his hands. "You caused quite the disturbance yesterday."

"That was your intention, wasn't it?"

"Indeed it was, although not in my wildest dreams did I expect it to turn out so well." He held up my rose as if to smell it, but his eyes were fixed on me. "Did you know that when an infant is born of half troll, half human blood, its magic never reaches half that of its troll parent? And if that child takes up with a human, the resultant child will have almost no magic to speak of. The fact of the matter is, if a child has less than one-eighth troll blood, it has no magic at all. It is as weak and unintelligent as a human, as susceptible to illness and injury."

I was silent. There was no mistaking his point.

"Magic," he continued, "is what makes us superior. Any act that diminishes it is an abomination."

"Except if such an act breaks the curse," I retorted, my anger rising. "Isn't that what you mean?"

"But it hasn't." He held out the rose. "So all you are is an abomination that has failed to serve any purpose."

The rose slipped through his fingers. I gasped, diving forward to catch it before it smashed against the paving stones. At my touch, it blossomed a dusky pink.

"You two thought you'd fooled everyone, didn't you?"

I stared up at him from my knees, fear filling me.

"And perhaps you did. Everyone, that is, except me." Reaching down, he took hold of my arm and pulled me to my feet. "I confess, you played the part of a hellion-bride quite well. And Tristan, well the boy has been playing something he is not for so long that sometimes I wonder if he remembers who he really is." He paused, considering his words. "You would know by now that all children receive an identical education until they are ten years of age, at which time they are educated by their respective guilds. Builders' Guild, Artisans' Guild, Bakers' Guild, Miners' Guild, and so on and so forth."

"Make your point, Your Grace." I tried to jerk my arm out of his grip, but his hand was as implacable as a vice.

"My daughter, Anaïs, she isn't guild-educated. No, I saw early in her life that she had a mind fit for a particular purpose. She is military educated, you see. She is strategic, ruthless, loyal, but…" He sighed. "She is still female – her emotions make her weak."

I fought to keep fury from rising to my face, but it was difficult.

The Duke leaned on his cane. His position and the way he watched my movements reminded me of a vulture. "Her emotions are what betrayed her. For weeks, she has sobbed herself to sleep every night, and Anaïs is not a girl prone to such behavior. There could be only one cause – that her dear Tristan had abandoned her for another girl. His wife."

I scowled. "That isn't what you said yesterday, Your Grace. Unless, of course, you were lying?"

His laughter echoed through the courtyard, mocking me from every corner. "Is that what I said? Are you sure?"

Even though I already knew the truth, my heart still sunk to know how thoroughly he had played me. Like a finely tuned instrument.

"A wise man once wrote that the truth spoken may not be the truth you think you hear. I would have thought you'd learned that by now, little bird."

"Leave her alone, Angoulême."

The soles of Marc's boots smacked against the stairs as he leapt down them two at a time. Striding across the courtyard, he stepped between the Duke and me. "He doesn't want you anywhere near her."

"I haven't harmed her in any way. I am well aware of His Majesty's laws."

"That doesn't mean you don't intend to." To my amazement, Marc shoved Angoulême backwards. "Leave, now."

The Duke's face darkened. "You dare lay a hand on me, you twisted wretch! I outrank you. In more ways than one."

"I'm under Tristan's orders not to let you anywhere near the Lady Cécile, and last time I checked, Your Grace, the heir to the throne outranked you. In more ways than one."

I felt the air around me grow hot, their magic manifesting and drawing together. "I'm not afraid to die, Angoulême," Marc said softly. "Are you?"

"You think you can best me, boy?"

Marc laughed. "No, but I think I can hold you back long enough for Tristan to get here. And I know he can best you. He'll tear your body into so many pieces that what's left won't amount to more than a smear of blood on the street."

Angoulême paled. "He wouldn't dare."

"Are you sure enough to tempt fate?" Marc's voice was chilly.

Without another word, the Duke spun on heels, hurrying up the steps and out of sight.

I tried to calm my racing heart. "He won't forgive you for this," I said.

"I'll add it to the list of things he'll never forgive me for," Marc muttered. "Are you all right?"

"Fine – I think he was just trying to scare me. And send a message to Tristan."

"He was expecting it." Marc shoved his hands in his pockets and stared silently at my piano for a long moment before speaking. "Cécile, I want to apologize for what I said to you in the labyrinth. How I behaved. It's just that…"

I held up a hand. "There is nothing to forgive." Slipping my arm through his, I sighed. "Let's walk. I need to be away from this space."

We wandered aimlessly through the glass gardens, which never ceased to amaze me: the detail blown into each plant, the thorns on the rose bushes, the pinecones and seedpods artistically scattered beneath the trees, the tiny drops of glass dew suspended beneath the tips of leaves. Unlit, they were a thing of beauty, but flooded with troll-light, they were magical, ethereal even. "How long did it take to create?" I asked, bending down to look at a gardenia that was so realistic, I half expected to smell its sweet perfume when I inhaled.

"Three hundred and thirty-seven years."

I smiled at his troll-like precision.

"Why didn't they use color? I've seen it in other glassworks in Trollus."

"You would have to ask someone in the Artisans' Guild, but if I were to speculate… it would be because they knew it would be a pale imitation of the real thing."

"Or perhaps they couldn't remember the colors," I said, closing my eyes and trying to visualize fields of green grass and vibrant wildflowers. Already it seemed something from another life.

"Perhaps."

"Don't you ever wish you could see it, Marc? Stand in the ocean and feel the water swirl around your knees? Feel the blast of winter snow coming off the mountains or the scorching heat of the summer sun? To walk through a field of golden wheat just before harvest, or gallop through a meadow sweet with the smells of spring?"

I sat on one of the stone benches scattered throughout the garden, the weight of memory heavy upon me. "Don't you ever dream of it?"

Marc looked away so that I could only see his profile, so handsome on its own. So like his cousin's.

"No," he said. "I don't dream of that."

"What do you dream of?"

His shoulders jerked as if I had slapped him.

"Pénélope." His voice rasped over her name like he hadn't said it in a very long time. "Every night. Every time I close my eyes." He sat heavily on the bench next to me, head in his hands.

Gently, I took his left hand and pulled off the leather glove he always wore. An inky black pattern scrolled across his fingers, still beautiful in its own sad way. "Will you tell me about her?"

He nodded. "She is… was, Anaïs's elder sister. But the only similarity between the two was their beauty. Pénélope, she was sweet and kind. Quiet. We were friends as children. I don't remember when it was that I fell in love with her. Sometimes I think I loved her all my life." His voice cracked and his fingers tightened over mine. "I wanted to marry her, but my father refused because she… It had recently come to light that she had the bleeding condition. Such things pass on to children."

I sighed softly. I had not known such a thing existed until I came to Trollus, but since I had been here, two boys had died from it. Blood that would not clot – the slightest injury could be fatal.

"So we became lovers, and were so for some time. I was a fool to allow it," Marc continued. "Perhaps if I hadn't, she might still be alive."

"She got pregnant, didn't she?" I asked softly.

"Yes." He swallowed hard. "She was happy. She believed she would survive it, but I knew." His shoulders slumped. "I knew it would kill her." He rose to his feet. "Let me show you something."

He took me to a small open space surrounded by glass rosebushes. At the center stood an ornate fountain, but instead of water, a blue liquid glowed faintly within the basin.

"Liquid Shackles," I exclaimed, hurrying over to it.

"You've clearly been spending too much time with Tristan," Marc chuckled. "It's called Élixir de la Lune."

"That's much prettier," I said, looking into the basin. "Where does it come from?"

"Watch."

We waited for a long moment, then seemingly out of nowhere, a large droplet fell into the pool.

"Stones and sky," I muttered. "Where did that come from?"

"You have to look from the right angle," Marc said. "Like this." Bending over, he tilted his head to look upwards. I mimicked him, gasping at what I saw. It looked like a circular window hanging in the air, but it was only visible when viewed directly. Looking through it didn't show me Trollus – it was a window to somewhere else entirely. I could see part of a rocky cliff, a faint hint of glowing blue dampening it. As I watched, a droplet slowly formed and fell, dropping between our heads to land in the fountain.

"Where is that place?" I wondered aloud.

"The moon."

I blinked at him.

"What you are looking at is a tear in the fabric of the world." He straightened upright again. "This liquid is the magic that bonds the moon to the earth. We harness its power to bind the hearts of two trolls. Or a troll and a human."

Holding out my hand, I caught the next drip as it fell and went to taste it, the memory of its sweetness vivid in my mind. Marc caught my hand. "Only once in a lifetime." Tilting my hand, he let the drip fall into the pool.

"In the southern half of the labyrinth, there is a small opening where the sky shines through. Very few know of its existence. One night, I stole a vial of Élixir de la Lune and the key to the gate from my father – the Comte de Courville has been its guardian for generations – and took Pénélope into the tunnels. She was terrified of the small spaces and afraid a sluag would come upon us, but she came anyway. We bonded under the full moon."

"I bet you got in a lot of trouble for that."

A hint of a smile touched his face. "Yes. But there was nothing anyone could do. The bond cannot be undone by any power in this world or the next."

He was quiet for a long time, and I dared not break the silence.

"We were together for sixty-three glorious days. Then she miscarried. The child died. Pénélope died."

Tears streamed down my face, but Marc's eyes stayed dry. He had long since run out of tears for his pain, I thought. Pain I could well imagine because I'd felt it myself. "How did you survive it?"

"I didn't want to live. I wanted to throw myself from the highest precipice. Cut my heart out with a knife. Dash my brains against the rocks. Anything. I didn't think I could live without her."

"So how did you?" I remembered how easily I had knelt down before the guillotine, ready to die rather than to live without Tristan. And ours was a new love, not one built over a lifetime.

"Tristan was there with me when she died. The instant her heart stopped, he tied me up with magic so I couldn't move. I fought him with everything I had, but even at fifteen, he was one of the strongest living. In the few moments he took to sleep, it required both the twins to hold me. He kept me tied up for weeks, forcing me to eat and to drink when I tried to starve myself. When I'd finally calmed down enough, he made me swear that I would live. Said I was his best friend, and his family and he needed me alive."

We were quiet for a long time, Marc remembering and me trying to take in what he had just told me.

"Does it get better?" I finally asked. "The pain? The feeling that a part of you is missing?"

Marc shook his head. "You just learn to live with it."

Fresh tears flooded my eyes and dripped down to stain the silk of my skirts. He had known she would die and the pain it would cause him, but he had bonded her anyway. It was the most incredibly brave and selfless thing I had ever heard – a love story such as songs were written about.

"Would you do it again, knowing what you know now?"

He smiled, eyes growing distant. "In a heartbeat."

We sat in silence for a long time, both of us lost in our own thoughts.

"Cécile, you asked me if I dreamed of the outside."

I nodded.

"Everything I have known and loved has been in Trollus. All my memories are of here. I belong here, in the dark. But you..." He took my hand. "You don't belong here, Cécile. This place is no good for you – you belong in the sun. And so does he."

Coming around the fountain, Marc gently kissed my forehead. "You must find a way." Then he turned and walked away, leaving me to struggle with a burden that seemed to grow heavier by the hour.

"How much of that did you hear?" I asked, once Marc was out of earshot.

Tristan stepped out from around a glass fir tree. "A fair bit," he admitted.

"It's rude to eavesdrop."

"I know." He walked over to the fountain and looked through the window to the moon. "You were afraid before."

"Angoulême paid me a visit." I turned my back on the fountain and smoothed my skirts down. "Mostly, I think he wanted to boast about the trouble he had caused. It seems he has known for some time that our behavior was an act."

"That vile malignant pustule!" Tristan hissed. "He's a

craven, dog-breathed, interfering weasel of a man!"

I waited for him to finish cursing before asking, "So, do we carry on as before? Is there any point?"

"I don't know." Tristan rubbed a hand through his hair. "I don't think I can go back to it, though."

I nodded, feeling much the same way. "Another strategy then?"

"Yes." He was feeling conflicted about something. He opened his mouth and then closed it again.

I frowned. "And whatever it is you are not telling me, now is the time to come clean. We can't have any more secrets between us, Tristan."

He sighed heavily. "I know, but we can't talk about it here. Come with me. I want to show you something."

With a mind to evade my guards, Tristan led me to a well-hidden gate at the rear of the gardens and then down a meandering path to the river, where we crossed one of the many small bridges. It was a long walk down the valley, and by the time we reached the fork in the river, my feet were sore and aching. The soldiers guarding the River Road eyed us from the opposite bank, but despite our lack of escort, said nothing as we turned to follow the water branching off to the right.

The tunnel we entered was loud with the sounds of rushing water, and soon the faint glow of Trollus faded away, leaving only my little light and Tristan's larger one to illuminate our path.

"Where are we going?"

"You'll see."

We walked a little further until the cave walls fell away and Tristan pulled me to a halt. The river water spilled down an incline worn smooth by the current, but to either side of its banks it was terraced with large steps. The structure was entirely flooded with water, forming a large, dark lake.

"The parade grounds." Tristan's light shot away from us, growing brighter as it traveled until it shone like a minute sun.

"Stones and sky," I whispered, trying to take it all in. I'd never seen a building so huge. Designed like a vast, circular theatre, tiered seating rose up from all sides, the topmost barely illuminated by Tristan's magic.

"The history books say that before the Fall, you could see the stadium from leagues away. It held fifty thousand people at capacity, and is the largest structure we ever built. Most of the army was here when the mountain broke, which is the only reason it wasn't crushed. A great deal of magic and pride.

"When King Xavier broke the hole the waterfall came through, he had not estimated the level of flow accurately enough and the River Road couldn't contain the water. Trollus flooded and he ordered a path blasted through so that it would flood the parade ground instead. The water seeps through the rocks at the far end, but I doubt anything much larger than a river trout could make it all the way to the ocean."

Taking me by the hand, he led me down the steps to the edge of the dark lake waters. A small boat was tethered to a stone pillar, and once I was settled, he untied it and jumped in next to me. The gentle current soon caught hold of the boat, and we drifted slowly across the lake. It might have been romantic, if not for our mutual anxiety. He had brought me here for a purpose.

I arranged the piles of pillows around me, waiting for Tristan to speak.

"I come here when I want to be alone," he finally said. "To think, or to sleep, sometimes. And because it is a good reminder for me."

Light flared, illuminating the structure and revealing walls carved and painted with scenes of war. Time had faded many of the images, but not enough to completely wash away the pictures of destruction and carnage. I stared at the legions of troll soldiers, men and women, their faces beautiful but cruel. Toppled cities, piles of corpses, humans groveling at the feet of their troll overlords. Humans in chains, bleeding and emaciated, their eyes downcast and devoid of hope.

I shivered, wrapping my velvet cloak tightly around me. "I read those history books you showed me, Tristan. I am not unaware of your dark past, and I realize that you think the curse is the only thing preventing history from revisiting itself on the world."

"If you know all of this," he gestured at the walls, "then why does it feel like you are pushing me to find a way to break it. Bloody stones, Cécile, if we are set free, all you will be accomplishing is replacing those faces with those of your friends and family. Is that what you want?"

"Do you think I haven't considered that possibility?" I snapped, those exact images rising up in my mind. "Do you think it doesn't terrify me?" I forced my hands to relax from their clenched grip, smoothing my sweating palms against my skirts. "The difference between us, Tristan, is that I don't see the future as set in stone. It has been hundreds of years! The trolls who committed those crimes are long since dead, and I don't think those living today should have to continue to pay for their sins."

"No, you think they should be released to commit their own."

"Why are you so convinced they will?"

"Do you honestly believe that if the curse was broken tomorrow that my father would be any better than them?" Tristan pressed his fingers against his temples in obvious frustration. "The desire for vengeance might very well make him worse than his predecessors."

"I know that," I said, leaning towards him. "That's why we wait until he's dead. We wait until you are king. Because I know *you* wouldn't do those things."

Tristan looked away. "You overestimate the power I have over them. I cannot control the actions of every one of my people, and even if I could, I am not immortal. All it would take is one angry troll to slaughter hundreds of humans. Thousands even. And that blood would be on my hands, because I would be the one who unleashed him."

"But what if you made them all promise not to?" I asked. "A carefully worded oath that would check any chance of violence."

A sharp laugh was my answer. "And who would they make this promise to?"

"You?"

"Ah." His eyes flicked up to meet mine. "Do you know what the best way for a troll to get out of a promise is?" He didn't wait for my answer. "To kill the one you made the promise to. I'd be a walking target – I wouldn't last a week."

"Then make them promise not to!"

He shook his head. "Then they would kill you. And if I made them promise not to, one of them would pay a human to do it. Trying to control them that way doesn't work."

I winced and stared down at my hands, trying not to let the futility of his words take me over. "Regardless. I think you underestimate them," I said softly. "I know I haven't been here a long time, but from what I've seen, most trolls do not desire violence and oppression – they've seen enough of it and that's why they are fighting for change now. It wouldn't just be you keeping the few bad apples in check, it would be everyone."

"And if you're wrong?" Tristan made a sharp sound of disgust. "What then? The witch may well have saved humanity with her curse. And in breaking it, we may well be sacrificing it. If the curse is broken, your kind will lose the only power they ever had over mine."

"But at what cost?" I argued. "There has to be a better solution."

"The witch found the only solution. I will not undo her work."

I stared at him, aghast. "You make her sound like she is some sort of saint, but let me assure you, she is not." I searched his stony expression. "Why do you insist on believing trolls are so evil?" And why did he seem so bent on proving he'd been painted with the same malevolent brush?

Tristan twisted away from my scrutiny, and the lights surrounding us blinked out, leaving only my own to light our passage across the lake. "I think it is in our nature to be selfish, and in our capacity to do a great many evil things," he eventually said.

"There are evil humans," I argued. "And I don't see you suggesting we be all locked up in a cave."

"How much damage can one human do? Even the Regent of Trianon, who commands a great army, could do nothing compared to one of us. One troll could reduce Trianon to rubble and kill all of its inhabitants. His magic could protect him not only from blades, but stop a bullet shot directly at him. Not even a cannon ball has the force to break through our shields."

"But why would a troll want to do those things?" My words sounded pitiful in the face of his logic. He was right. Trolls had the potential for great destruction. But I did not see evil as part of their nature. "Not all of them are Angoulême!"

"But enough of them are," he said, gently. "And I can't execute hundreds of my people because of what I think they might do, Cécile. It's better this way. Once we gain control over Trollus and I can complete my plans, it will be possible to live here without magic. Perhaps as generations pass, the troll blood will become diluted enough by humans that the witch's curse will no longer be effective." He took my hands in his. "We are too powerful for this world – it is better that we remain caged."

"Too powerful for this world because you don't belong here," I said, pulling out of his grasp. "Maybe you should go back where you belong."

Tristan grew very still. "We can't. Otherwise I would send them all back in an instant."

My breath caught. I had not expected him to be frank. "Where?"

"Here, but not here. The in-between place of shadow and light."

"Well, that's certainly vague." I scowled at him. "Does it have a name?"

He nodded gravely. "It does, but it's better you don't know it. There is power in a name, and I'd rather not bring their attention down on us at the moment."

"Who?" I demanded. "Are there other trolls there?"

"Yes, although I suspect they'd object to being called so." He grimaced. "Humans were the ones to first call us trolls and we encouraged the moniker because it held no power over us. But it is not what we are."

I pressed my hands to my temples. "What are you then?"

Tristan shook his head. "It is best that you don't know."

Always with the secrets. It seemed he knew everything there was to know about me, but every time I peeled back a layer of his mystery, another lay beneath. It made me angry that he always kept me in the dark. He seemed to think it was for my own good, but I wasn't a child. I deserved the truth. Whether because of the look on my face or the anger he sensed from me, Tristan started talking.

"Those of our kind have always been able to move between worlds or wherever we pleased, and usually caused a fair bit of trouble wherever we went," he said. "Fourteen hundred years ago, my ancestors came to this place, the Isle de Lumière, and fell in love with the gold." He thought about it for a minute. "Love isn't even the right word. Obsession is probably better. But they could not bring it back with them. There is no gold in... where they were from."

Reaching into his pocket, Tristan pulled out a gold coin, turning it over in his hand. "Neither, as it turns out, was there iron. But here, there is iron in everything. In the water. In the plants and animals we eat. In your blood." His eyes flickered away from the coin to meet mine. "They discovered they had been here so long that they couldn't go back. The iron infecting their bodies wouldn't allow it. And in staying, they lost their immortality."

He pulled back the sleeves of his coat and shirt, revealing the scars on his arm – the only scars he had at all. "We are sensitive to iron still. Injuries caused by steel heal slowly. If they are bad enough, we can bleed to death."

I clapped a hand over my mouth. "I'm so sorry – I didn't know."

He grinned. "Despite what you might think, I'm not so vain as to prefer death over a few scars." But the smile was short lived, slipping from his face as he placed the coin back in his pocket. "Bound to this world, they set to conquering and enslaving its inhabitants. They were unstoppable until that fateful day that Anushka brought down the mountain."

I frowned. "What about all the trolls who weren't here? What happened to them?"

"Almost every troll was," Tristan said. "It was King Alexis's birthday. But those who were not found themselves inexplicably drawn back to Trollus until everyone was bound within its confines."

"And what about your nameless brethren from the nameless place you come from? Do they still visit this world?"

"They dare not. Coming to this world means getting caught up in the curse. But they are watching."

"Ah." I stared into the depths of the dark water, understanding sinking in. He wasn't protecting me by keeping the knowledge secret, he was protecting himself. From me. "So Anushka knew the real name of your kind. And because of what she did with it, you don't trust me enough to tell it."

"Yes." He said it so simply, the admission that he did not wholly trust me, and it stung.

"The sluag," I said, pushing aside the hurt. "They come from there too?"

He nodded. "Yes, although they are minions of the dark court. It's possible they followed us here on their own, but I suspect *she* sent them. And keeps sending them, which is why we can't seem to get rid of the damn things."

"She?"

He traced a finger around the hilt of the sword, obviously considering how much he wanted to tell me. "The in-between spaces is ruled by two courts. My many-times-great uncle is the King of Summer. *She* is the Queen of Winter."

A shiver ran through me, and I swore I could smell the scent of ice and frost on the air. A memory tickled the back of my mind, but for the life of me, I could not bring it into focus. "I assume she must remain nameless."

His fingers tightened around the hilt.

"You say there is power in a name, but I know yours and it doesn't seem to do me any good."

The silence hung long and heavy. But I could feel his guilt.

"Or not." My voice cracked and I clenched my teeth.

He sucked in a breath. "You know what I am called, but not the name that binds me."

I recoiled away from him to the far end of the boat, but it wasn't far enough. "Take me back," I hissed. "I've had enough of this – I don't care to be near you right now. I am tired of your deception."

"Cécile, please." He reached for me, but I clambered to my feet, causing the boat to rock wildly. "I'll swim back if you don't turn the boat around."

He withdrew his arm. "Please, Cécile, let me explain."

I watched him warily.

"If you knew my true name, you would have complete and utter control of me," he said softly. "You'd be able to compel me to do whatever you wished, and I would have no choice but to do what you ordered, whether that be to slaughter one or slaughter thousands. I would have no liberty – I would be your slave." He grimaced. "I'd be a weapon."

"And is that what you think of me," I replied, gripping the edge of the boat for balance. "That I would use you that way?"

His shoulders trembled. "I don't know!" The water of the lake surged and the boat plunged up and down, threatening to overturn.

I fell to my knees on the cushions. "Tristan!"

He jerked, looking around as if surprised at what he had done. Then he bowed his head. "I'm sorry." The water stilled, becoming as smooth as glass, the effect managing to be somehow more frightening than the waves. "I wish I was not what I am." His voice was twisted with anguish. "I wish I was not who I am. I wish I had met you in different circumstances, in a place far away from here, where there was no magic, politics, and deception. Somewhere where things could be different between us. I wish I was someone else."

He raised his head. "But I am what and who I am, and all the wishes in the world will not change that."

All my anger fled and I sank down onto the pillows, my fingers twisting the tassels on one of them as his words sank in. And with them came the understanding of the enormous responsibility that came not with his birth or position, but with *what* he was. And there was nothing that could change that. Yet still I had to ask. "How do you wish things were between us?"

One corner of his mouth turned up. "How can you ask that? You know how I feel – you feel what I feel."

I shook my head. "Sometimes it's hard to tell what emotions are mine and what are yours. There were times that I thought maybe you…" I sighed. "But then I'd decide it was my own wishful thinking."

"I did." His voice cracked and he swallowed hard. "From the beginning, I wanted you. But that first night – you looked at me like I was a monster. You were terrified that I was going to make you…" He broke off, his face tightening.

"And later." He sighed. "Being around you was the sweetest torture. I wanted to touch you, hold you, kiss you. I wanted all of you." His shoulders slumped. "But I was afraid of what would happen if I gave in to my desire. If I let myself love you."

"You were afraid it would break the curse?"

"That was only part of it." I barely heard him speak his voice was so quiet. "I was afraid… I am afraid of loving you, knowing that someday you will go and leave me here."

I shuddered, blinking fast to hold back tears. "That's not how it's supposed to be." It certainly wasn't how I'd imagined it. In my mind's eye, I had always thought of us gaining freedom together. Walking out into the sun together. But that wasn't what Tristan envisioned – he saw me leaving on my own and never turning back.

"There were so many things I wanted to show you," I whispered. "Things you have never seen."

"What sort of things?" he asked softly.

I thought about it for a moment. "I wanted you to see the world as it changes through the year, not the perpetual sameness it is here."

"Describe it to me? Tell me about winter."

I lay back on the silken cushions, closed my eyes, and remembered. "My father's farm is far enough up the mountain slopes that in winter, the snow can pile so deep that only trees and houses stick out. Tiny flakes of ice fall from the sky and melt on the tip of your tongue. On the most bitterly cold days, the air is at its clearest and you can see for leagues, all around."

The boat rocked as he shifted, my skirts pressing down against my legs as he knelt over me, his weight pressing my hips into the cushions. The clasp of my cloak opened with a click, the velvet soft against my skin as he pushed it back, baring my shoulders. His fingers trailed over my collarbone, leaving hot flames of desire in their wake. I felt his breath, warm against my throat, and I gasped, my heart beating so hard I was certain he could hear it. "And spring?" he whispered in my ear, his hair brushing softly against my cheek.

A smile curved over my lips. "The days get warmer, bit by bit. The sun shines. The snow starts to melt, and water runs in rivulets down the icicles hanging from the eaves. Bits of green start to poke through the snow and buds form on the tree branches. Then, in what seems like an instant, all the snow is gone and replaced by lush grass greener than any emerald, more vibrant than anything an artist could paint. The rainstorms come, blocking out the sun and turning midday to dusk. Lightning flashes across the sky and thunder echoes across the mountains. The spring rain comes down so hard and heavy that it soaks you to the bone in an instant, and the seas boil with the ferocity of the winds."

Tristan's lips brushed against the pulse in my throat, and it felt like I had my own storm raging inside of me. My whole body trembled as he kissed a line of fire up my neck, to my jaw, and then rested his cheek against mine. "Summer?"

"I can't remember," I murmured, my mind a chaos of emotion.

"Yes, you can." His fingers ran up my sides, separated from my skin by only a thin layer of silk.

I squeezed my eyelids tighter and tried to think, tried to visualize the land, but all I could see in my mind's eye was Tristan. All I could feel was passion, both mine and his, burning like a beacon on a starless night. I wanted him, needed him. Nothing else would satisfy the hunger building low in my belly.

"Flowers," I whispered. "Fields of wildflowers, every color of the rainbow. The animals grow shiny and fat and the fields of wheat grow tall and golden. The warmth drives away the memory of winter and the air is so heady and wet that each breath is like a drink of water. And the sun." My voice trembled and I wrapped my arms around his neck, burying my fingers in his hair. "The sun rises every morning like a god on fire, flushing your skin pink, giving life to everything, until he disappears beyond the horizon every night."

Behind my closed lids, my eyes stung and I bit my lip. Tristan stroked my hair and I opened my eyes, staring into his soul, which was filled with all the sympathy, sorrow, and longing that I felt in my heart. For what I had lost. For what he had never had. And for what he never would have, if I did what he'd asked and abandoned my quest to break the curse.

"I love you, Cécile," he said, and my breath caught. It was one thing to feel it, and quite another to hear the words from his lips.

He kissed me, gently at first, and then harder as his control vanished. My lips parted, and the kiss deepened, opening up a floodgate of heat that tore through my body. Rational thought slipped away, and all that was left was need and desire. I felt his hands on me and I tore at his coat, pulled off his shirt and dug my fingers into the hard muscles lining his back, felt his breath hot and ragged against my lips and at the plunging neckline of my dress. The air was cold against my legs as my skirts rode up, and I wrapped my ankles around him, pulling him down against me. All I wanted was him. And I wanted everything.

The hilt of his sword dug into my ribs, and I grabbed at his belt, fumbling with unpracticed hands with the buckle.

"Cécile, stop." I barely heard him. My body felt like a wild thing, completely out of my control.

"Cécile!" He caught hold of my wrists and pinned them down against the cushions. "Enough. You overestimate my degree of self-control."

I looked up at him, hurt and confused. "Why should you need any? We're married. I am yours, and you," I said, "are mine." I struggled against his grip, but he was stronger than I was. Stronger than any human possibly could be. "Have we not sacrificed enough?"

His lips pressed down, warm and sweet. He rested his forehead against mine. "I want you. I've wanted this for so long." He bit his lip. "But there could be consequences of… that."

The chaos retreated from my mind, replaced by the cool feel of logic. "You mean a child?"

He nodded and let go of my wrists. "If we had a child, it would be as bound to this place as I am." Smoothing back the hair from my face, he said, "Then what would you do? Stay out of obligation and give up life on the outside? Or be like your mother, and only visit when the mood strikes you?"

I jerked away from him. "Don't say that – I'm nothing like her."

He sat back on his heels, his face unreadable, and the combination of our emotions was a tangled web that I was having difficulty sorting through. I stared at him, and eventually it came to me: anticipation. But of what? What did he want me to say?

"You need to decide what life you want," he said, his eyes searching mine.

I covered my face with both hands, frustrated. "I can't do this, Tristan. I'm not like you – I can't plan out every moment of my future, every decision I'm going to make."

Silence.

"Of course not." His voice was cold, but the shock of his grief stung through me like an icy spear. "After all, you never chose to come here. Never chose any of this. Who could blame you for wanting to leave? And what sort of fool am I for wishing that you would stay?"

A chill swept through me. "Tristan, that isn't what I meant!" But he was already pulling his shirt over his head, the boat moving swiftly under an invisible force back to the tunnel entrance.

"I love you," I pleaded, but the words sounded weak even to me. "I wouldn't leave you here alone."

"So you say." His voice was emotionless, posture stiff, but the pain I had caused him made me sick. "But you're human, Cécile, so why should I believe anything that comes out of your mouth?"

"Tristan." I reached for him, but he turned away, moving to the front of the boat.

"We need to go back. They'll be missing us by now."

The boat bumped against the steps, grinding to a halt, and Tristan leapt out. It was magic, not his hands, that lifted me out of the boat, and it was magic that steadied me as I climbed the slippery steps back to the tunnel. After everything that had happened to us, it seemed that words from my own lips had done the most damage of all.

CHAPTER 29
Tristan

I stared bleary-eyed at the trunk of the tree, absently letting my power flow without providing it much direction. "Please, just hold it up," I mumbled. "I don't care how you go about it, just don't drop any rocks." It was the wrong way to manage the magic – the structure was architecturally complex, and with the amount of activity in the earth as of late, it required my full attention. Which was rather difficult, given that Cécile was the center of my every thought. Every day, every hour, every minute. Every bloody waking breath, which was a substantial number of breaths, considering I'd rarely had more than a few consecutive hours of sleep in the time since she'd arrived.

Which had clearly caused me to lose my mind. What other explanation could there be for my hoping she would stay? We'd kidnapped her from her family and forced her to marry someone she didn't even know. Something that wasn't even human. I'd treated her dreadfully for nearly our entire marriage. And still she'd saved my life. Told me that she loved me.

But what did that even mean?

Cécile could lie. I'd watched her do it countless times. The tiny little mistruths she employed without any real intention of being deceitful. It wasn't in her nature to be manipulative or devious; but it was in mine. How many secrets was I keeping from her? Layers and layers, I thought. Many were those of my people, but some were mine alone. She knew it, too. Knew that I kept her in the dark, and still she trusted me implicitly. I could see it in her eyes: a blind, unfaltering faith that I would never hurt her, despite my having done exactly that on so many occasions. She lived in the present, always running off in the heat of the moment and saying exactly what she thought, rarely considering how the things she said or the decisions she made would affect the future. I was the exact opposite. Almost every action I took or decision I made was designed to affect circumstances months, years, even decades down the road. I'd always thought it was the prudent way to live, but now I feared I would wake up one day an old man, with my past wasted and no future left to live. Loving her had changed me, pulled me into the present and made me want to give myself to her as wholly and completely as I could.

But I was who I was, and I could not let go completely. Could not trust her the way my heart wanted to, because I could see the way it would go. I would give her everything I had, love her with every breath of my being. I would have months, perhaps even a year of happiness before my other plans came to fruition. Then I would be bound by my own promise to let her go, and she would leave. Closing my eyes, I watched a specter of her future self walking down River Road and out onto the beach, never looking back. The pain was worse than a spike of iron through the heart.

My mind, always attuned to where Cécile was, sensed that she was on the move. The dull throb of her misery – misery that I had caused – was a beacon allowing me to trace her progress from the palace down into the city. I didn't like her out and about like this – the people had mixed feelings about her. Abandoning the tree, I hurried down several flights of stairs and across a bridge into the merchant district. Though she was shorter than everyone around, I caught glimpses of red hair as she walked slowly through the crowd, her guards following a few paces behind. She didn't seem to realize that I was following. I could think of countless instances when she'd been so lost in thought that I could have walked up and tapped her on the shoulder before she'd notice me. How many times had I followed her through the glass gardens listening to her sing? How many times, and never once did she seem to sense I was there.

Or maybe she just didn't care.

Turning down an alley, I rounded a corner to get a better view of the market and froze. Cécile was talking to Jérôme Girard's son, Christophe. Almost without thinking, I ordered my magic to dim, letting the shadows wrap round me like a cloak.

So you can better spy on your wife.

Christophe handed her a peach, and I watched her bite into it, the yellow juices trickling down her slender fingers. She was at ease with him in a way she wasn't with me, and it was obvious that he fancied her from the way he twitched about, the color on his cheeks, and the way he peeked down the bodice of her dress when she wasn't looking. I felt a scowl rise to my face. He was good enough looking, I supposed. Shorter than I was, but broader, with the thick muscles all the farmers seemed to have. His hair was the color of the hay his mule was munching on, and brilliant blue eyes shone out of his tanned face. Normally he was the smiling sort, which always put me on edge – anyone who smiled all the time clearly suffered from a mental imbalance – but today his mouth was set straight in a frown. Whatever he was telling Cécile had upset her – I could feel her anguish thick on my mind – and I watched her drop the peach then bury her face in her hands. What had he said? I'd have heard about it if something had happened *outside,* so it wasn't to do with her family. He was probably making up some lie about me or Trollus – something that would turn her against us.

I fought the urge to go to her side, to tell Christophe to bugger off while I comforted my wife. My Cécile. Mine.

For now. Until she leaves you to rot in the dark.

I shuddered, suppressing the thought. They were arguing now, but I couldn't hear their words. If I used magic to amplify them, everyone near the alley would hear them as well. What he was telling her was eliciting surprise and bewilderment, which meant more lies. Cécile closed her eyes, and I saw her lips form my name. *Tristan isn't...* I couldn't make out the rest. I wasn't what? What lies was he telling about me? Or worse, what truths?

My hands balled into fists of frustration as I watched the human boy reach down and take her hand, his thumb stroking her knuckles. I could see plainly on his face that he wanted to do more. And she didn't pull away. She was conflicted. My chest felt hollow and I could feel my breath coming in short little gasps. He was going to take her away from me. Fury like nothing I had felt before filled the space where emptiness had once been, and I strode out into the market.

Cécile's guards started in surprise as I pushed past them. "Don't interfere," I hissed. "In fact, make yourselves scarce. I'll handle this one."

CHAPTER 30
Cécile

Christophe handed me a peach from a basket in the cart and I bit into it, relishing the sweet juices that filled my mouth and trickled down my fingers. "Summer is nearly gone then?" I asked, eyeing the cart full of produce.

"Aye. Harvests have already begun." He frowned, his tanned skin crinkling a bit around eyes as blue as my own. "Just one endless season down here, I reckon."

I shrugged. Snagging another peach from the cart, I sat down on the fountain edge and bit into it. Chris moved over to sit next to me, but the dark glares on my guards' faces made him lean against the wagon instead.

"Have you seen my family? Are they well?" It was information I probably could have gotten from the trolls' many spies, but it was better coming from Chris, who knew me. Knew my family.

"I saw Fred in the Trianon markets a week ago," Chris said, picking at one of his fingernails. "He's not been back to the farm much, I don't think, though he says your father and gran are well. I think he..."

"You think he?" I prompted, curious.

Chris sighed, letting his hands fall to his sides. "I think he blames himself for not being in Goshawk's Hollow – thinks if he'd been riding with you, nothing would have happened. And it's been so long now. No sign of bones, but also no word from you, so everyone thinks that you're..."

"Dead."

He nodded and lowered his voice. "I'd tell him otherwise, if I could, but I can't even get my lips to form the words. Makes me sick to my stomach to even try. I'm sorry, Cécile."

I stared at the half-eaten peach in my hand, not feeling hungry anymore. It was one thing to know that my family missed me, but quite another to know my brother blamed himself for my disappearance.

"Fred was talking about resigning his post with the Regent to go looking for you. Now he was drunk as a skunk when he told me this, mind you," Chris added, "but I know for a fact that your mother has offered a reward for any news about where you are. I think it's she who's pushing him to it."

I buried my face in my hands. "He can't do that. All he ever wanted was to be a soldier!" From between my fingers I mumbled, "My mother, she... she was upset that I left?"

"Aye. Tore up her apartments in the palace and then had the Regent send soldiers out to scour the countryside for you."

"She did?" I looked up, stunned. Never in my wildest dreams had I thought my mother would be so grieved by my loss.

Chris nodded and to my surprise, he knelt down in front of me. I inhaled, and I could smell the tang of ocean spray, the sweetness of hay, and the hint of sweat from exertion under the sun. He smelled human. He smelled like home.

"She's offered fifty gold pieces for word of you, Cécile. And she's a wealthy woman – she could pay more. Enough to buy you from them."

I felt suddenly cold and the peach fell from my stiff fingers, rolling next to the wagon wheel. "No."

"Just think it through, Cécile. The trolls love their gold. Your mother could pay them whatever it is they wanted, you could swear magic oaths to keep your mouth shut about Trollus, and you'd be free."

"No." It was the only word I could manage.

"It could happen, Cécile," Chris insisted, mistaking the meaning of my refusal. "For trolls, there is always a price. We just have to figure out what yours is."

I shook my head rapidly. "No, Chris. I don't want to leave."

His eyes widened. "Why?"

"I won't leave Tristan. Not for anything." I met Chris's stunned gaze. "I love him."

Shock turned to disgust and he recoiled back on his heels away from me. "You can't be serious."

"I love him," I repeated. "I won't leave. Ever."

"How can you love one of them?" he asked, his face twisting like he had bitten into something bitter. "They're monsters, Cécile. Wicked, nasty, selfish, greedy monsters. I've seen them slit a man's throat for whistling at one of their women. I saw another man smothered with their magic because they thought he'd lied to them. Oh, some of them might be pretty enough to look at, I'll give you that, but inside they're as cold as steel." He glanced at my troll guards who, although they were too distant to hear our words, looked none too pleased with the exchange. "Cécile, they aren't even human. He isn't human. You might as well be in love with a pit viper."

I jerked back, furious. "You don't even know him – Tristan isn't like that."

"I've been coming to Trollus almost all my life, Cécile. My father has been coming here for nearly all of his, and his father before him, and his father before that. You think you know them, but you don't. They are pure evil."

"You are wrong to think they are any worse than we are," I argued. "And wrong to say we rule ourselves anymore benevolently than the troll kings have ruled their subjects."

"You've lost your mind," Chris hissed. "They enslave their own. Murder their own. They are incapable of any sort of decency."

I closed my eyes. "Tristan is different. He wouldn't hurt anyone. He loves me." My voice sounded plaintive and pathetic. I had no ground to stand on – I knew the trolls' dark history. It had been Tristan who'd told me of it. But in my heart, I knew he was different. He wasn't like the kings of past.

Chris closed his hand over mine. It was warm, but not in the feverish way of the trolls. He turned my hand over and our fingers linked: his tanned and calloused from years of labor in the fields; mine, pale as marble and buffed smooth by my maids. "Cécile, you must leave this place. Already you've changed, faded." His dark thumb brushed over my skin. "Trollus is killing you."

White-hot fury lanced through my mind with a force that sent me reeling.

"Get your hands off of her," said a voice behind me.

Chris raised my hand, kissed my knuckles gently and then got to his feet. Very brave, but also very stupid. Which he probably realized when a fist of magic hammered into his stomach, tossing him against the wagon. The mule brayed unhappily, pinning its ears against its head.

I was on my feet and between them in a flash. "Stop it!" I pressed my hands against Tristan's chest, trying to keep some distance between the two. "He's telling me news about my family."

Tristan didn't even look at me – his eyes remained fixed on Chris. "She doesn't need to speak to the likes of you to have news about her family."

"The likes of me?" I heard Chris come up behind me, and I turned, slamming a hand against his chest to keep him from coming any closer. "Let it go, Chris," I warned, but he paid no more attention to me than Tristan had.

"The likes of me is the same as the likes of your wife," Chris snapped. "I've known her all her life. I know her father and her grandmother. I'm friends with her brother. I've danced with her at festivals and walked her home from her lessons in town. We're the same people."

"She is nothing like you," Tristan sneered, his tone making me flinch. It made him sound like his father. "She is my wife. She is Princess of Trollus, and you are not fit company for her."

"She's your prisoner."

Tristan showed no visible reaction, but I felt Chris's words strike him to the core.

I turned, pressing my back against Tristan and pulling his arm around me. "That isn't true Chris. I told you – I'm here because I want to be."

"That true, my lord? Does she have the choice to leave if she wanted to? Has she ever had the choice?"

Tristan was silent. I could hear his heart beating furiously where my head rested against his chest.

"Just as I thought." Chris's face was dark with anger. "You stole her from her kin and now she's your prisoner. She might say she loves you, but I don't believe it for a minute. You've either put some magic on her mind or she's just saying it because it's what you want to hear!"

"That isn't true!" I shouted. "You shut your mouth, Christophe!" I looked up at Tristan. "It isn't true. You know I love you." He refused to meet my eyes, but his grip around my waist increased, drawing me tight against him.

"We have no such magic." His sword slithered as he pulled it out of its scabbard. "I could have your head for this, boy. Or perhaps cut you open and leave you on the street to die, slowly. I could kill your father for bringing such an insolent brat into my presence." His grip on my side was becoming painful, his fingers grinding the bones of my corset against my ribs.

I closed my eyes, fear building in my gut. This wasn't Tristan I was hearing. It was his father's voice, and the voices of all those horrible selfish kings before him. The voice of a troll.

"No," I whispered. "Please, don't."

"Aye, you could," Chris said, and I saw the first traces of fear on his face. Then he looked at me, "Seems to me he's just like all the rest of them, Cécile."

"You have no right to use her name," Tristan snapped, and I gasped against the pain in my side.

"You're hurting her!" Chris shouted.

Everything happened too quickly. Chris swung his fist at Tristan's face, but it bounced off a shield of magic. Tristan pushed me out of the way, and my feet tangled in my skirts as I fell in a heap. Neither of them noticed.

"Can't even fight like a real man!" Chris shouted. "Always hiding behind your magic."

"Hardly," Tristan replied. Then he punched Chris in the face. Chris staggered, and then with a shout, leapt forward, knocking Tristan backwards. They grappled on the ground, both of them landing heavy blows and neither of them paying any attention to my pleas for them to stop. Chris was older and his body was heavy from muscle that only hard labor could bring. But his was human strength. It was only a few moments until Tristan had him pinned, fingers latched tight around Chris's throat.

"You're killing him," I shrieked, pulling at his wrists, trying to make him let go. "Tristan, stop this! Please!" I pounded my fists against his shoulders, dug my nails into his arms, but it was as if I were invisible. Chris's face turned purple and his attempts to dislodge Tristan's hands grew as weak and ineffective as my own. "Please stop!" I begged, but he wasn't listening to me. So I screamed, my voice echoing through Trollus.

Boots pounded towards us and several trolls, including my mysteriously absent guards, appeared. Chris's father was with them. "Stop them!" I shouted.

Jérôme tried to run forward, but one of the trolls

snatched him off his feet. He dangled helplessly in the air, terrified eyes on his dying son. "Help him," I screamed.

The trolls exchanged amused glances with each other and one of them shook his head at me. They wouldn't help. If their prince wanted to strangle a human boy, why should they stop him?

I grabbed hold of Tristan's shoulders again and pulled with all my strength, but it wasn't enough. Chris was going to die, and I was powerless. Dropping to my knees, I pressed my lips to Tristan's ear. "I will not forgive you if you do this. I will never forgive you if you kill him."

I felt realization click in his mind, rage fleeing in the face of horror and guilt. His hands jerked away from Chris's neck and he stared at them as if amazed at what they'd been doing. Then he rose smoothly to his feet.

Chris rolled on his side, gasping for breath, redness receding from his face. "Are you all right?" I asked, touching his shoulder. He jerked away as if I'd burned him.

"So strong," he rasped out. "How can anyone be that strong?"

"They all are, you idiot," I whispered.

His eyes flickered up, looking over my shoulder at Tristan like a sheep watching a wolf. "Then the witch was right to lock them down here – nothing could ever stop them."

"He's right."

I looked at Tristan, who stood with his arms crossed, his face bleak. "No, he isn't," I replied. I made my voice firm, but it would be a lie to say I was as confident about that fact as I had been an hour ago.

Tristan refused to meet my gaze, instead, he gestured to the troll holding Jérôme. "Let him go."

Jérôme staggered as the magic released him and hurried over to his son. Chris was on his feet now, holding onto the edge of the wagon to keep his balance. Jérôme cuffed him hard. "Blasted fool! What were you thinking?" He turned to Tristan and bowed. "My deepest apologies, Your Highness. The lad is young, impulsive."

Tristan didn't reply, only watched me in silence. Reaching into his pocket, he tossed a gold coin through the air at Jérôme, who caught it. "For the peach she ate."

Jérôme looked at the coin glittering in his palm. Then he tossed it back. "We've already been paid for the load, my lord. Market rate, not a penny more, not a penny less." He inclined his head to Tristan. "We know your rules, and we follow them." The last bit I was certain he directed at his son, but if Chris heard, it did not register on his face.

"You're a good man, Jérôme," Tristan said, voice heavy as he turned away from us.

I watched the trolls make way for him as he strode out of the market, and then I glared at Chris. "You're wrong about them. You're wrong about him." Grabbing up my skirts, I ran after Tristan, guards hot on my heels.

I found him in a tavern that did not normally cater to noblemen. Not that it was rough or run down – nothing in Trollus was – but it carried the less expensive products that appealed to the working class – the half-bloods. Noon had not yet passed, and the room was empty except for Tristan and the proprietor, who was drying a glass with the vigor of an anxious man. "Something to drink, my lady?" he asked as I made my way through the tables. I shook my head and sat down across from Tristan. A glass with amber liquid sat in front of him untouched, the sharp scent of whiskey rising up to assault my nostrils. A dark bottle sat corked next to his hand.

"My gran always said that drink might make you forget your problems, but it doesn't solve anything," I said. "Besides, I've never even seen a drunk troll."

"Your gran had a lot to say." Tristan swished the liquid around the glass and tossed it back.

"Most grandmothers have a lot to say. And they are usually right."

"Perhaps I'd be wiser if mine were still alive to fill my ears with such helpful proverbs."

He reached for the bottle, but I pulled it away. "No."

His hand dropped to the table. "You should go, Cécile."

"No." Every inch of me felt cold beneath the weight of his misery.

"I hurt you. I nearly killed your friend for speaking the truth. For touching you." He rested his chin in his hands. "He was right. Everything he said was true."

"Not everything," I whispered. "I love you, Tristan. I want to be here with you."

"I should have distracted your guards and let him steal you away in his wagon," Tristan said, his eyes blank and distant. "He fancies you – has for a long time, I think. He'd make a good husband. You could live on a farm with golden wheat fields and have golden-haired babies." He sounded almost wistful.

"No!" Tears trickled down my face, my misery magnifying his until I felt overwhelmed.

"Under the sun, with your family. That's where you belong."

Every inch of me hurt. I couldn't think, couldn't breathe. Tristan was going to send me away because he thought that deep down it was what I wanted. He would think he was doing it for my own good, that I would be happier. But the thought of never seeing his face, or feeling the heat of his skin against mine, his lips against my lips, caused greater pain than any torturer could devise.

"I was planning on leaving them anyway, and besides…" I struggled to articulate myself. Even if ten years passed between now and the time I saw my family, they'd still be my family. They'd still love me as much and the same way as they always had. But if Tristan and I were parted for ten years? What was between us was new and fragile. Time would not leave it unscathed, and the thought of losing it broke my heart. "You're more important to me now," I finally said.

My words finally snapped him out of his miserable reverie, and his eyes focused on me. "You don't mean that. The distance would diminish the bond. You'd think about us less and less until one day your time in Trollus would seem like a bad dream that left a strange mark on your hand."

I wiped the wet streaks off my face with my sleeve and met his eyes. "And would you forget about me? Would the memory of the human girl you married and loved fade away until it seemed like she was just a bad dream?"

His eyes darkened and he looked away. "No. Never."

"Then how can you believe I would forget?" I reached for his hands, but he pulled them off the table. "I love you, Tristan. Given the choice, I would stay. You must believe that."

"I can't." His voice was so quiet I barely heard him.

"Why?" I slammed my fists down on the table. "Why can't you believe me? Why don't you trust me?"

"Because you're human, Cécile. You can lie, even to yourself."

I wrapped my arms around my torso, trying to ward off the sorrow and misery like it was the cold.

"Go, Cécile. I need to be alone. I need to think."

The bench scraped against the ground when I pushed it back, but that was the only sound in the room. I walked to the entrance and opened the door, but it was as far as I could stand to go. From round the corner, I heard Tristan ask the tavern keeper for paper, pen, and ink. I stood frozen in place, desperate to know what he was writing. A note to put in my pocket when he shoved me in a cart destined for outside? Or something else?

"Take this to Lady Anaïs," Tristan said, and I felt as if someone had punched me in the gut. Shutting the door softly, I hurried down the street so that the troll delivering the message wouldn't see me. Wanted to be alone, did he? More like he didn't want to be with me. I had to believe him when Tristan said he harbored no feelings for her, but they were still the closest of friends, and it hurt that he'd rather turn to her for comfort than me.

Wiping all evidence of tears from my face, I attempted to walk with purpose. But I had none. Instead I wandered through Trollus, doing my best to ignore the curious and often dark looks from the trolls who saw me pass and on the faces of my grumbling guards, always two paces behind. Eventually I wound up at the door of Pierre's house. Knocking, I waited a moment, and then went in. "Pierre?"

"Lady Cécile!" The little troll rolled in on his stool, a wide grin on his face that fell away when he saw me. "What is the matter, child?" Stacks of paper lifted off the only other chair in the room and settled on the ground. "Sit, sit!"

"So sad!" He rolled next to me and took my hand, patting it gently. "I am thinking it is because of the altercation between His Highness and the human boy, am I correct? Gossip – it travels fast in Trollus."

I nodded miserably, my heart listening to Tristan's emotions. Misery was gone now, and in its place was grim determination. I bit my lip and tried to keep my composure. Tristan was coming this way. It wouldn't be long now.

"Young men in love, they are all fools. Trolls and humans, it makes no difference."

"He almost killed him, Pierre."

The little troll's face looked grim. "I heard as much." He sighed. "Not a fair fight – it never is between trolls and humans. Strength from another world."

My ears perked up at that. Perhaps Pierre would not be so reluctant to divulge information about their history. "Is that where trolls come from? Another world?" I feigned ignorance to see what he would say.

He smiled and pressed a finger against my lips. "Some things are better left a mystery, non?"

The little glass balls representing the planets and moons rose up in the air and began to circle the glowing sun. I watched with fascination as they circled round and round, wondering to which one trolls might belong. Then they all fell away, until only the moon and the sun were left. They circled each other, both equally bright, one silver and one gold. Like Tristan and I.

"Pierre, if the curse were broken, do you think the trolls would go to war with the humans to take the Isle back?"

He looked away from me, his brow furrowed. "Yes," he said. "With Thibault as king, I think freedom would mean much bloodshed for humanity."

"But what about Tristan?"

"Tristan is not king yet."

"But he will be, one day," I persisted.

The little troll was quiet for a long time. "I do not know what he would do," he finally said, the moon and sun settling into his hands. "I think that might very much depend on you, my lady."

I closed my eyes. It was an answer, but not one that helped me at all. "Pierre?"

"Yes, my dearest lady?"

"If you had the chance, would you leave Trollus to go above?"

I didn't need to open my eyes to know he was smiling. "Oh yes, Cécile," he said. "I would very much like to see the planets, the stars." He sighed. "I would climb the highest mountain, build the greatest telescope that ever existed, and I would watch them until my light went out."

A ghost of a smile drifted across my lips. "Thank you, Pierre."

"What for, my lady?"

"For giving me the answer I needed."

The door slammed open and I turned to look at Tristan. "You need to come with me, Cécile. Now."

My time was up.

CHAPTER 31
Cécile

"Hang back," Tristan snapped at my guards as we left Pierre's home. "I'll not have you eavesdropping on my every word."

They gave each other concerned looks, but the expression on Tristan's face was enough to triple the distance at which they normally followed me.

"Where are we going?" I asked, although in my heart, I already knew. Tristan wanted me to leave. As much as he might love me, he would never trust me; and without trust, our love was doomed.

"River Road," he muttered under his breath.

I wanted to argue with him, plead for him to let me stay. But what was the point? I couldn't make him trust me. I had no way to prove that, despite having been brought to Trollus against my will, it would now be against my will to leave. Knowing my feelings was not the same as knowing my thoughts. "The guards won't let me pass."

"No. But they won't stop Anaïs."

I stared up at him, confused. "What?"

"You'll see."

Tristan led me through a series of alleyways, and then stopped at a door in the back of a building. At his knock, a man opened the door and bowed deeply. "My lord. My lady." His chocolate-brown hair marked him as part human, but Tristan did not introduce us. The man gestured to the entrance of another room, but did not follow us in.

"About time. Do you think I have all day to waste sitting around waiting on you?" Anaïs reclined on a sofa, smirk firmly in place. I scowled at her and her grin grew even wider. "No need for that, Cécile. I am doing you a favor, after all."

"No, you are not," Tristan snapped. "You are doing me a favor and it is from me whom you will collect."

She got to her feet and made her way to Tristan's side. The parlor seemed too small to contain the three of us. Anaïs was too close, and the satisfaction on her face made me want to hit her. Not that that would go well.

"You don't do anything that doesn't benefit you in some way, Anaïs." I felt too drained, too tired, to deal with her today. Even at my best, she was better. "This is no favor."

"As you like." Anaïs laughed. "Turn around, Tristan. I'm not your wife. Yet." A wink accompanied this last bit, and the urge to strike out became almost unmanageable.

"Get on with it, Anaïs," Tristan said darkly, but he turned around.

"Help me," she said, turning her back to me. "We need to switch dresses. I'd never wear something like that."

"It's going to take more than a dress for anyone to mistake the two of us," I replied. But I began undoing the gold buttons running down the back of her gown. Her skin felt soft and overheated beneath my fingers, the lace of her undergarments reminding me of the tattoo on Marc's fingers, black against porcelain white.

When she was unbuttoned, I pulled off my own dress, needing no assistance to extract myself from its forgiving design. When she turned around I flushed, profoundly grateful that Tristan had his back turned. Fully clothed she was the most beautiful girl I had ever met. Half-naked, I was certain she was every man's fantasy. Beside her, I felt like the troll. Shorter, plumper, with a smaller chest and a bigger behind.

We put on each other's clothes, her dress so tight I could hardly breathe and mine hanging off her slender frame. Then she pulled off her shoes and as she settled onto her bare feet, I realized she wasn't all that much taller than me after all. "You're short for a troll."

She raised one finger to her lips and then handed me the shoes. "No one needs to know that."

I put them on, wobbling on the high platforms and wondering how I would get more than two steps without falling. In the meantime, Anaïs pulled a black wig out of her bag, along with a golden-framed mirror. "Hair is tricky," she muttered.

It took a bit of doing to get all of my red hair tucked beneath the wig, and my ribs began to ache from my extra-tight corset. Sweat trickled down my back as I took one shallow breath after another. Anaïs held up the mirror and examined her face. "Now for the illusion," she said, and her brow furrowed in concentration. I watched in amazement as her black hair turned red and her features shifted until the girl looking back at me was my mirror image.

"Now, for you."

Warm magic washed over my face, but otherwise I could feel nothing. "Done," she said, my face smirking in a way that betrayed the girl lurking underneath. I'd never make that face. She handed me the mirror and I held it up to my face. An unhappy looking Anaïs stared out at me, silver eyes and all.

"You shouldn't frown like that," she said. "You'll get wrinkles."

I lifted my hand and made a gesture that was extremely unladylike.

Blue eyes widened and Anaïs-as-me shrugged. "Just saying. Tristan, you can turn around now."

He turned and looked from one of us to the other. "It will do." He took my hand and squeezed it in a way that was probably meant to be reassuring. But it wasn't. All this costuming and deception was just a step in the process of us being torn apart. "Please don't make me do this, Tristan," I whispered. "I don't want to go."

He shook his head. "I have to know, Cécile." He bent to kiss me, but I turned away, not fond of the idea that he'd be kissing Anaïs's face, not mine.

"This is all very touching," Anaïs said, interrupting. "But my magic tends to grow bored and wander if unattended. You've got maybe half an hour with my face and then it will fade."

Tristan nodded. "Where will you be?"

"In the glass gardens, wandering around and looking forlorn."

"Are you certain you want to do this, Anaïs?" Tristan and Anaïs stared at each other for several long moments. I flinched at their familiarity. It was something he and I had never had. "He won't let you off easily for helping me."

"I've never said 'no' to you, Tristan. Never denied you anything." She lifted her chin defiantly. "And I never will." They exchanged more long looks, and then Anaïs turned and walked out, comfortable in my flat shoes.

Tristan waited a few moments and then took me by the arm, leading me back into the city and down the valley towards the River Road. I walked blindly, not seeing anything or anyone. It took every ounce of control to keep my face serene, my steps even on Anaïs's impossibly high shoes. "Don't say anything," Tristan muttered. "They'll recognize your voice."

My nerves reached a fevered pitch as we approached the heavily armed and very imposing trolls standing to either side of the gate. They bowed low and one of them lifted the heavy bar holding the gate shut. It swung open silently on greased hinges.

"Haven't noticed any fallen rock, my lord," one of the trolls said.

"There's never a problem until there is," Tristan said, his arm drawing me forward.

The incline of the road was steep, the rock smooth, and everything was slick with water. We hadn't gone far when I was forced to take off my shoes and walk barefoot. The road was perhaps ten feet wide, and the river, white with rapids, flowed only a few feet below.

Tristan didn't look at me as we walked, but he did let go of my arm to take my hand instead. I held on as tight as

I could, trying to memorize the way his skin felt beneath mine, the way his thumb rubbed the tops of my knuckles. Every step I took was one closer to the moment he'd make me leave him. When I saw the glow of sunlight appear ahead, fear lanced through me. It was the end of the tunnel. It was the end of us.

And the fear wasn't just mine. Tristan's dread had grown into something close to terror as we neared the light at the end of the tunnel.

"Will it do anything if you get too close?" I asked, suddenly uneasy.

Tristan jumped at my voice. "No," he said. "No, it isn't that." Suddenly, he stopped and held up his hand, knuckles rapping against something that sounded like glass but which I suspected was infinitely stronger. "No. It isn't that," he repeated. Then he staggered back away from the barrier with a groan, and slumped against the wall.

"Tristan!" I dropped to my knees in front of him, terrified the curse had hurt him somehow. He grabbed hold of me and pulled me close. Tugging off the black wig, he buried his face in my hair, his whole body shaking. "I can't lose you," he whispered, and I felt him brush away Anaïs's magic so that I was myself again.

"Then why are you doing this?" I demanded. "Why did you bring me here?"

"Because I can't live this way, Cécile. I feel like I'm losing my mind. I live every moment on edge, thinking that I'll turn around and you'll be gone. I never know whether you're telling me what you feel or what you think I want to hear. I need to know that you're here by choice, not because you were never given one." He pulled away so that he could look at me, and I saw his eyes and cheeks were streaked with tears.

I brushed one of them away, staring at the gleaming droplet sitting on my fingertip. "I didn't think trolls could cry."

He blinked. "Another myth?"

I shook my head. "No, I... When I first came, I thought trolls didn't feel sorrow like we do. Pain like we do. Loss like we do." I pressed the tear to my lips, tasting its sweet saltiness and thinking of all the many times the trolls had proven that notion false. "I was wrong."

We sat on the road for a time, my head resting against his chest, both of us watching waves crash against the shore, pushing the river in and then drawing the flow out. A warm breeze blew into the tunnel, smelling of salt and seaweed, carrying with it the sound of gulls. This was the closest Tristan would ever get to the world outside of Trollus. This one small and unchanging view of the ocean.

"Tristan?"

"Yes?" He was voice was raspy, thick with emotion.

"Are you really giving me a choice? You won't argue with what I decide?"

He squeezed his eyes shut and shook his head. "I won't stop you."

"And if I want to stay, you'll let me? You won't make me leave?"

His eyelids twitched against his cheeks, but he didn't open them. "It is your choice to make."

I kissed him hard, drinking in the taste of him. I felt punch-drunk and reckless, willing to say whatever it took to keep him from making me leave. "Then I'm staying. I want to be with you – forever." In the back of my mind, I knew I wasn't considering the full extent of my words, but I had faith Tristan would succeed in everything he set out to accomplish. That perhaps it would take a year or two, but my isolation from the world would not be a permanent thing. It couldn't be.

He held me against him, hand stroking my back, but I didn't feel the sense of relief from him that I had hoped for. "You are impetuous, love," he said softly. "You think with your heart, not with your mind."

"So?" My voice was muffled against his chest.

"You can't make the decision here. Troll magic is too thick. Half of what you feel is what I feel. You don't know what you want."

"Yes, I do!" I shouted against him, my voice muffled by the fabric of his shirt. "I want you." I dug my nails into his shoulder, inhaling the clean scent of him. "I want you."

With me clinging to his shoulders, Tristan got to his feet. Then he took hold of my wrists, gently tugging them free, and pushed me through the barrier. I stepped through the sticky thickness, and the roar of emotion in my mind subsided into a faint murmur. I gasped aloud, hating the loss, and I tried to go forward again, back to him. But Tristan held up one hand. "Go out into the sun and remember all the things you would give up for a life with me. If you decide not to come back, then…" He swallowed hard and tossed me a heavy purse that clinked when I caught it. "This should keep you for a time."

"And if I decide to come back?"

"I'll be waiting."

I turned and looked out towards the ocean. The river poured into a small cove that had once been the harbor of Trollus before time and breaking mountains changed the coastline. Where I stood was still partially in shadow from the overhanging rocks. The trolls were cursed to darkness even here.

I started walking to the beach, picking my way carefully over the rocky cove until the summer sun hit me like a wall of heat. I turned my face to the sky and stared at the yellow orb, my eyes burning from the pain of so much light. Then, I started to run. Faster and faster, my feet sinking into the wet sand until I reached the water's edge. Catching my skirts up high, I waded in, relishing the feel of wide open space as the salty water slammed against my shins. I spun in a circle, my burning eyes taking everything in. The seagulls flying high above me. The mountains a virulent green, with the exception of the broken one, its veins of quartz and gold glittering. I ran down the beach to the edge of the rock fall and up a path until I reached grass. I flopped down, gasping for breath. Everything was lush with the peak of summer and I basked in the warmth, letting it soak into my bones. Everything around me was bright and alive, and I realized Tristan was right: I had missed it.

But would I miss him more?

Curling around onto my side, I rested my head on my arms and plucked blades of grass. "Think, Cécile!" I ordered myself. But it was hard, because Tristan's sorrow was a hard knot of pain in my mind. "You think I've left," I whispered to a little wildflower growing just out of arm's reach. A big part of me wanted to leap up and run back to him, but would I regret my impulsiveness later?

Think about what you'd be giving up to be with me. Tristan's voice echoed in my head.

My freedom, for one. If I turned my back on Trollus, the possibilities were endless. I could go back to the farm to live with my father. I could travel to Trianon to live with my mother at court. I could sing on the great stages, or travel across the strait to see the continent. If there was one thing my time in Trollus had helped me do, it was to conquer my fear of the unknown. Up here, I could do anything. I would do anything.

Alone? I grimaced. I had my family and friends in the Hollow, but it wasn't the same. Gran was getting on in years, and my father was busy with the farm. My brother was busy with his soldiering, and it would not be long before he married a girl and started a family of his own. Fred would inherit the farm and all the land when father passed, and there would be no place for me anymore. A new wife wouldn't want her husband's younger sister living with her.

I sighed, the idea of growing old alone heavy upon me. Never again to be kissed or touched by a lover. To remain a maid until I was wrinkled and grey and beyond caring about such things. Maybe Tristan was right. Maybe I would forget him in order to have a life with someone else.

Unbidden, the feel of Christophe's hands came to my mind. The rough, calloused hands of a farmer. His blue and so very human eyes. He was certainly handsome – all the girls fought for turns to dance with him at festivals. Kind, thoughtful, and hardworking, he would make someone a good husband. Make me a good husband? I imagined what it would be like to hold his hand while we walked; how it would feel if he kissed me out under the stars. What it would be like if I wed Chris and let him take me to his bed?

My mind recoiled at the very idea of it. It wasn't that Chris disgusted me, but the thought of doing any of those things with anyone but Tristan made me sick to my stomach.

Getting to my feet, I walked down the beach until I reached the eastern edge of the rock fall. Then I made my way up the slope until I reached the edge of the massive wooden bridge built years ago that spanned the rock. From here, I could see the entire extent of the fall that stretched between Forsaken Mountain and the beach, and it seemed impossible that an entire city resided beneath. I started across the bridge, stepping carefully to avoid getting splinters in my bare feet. When I reached the point above River Road, where Tristan waited for me, I stopped. If I continued east on the road, I would eventually reach Trianon. West and then north would take me back to the Hollow.

Choose.

Hoof beats sounded on the wooden bridge. A rider was coming towards me on a big white horse. When he saw me, he pushed the horse to a gallop, rapidly covering the distance between us. Then he pulled the horse to a stop so sharply that it reared up.

"My lady! What are you doing on the road all alone! It isn't safe."

I took in his clothing and the quality of the horse – a wealthy landowner, or perhaps a minor nobleman.

"What do I have to fear?" I asked, leaning back against the railing. The answer was: plenty. I was unarmed, and Tristan was beyond reach.

The man's eyes raked over me, taking in my jewels and finery. "A beauty like you, my lady?" He smiled. "Ravishment, at the very least."

I raised an eyebrow. "Surely a man of your quality would never consider such a thing, sir?"

He inclined his head. "I'd take off the head of any who tried, lady." He reached down with one arm. "Let me take you back to the city."

I stared at his hand. This was my chance, if I wanted to take it. Once I was in Trianon, there would be no turning back.

I shook my head. "Someone is waiting for me."

The man laughed. "Lucky man. And good day to you, lady." He clucked to his horse and cantered down the road. I waited until he was out of sight before walking back along the bridge and down to the beach, where I sat in the sand for a very long time. There were so many things I would be giving up if I went back to Trollus, but there was a lot I would be leaving behind if I didn't. Not just Tristan, but Marc and the twins, and all the other trolls I'd met and befriended in my time beneath the mountain. Trollus had its dark side, but there was so much about it that I loved, a world of opportunity in one small city – and once Tristan was king, he'd wipe away the darkness, leaving only light.

And there was the matter of the half-bloods to consider. I felt I owed it to them to try to enact the change they so desperately needed, to give them a chance at having lives worth living. The thought of leaving the miners in their current circumstances filled me with guilt, especially given that they already thought I'd tried to abandon them once.

I poured sand from one hand to another, weighing and measuring, but it was hard to value matters of the heart. When I finally stood, the choice was clear.

I started back towards the mouth of River Road. Tristan must have heard, or at least felt, my coming, because he got to his feet and leaned against the invisible barrier. This place, like twilight or dawn, was a bridge between darkness and light. A place where both fought for domination, but neither ever truly won. Here, Tristan looked more human than I had ever seen him. His troll-light had disappeared, and his eyes, while still unnaturally silver, did not glow. The otherworldliness had diminished. I wondered, as I walked towards him, if out in the brightness of the sun, he would seem as mortal as me. He was still beautiful, handsome, like something out of a dream, but the coldness of that perfection was softened by anxiety, fear, and hope. Painful, painful hope.

As I reached the edge of the barrier, I stopped and looked back. The waves crashed towards me, the tide coming in; and even in the shade, the sun warmed my bones with a heat never felt in Trollus. My world. My life. My choice.

I cleared my throat. "I've made my decision."

CHAPTER 32
Cécile

My love.

"I choose you." I stepped through the barrier, pushing him back and away from it. The second I was through, his emotions hit me like a tidal wave. Relief, happiness, and most of all... love. I drowned in it. We both did.

"Cécile." He pulled me into his arms, kissing me hard and without any reservation. We both slipped to our knees, and I gloried in the feel of his lips on my lips, my cheeks, my throat. Golden buttons rained across the stones as he lost patience with them and tore the back of the dress open, purple silk sliding down my body to pool at my waist. I pulled off his shirt and tossed it aside, so there was nothing between us but the silk and stays with which Anaïs had so cruelly laced my ribs. The frenzy of Tristan's kisses faded, his lips pausing on the spot above my frantically beating heart. I felt his fingers trace down my silk-lined body. "How do you breathe in this?" he murmured.

"I can't," I gasped. "Take it off."

A cough echoed through the tunnel and both of us froze. Looking over my shoulder, I saw a young troll guard standing a few paces up the tunnel, his eyes fixed on the ground at his feet. A squeak of horror escaped my lips, and I jerked the dress up around my torso, trying to reclaim some vestiges of my modesty.

"Your timing is dreadful," Tristan said.

"Sorry, my lord," the guard said, hazarding a peek at me. "She really isn't supposed to be down here."

"And you really weren't supposed to interrupt," Tristan said, the corners of his mouth turning up. "I'm willing to forgive the latter, if you pretend you never saw the former."

"Yes, my lord!"

"Now how about you start walking back up the tunnel, and we'll be along shortly."

The guard shot an anxious look at me. "She won't leave, will she?"

"No," Tristan replied. "She is coming back with me."

"Anaïs won't be happy about this," I said after the guard had departed, examining the torn gown.

"Likely not," Tristan agreed, pulling his shirt back on and eyeing the dying glow of the setting sun. "We need to get back."

I put the torn dress on as best I could, and with one hand gripping Anaïs's shoes and the other Tristan's hand, we started back up the River Road.

Despite being uphill, the journey back to Trollus was much pleasanter than the descent towards the beach. An enormous weight had been lifted off Tristan's shoulders and his happiness mirrored mine. Everything was going to be all right now that he knew I wasn't secretly searching for a way out. He trusts me now, I thought, and I found that I valued this gain as much as his love.

When I saw the glowing orbs of the guards ahead, I only felt a little bit nervous. "They won't be terribly angry, will they?" I asked Tristan.

He frowned. "Hard to say."

The lights started towards us. The young troll guard was waving his hands about as he explained what was going on to his fellows.

"Sorry about the bit of deception, boys," Tristan said, throwing a companionable arm around the shoulders of two of them. "No need for anyone other than the six of us to know about this little adventure, is there?"

The older trolls grumbled a bit, but agreed to keep silent.

The younger was staring at me hard. "But if you're here, then…" His gaze drifted back to the gate. "Then that's…" He grimaced. "I don't think it's us you need to be worrying about."

We stepped through the gate and I saw Anaïs-as-me waiting only a few paces beyond, her face anxious. The anxiety fled when she saw us, as did my features. Red hair became black; round cheeks sharpened; and blue eyes became silver ones, filled with rage. I watched her take in my disheveled appearance, and the realization of what that meant dawned on her. "I take it you decided to stay." Her voice was harsh.

"I decided to stay," I agreed, but as I reached for Tristan's hand, my feet flew out from beneath me and I toppled to the ground. My first thought was that she'd hit me with her magic, but then I realized everything around me was shaking. The trolls were on the ground, too, falling bits of rock and dust bouncing off magical shields.

"Earthshake!" someone screamed.

Tristan's arms pulled me close, his body and magic protecting me from anything that might fall from above. "Hold, hold, hold," he repeated over and over again, his eyes locked on the magic of the tree that was all that held a million tons of rock from falling down on our heads. The rocks were moving, sliding and slamming against each other, and the noise drowned out even the sound of the waterfall.

As soon as it had started, the shaking stopped. We all rose to our feet, eyes on the shifting rocks above. Then the unthinkable happened. A boulder the size of a house slipped through the thick layers of magic and crashed downwards.

"No!" shouted Tristan, and he reached forward as though he might catch it. But even magic can move only so quickly. The rock smashed into the city.

The screaming began. Screams of terror, pain. Screams of those who had just lost loved ones beneath the weight of the rock.

"I have to..." Tristan looked at me with wild eyes and then at Anaïs. "Take Cécile back to the palace." Then he grabbed her by the shoulders. "On your life, you keep her safe. Promise me!"

She stared at him dully. "I promise."

Then he was off running towards the screaming. Anaïs took hold of my arm. "We need to go. The palace has a thousand years of magic reinforcing its walls – it is the safest place for you." She looked back at the guards. "Start moving everyone to higher ground. The tides may rise against us."

Her hand latched around my wrist and we ran through the city. The streets were thick with trolls, all of them crouched around the many pillars of the tree, their faces tense with concentration and fear.

"What are they doing?" I shouted over the sounds of screams and shifting rock.

"Flooding the tree with power!" Anaïs shouted back.

"Will it work?" My eyes were on the massive rocks shifting above us.

"He won't let it fall."

The ground shook again – not as badly as the first time, but it was enough to knock me from my feet. Anaïs caught me, her body taking the brunt of our fall, but my knee smashed against the ground, and blood instantly began dripping down my leg. I felt Anaïs's magic wrap around me, tiny stones bouncing off it as she held me tight against her. All around us, glass was shattering beneath the bits of falling rock. Not only was I afraid, but Tristan was afraid, and that made it worse.

When the shaking eased, Anaïs pulled me to my feet and started running again. She protected me at her own expense, shoving aside trolls who got in our way and wrapping me in magic whenever the world trembled. My skirts clung to my bloody knee, but my fear numbed the pain.

"Why are you helping me?" I asked as we clutched each other during another violent tremor.

"Because if you die, he will die," she hissed in my ear. "And if he dies…" Her eyes rose skyward, but whatever she'd been about to say died on her lips. "We must get back inside." Together we ran into the palace. It was empty.

"Where is everyone?" I asked as I followed Anaïs through the corridors.

"Helping." The shortness of her tone made me realize how much she resented not being out there herself. "Everyone who can walk. Except for you and me, that is."

I had never felt more useless in my life.

"You can go, now, if you want. I'm safe enough here alone." Or maybe not. I could feel blood running down my shin.

"I'll stay until I'm told otherwise." Anaïs flung the doors to my room open and walked over to my closets. "Take off that dress – we can't have you running around half-naked."

"Sorry," I mumbled, pulling the ruined dress off my shoulders and laying it carefully across a chair. The gash on my knee was a nasty looking thing. Grabbing a handkerchief, I tried considering how best to bandage it. "Perhaps it can be mended."

"As if I would ever wear it again." She emerged with a gown of yellow brocade. "Here. You look pretty in this color." She pursed her lips. "Why are you bleeding?"

"I cut myself when I fell."

She walked over and examined the injury, and to my surprise, she began to tremble. "Why hasn't it stopped bleeding yet? What's wrong with you?"

I jerked away. "Because I'm not a troll, you idiot. I'm hardly going to bleed to death, but this needs to be stitched."

"What?"

"Stitches. You can sew, can't you?"

"You want me to sew your skin?" Her expression was one of incredulity.

"First boil this water." I set a basin of water out, and it started bubbling within moments. I reluctantly set to cleaning the wound, my head dizzy from the pain. "Stitch," I commanded, but the moment she pressed the needle against my flesh, I gasped in pain and jerked back. "Sorry," I muttered. She made a second attempt with the same results. The third time I dug my nails into the upholstery and clenched my teeth so hard I thought they might crack.

"I'll be quick," she said, ignoring the tears flooding down my face.

Once we were through and I'd composed myself, I pulled the yellow gown on, balancing myself against the furniture when the room shook from another tremor. Anaïs flung open the curtains, went out onto the balcony, and looked up at the rocks. "If it were going to fall, I think it would have done so by now."

She came back into the room and began placing fallen books back on the shelves. I helped her, and together we put the room back into some semblance of order. When we were finished, I sorted through smashed glassware for two unbroken cups and poured us both a heavy measure of wine.

"Thank you," she said, sitting on one of the chairs and demurely crossing her ankles.

"I'm sorry," I blurted out.

"I've plenty of dresses, Cécile." She took a mouthful of her wine, watching me. "Although since you stole Lessa from us, I've had to stand for my own fittings. It's most bothersome."

"I don't mean about the dress." And I had no intention of apologizing about Lessa.

"Oh." I saw the dark red liquid in her cup slosh as though there'd been another tremor, but the room was still.

"You thought I'd leave today, given the chance. That was why you helped us, wasn't it?"

"I always help Tristan when he asks something of me," she said, composure restored.

"You'd have helped even if you'd known I wouldn't leave?"

"I've never said no to him before."

I set my glass down on the table untouched. "Enough with these vague answers. You thought I would leave and that's why you helped. Yes or no?"

Her eyes darkened. "Yes."

"Because if I were gone, he would spend more time with you?"

"Yes."

"You love him?"

She drained her glass and slammed it down next to mine, cracking it. I felt power and magic roil through the room. She could snap my neck without moving. Toss me so hard against the wall my bones would shatter. But I wasn't afraid. As much as she might hate me, she wouldn't, couldn't, break her word to Tristan.

"Yes."

"Because if I were gone, then there'd be a chance he would be with you instead?"

"No."

"You're lying!"

Anaïs shook her head and the weight of power in the room fell away. "I cannot lie. If you'd asked me if I desired to be his wife, my answer would have been different. But it has been a long time since there was a chance of that happening." Reaching for my untouched glass, she drained it. "For one, he has never felt that way about me. And two, I am flawed. Unfit. And there was nothing I could do to make up for it."

I choked back a laugh of astonishment. "If you're flawed, what does that make the rest of us? I might not like you very much, Anaïs, but you're still the most beautiful girl I've ever seen."

"And I might as well be the most ugly for all the difference it makes." She touched her chest. "My flaw lies within."

Hefty personality flaws didn't matter much to men when the outside was pretty, I wanted to say; but I didn't think that was what she meant.

"You know about my sister? How she died?"

I hesitated, then nodded. "Marc told me. She bled to death."

She scowled. "He would know. Regardless, since she had the blood sickness, I have it too."

I shook my head. "You got your fair share of scrapes during the earthshake and they've already healed. If you had the sickness, that wouldn't have happened."

"Just because it hasn't manifested doesn't mean I don't have it, Cécile. It's in me. I'd pass it down to my children." Her shoulders slumped. "I am an unfit wife, for the future king or for anyone. I have been told so to my face by the King himself." I watched as all her cool composure fell away, her body trembled with unshed tears. "I wasn't good enough to marry Tristan. I am not good enough to marry anyone. No one will even touch me for fear of tarnishing my reputation. I will always be alone."

A knock at the door interrupted her.

"Yes?" I called out, feeling rattled by the swell of sympathy Anaïs's confession had inspired in me. The door opened and Victoria walked in, shoulders bent with exhaustion.

"Well?" Anaïs snapped. Her composure was back in place again, and I half wondered if I'd imagined her losing it in the first place.

"Six dead in the city, a dozen more injured. Two mineshafts collapsed – we think there are five gangs of half-bloods trapped, but there could be more. Miners' Guild is waiting for the tremors to finish before they go after them, but there isn't much hope of reaching them in time."

I gasped and leapt to my feet. "We have to help them! They have no way to get themselves out."

"She's right." Anaïs got to her feet and began pacing back and forth like a caged animal. "They may not have much time."

"No sense risking more lives. We don't even know if they are still alive," Victoria said, picking through broken glass, trying to find an unbroken cup and eventually giving up.

"It's worth the risk," Anaïs argued. "I'd do it myself if I didn't have to stay here to mind the human."

"Go then," Victoria said. "I'll stay with Cécile. You're probably the only one left in the city who isn't nearly drained, and no doubt she will prefer my company to yours."

She didn't need to be told twice. Without a backward

glance, Anaïs bolted out the door and I watched resentfully as she went. She could move rocks the size of horses with the flick of a finger, dig out miners buried beneath the mountain. She could save lives, and all I could do was sit here and wait. Worse yet, both Victoria and Anaïs could be out helping, but instead their magic was wasted on minding me.

"I feel so useless."

"No one is expecting you to help, Cécile," Victoria said, her voice sympathetic. "This is work for trolls."

I sighed. "Let me find you an unbroken glass, then. I can do that much at least."

With my little ball of magic in tow, I wandered from room to room, picking my way through overturned furniture, fallen items, and broken glass. The entire palace looked like a dollhouse that someone had picked up and given a good shake.

Spying an unbroken goblet on the floor, I called out, "I've found you a..." but then trailed off as I looked through the doorway. My friend was leaning back in a chair, mouth open, the sound of gentle snores filling the room. "Glass."

Walking out onto my balcony, I looked down at the city. It was darker now. The trolls were all spent and had retreated to their homes. The tree was flush with power, the pillars, arches, and canopy visible even to me. It was up to the builders now to direct the magic to best balance the load. Up to Tristan.

I could feel him, so I knew that he was well enough. Anxious and tired, but unharmed. My knee ached unmercifully, but I tried to ignore the pain as best I could. I didn't want Tristan coming back here because he thought I was hurt when his people desperately needed him. I racked my brain for what should be done to treat it, berating myself the entire time for not paying more attention to Gran. Why couldn't I be strong like a troll, not... fragile. Human.

Tiptoeing around Victoria, I extracted Anushka's grimoire from its hiding place. Flipping through the pages, I found her healing spell, but the plants were not native to the Isle. Turning to the last page, I stared at the word *curses*. Once again, I hoped for inspiration to come. For some answer that would save all the good in Trollus while protecting the world from the bad. But as before, there were no answers.

"Victoria," I said quietly, deciding it was time to wake her. She didn't even twitch, so I walked over and shook her shoulder. One eye opened and regarded me blearily, and I watched as realization struck and she leapt upright. "Cécile! My apologies!" She looked around wildly. "Has something happened?"

"Nothing," I said calmly. The last thing I needed was for her to overreact like Anaïs had. "I cut my knee during the earthshake. It isn't that bad," I added quickly when her eyes widened. "Anaïs stitched it up, but I need some herbs to clean it properly." I listed off several. What I really wanted was an opportunity to go to the library. There had to be more grimoires in that vast collection of books, and maybe there was one with a spell I could use to fix up myself.

Victoria nodded uncertainly. "The kitchen, perhaps? *Anaïs* stitched you up?"

"The kitchen is a good place to start," I said, pulling on my cloak. "And yes, she did." Opening the door, I walked out into the hallway. "It turns out she isn't as awful as I once thought."

Victoria was utterly useless at helping me find anything in the kitchen – not that I was overly surprised. "What about this?" she asked, holding a sprig of rosemary. "Smells nice."

I shook my head and took the sprig from her. "Sit over there and wait," I said, scanning the shelves filled with spices and herbs. The palace's kitchen seemed to have everything but what I was looking for – most likely because what I was looking for didn't go in a pot for flavor.

"Élise, where are you when I need you?" I muttered as I moved deeper into the kitchen, which was devoid of life. Everyone was out helping fill the tree with power – including both my maids. I could hardly begrudge them their absence, but they would have been useful in my search. They both had minds like steel traps. If they'd ever seen comfrey or calendula or any of the other herbs that I could use, they'd remember.

Remember.

I glanced down at the sprig of rosemary in my hand, the smell of it triggering my recollection of a spell in Anushka's grimoire. Making sure I was out of Victoria's sight, I motioned for my light to come closer and flipped through the pages until I found what I was looking for: a spell for retrieving lost objects. "The incantation can be performed to help retrieve the memory of where the object was last seen," I read softly. "The memory is pulled into the mind of she who casts the incantation."

Neither of my maids had precisely lost what I was looking for, but I thought the spell might do. That is, if earth magic worked on them at all. They were half-human, but would that be enough? Never hurts to try, I thought to myself.

Firstly, I tracked down paper, pen, and ink. After giving it a bit of thought, I wrote *clove oil* on the paper and then rolled it up. Next, I needed something belonging to one of the girls. I looked myself up and down. Élise had lowered the neckline on the dress I was wearing – that meant the work was hers. I hoped that counted. Carefully, I pulled loose the piece of thread and wrapped it around the bit of paper, followed by a twist of rosemary. "Water," I mumbled, finding a basin and filling it to the brim. From what Martin had told me about human magic, I understood that a witch drew power from the four elements, in this case water, but I didn't understand why. Nor did I know why certain herbs were used in certain spells, but not others. Her grimoire was like a recipe book that told me how to perform certain spells, but I had no idea how or why they worked. And I didn't have time to figure it out now.

Looking over my shoulder, I checked to make sure Victoria hadn't moved from the spot where I left her. But my friend was slumped in a chair, chin resting on her chest. I could faintly hear the sound of her snores.

Speaking in a quiet but firm voice, I recited the strange incantation, substituting Élise's name and clove oil in the appropriate spots. Eleven times, I repeated the phrase. On the twelfth time, I threw the rosemary-wrapped package into the basin. On the thirteenth repetition, I touched my finger to the water. The sound of waves roared loudly in my ears, and the package began to rotate around the basin. Faster and faster it spun, and with each turn, I felt magic flood up into me. I pulled my hand from the water and the contents stilled. Nothing. I could see nothing. Either the spell hadn't worked because Élise wasn't completely human, or she had no memory of what I'd asked for. Or maybe the thread I'd included didn't count as hers. There were so many factors, and I had no way of knowing which one had interfered.

Sighing, I reached for the basin, but pulled back when an image appeared in the water. It wasn't my reflection. I watched wide-eyed as a pair of hands folded linens and stacked them on shelves. The same hands then picked up a dark bottle and carefully tucked it in next to the folded sheets. This was a memory. This was Élise's memory.

Clapping my hands together, I crowed with delight.

"What's going on?" Victoria shouted, the chair she'd been sitting on clattering to the ground.

Snatching the water-soaked package out of the basin, I shoved it in my pocket and spun around. "Nothing," I said, wishing for a moment I could be truthful to my friend. "I just remembered where to look. In the laundry room."

Victoria tilted her head slightly and pursed her lips. "And when, precisely, was the last time you visited the laundry?"

Never. I grimaced. "Do you know where it is?"

"Of course I do," Victoria replied. "But I'm not going to show you until you tell me the truth about whatever it is you're lying about."

I wiped my hands on my skirts and stared at the floor. Tristan had told me to keep my magic a secret – that it would be dangerous for anyone to discover I was a witch. But this was Victoria, and I couldn't imagine a circumstance where my friend would ever try to harm me. It was Tristan who never trusted anyone, not me. For me, it was second nature to have faith in my friends – to believe they'd do right by me no matter what. And maybe that was stupid. But I didn't want to live in a world where I couldn't trust those closest to me. "I did a spell," I said, handing her my water-soaked package. "It told me where to look."

"So, you're a witch?"

"Yes." I hazarded a glance up to see how she was reacting. Victoria had a smile on her face.

"Well," she said, pausing for a long, dramatic moment. "There are worse things to be – things that rhyme with witch. And at least you aren't one of those."

A wave of relief passed over me. "I certainly hope not."

She slung an arm around me, squeezing me so tight I wheezed for breath. "Rhyming is as good as alliteration, you know. Possibly better. Now let's go find what you're looking for."

CHAPTER 33
Cécile

The next morning, I set out to see if I could learn anything more about the nature of human magic. As much as I'd been successful the night before in lifting the memory from Élise's mind, I didn't understand anything about what I was doing.

Trollus was a mess. Broken glass and pieces of rock littered the streets, and enormous waves from the ocean had pushed the river back, causing its banks to flood. Trolls were busy at work trying to clean everything up, but it would be a long time before the beautiful city was back to its usual glory.

With Élise at my side, I headed to the library. I hoped that Martin would be there, because I would be at a loss to find anything in the massive building.

"Oh dear," I said, looking around with dismay. There were books everywhere.

"My lady!" Martin came around the corner, an armload of books floating behind him.

"I came to see if you had any other... er, grimoires," I said, casting a backwards glance at Élise. The girl was already asking one of the other librarians if she could help. "But I can see that you are rather busy."

"Not at all, my lady. I had set some aside for you, but I haven't had a chance to send them over. My apologies. I'll go get them for you straight away." He bowed to me, but I noticed his eyes were on Élise.

"You'll keep her occupied while I read?" I asked, trying not to grin.

"Certainly, my lady. Miss Élise is always a pleasant conversationalist."

The corners of my lips twisted up despite my best effort. Élise was as quiet as a mouse, but perhaps that made her well suited for a librarian. Mostly, I was pleased to see that Martin was willing to overlook the fact she was half-human. I settled down at a table and picked up the first of the three books. It was almost entirely dedicated to love potions, the prevention of pregnancy, and predicting the weather. The second and third were focused on healing remedies and magic, but they were all clear that healing could not be done on oneself. So much for that idea.

None of them used blood or sacrifice, and none of them mentioned curses. And much like Anushka's grimoire, none of them explained why certain elements and plants worked better for certain types of spells. The only truly interesting thing the books taught me was that witch magic was passed down from generation to generation, but only manifested itself in women. Ability and strength varied between women, and many lived their whole lives never knowing they possessed the power. Which was certainly the case in my family.

Leaning back, I rubbed my tired eyes, trying to ignore my sore knee. I'd cleaned it last night with the oil my spell had led me to, then again this morning, and it had scabbed over. It didn't need magic, it just needed time to heal. Coming here had been a waste of my morning. None of what I'd found was helpful. I wasn't helpful. Anaïs could dig trolls out of collapsed mines, but the best I could come up with was how to put boils on someone's bum. And I couldn't even do that to the King, because earth magic didn't work on full-blooded trolls. And I didn't exactly have a supply of troll blood on hand, nor did I expect any of them to provide it willingly.

Suddenly, I jerked upright. When Christophe had accused Tristan of using magic to make me love him, Tristan had said that such things were not the magic of trolls. I stared at the grimoires and mentally skimmed through the pages of Anushka's book. Witches could make you fall in love, heal a wound, or bind you to a place, but their magic always affected the flesh or mind. While a troll could lift a rock, create light, or toss you across the room, they couldn't make you sick or cause you to fall in love: their magic was primarily tangible.

"Anushka didn't break the mountain," I whispered. She had been caught up in the rockslide as much as the trolls, and whatever had driven her to curse the trolls to eternal captivity had happened during the four weeks it took to dig out the city. But what? What had they done to make her turn to such evil? And if she hadn't broken the mountain, then who had?

Élise abruptly appeared, and to my surprise, she sat down heavily across from me.

"What has happened?" I asked, her bowed head filling me with anxiety.

She looked up, eyes glistening. "It's Tips. He snuck into the mines with one of the day-shift gangs to help them meet quota." Élise squeezed her eyes shut. "He was pinned by a falling rock. The rest of the miners got him out, but his leg was crushed."

I blanched. "Is he healing?"

Her tears fell faster and faster. "Anyone else would have been, but he's mostly human. He heals like a human." She looked up at me. "They don't think he's going to make it – and even if he does, he'll never walk again. The guild will put him in the labyrinth for certain."

My stomach tightened, and I gripped the edge of the table hard, breathing deeply in an attempt to control my hammering heartbeat. My eyes fixed on the stack of grimoires in front of me, two of which I knew contained spells for healing humans. Spells that I knew would work on half-bloods. "I'm not going to let him die," I said, my voice hoarse.

"There isn't anything you can do," Élise sobbed, her shoulders shaking.

There wasn't anything I *should* do. Tristan had been right when he said that bravery and wisdom made poor bedfellows. It had been one thing to tell Victoria, but if I helped Tips, everyone would know I was a witch. And the trolls hated witches – they'd been hunting them down for centuries. It would not surprise me in the slightest if some of them demanded I be burned in the streets when they found out, no matter the risk to Tristan. I bit my lip hard.

Risking my life meant risking his, but if I did nothing, Tips was a dead man, that much was certain. And I couldn't quietly stand back and let that happen, even if it was the smart thing to do.

Picking up the two grimoires, I rose to my feet. "What," I said softly, "would you say if I told you I *could* help?" I swallowed hard, knowing I wouldn't be able to turn back once the words were out. "What would you say if I told you I was a witch?"

CHAPTER 34
Cécile

I kept my hood up and my head down as I made my way from the library towards the Dregs. My light bobbed about in front of me and, unless anyone looked closely, I'd be mistaken for a troll. I was alone – Élise had gone in search of the ingredients I needed for the spell, but not before she'd convinced Martin to let us out the small back entrance. I didn't need my guards following me – the fewer who knew about what I was going to attempt, the better.

Knocking on the door to the miners' dormitory, I glanced surreptitiously up and down the street, hoping no one would notice my finery and question what a noble woman was doing at the door to a half-blood home. But everyone nearby walked with the hunched shoulders of weariness, too set on their own business to pay me mind. I was still relieved when the door swung open.

"Your Highness!" said the girl who answered, her eyes wide with surprise. She started to curtsey awkwardly, but I held a finger up to my lips and gently pushed her inside. "I'd rather no one know I am here," I said, shutting the door behind me. "Where is Tips?"

Her face tightened. "This way."

The smell of blood and sweat assaulted me the second I entered the room, but it was the sight of Tips lying on the bed, face contorted with pain, that made me feel sick to my stomach. The other miners in the room rose to their feet when they saw me, but not before exchanging confused looks with each other.

"Hello, Princess," Tips said weakly. "I can't say I expected to see your pretty face again."

I smiled. "Why would you say such a thing – do you think I am such an inconstant friend?"

He laughed. "Never that – I'm afraid that I am the one you can't be counting on these days." He made a small gesture with one hand towards his covered legs.

Taking a deep breath, I raised the edge of the blanket. I immediately clenched my teeth to hold back the bile threatening to surge up my throat. From the knee down, the pulverized bone and flesh was barely recognizable as having once been a leg and foot. "God have mercy," I whispered, lowering the blanket.

"I'm not so sure your god has much time for us," Tips said through clenched teeth.

"Why not?" I asked, settling into a chair next to the bed. "You're nearly as human as I am." I turned my head to address the other miners. "Could you please leave us alone for a bit? I need to speak privately with Tips."

Nodding, they all started to leave the room. "Send Élise up when she arrives," I added, praying that would be soon. Once they were gone, I pulled the grimoires out of my pocket, flipping through the pages until I found what I was looking for. This wouldn't be simple. And it would be far from perfect.

"If you're thinking that you being here will stop the guild from ridding themselves of me, you're wasting your time," Tips said, his one eye fixed on the ceiling. "They won't bother with the labyrinth – I'm done for without it."

"Not if I have my way, you aren't," I muttered, my eyes fixed on the page, praying that I wasn't being falsely optimistic.

The sound of him shifting on the bed caused me to glance up. Tips was staring at me, his one eye filled with anger. "What exactly do you think you can do to stop me from dying, girl? Your false hope is no kindness to me."

"It isn't false hope," I replied. "I intend to heal you with magic. Human magic."

His eye widened. "You're a witch!" Despite the incredible amount of pain he must have been in, a smile stretched across his face. "I knew there had to be more to you than meets the eye."

"I suppose we'll find out," I said. Footsteps pounded up the stairs and, seconds later, Élise came into the room. She smiled encouragingly at Tips as she handed me a sack of supplies.

"Did you find everything?" I asked.

She nodded and set to helping me spread the various plants and herbs out on the floor next to the basins she had brought. Once we had everything arranged to my liking, I sat back on my heels and took a deep breath. "Tips, there is something I need to tell you before we start."

He gave a slight nod.

"This grimoire," I began, "it tells me that spells can only speed along that which is humanly possible to heal." I took a deep breath. "Which means that although I can save your life, I can't save your leg."

Élise pressed a hand to her mouth, but Tips didn't flinch. "What do you plan to do?"

I dug my fingernails into my palms. "I think if we take the leg off just below the knee that I can heal the... stump." Sweat broke out on my forehead – it had been one thing to think it, another to say it.

"You think?"

"I've never done this before," I admitted. What I had done to Tristan had been something different – I'd somehow channeled his magic, not the earth's. But comparing Tips's and Tristan's magic was like comparing a drop of water with the entirety of the ocean. His power wasn't capable of managing this injury, even if I could replicate the circumstances.

"You want to cut off my leg." His face tightened and a bead of sweat ran down his forehead to soak into the pillow.

"It is our only option," I said. "The only way you are going to live."

"Live?" He snorted. "Even if this works, what good will I be?" he asked bitterly. "What good is a miner with one leg – you'd be saving me from death only to see me sent off to feed the sluag."

"Don't say that," I snapped, rising to my feet. "Your worth isn't determined by your leg – it is determined by your heart and your mind. It is determined by what you do with your life."

"Pretty words." He turned his head away from us. "Just let me die."

"No!" I shouted. "You listen to me, Tips, and you listen well. It isn't your leg that can smell gold. It isn't your leg that has ensured your gang never missed quota. And it isn't your leg that all your friends chose to have as their leader. They need you, Tips. Without you, it will be your friends who will be facing the labyrinth." I took a deep breath, trying to calm myself. "The odds have been stacked against you from the day you were born, yet here you are. Alive. And having persevered through all of that, how dare you turn your head and tell me to let you die. You're better than that." My voice trembled. "You once told me that power doesn't determine worth. Well, neither does a leg."

He kept his head turned away from me, and the silence hung long and heavy.

"You make a compelling argument." His voice was choked, and when he turned his head, I could see the gleam of tears on his cheeks. "Do it then."

I nodded and looked at Élise. "I'll need your help."

It seemed my mind stepped back and away from what it was witnessing as I carefully mixed the spell's ingredients into the basin, following its instructions to the letter. "I need fire," I muttered, and Élise held out her hand, silver flames blossoming from her palm.

I stared at it for a minute. "Real fire," I said. Tearing a blank page from the book, I rolled it tightly then held it to her troll-fire, nodding with satisfaction as it flared up with yellow and orange flames. Holding the burning paper above my mixture, I turned my attention to Élise. "Are you sure you can do this?"

She licked her lips, and I could see her hands were trembling. "If this doesn't work, he'll bleed to death in moments."

"If this doesn't work, I'm dead anyway," Tips said. "This isn't the time for you to turn prissy on me, Élise."

"All right," Élise whispered. "Then I'm ready."

Tips twitched slightly as her magic bound him to the bed and the ambient sounds of the house faded as she blocked us off – the last thing we needed was for Tips's screams to draw attention down upon us.

"Bite down on this," I said, putting a spindle we'd broken off the chair back between his teeth. "Close your eyes."

"When I put my hands in the basins..." I broke off and gave Élise a hard look. Her lips tightened, but she nodded.

Touching the burning paper to the mixture, I jerked back as it burst into flames. Then I began the incantations. Eleven times I repeated the words, and on the twelfth time, I plunged one hand into the burning mixture and the other into a basin of water. Power flooded up my arms, filling me, and then spilling over. I nodded at Élise.

Troll magic sliced through flesh and bone like a surgeon's scalpel, blood spraying in all directions, and Tips screamed once. Leaning forward, I grasped hold of the bleeding limb and said the incantation for the thirteenth time: "Heal the flesh." At the touch of his blood, I could feel a faint hint of his alien magic, but I passed it by, knowing instinctively that he was a child of *this* world. The earth's power drained out of me and into Tips, recognizing him. Amazed,

I watched as pink skin sealed over the wound, paling and hardening into tough scar tissue before my very eyes. Then exhaustion hit me, and I fell backwards to lie on the cold, wooden floor.

"Cécile!" Élise's face appeared above me. "Are you all right?"

"Yes," I croaked, although I was not entirely sure that I was. "Is Tips alive?"

She moved out of my line of sight. "He's alive," she exclaimed. "Unconscious, but alive. And the wound is healed over as though it were half-a-lifetime old."

Coming back over to my side, Élise helped me to my feet, releasing the magic blocking sound as she did. Screams instantly attacked both our ears.

"Stones and sky," I said, clinging to her arm. "What is going on out there?"

"I've no notion," Élise said, her eyes wide. "We would have felt it if there had been another earthshake."

We both jerked at the sound of an explosion, followed up with more screams and the sounds of running feet.

The door burst open followed by one of the miners. "Lord Roland is on the loose," he panted. "He's tearing apart the Dregs. You need to get out of here now." His eyes fixed on Tips, who was only now rousing. "How in the…"

"There is no time for that now," I snapped. "Take Tips with you. Get him somewhere safe. Élise, you help him."

Not waiting for their answers, I bolted down the stairs. Roland was hunting half-bloods, I knew it. And who knew how many he would kill before someone powerful enough arrived to stop him. I needed to distract him, buy Tristan or Anaïs enough time to get here and for the half-bloods to flee. Roland wouldn't hurt me – insane or not, he'd know that harming me would harm his brother. I was the only one close enough who had a chance of stopping him.

The lower level of the house was empty, but the streets were full of panicked half-bloods running for their lives. I fought against their flow, jostling against their greater strength while I ran towards the sound of screams. Then abruptly, I was alone, their footsteps fading into the distance behind me.

A young troll stood in the center of the road ahead of me, an older half-blood pinned to the ground at his feet. The half-blood screamed and thrashed, trying to escape, while the boy watched with interest.

"Your Highness!" The words were out of my mouth before I could think. "Lord Roland."

The boy looked up, and the blood in my veins turned to ice. It was not the resemblance to Tristan – I'd expected that. What made me want to run as far and as fast away from this creature as I could were his eyes: they were cold, completely devoid of empathy or compassion. Or sanity.

"Hello, Cécile." He cocked his head to one side, watching me with undisguised malevolence.

I curtseyed, my knees shaking. "You know who I am, then, my lord?"

"Oh, yes," he said. "I've heard a great deal about you. You are the human that my brother Tristan is bonded to."

"Yes, I am," I said, his recognition not bringing any relief to my fear, because what was looking at me was utter evil.

"My foster father told me that Tristan loves you – is that true?"

I nodded, forcing myself to hold his gaze. The longer we talked, the more time the half-bloods had to get away. "And I love him."

Roland scrunched his face up as though he had smelled something foul. "Well of course you do, that makes perfect sense." He shook his head, his brow furrowing. "It's him that I don't understand."

This creature didn't understand love at all.

During our exchange, Roland had released the half-blood, and the man was now trying to crawl away. His motion caught the Prince's attention, and his face twisted. "Vermin," he hissed. Raising one hand, he brought it down fast, and the man collapsed against the street with the sound of crunching bone. I swayed on my feet.

"Where is my brother now?" Roland asked, stepping over the corpse and walking slowly towards me.

"Very near," I lied. Tristan was indeed coming this way, but it would take long minutes before he arrived – and that was time I was beginning to suspect I didn't have. "I am sure he will be pleased to see you."

"I doubt that." He bolted towards me, and before I could move, he had me by the wrist. Even though he was shorter and slighter than me, with one twist of his wrist he had me on my knees. He ignored my groan of pain, carefully inspecting the silver tattoo on my fingers. "He is near, you say?" His childish giggles filled the street. "Not near enough, I say!"

"If you hurt me, you hurt him, you know that," I pleaded. But what did that mean to this remorseless creature. He didn't care about his brother – he didn't care about anything but himself.

"I know that very well," Roland said, shoving me back. He closed his eyes and, for a moment, he was a beautiful little child. Then he opened them again, and it was like looking into the eyes of a devil. "And when I am king, I will be certain not to bond something as weak as you. Or anything at all."

I clambered to my feet.

"Roland, stop!"

It was Anaïs's voice, but she was too late. As I turned to run, magic slammed into me, crushing the wind out of my lungs and sending me flying through the air. My body slammed against the ground and, after that, all I knew was pain.

CHAPTER 35
Cécile

When I awoke back in the palace, it was to an agony that told me instantly my injuries were grievous. Mortal. It hurt to move – it hurt even to breathe – and I was so very, very cold.

"Cécile?" Tristan was sitting at my bedside, his eyes rimmed with red. "I am so sorry."

I licked my parched lips. "It isn't your fault."

"Yes, it is." His voice was bitter. "Anaïs warned me something like this would happen – she told me to take care of Roland before he got any more powerful, and I refused."

"You couldn't have known," I whispered, unable to manage anything louder.

"I knew he was dangerous," Tristan said sadly. "I was just too much of a coward to do anything about it."

He pushed my hair back from my face. "But I won't make the same mistake twice – I'll deal with him and, when you're better again, Trollus will be safe for you."

"Tristan," I said. "I think I need help. From a doctor. It hurts to breathe."

He bit his lip. "We don't have doctors."

I knew that. Trolls didn't need them. "It hurts."

His jaw tightened. "It will get better."

I gave a slight shake of my head. "I'm not a troll," I said, unable to keep the bitterness from my voice. "I am only human. Mortal and breakable. There is no one here with the skills to help me. I'm afraid…" I broke off, coughing weakly.

He took a deep shuddering breath, and his trepidation grew thick as he slowly pulled the glove off his left hand. His lovely eyes fixed on the golden lace tattooing his hand. The vines, once so bright and vital, were dull and tarnished. "I was afraid to look," he said. "I was afraid this is what I would see."

"I'm dying," I whispered. My voice was calm and completely incongruous with the riot of terror and anger in my head. I did not want to die. Only a day ago, it had seemed my future spread ahead of me like a wild, passionate, and unexplored sea, and I was the captain at the helm, eager to see where the winds would take me. I was in love, and I was loved. I'd never felt more alive and happy, and now it was all going to be over. My lower lip trembled and I clenched my teeth to make it stop. It wasn't fair. Trollus was full of magic – magic capable of doing the impossible, but powerless to help me in this. An angry noise escaped my lips. "It isn't bloody fair," I swore. "This wasn't how it was supposed to be."

My chest spasmed, and I hissed in pain. "I'm sorry," I said through clenched teeth. Because that was the worst of it – not only was I going to die, I was going to bring Tristan down with me.

"No," he said, rising to his feet. "No!" He picked up a decanter and threw it, then backhanded a vase off his desk. I watched in horror as he set to destroying everything fragile in sight.

"Tristan, stop!"

He froze, turning back towards me. A shard of glass had sliced open his cheek and one drop of blood trickled down his skin before the cut sealed over. "There isn't anyone here with the skill to help you. But somewhere else there is?" He turned. "Could other humans help you?"

"I don't know. Possibly a surgeon could." There is always hope, I thought, remembering Pierre's words. Hope that I might live, and that my future with Tristan wouldn't be cut short. But my hope was diminishing.

"There are always humans coming and going. They're always wanting to sell something. Always wanting our gold." His face set in determination. "One of them will be able to help you."

Anaïs must have been waiting outside, because she came in right after Tristan left.

"Tristan said he was going to find you a surgeon," she said, sitting next to the bed. "And medicines to help you heal."

I said nothing, but something in my eyes must have told her what I was thinking. "They can help you, can't they?" she pleaded.

I gave a slight shake of my head. "I don't think so. A witch could, maybe." But Tips was an all too recent reminder that even witches had their limitations.

"There are no such creatures in Trollus." Anaïs gripped the sides of her chair so hard the wood creaked. "Except, it turns out, you. The whole city is talking about what you did for that miner." Her eyes brightened. "If we got you the same materials – couldn't you heal yourself?"

"No." I mouthed the word, feeling short of breath. The pain in my side was sharp and internal. "I'm dying." The words came out silently.

"No!" Anaïs shouted, leaping to her feet. "You can't die! If you die, he…"

"Do you think I don't know that?" I said, sucking in a painful breath to make myself clear. "I know what it feels like, Anaïs!"

I started coughing, the pain of the motion so intense it made me dizzy. It was a long time before I could speak again, and Anaïs was forced to lean close in order to hear me. "I need your help, Anaïs. I don't trust his father, and the twins told me you're the only other one as powerful as Tristan. You have to keep him alive. I know he did it for Marc, so can't you do the same for him?"

Her shoulders slumped and my hopes fled. She shook her head. "There is a reason they have ruled us for so long, Cécile. There are none in this world as powerful as the Montigny family – I wouldn't have a chance of stopping him. Only his father could restrain him, and even then, it would be a struggle."

I tried to take shallow little breaths, but I could taste blood on my tongue. "Is there no other way?"

Anaïs grimaced. "With iron."

I frowned.

She hesitated as though the information was a great secret. Perhaps it was, if it were something that could control their magic. "It is a method usually only used to bind prisoners until the time of their execution. Sometimes it's used as a punishment," she said. "The troll is physically restrained and iron spikes are driven into the body. The metal interferes with our magic – if enough are used, he might be controllable."

A shudder ran through me. She'd have to torture him to save him.

"He'd have to agree to it beforehand, though," she said. "And he won't."

I bit my lip. "Is it the only way?"

"Yes." She closed her eyes, but glittering tears forced their way through her black lashes. "Except for one thing. He has my true name."

I squeezed my eyes tight, giving her a slight nod so that she would know that I understood the implications of that knowledge. Tristan had complete control over Anaïs – and in this situation, he would use it.

"The same goes for Marc and the twins," she said bitterly. "He has the name of anyone we dare ask who is powerful enough to do it."

But what if I could handicap him enough that a less powerful troll might be able to control him. Could I do it? Did I have the strength?

"There's a book hidden in the garderobe."

Frowning, Anaïs went into the side room and came back holding the grimoire. "What is this?"

"Anushka's grimoire," I said. "There are spells in here for use against trolls."

Anaïs recoiled. "Blood magic!"

I nodded and explained the spell that would cut a troll off from his magic.

"Can you make it work?" she asked, eyeing me warily. "Using my blood?"

"I hope so."

"I prefer certainty to hope." She made a face. "What makes you think you are even capable of subduing one of us? And not just any Fa..." She broke off. "Not just any troll. The most powerful troll in this world."

I blinked. "I could test it on you, I suppose." My eyes met her metallic gaze. "If I can cut him off from his magic, a less powerful troll could restrain him. Stick him full of metal until he is sound enough of mind to be set free."

She looked ill.

"You'll help me, won't you?" I asked, trying to keep my voice level.

"I will do what it takes," she said. "Whatever it takes to save him."

Relief flooded through me.

"It doesn't need to come to that, though." Anaïs squared her shoulders. "We can get you help. Get you another witch who can fix you with magic."

"If the King allows it," I replied. "I think he might rather see me die than allow another witch in this city."

"He wouldn't dare – he knows the risks it entails."

"There is always Roland," I said softly.

Magic prickled over my skin as Anaïs's anger rose. "If it comes to that, we are all of us doomed."

When Tristan eventually returned, it was with Jérôme and Christophe trailing along at his heels. "Oh, my dear girl," the weathered old farmer said upon entering the room.

"What has happened to you?" Pulling back my layers of blankets, he rested a hand on my forehead and then laid his ear against my chest, listening to the rapid thudding of my heart. Then, very carefully, he felt along my side, quickly withdrawing his hand when I squealed in anguish.

"This is far beyond my skill, or that of any of the others who do business with you, my lord," he said. "Her ribs are broken, and I suspect she is bleeding internally. She needs a skilled surgeon, and soon, for there to be any chance she'll live."

"She needs her grandmother," Chris said from where he stood in the corner. He pointed a finger at Tristan. "I told you this place would kill her."

"You bring her grandmother, then," Tristan said. "Just name your price – I'll pay."

"Only a troll would try to put a price on something like this," Chris said, not bothering to hide his disgust.

"Shut your fool mouth," Jérôme snapped at his son. "We'll bring her grandmother, my lord. If we ride fast, we should be back here by morning."

"Or not." The door clicked shut. "The grandmother is a witch – and it seems we already have one too many of those within the confines of this city."

Jérôme and Christophe dropped to their knees. Anaïs's grip on my hand tightened, and Tristan spun towards the door.

As soon as I heard the King's voice, I knew my time was up. He wanted me dead, and this way it would happen without him even muddying his hands. I would be just another human who succumbed to the darkness of Trollus.

"Have you lost your mind?" Tristan shouted. "She's injured! If we don't help her, she'll die!"

Thibault tsked through his fat lips. "Tragic, to be sure, but such is the way of life. The strong flourish, the weak perish. It is not our way to interfere." He walked over to the bed and leaned over, cold eyes taking in my weakness. I felt like a small, injured creature under the eye of a hungry vulture. "Pathetically weak," he said, turning away. "I am sure we can find you something stronger."

Tristan's eyes bulged with fury. "She is my wife," he howled at his father.

"Your Majesty, you must reconsider," Anaïs gasped. "If she dies..." Her eyes flickered to Tristan.

The King chuckled. "Never fear, Anaïs. I won't let my boy die. If I have to tie him up for months and force-feed him gruel myself, I'll do it."

Even though he was discussing my impending death, I felt relief at the King's words. He wouldn't let Tristan die. Tristan wouldn't have to endure torture in order to survive. But while this knowledge relieved that anxiety, it did nothing to quell my fear of what was to come for me. I did not think I could stand it if the pain got much worse, but the thought of losing consciousness was worse. I didn't want to lose my last moments. I wanted to live. Clenching my eyes shut, I prayed for a higher power to intervene and keep this hour from becoming my last.

"No," Tristan said, the word ripping me out of my reverie. "I won't live without her."

His father smiled. "How poetic. Unfortunately, kings and their heirs cannot afford such romanticism, Tristan.

When she dies, you'll take a nice troll girl to your bed, one of my choosing." He shot Anaïs a nasty grin. "Not you, bleeder, so don't get your hopes up. A nice, unflawed one. Once she produces an heir or two, you, Tristan, can drown yourself in the river for all I care. It won't matter. You won't matter."

"You're a monster," I said, my words barely loud enough to hear.

Thibault leaned down over my bed, his breath hot and smelling of garlic. "Yes, but you knew that before you even came, didn't you, Cécile?"

I cringed away from the creature above me, for the King was like a thing of nightmares. The beast hunting in the midnight spaces, beneath bridges and in forest caves. Always watching and always waiting for the chance to strike.

He pressed a hand against my forehead. "You are in a great deal of pain, I think." He looked at Jérôme, as if noticing him for the first time. "Do you have something you can give her? No need for her to spend her last days in agony."

Jérôme's face was white from fear. "Yes, Your Majesty."

The King turned his attention back to Tristan. "You will do nothing to interfere, do you understand?"

"I hear you," Tristan said. "But I far from understand why you are doing this."

"All that matters is that you obey." The King strode from the room, slamming the door shut behind him.

"I'm sorry." My voice was quiet, even in the silence of the room.

"I won't let you die," Tristan said, the words almost a groan. In two strides, he was next to the bed, his forehead pressed against mine. Magic enveloped us, blocking our words from the others in the room. "I can't lose you." His words were muffled against my hair. "I won't."

"There isn't anything you can do," I said. "Except to let me go and promise me you'll live." It took every ounce of control for me to keep my voice calm and reasonable. I wasn't even certain why I bothered, because I could see my anguish reflected in his eyes. He felt it too.

"No."

"You aren't making this any easier for me by saying that," I said, my fingers clutching at his shirt. My voice cracked, and a sob racked my body with pain.

"It is the truth." I could hear his heart thundering against my ear, feel his misery and fear. "I should have made you go when I had the chance."

"It wasn't your decision to make." I kissed him hard, clinging to him with what little strength I had left. "I would never choose to leave you."

"Isn't that what dying means?" Bitterness echoed through me. "Leaving?"

"But not by choice." I tried to breathe and calm myself – to bury my sorrow beneath my desire to ensure Tristan remained alive. It was the last thing I had any control over, and I clung to it like a shipwrecked sailor to the debris of his vessel.

"Does it make a difference, if the result is the same? I'm going to save you," he muttered. "No matter what the cost."

He gestured to Jérôme. "Give her something for the pain." Then he motioned to Anaïs and Christophe, who both followed him across the room, their words cloaked by magic.

Jérôme stirred a mixture of herbs into some water. Lifting my head with one hand, he poured the liquid into my mouth. It tasted foul, and I struggled to swallow it back. "This will help you rest easy."

"What are they talking about?" I asked, my eyes fixed on Tristan. He was writing something on a piece of paper.

"I don't know," Jérôme said. "I'll leave these herbs for you. Take as much as you need to numb the pain." His eyes met mine. "Take them all when you feel you cannot bear it any longer."

My attention flickered back to Tristan. He handed Chris a folded and sealed letter, which Chris tucked into the pocket of his coat. They both wore grave expressions. Chris nodded at whatever Tristan was saying, and to my astonishment, they clasped each other's shoulders. Tristan turned to Anaïs, and I watched them silently argue, she shaking her head while he gestured wildly. Eventually she nodded, and Tristan came back over to the bed.

"We are going to take you out of Trollus," he said. "We cannot get anyone here to help you in time, but I believe we can smuggle you out."

"You can't send me away!" Hot tears filled my eyes, making Tristan's image blur. Everything was blurry. Jérôme's medicine was taking its effect, making both my mind and body numb. "You can't, you can't," I repeated, searching for words to convey what I was feeling.

"He's going to come with you, Cécile," Chris said. "You don't need to worry. We've found a way that he can leave."

"What? How?" Exhaustion crept over me like a blanket of fog, my eyelids drooping. Neither Chris or Jérôme answered as they walked quickly from the room.

"Don't worry about how," Tristan whispered in my ear, his breath warm. "Just know that I would never choose to leave you. Rest now – we leave tonight."

In a haze, I watched Tristan walk swiftly to the curtains. Bending down, he tore open the stitching and extracted the papers I had carefully sewn in. All this time I had assumed he'd moved them to some secret place.

He tucked the plans into his coat and, without a backward glance, hurried from the room.

CHAPTER 36
Tristan

I walked swiftly through the streets of Trollus, but in truth, it took every ounce of control not to run. I could not risk showing the urgency of my situation – my desperation – or they wouldn't give me what I needed.

The city was dusty and littered with debris, and the faces of those tasked with the cleanup were equally filthy and exhausted. But that didn't stop them from noticing my signal when I paused to light the lamps that marked the outskirts of the Dregs. Several of them stopped their tasks and walked briskly in opposite directions. It would not take them long to convene those I needed.

But first I needed to take care of those who were following me.

I wandered slowly through the Dregs for a good quarter hour, pretending to examine the damage my brother had done, before deciding I had given everyone enough time. Turning a corner sharply, I stepped into a doorway and waited. Moments later, I heard the steps of Angoulême's men scraping across the stones. I coughed as they passed and tipped my hat as they turned. "I need a bit more privacy than usual today," I said, and immediately trussed them up with magic, depositing them in the house behind me.

It took me only a few minutes more to reach the familiar tavern. "My lord," the proprietor said, bowing low before bolting the doors behind me. "How is the Princess?"

"She will be fine," I said. She would be – I just needed to get her out of Trollus to someone who could help.

"That is good news," the man said, smiling. "We owe her for what she did today."

Yes, they did.

"Is everyone here?" I asked, walking towards the stairs.

"They are."

"Good. Keep watch."

I started speaking as soon as I entered the room – there was no time to spare. "Thank you all for coming," I said. "I am gravely sorry for the actions my brother took today. I see now that he is a menace that will soon grow out of the bounds of control, and it is my intention to deal with him in a permanent fashion as soon as it is expedient to do so."

They all stared at me silently, showing no reaction to my declaration, so I continued. "But that is not why I am here. As you all well know, the curse remains in effect. No one with troll blood in his veins may pass the boundaries of Trollus. Yesterday was a demonstration of our most immediate and urgent peril – the thousands of tons of rock balanced above our heads with magic. Montigny magic. Without our power, our skill, Trollus and all its inhabitants would be doomed." I was at the front of the room now. Slowly I turned around and stared down the dingy cellar full of half-bloods. "And it is this unfortunate truth that has always been the limiting factor in your cause. You. Need. Us."

Their faces darkened and the room filled with angry whispers. "A truth we hardly need reminding of!" someone shouted, "You promised a solution!" yelled another voice.

"Indeed I did," I said. "And I am meeting with you today to offer you that solution." Slowly, I withdrew the plans from my coat. "These documents contain detailed plans for the construction of a physical structure that would eliminate the need for the tree. It would eliminate your need for us."

Silence.

"I will build this structure for you, but it will have a cost."

"We've already promised safety for those on your list," the half-blood called Tips snarled. His pant leg was knotted below the knee, and he had an arm slung around one of his friends for support. He was the reason Cécile had been in the Dregs – he owed her. "What more do you want?"

I hesitated. They knew she'd been injured, but not how badly. If any of them knew the dire straits Cécile was in, no one would agree to my proposition. But it was the only chance I had. "You did not promise *my* safety," I said. "Understand, by leading this revolution – by building this structure – I will be gaining many powerful enemies. If it were only my life I were risking…" I stared down at my carefully constructed diagrams – the result of years of research. "But circumstances have changed. If my life is in jeopardy, so is that of the Lady Cécile. And that, sirs, renders our prior agreement unacceptable in my eyes. I need assurance that she will at least be safe amongst you and yours."

"That girl saved my life today," Tips said. "Saved the lives of countless half-bloods by going up against that devil of a creature you call a brother. Do you think there is anyone here that would lift a finger against her?"

I wasn't concerned about any of them harming her – what I was concerned about was whether they'd risk their own necks to save her. I did not trust them enough to take the chance.

"That's your price then," Tips said, his hand balling into a fist. "To put your life and Cécile's on the list of untouchables in exchange for some papers. To ensure her safety amongst your *comrades*?" I did not miss his emphasis on the final word. He shook his head angrily.

"No," I said. "I want something else from you."

My gloved fingers contracted slightly around the roll of paper, and in my mind's eye, I visualized the blackening bonding marks tracing across my skin. I had to save her. There was no cost too high.

"In exchange for these documents and my promise to do everything in my power to ensure their construction, I want the true name of every half-blood in Trollus." I would have asked for the name of every known sympathizer, but I didn't have that kind of leverage over those of full blood. The half-bloods would have to do.

Silence.

"You would have complete control of us," Tips finally said. "More control than even your father has now."

I tilted my head to one side as though considering his words. "I promise never to use your names except in the defense of Cécile. And you have my word that I will never reveal any of them – not even on pain of death."

They began to exchange weighted looks with one another. "We need time to decide," Tips said.

"Decide now," I snapped. "Or any chance of you ever having freedom will go up in smoke." White-hot flames rose from my outstretched palm, and I held the plans above them, watching as the edges began to singe.

Groans of dismay filled the air. I was playing off lifetimes' worth of desperation, offering what they wanted more than anything in the world in exchange for the one thing no troll gave up lightly. The question was, once I had the names, would they be enough?

CHAPTER 37
Cécile

The next several hours passed in a haze of semi-consciousness. I was aware of Anaïs's presence, of Tristan's aunt ordering that I be cleaned up so that I might die with dignity, of my maids holding my body rigid with magic while they laced me into an elaborate evening gown, and of the weight of the jewels they fastened to my ears, wrists, and throat.

Of the King arriving, a liveried Lessa trailing at his heels.

"Leave us," he barked. Zoé and Élise dashed from the room, but Anaïs remained. "I won't let you hurt her," she said, her shoulders set.

"If that was what I intended," he said, "do you think you could stop me?"

"Then I'm going to go get Tristan," she said, and bolted from the room.

The King waited until the door slammed shut behind her and said, "Please do, Anaïs. Please do." Then he jerked his chin at Lessa. "Follow her." A faint smile rose to her lips as she hurried off.

I watched, frozen, as the King came across the room towards me.

"Do not look so afraid, Cécile. Right now you are more useful to me alive than dead." He smiled. "I have a witch-woman waiting to heal you once Tristan makes his move."

What was he talking about? My sluggish mind tried to puzzle out the meaning of his words. If he had someone here who could heal me, what was he waiting for? Alarm bells went off in my head.

"He never made mistakes before you arrived," the King mused, the bed groaning as he settled his bulk on the edge. "Now he behaves rashly, making decisions based on emotion rather than logic. Which has served my purposes, but is not a good quality in a future king. He will learn much from suffering the consequences."

"You've been manipulating him," I said, my words sticky and thick on my tongue. "If you knew he plotted against you, why didn't you stop him? Why did you let it go so far?"

"I've been training him," the King clarified. "This plot will fail, but he will soon begin afresh. Perhaps he will fail again. And again. But one day, he will wrench the crown from my cold dead hands and, by then, he will be the man he needs to be to rule Trollus. Not a sentimental, idealistic boy."

The loud clamor of the bells signaling the beginning of curfew sounded, echoing through the room.

He sighed. "You see Cécile, as a child, Tristan was entranced by humanity." He twisted a golden ring around one thick finger. "He was constantly sneaking out of the palace to go see the human traders in the market; was always pestering them with questions and playing with their animals. As he grew older, his minders constantly found him at the end of the River Road, staring at the world beyond. He had no interest in politics or in the concerns of our people, and it grew increasing clear to me that his sympathies lay contrary to my own. But no matter how hard I tried to bring him to heel, he would not bend. He was too secure in his position as my sole heir."

"So you had another child to replace him?" I whispered.

The King shook his head. "Only to threaten his position. But do you know what he said when his brother was born?"

I shook my head.

"That he was glad to have a brother because now he wouldn't have to be king." The memory brought fury to his face. "As if being a king were a choice! So as punishment, I made him watch as I tore one of his favorite humans, a charming little old man, to pieces. I told him that if I ever caught him associating with the traders again, I would kill whoever it was. And he wept, but by the very next day, he had begun his pursuit of the crown."

The door opened and a troll I did not recognize hurried inside. "Your Majesty, the half-bloods are rioting in the streets," he gasped.

"Indeed." The King's face was neutral – he'd expected this. "Order them contained, but keep casualties to a minimum. Do you understand?"

The troll's eyes widened. "But they've gone wild, sir. I do not see how we can contain them without violence."

The King rose to his feet. "I do not desire my people

killed," he snapped. "Let that be known. And see that they are contained peaceably. They are not acting under their own volition."

The troll nodded rapidly and bolted from the room.

"Already he grows harder," the King mused. "He has promised the death of his own brother. He has deceived his followers in the worst of ways to further his own ends. He is sending men to their deaths to protect a life he considers more important than theirs. And he is right. You, my little witch, are the key to our freedom."

"No," I whispered, my heart filling with horror. "You lie."

"I cannot lie." The King cocked his head as though listening. "He will not be long now."

Sure enough, my ears caught the sound of boots pounding down the hall, and I could feel Tristan coming towards us. I opened my mouth to scream a warning, but magic muffled my attempt. "You see, Cécile, I will break him as many times as I need to in order to make him the heir I need him to be." Picking up a pillow, he loomed over me.

The door flew open.

"Get away from her," Tristan shouted, and magic slammed his father away from the bed. The King howled with laughter and Tristan staggered back beneath the onslaught of invisible fists.

"You're a fool, boy," he cackled. "Ordering a rebellion now, when you are at your weakest. If only you'd waited, you might have had a chance."

The air grew so thick with magic that I could scarcely breathe. And it was getting hotter, the temperature rising until the room blistered with the heat of an oven. I lay paralyzed on the bed, helpless. All I could do was watch.

To my eyes, it was a battle of invisible weapons made known only by their effects. Blades of magic slashed through the air with a whistling sound, clattering against magical shields like steel on steel. Tristan and his father both landed blows, jagged wounds opened on pale skin, healing over seconds later, leaving only bloody smears to show they'd been injured at all.

But blind to the magic as I was, it was still clear to me that Tristan was losing. The fear and exhaustion I felt in my mind were reinforced by the dark shadows on his face, the tearing gasp of his breath. Sweat plastered his dark hair to his forehead, and I hissed in terror as the King landed a blow on his arm, sending him staggering. Too many sleepless nights, the sluag attack, and the effort of shoring up the tree had taken their toll.

"Enough of this," the King muttered, and the air around me seemed to compress as magic surged across the room, crashing against Tristan's opposing force like a thunderclap. I struggled to breathe – the air was burning hot, searing my lungs with every gasp I dragged in. My body twitched and jerked, my fingers clutching at the blankets in a feeble attempt to drag myself off the bed to find a weapon. Something, anything, that could help. Tristan fell to his knees, his face twisting, while his father wasn't even winded.

I watched in terror as the King, never removing his gaze from Tristan, pulled a knife from his belt and threw it at me.

"No!" Tristan screamed. The knife clattered against a wall of magic, dropping harmlessly to the bed. But the damage was done. I sobbed in terror and pain as the King's magic pinned Tristan against the wall. He gasped soundlessly, his fingers clawing futilely at the magic choking his throat.

"Pathetic," the King sneered. "Just like your little army dying out in the streets against their wills."

Tristan slumped against his father's magic. Pain filled his eyes as they locked with mine, his mouth moving soundlessly to form the words, "I'm sorry."

Sucking in a mouthful of the burning air, I screamed. The sound was shrill and terrified, like a dying animal.

Then Anaïs was there. Dressed in boy's clothes, she smashed through the glass-paned doors like a warrior maiden of legend. She rolled to her feet, the force of her magic sending the King staggering into the corner. Tristan fell away from the wall, his chest heaving as he sucked in precious air. The air in the room compressed again as their joint power dueled with the King.

It did not take long. As Angoulême had said, Anaïs was military trained. And unlike Tristan, she was utterly ruthless.

"Got him," Anaïs shouted with triumph, and my ears popped as the battle ended. The King slumped to his knees, holding up one hand in apparent defeat.

"Now it is your turn to do what I say," Tristan said, striding across the room. "You'll let us bring help for Cécile. You won't interfere or threaten her life anymore. And I want your word on it."

"And if I refuse?"

Tristan's face hardened. "Then you die."

Thibault cowered before his son. "You won't kill your own father," he pleaded. "That would make you a monster – not the sort of man your dear wife wants you to be."

Tristan's face turned in my direction. I saw the King reach for something on the floor and shouted a garbled warning. The lights flashed out, including mine, and all I could hear was the crash of something heavy hitting the floor, a wet thud, and a soft cry of pain. One orb of light flickered back into existence: the King's. Tristan lay on the floor, conscious, but bound with cords that glowed when he fought against them. Anaïs lay against the far wall, a sluag spear embedded in her chest.

"It seems you are to face the same fate as your sister," the King said, walking over to caress the side of Anaïs' face. "Pity. You were a lovely thing to look at."

She spat, a glob of spit which flew through the air only to be brushed away by a bit of magic.

He frowned. "Foolish girl." Grabbing the haft of the steel spear, he jammed it the rest of the way through her chest. Anaïs tried to scream, but it came out as a gurgle, blood staining her lips. Her fingers latched on the spear, but she did not pull it out. The King laughed and turned from her to me.

I was terrified. Dying was an easy thing to accomplish, effortless in its agony. It was living that was hard, requiring endless toil and labor, and for all one's efforts, it could be stolen in an instant. My entire time in Trollus had been one long struggle at death's doorstep. But instead of breaking my will to live, it had made me stronger. I wasn't just fighting for my life, I was fighting for Tristan's.

Nor was I completely powerless.

"Poor Cécile," he said. "Poor fragile human, how you suffer so. I want to let you live, but I feel you will forever be a liability for him."

I saw Tristan shout something, but heard nothing – the King had blocked away the sound of our voices. But not Anaïs, she was closer.

"You've no intention of letting me die," I choked out. "Why else bring a witch into Trollus to save me?"

"True," the King said, stepping in between Tristan and me so that we were blocked from each other's sight. "But Tristan doesn't know that – and even here, he controls the actions of his half-breeds on the streets. He has their names. I want this played through to the end. I want to see how far he will go."

The half-bloods were dying in the streets for me – I had to do something.

"I opened Anushka's grimoire," I whispered. For all the politics and intrigue between Tristan and his father, I knew that the King's desire to break the curse trumped them all.

He hesitated.

"I know her secrets – the magic she used against the trolls. If you stop this now, I'll tell you everything."

The King laughed. "Oh? If you have the witch's spells, why don't you use them now?"

The smell of blood was thick on the air, heady and metallic. Anaïs moved, the end of the sluag spear dragging against the carpets. I didn't dare look in her direction, though. I could only trust that she would know what to do.

"You're lying," he said, leaning over me. "You know nothing."

My breath came in short, shallow gasps. With every minute that passed, more people would die. And I had only once chance to end this.

"I know enough to stop you," I whispered.

A cup flew across the room and blood splattered against the King's face, hot droplets raining down onto my cheeks. The northern words felt foreign on my lips, but I instinctively knew what they meant.

Bind the light.

I felt strength surge into me, rising from the earth beneath us. Wind rushed through the room, cold and fresh, pushing away the burned stench of the battle. But as it had when I healed Tristan in the labyrinth, it was from the blood that I drew power, directing the strange magic in a way no troll could use it.

"Not possible," the King hissed.

"Sometimes," I whispered, "the truth hurts."

The King collapsed backwards, Tristan's magic binding him to the floor and muffling his curses.

"Cécile!" Tristan was at my side in an instant. "Are you all right?"

I shook my head. "Help Anaïs."

I watched as he knelt beside her, blood running in bright red streams down the steel sluag spear. "Anaïs?"

She opened her eyes. "Kill him, Tristan. Now, while you have the chance."

I watched him turn to look at his father. From my position on the bed, I couldn't see the King, but I could well imagine the fury in his eyes. Cut off from his magic by my spell and physically restrained by Anaïs's and Tristan's magic, he was helpless. Yet I doubted he was afraid – for all his faults, cowardice was not one of them.

Tristan drew his sword, examining the sharp steel edge

as though he'd never seen it before. "I can't," he whispered. "Not like this."

"He'll eventually break free, Tristan. You have to do it now," Anaïs argued, her voice strained. I closed my eyes, her words faint noise in the background of my mind. She was right, but I knew that Tristan wouldn't be able to kill his father. Not in cold blood while he lay helpless on the floor, no matter how much the King might deserve it.

"Then let me do it!" Anaïs's words interrupted my thoughts and I opened my eyes.

"No," Tristan said, his voice resolute. "You will not."

Anaïs slumped lower against the wall. "I need you to pull the spear out, then. It's troubling my magic." Her hand stretched out in front of her, fingers reaching for something invisible.

"You'll bleed to death," Tristan argued.

"I'm as good as dead, and if you think otherwise, you're a blasted idiot." She smiled, beautiful as ever, despite the gore. "I'll keep him bound for as long as I can, buy you some time. Now go."

Tristan remained frozen, face full of indecision.

"I can't leave you like this," he said.

"You owe me a good number of favors, Tristan, and I'm calling them in now. Get Cécile out of here, and leave the slate between us wiped clean."

Tristan nodded slowly. "You've never failed me, not once."

"And I don't intend to now," she whispered. "Go, and live."

I watched in silence as Tristan took hold of the spear haft. "I'm sorry," he said. "For everything. For not being able to give you what you wanted, for not..." His voice broke.

"For not giving you what you gave me."

"Don't," she whispered.

He shook his head. "You deserved better."

"I love you," she said, her tears turning the blood on her lips from red to pink.

Tristan's hands trembled around the spear. "Anaïstromeria," he said, the name spoken as though it were an invocation. Her pupils dilated, fixing on him with a preternatural intensity.

"No more tears," he commanded, and her eyes immediately dried. The words he spoke after that were in a language I'd never heard before – one not of this world. But I could tell from his tone they were a valediction – a final farewell between friends. When he finished speaking, Tristan leaned forward and kissed her. When he pulled back, the spear came with him.

The keening wail of pain made me cringe.

"Go," she gasped. "There isn't much time."

Tristan came over to my side. "He knew everything," I choked out. "I tried to warn you, but…" A racking cough tore through my chest. "He has a witch somewhere in the city."

Tristan's eyes flicked over to his father. "He'll never tell me where. It's better we leave Trollus now, while we have the chance."

A small, satisfied little smile rose on the King's face.

Tristan carefully wrapped my torso in magic to keep my ribs from moving, then scooped me up off the bed, my dying, drugged body limp in his arms. "Thank you," I whispered to Anaïs as he walked to the broken window.

"I didn't do it for you," she said.

"I know," I said. "Thank you anyway."

Over Tristan's shoulder, I saw the King on the ground, held in place by magic. As I suspected, there was no fear in his eyes, but what sent a thrill of terror through my body was the calm thoughtfulness on his face. It made me afraid that despite how things appeared on the surface, the situation had still gone according to his plans.

Tristan stepped out onto the balcony and through the sound barrier. Shouts and screams filled the air.

"I ordered the sympathizers to start the rebellion."

"I know," I croaked. "You need to make them stop."

"Not yet," he muttered, hurrying over to the wall. "Victoria? Vincent?"

"Here!"

I rose up into the air and felt another set of magic hands catch hold of me, lowering me down until I was in Vincent's big arms. "Don't you worry, Cécile," he said, grinning. "We'll get you out of here."

Tristan dropped down next to us and took me back in his arms. "Marc's waiting?"

They nodded.

"Let's go then."

"The fighting's thickest down at River Road," Victoria whispered as we ran down dark alleys, making our way stealthily through the city. "They think that's the way you'll try to take her, so we engaged them there to keep up the ruse."

I heard magic break against magic, sword against sword. The screams of the dying hung in my ears, blood flashing in my eyes. Dying because of me. Dying because Tristan had ordered them to. But it all seemed to be part of a dream. My delirium.

I saw Marc by the gate to the labyrinth, the key glittering in his hand.

"Come with us, come with us," I mumbled, trying to grab hold of him, but he seemed so far.

"Hush now, Cécile," Marc said. "You know my place is here."

"But I don't want to leave you behind," I sobbed. I didn't want to leave anyone. The lights of Trollus gleamed in swirling blurs as I tried and failed to focus my eyes. Then the city was gone and we were running through the labyrinth, Marc's last words chasing behind us: "Goodbye, Princess."

The twins were with us, Victoria ahead, Vincent behind. I half-listened to them talking as they navigated the dark tunnels and narrow crawlspaces, Tristan's magic clutching me tight against him with every step he took. Then I dreamed of above. Above, above, with Tristan.

"It will be warm," I whispered. "I'll teach you to ride a horse and we will travel anywhere we like, you and I. No more monsters, nothing to separate us. We will be together forever."

His lips brushed my forehead. "Hush, love. You know you must be quiet here."

I fell asleep, and when I awoke, we were alone. "Where are Victoria and Vincent?" I asked. I tried to look around, but it hurt to move.

"They're buying us time," Tristan said.

"Surely they'll come with us," I said. "They'd like to go hunting and to travel about telling their jests to everyone."

"Perhaps they'll come later," Tristan said.

I dreamed again, only this time it was of a place of such brilliance that my eyes stung if I gazed at any one thing for too long. The green of the grass beneath my feet, the red of the roses on the bush, the blue of the sky above. The colors were familiar, but somehow more vibrant than anything I'd seen before. The air was sweet on my lips, the faint breeze smelling of summer and spice. All around me danced folk with a beauty and grace beyond reason, their curious eyes glowing like jewels. Hair and skin of every color of the rainbow, their lithe bodies were dressed in mists that swirled with them as they danced circles around me.

"Who is she, who is she?" they sang with voices so sweet they brought tears to my eyes.

"A mortal dreamer," one whispered, her fingers catching in my hair and yanking hard. They laughed and descended on me, sharp nails raking across my skin and driving me to my knees. I screamed, but when I tried to run, I found myself dancing instead.

"Dance with us, mortal," they laughed. "Dance for eternity."

"Stop."

A voice thundered through the meadow, and all the creatures around me fell to their knees. I turned and flung a hand up to block the brilliant golden light radiating from the man standing in front of me. Through my fingers, I saw a woman at his side, her skin pale, hair an inky black and eyes the color of verdelite.

"She is consort to the mortal prince," the man said, and the meadow filled with whispers. "Why are you here?"

"I don't know," I whispered. "I can't remember."

The woman at his side laughed, her voice cruel. "Come to beg a favor, but forgot what it is?"

The creatures in the meadow echoed her laughter. The golden man did not. "Is it a favor when our purposes are aligned, wife?" he asked softly.

"Yes." I cringed at the harshness of her voice. "A favor given is a favor owed."

"But I don't even know what I need," I said.

The man smiled and I fell to my knees at his feet. "What you seek is the name of that which you most desire." He tilted his head in a way that was oddly familiar to me. "If you choose to use it, then you will be in my debt." He bent down, the warmth of his breath like a summer wind against my cheek, and he whispered a single word in my ear.

"Cécile, wake up!"

Tristan was leaning over me, his eyes wide and wild.

"We're here."

I blinked at him. "I was dreaming. Of a place of endless summer..." I trailed off, taking in our surroundings through bleary eyes. It was the entrance to the labyrinth that Luc had brought me through what seemed a lifetime ago. Water lapped against the rocks, but it was much lower than before, the heat of summer drying up the pond, making the cavern seem huge. Tristan sat at the edge with me cradled in his lap, my little light following his larger one around the rocky ceiling like a lost puppy.

"What are we waiting for?" I asked.

"Dawn," he replied. "Look."

Faint light was glowing in the water, growing in strength with each passing moment. The lip of the cave wall was only barely submerged. I could see that now. During times of drought, it might even be possible to enter the cave without getting one's feet wet. I thought I could hear the sound of voices; the loud whinny of a horse.

"Is it time, then?"

"Yes." But he didn't move, only held me tighter, his face buried in my hair.

"Tristan?"

He turned his face to me, and it was streaked with tears. I wanted to wipe them away, tell him that everything would be all right, but my body was locked stiff with pain.

"Promise me you'll get better," he whispered. "Tell me you'll grow strong again. That you'll gallop on horseback through summer meadows. Dance in spring rains and let snowflakes melt on your tongue in winter. That you'll travel wherever the wind takes you. That you'll live." He stroked my hair. "Promise me."

Confusion crept over me. "You'll be with me, though. You'll do those things too?"

He kissed my lips, silencing my questions. "Promise me."

"No," I said, struggling against him. "No, you said you were coming with me. You said. *You* promised." He had to be coming with me – he said he was, and Tristan couldn't lie. Wouldn't lie.

He got to his feet and stepped into the water. I tried to struggle, but he was too strong. "Tristan, no, no, no!" I tried to scream, but I couldn't. I tried to hold on to him, but my fingers wouldn't work. The cold of the water bit into my skin and I sobbed, terrified. "You said you would never leave me!"

He stopped, the weight of his sorrow greater than any mountain. "And if I had the choice, I never would. I love you, Cécile. I will love you until the day I take my last breath and that is the truth." He kissed me hard. "Forgive me."

Tristan shoved me under the water. I came up on the other side, gasping for breath, sunlight stinging my eyes. The weight of my skirts pulled me towards the bottom and I didn't fight it. I drifted down, my eyes searching for the opening, for the way back, but there was only rock. I pounded my fist against the illusion, but it would not yield. I let my body go limp, let it sink until my feet brushed the bottom. He could see me – would know what I was trying to do. He'd have to drop the illusion of rock and let me come back or watch me drown.

Then an arm closed under my arms, pulled me upward. My head broke the surface and I choked on water and blood.

"I've got her!" It was Christophe's voice.

"No!" I coughed. "I have to go back, I have to go back." But my words were silent. I couldn't breathe.

"It's all right, Cécile." He was pulling me to shore, away from Tristan. I felt more hands grab hold of me, lifting me out of the water. I heard Jérôme's voice. He was trying to soothe me, but the words meant nothing. I had to go back. Tristan was trapped. He was in danger. Once someone washed the blood off the King, his power would return and Tristan would be at his mercy. I had to go back.

"Tristan." My lips formed his name and I reached out towards the rocks. I could feel him there, waiting.

"We need to get her home," Chris said. "She hasn't got much time."

Hands lifted me into the air, the sound of a horse whickering beneath me faint in my ears. Then I was moving, faster and further away.

CHAPTER 38
Cécile

Burning light pierced through my eyelids, and I groaned, turning my face to the side. Rough homespun sheets rasped against my cheek, and the smell of smoke assaulted my nostrils. "Something's burning." My voice sounded slurred, even to my own ears.

"She's awake."

A familiar voice. "Gran?"

"It's your gran, dear. You're home safe now." The mattress sunk beneath her weight as she sat next to me. "Do you remember what happened?"

My memories came crashing back: Tristan carrying me through the labyrinth, begging me to forgive him, and then doing the unforgivable. A sob tore from my throat.

"Joss, go warm up some of that broth for your sister."

The door opened and shut.

"When Christophe and Jérôme brought you here, you were almost beyond my power to save. You've been unconscious nigh on three days now."

Three days! My heart leapt. The King had been far from

464

dead when we left him, and there was nowhere in Trollus safe from his wrath. My breath came in short little gasps. I couldn't feel him. Tristan wasn't there. My mind was empty.

"Cécile, calm down. You're safe now."

Gran's words barely registered as I fumbled with the blankets, my eyes stinging and watering in the sunlight. Finally I got my hand free of the sheets, my gaze latching onto the silver lacework gleaming across my knuckles. "Thank God," I whispered and collapsed back against the sheets. As my panic receded, I realized I could feel Tristan in my mind, just faintly. He was miserable though, and in pain.

"Cécile, where have you been? We searched everywhere for you; for weeks, months! We thought you were dead!" Gran said.

"I... I..." I didn't know what to say. "Can you please close the drapes?"

She did as I asked and, in the dimmer light, I could see my grandmother had aged. Deep lines creased her face and her normally upright shoulders were slumped. "Christophe told me they found you on their front porch and brought you straight here," she said softly. "But your dress was soaked through." Her eyes met mine. "It hasn't rained in more than a week. And you hadn't any shoes, but your feet were clean." A shudder ran through her and she turned away. I'd never seen her cry before.

"Luc took me," I said softly. "He caught me on my way home from town."

Gran spun around. "You've been in Trianon this whole time?"

"No," I said. "He sold me."

Her eyes widened. "But who..." Whirling around, she crossed my room and flung open the chest of drawers. Rifling around, she extracted something from a leather purse and examined it closely. Her breath hissed through her lips and a coin bounced against the floorboards. "Troll gold. I know it by the weight."

"Yes." I awkwardly pushed myself into a seated position, my ribs stiff and sore.

"They're monsters." Her voice trembled with fear.

"Some of them," I agreed, swinging my legs around. "But most of them are rather charming."

Gran stared at me in horror. "What did they want with you?"

The door swung open and Joss stuck her head in. "Girards are here."

"You should go down and greet them," I said. "I'll dress and be down shortly."

"You shouldn't be up," Gran said. "You need to rest."

"I'll be fine. Go ahead."

I waited until they were down the steps and then pulled on one of my old dresses, my body stiff and uncooperative. There was a long scar running down my rib cage, pink and fresh. Magic had been used to heal me. My grandmother's magic, if what the King had said was true. But I had no time to think about that now. Stepping quietly across the floor, I made my way down the hall and into my father's room. I pushed open the window, climbed out onto the shed and jumped to the ground. My knees buckled and I tumbled into a heap, breathing hard. I didn't have time for this. I needed to get back to Trollus now. Tristan was hurt because of me. I had to help him.

Sneaking around to the front of the house, I eased the reins of Chris's horse loose from the post and swung into the saddle. The door opened and Chris looked out, his mouth dropping open when he saw me. "Cécile, no!"

"I have to," I whispered. Wheeling the horse around, I slammed my heels against its side and galloped out of the yard.

I didn't get far. By the time I reached the tree line, Chris had caught up to me on his father's horse. Reaching down, he grabbed hold of my reins and pulled the two horses to a halt.

"Have you lost your mind?" he shouted.

I kicked the horse's sides and tried to pull the reins free, but I was already exhausted from the short gallop, my injured side screaming from exertion. "I need to go back!" The words came out in a choked sob. "He's hurt. I have to help him."

"How?" Chris swung down from the saddle and pulled me off the horse. "What do you possibly think you can do? Ride back into Trollus and demand they let him go? He can't leave, Cécile. He's as stuck there as the rest of them."

"You can't expect me to do nothing!"

"That's exactly what I expect you to do. That's exactly what Tristan expects you to do." He grabbed my chin and forced me to look at him. "If you go back, everything he did, everything he sacrificed to keep you alive will be for nothing. You can't help him, Cécile, but you can ensure his sacrifice was worthwhile."

"Of course you would say that," I hissed. "You hate him. You're jealous of him. Don't pretend you'd shed a tear if you found out he was dead."

Chris abruptly let go of me. "Is that what you think of me?"

I looked away, lowering myself on weak knees to the ground.

"You think I'd see someone dead because I was jealous?"

"Then prove me wrong." My voice was barely audible. "Help me save him."

"Letting you go back would be the exact opposite of helping him," Chris replied, blankly watching the horses wander off to graze. "He made me promise to keep you safe, but even if he hadn't, I still wouldn't let you go. Hate me if you want to, but I'm not letting you throw your life away for a troll."

"You shouldn't even be able to speak his name." I dug my fingers into the dirt. "You shouldn't be able to talk about anything to do with Trollus."

"He released me from those oaths. And he told me to give you this." He dropped a folded letter onto my skirts, its golden embossed seal glittering under the sun. Tentatively, I picked it up and pulled it open, the sight of Tristan's familiar script causing a pain in my stomach.

Cécile,

There is much I wish to say to you – so much, that if I had hours, even days, to write this letter, it would not be enough. All the words in this world and the next are not enough. But even as the ink on the page dries, you are dying. I have no more time than to tell

*you that I love you, and on the hope that you survive
to read this, to warn you. You must never return to
Trollus. Only death awaits you here...*

My eyes skimmed the rest of the page, and then again, the
page shaking between my fingers.

"He's giving you the chance to start over, Cécile." Chris
knelt next to me and pushed the trembling page down into
my lap. "You can have a life here, if that's what you want.
Here, in the Hollow."

I knew what he was thinking, though the words
remained unspoken. With dull eyes, I watched my family
hurrying towards me. Chris was right: the right decision
– the safe decision – would be to stay in the Hollow. To
one day get married and have children and forget about
Trollus. To forget about magic. To forget about Tristan.

You must never return to Trollus...

My eyes turned southward, towards the ocean and towards
Trianon. Trollus might be forbidden to me, but there was no
power on this earth that could make me forget. Or make me
give up. I wasn't powerless – far from it. I had witch magic in
my blood strong enough to stop a troll, and that had to mean
something. Who knew what I could accomplish with a little
practice. And while I was learning, my hunt would begin. I
wasn't certain where I'd find her or what I'd do when I did,
but there was one thing I knew for certain.

The witch must die.

Acknowledgments

I can say without a shadow of a doubt that this novel would never have come into existence without the love and support of my family. Thanks Dad, for reading fantasy novels to me before I was old enough to write a sentence, and then for editing those sentences when I was finally wise enough to write them. Thanks Mom, for being supportive when I made the unexpected and inexplicable decision to become a writer – you've been my #1 cheerleader. And thanks Nick, for keeping my ego in check – no one makes fun of my characters quite as well as you.

A very special thanks must go to my tireless agent, Tamar Rydzinski, who plucked me from obscurity based on a logline and two hundred and fifty words. You helped make my dream a reality, and for that I will be eternally grateful.

To my editor Amanda Rutter, thank you for falling in love with my trolls and giving me the amazing experience of seeing my book on the shelves. I'm looking forward to working with you and the rest of the Angry Robot/Strange Chemistry team over the coming years.

My endless gratitude goes to those who have stuck by me during my journey to publication. To Donna, for buying me countless lunches at Earl's and always listening to my drama; to Lindsay, for your ceaseless enthusiasm and salesmanship; to Carleen and Joel, for kindly feeding and employing the hermit who lived in your basement for five months; and to all my friends who kept dragging me out of my writing cave so that I could still claim to have a life.

And last but by no means least: Spencer, thanks for discovering – much to your own surprise – that you've a penchant for somewhat crazy writers who can't cook. My heart and my stomach would be in a much worse state without you.

COMING SOON
Hidden Huntress

Read the opening here...

CHAPTER 1
Cécile

My voice faded into silence, though the memory of it seemed to haunt the theatre as I slumped gracefully, trusting that Julian would catch me, however much he might not want to. The stage was smooth and cool against my cheek, a blessed relief against the heat of hundreds of bodies packed into one place. I tried to breathe shallowly, ignoring the stench of too much perfume and far too few baths as I feigned death. Julian's voice replaced mine, and his lament echoed across my ears and through the theatre, but I only half-listened, my attention drifting away to fix on the all-too-real sorrow of another. One far out of reach.

The audience erupted into cheers. "Bravo!" someone shouted, and I almost smiled when a falling flower brushed against my cheek. The curtain hit the stage floor, and I reluctantly opened my eyes, the red velvet of the curtains pulling me back into an unwelcome reality.

"You seem distracted tonight," Julian said, hauling me unceremoniously to my feet. "And about as emotive as my left boot. She won't be best pleased, you know."

"I know," I muttered, smoothing my costume into place. "I had a late night."

"Shocking." Julian rolled his eyes. "It's tiring work ingratiating yourself with every rich man in the city." He took my hand again, nodded at the crew, and we both plastered smiles on our faces as the curtain rose again. "Cécile! Cécile!" the audience shouted. Waving blindly, I blew a kiss to the sea of uniform faces before dropping into a deep curtsey. We stepped back to let the rest of the cast take their bows before coming forward again. Julian dropped to one knee and kissed my gloved fingers to the roaring approval of the crowd, and then the curtain dropped for the final time.

The moment the fabric hit the stage floor, Julian jerked his hand away from mine and rose to his feet. "Funny how even at your worst, they still scream your name," he said, his handsome face dark with anger. "They treat me as though I am one of your stage props."

"You know that isn't true," I said. "You've legions of admirers. All the men are jealous, and all the women wish it was them in your arms."

"Spare me your platitudes."

I shrugged and turned my back on him, walking off stage. It was two months to the day since I had arrived in Trianon and nearly three since my dramatic exit from Trollus, and despite arriving with a plan I had thought was good, I was still no closer to finding Anushka. Julian's jealous theatrics were the least of my concerns.

Backstage was its usual state of organized chaos – only now that the performance was over, the wine was pouring more liberally. Half-dressed chorus girls preened at Julian, their overlapping words barely intelligible as they rained praise upon his performance. I was glad for it – he didn't get the credit he deserved. Me they ignored, which was fine, because all I wanted was to be alone. Eyes on my dressing room, I wove through the performers until the sound of my name stopped me in my tracks.

"Cécile!"

Slowly, I turned on my heel and watched everyone scatter as my mother strode through the room. She kissed me hard on both cheeks and then pulled me into a tight embrace, her strong fingers digging painfully into the long livid scar where Gran had cut me open to set my ribs. "That was positively dreadful," she hissed into my ear, breath hot. "Be thankful for small mercies that there was no one of taste in the audience tonight."

"Of course not," I whispered back. "Because if there had been, you would have been the one on stage."

"Something you would be grateful for if you weren't so ignorant." She pushed away from me. "Wasn't she brilliant tonight!" she announced to the room. "A natural talent. The world has never known such a voice."

Everyone murmured in agreement, a few going so far as to clap their hands. My mother beamed at them. She might criticize me until she was blue in the face, but she wouldn't tolerate anyone else saying a thing against me.

"Yes indeed, well done, Cécile!" A man's voice caught my attention, and looking around my mother, I saw the Marquis strolling across the room. He was a bland man, as remarkable and memorable as grey paint but for the fact he usually had my mother on his arm. I dropped into a curtsey. "Thank you, my lord."

He waved me up, his eyes on the chorus girls. "Wonderful performance, my dear. If Genevieve hadn't been sitting right next to me, I would have sworn it was her on stage."

My mother's face tightened and I felt mine blanch. "You are too kind."

Everyone stood staring mutely at each other long enough for it to become uncomfortable.

"We'd best be off," my mother finally said, her voice

jarringly cheerful. "We're late as it is. Cécile, darling, I won't be home tonight, so don't wait up."

I nodded my head and watched the Marquis escort my mother out the back entrance. I wondered briefly whether he knew she was married to my father, and if he did, whether he cared. He'd been my mother's patron for years, but I hadn't known he existed until I came to Trianon. As to whether my family had been kept from that knowledge or my family had kept the knowledge from me, I couldn't say. Sighing, I made my way to my dressing room, closing the door firmly behind me.

The small room was stuffed to the brim with flowers, the scent of them cloying. I shoved a few wilted bouquets into an already overflowing bin, and the cynical side of me expressed a moment of gratitude that winter would soon be upon us and flowers would become an expensive commodity. They made me think of the glass gardens, and I didn't need any more reminders of Trollus.

Sitting down on the stool in front of the mirror, I slowly peeled off my stage gloves and picked up a short lace pair that I habitually wore to cover my bonding marks. The silver of my tattoo shone in the candlelight, and my shoulders slumped.

How much torture could a person endure before breaking? A knot of continuous pain sat in the back of my mind – pain laced with wild fear and anger that never diminished, never seemed to sleep. A constant reminder that Tristan suffered in Trollus so that I could be safe in Trianon. A constant reminder of my failure to help him.

"I'm sorry," I whispered, wiping away the salty droplet beading on top of my waxy makeup.

"Cécile?"

I twisted around, instinctively covering my bonding marks with my other hand until I saw it was Sabine, and then I let my arms drop to my sides. Her brow furrowed when she saw my tear-streaked face, and she came the rest of the way inside, shutting the door behind her.

Despite her parents' protestations, my oldest and dearest friend had insisted on coming to Trianon with me. She'd always been a talented seamstress and had a knack for hair and cosmetics, so I'd been able to convince the company to hire her as my costuming assistant. While I had been recovering, my family had told everyone in the Hollow that I'd gotten cold feet about moving to Trianon and fled to Courville on the southern tip of the Isle. But keeping my secret from Sabine had never been an option. After what she'd gone through during my disappearance, allowing her to believe that I'd let her endure all that hurt because of performance nerves would have been a slap in the face.

"You weren't all that bad," she said, fastening my gold necklace before dipping a rag in some cold cream and setting to work removing my makeup. "In fact, you weren't bad at all. Just not your best. Who could be under the circumstances?"

I nodded, both of us aware that it wasn't my mother's words troubling me.

"And Genevieve, she's being a right old witch to say otherwise."

Apparently my mother's whispered criticism had not gone unheard. "She wants the best for me," I said quietly, not knowing why I felt the urge to defend her. It was a childhood habit I couldn't seem to break.

"You'd think that, you being her daughter and all, but..." She hesitated, her brown eyes searching mine in our reflection. "Everyone knows she's jealous of you – her star's setting while yours is on the rise." She smiled. "It looks better on stage when it's you playing Julian's lover. Genevieve is old enough to be his mother, and the audience, well they're not blind, you know?"

"She's still better than I am."

Her smile fell away. "Only because your passion has been stolen by what's happening to him."

She never said Tristan's name.

"If you sang how you used to before..." She huffed out a frustrated breath. "You worked so hard for this, Cécile, and I know you love it. It makes me angry knowing that you're throwing your life away for the sake of some creature."

I'd been so angry the first time she picked this argument; hackles up and claws out in defense of Tristan and my choices. But I'd come to see events from Sabine's perspective – as a story plucked from the imagination. All that resonated with her was the worst of it, which made my decision to put aside everything to try to free my captors incomprehensible to her.

"It's not only him I'm trying to help." Names drifted through my mind. So many faces, and all of them relying on me. Tristan, Marc, Victoria, Vincent...

"Maybe not. But s him who's changed you."

There was something in her tone and the set of her jaw that made me turn from the mirror to face her.

"You might be hunting this woman for the sake of them, but you've stopped living your life because of him." She dropped to her knees in front of me and took my hands in hers. "It's because you're in love with him that you've lost your passion for singing, and I wish..." She broke off, eyes fixed on my hands.

I knew she wasn't attacking, that she only wanted what was best for me, but I was sick of defending my choices. "I'm not going to stop loving him for the sake of improving the caliber of my performance," I snapped, pulling my hands out of her grip and a second later regretting my tone. "I'm sorry. It's only that I wish you'd accept that I'm set on this path."

"I know." She rose to her feet. "I only wish there was more I could do to help you find happiness."

Find happiness... Not find the witch. She'd been clear when we'd come to Trianon that she'd have nothing to do with freeing the creatures that had ruined my life.

"You do enough by listening." I caught hold of her hand and kissed it. "And by keeping me in style."

We stared at each other, both of us keenly aware that the awkwardness between us was new and strange. Both of us longing for the days when it hadn't existed.

"Come out with us tonight," she said, the words spilling from her mouth in one last desperate plea. "Just this once, can't you forget the trolls and be with us lowly humans? We're going to have our fortunes told in Pigalle. One of the dancers heard from a subscriber that there's a woman who can see your future in the palm of your hand."

"I'll not hand my hard earned coins over to a charlatan," I said, forcing lightness into my voice. "But if she happens to have red hair and blue eyes, and seems wise beyond her years, do let me know."

If only it could be so easy...

angryrobotbooks.com